November 30, 2021

For Robin,

From the Grey Lady with my very best wishes!

Shep

NANTUCKET
A Winter's Idyll
NOCTURNE

Also by Steve Sheppard

TOURIST TOWN
A Nantucket Idyll

NANTUCKET NOCTURNE

A Winter's Idyll

by STEVE SHEPPARD

Nantucket Nocturne, A Winter's Idyll

Capaum Pond Publishing
First edition

This is a work of fiction. Names, characters, places, and incidents are either the product of the author's imagination or are used fictitiously. Any resemblance to actual persons, living or dead, business establishments, events, or locales is entirely coincidental.

Cover art: Karin Ganga Sheppard

Book design: Kimberly White

ISBN: 978-0-578-30130-3

For Blaise and Liesel
Nantucketers

with love

TO THE READER:

As with *Tourist Town: A Nantucket Idyll*, the characters and circumstances contained herewith and herein aren't real, no matter how many islanders insist otherwise.

The Nantucket history, however, is verifiable.

As baseball sage Casey Stengel often said:
"You could look it up."

THE AUTHOR

What wonder, then, that these Nantucketers,
born on a beach, should take to the sea
for a livelihood!

— Herman Melville, ***Moby-Dick***

Dionis — watch that train go. Dionis — if you listen hard you can still hear the whistle blow.

— from the song ***Dionis*** by Erik Wendelken

A dream you dream alone is only a dream. A dream you dream together is reality.

— John Lennon

Never trust hunches; the stars are safer.

— Bret Maverick

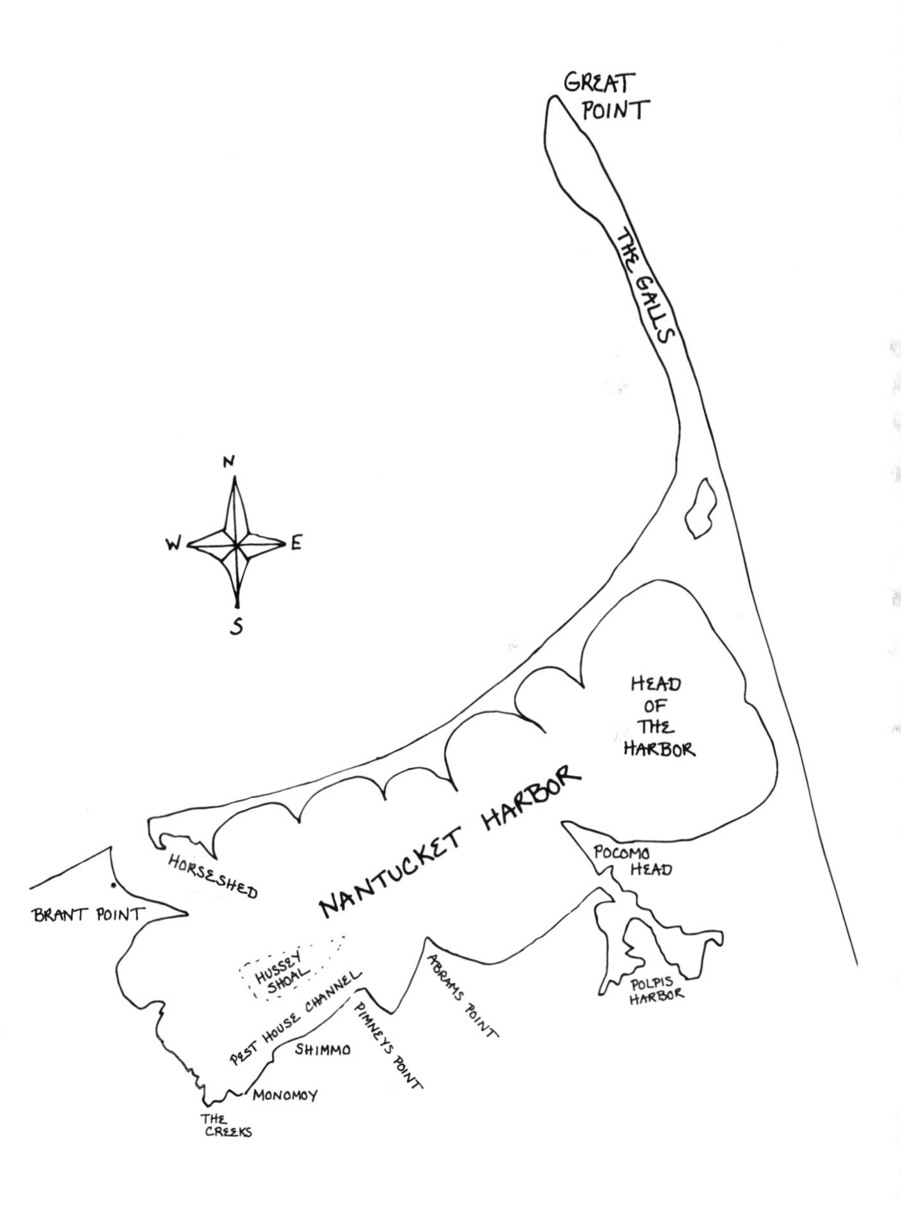
GREAT POINT
THE GALLS
N
W
E
S
HEAD OF THE HARBOR
NANTUCKET HARBOR
HORSESHED
POCOMO HEAD
BRANT POINT
HUSSEY SHOAL
PEST HOUSE CHANNEL
ABRAMS POINT
POLPIS HARBOR
PIMNEYS POINT
SHIMMO
MONOMOY
THE CREEKS

Chapter One

THE FOG was unexpected, but welcome. Gliding slowly but purposefully past Abrams Point, the rower can't believe this lucky break. It had been planned for a moonless night, but the added cover of thick fog is most appreciated.

In the still silence of the upper harbor, the rower stops and listens. Nothing. Not even a ripple on the water. The spot is nearby.

It had been discovered many years before, a shoal about two hundred feet from the beach that revealed itself at low tide. Now, the rower scouts the spot, with stealth, and it remains as it was before — hidden, undiscovered; untouched. No one came to this small, secluded inlet up harbor; not in summer, fall, winter, spring; not at dawn, not at dusk. It was perfect.

It was far enough offshore that you wouldn't walk to it, not even with waders, but it was surrounded by such shallow water that motorboats steered clear.

To get there, you really had to want to get there, and the only way that made sense to get there was by rowing.

It had to be buried here.

Chapter Two

PAST THE cusp of middle-age, yet still hale, hearty, and most assuredly salty, Clarence "Digit" Hathaway walks steadily on the sidewalk of upper Main Street, past the noble houses of the whaling merchants and shipowners — the once ruling classes of the island — going home. There is no one else but him, the handsome houses, and the fog. He especially enjoys walking through this part of town in the fog, enveloped in the shadowy, cloud-like greyness as if he is living out of time, as though the past, present and future all exist as one. It would not have surprised him had an ancient mariner materialized from the mist, puffing on a pipe, nodding a reserved hello.

The sailors of old didn't have to think about parking their cars in summer, of course, which was why Digit was walking. It was easier to walk than deal with traffic. Just yesterday he was about to back his pickup out of a spot near the docks when a visiting foursome, pushing a stroller, walked right behind him, looking only at their cell phones, oblivious to his backup lights. He didn't say anything, just waited patiently, but, man, did they take their time. And then, as he was turning onto a one-way street downtown, a bicyclist, going the wrong way, pedaled right at him.

"Is everybody's brain on vacation?" Digit said to himself as he took a deep breath.

Which was why he was looking forward to October, his time of year, the "off-season," the fall, scallop season. Not just because everybody's brain was on vacation, but because he wanted his island back.

"So just what *do* you do in the winter?" He'd heard this question — in one form or another— all his life: either from a visitor asking directions, or a college kid newly down for the summer, or, more recently, from a caretaking client recommended to him. "Oh, you know," he'd say, "this and that," not wanting to let anyone in on the secret — that winter in many ways was the best time of year. His father would answer the question by saying that both his children were born in the summer — a joke his friend Addie McDaniel retold on his bus tours. What Digit never said was that winter was when the island, as if at rest, renewed itself; when the islanders happily reclaimed Nantucket as their own. If each season had a song, winter's was a nocturne: pensive, dreamy, dusky.

His island. He wasn't sure when he'd become so possessive, so clinging to the lifestyles and traditions he was born into. Didn't he have some claim to the island by birthright? He never used to think so, not when he was growing up: it simply was that he was a Nantucketer.

But after all, his family had lived on the island for generations, most of them making their living from the sea, right back at least to his great-great-great grandfather, James Hathaway, a whaling captain who'd made three trips round Cape Horn.

He supposed Marsha's leaving him had something to do with his neediness; his newfound desire to establish his rights, stake his claim. She was from the island, too, had been part of his life for decades, and although his initial reaction to her divorce request had been 'good riddance,' that was more out of shock than anything, a defensive posture. Time had elapsed, the months slowly passed, and he missed Marsha, more than he ever thought he would. Part of him was gone with her.

At least he'd held onto his house, which he'd inherited from an aunt, and at least he had his best friend, Addie, living with him, along with Addie's girlfriend, Verona.

Addie and Verona, now there was a pair, Digit thought, as he crossed Main Street at the Civil War monument and continued up Milk Street. Those two were meant for each other.

But so were he and Marsha, he'd thought.

Chapter Three

ADDIE McDANIEL had almost made it through another season. Now, lying across the rear seat of his tour bus, he pondered his options.

August's end meant fewer visitors, so there was time for a quick lie down, or even a short nap, between tours. After Labor Day the day- trippers would be replaced by tour groups — charters from visiting cruise ships or excursion companies that included the bus tour in the package price. As in summer, there would be no time for naps once the charter season got underway. He was just about to nod off in euphoric cogitation when a rap came at the side window. "Who the hell . . .?"

Addie rose onto his elbows and looked out at what appeared to be a disembodied clown's head floating in air. He slid the window open.

"How many?" the head wanted to know.

"How many what?"

"How many coming over on the next boat?"

"How should I know?"

The clown's head smiled a yellow-toothed smile bordered

by lips ringed in bright scarlet. "Okay," it said. "Have a great day."

There'd be no relaxing on the bus today, not with clowns knocking on the windows, so Addie went into the office.

It was a small office, a former shanty, a fishing shack, with a ticket counter and behind it a desk, where his boss, Ken, studied some kind of paperwork and smoked a cigarette. Ken had to be the last person in America who could still smoke on the job.

"What's up with that clown?" Addie asked Ken.

"He's trying to sell ice cream, I think," Ken said with a slow exhale, not looking away from his papers. Ken never got too excited about anything. He was the best boss Addie'd ever had, not that he'd had many bosses in his life. There was a side counter with pamphlets and maps that Addie hoisted himself onto. "What are you up to this winter, Ken?"

Ken turned around in his chair, stubbed out his cigarette in the ashtray. "Heading back to Florida."

"What do you do down there?"

"Nothing." He lit another cigarette and lightly inhaled. "You collecting unemployment again?"

"Yeah. Although they make it harder now to have a job on the side. They're checking up on people working under the table."

"I've heard that," Ken said. "I ever tell you about when I collected, when I used to live here in the winter? There was an unemployment office in town, just a room really, and we'd file in to report our job searches — with every one of those potential jobs shut down for the winter, of course. I'd show up right after I scalloped, still in my boots and fishing gear. I'll never forget one day where it was busier than normal, and we had to wait our turn. All of a sudden Fred Lopes calls out: 'Can you hurry it up, Leon? I've got to get to work.' "

"It's not like that anymore."

"What *is?*" Ken turned to his office window. "You'd better get out to your bus. They're here."

And as Addie headed back to his bus, there was the clown, leading the parade of tourists and humming "Whistle While You Work" through his yellow teeth and waxy red smile.

"There's got to be a better way to make a living," Addie thought as he waited outside his bus doors for the first passengers to arrive.

Chapter Four

ON A warm, late summer twilight, Verona, alone, sits on a blanket and waits for darkness. Ever since she had regained her memory she found herself reflexively looking heavenward — seeking solace, she supposed — which led her here, eventually, to the beach, at night, studying the stars.

It seemed like a dream, the months she lived not knowing who she was, or where she came from. Yet, fantastically, all of it was clear, she remembered it all: the times before, during and after her loss of self. It had been a gift, she realized now, the unknowingness, and because she had given herself over to it, she had gained so much, had learned to trust again, and had found new love with Addie McDaniel.

When she'd had amnesia — for she supposed that's what it was; she'd never consulted a doctor, nor anyone for that matter — she accepted it as a new beginning, a second chance at life. When she'd woken on a bench on Straight Wharf, it was as though a veil had been lifted, a curtain drawn on a new life; one without memories, or doubts, or regrets. She clung to that dream as though it was a life raft: if her past was to be shipwrecked, she would embrace being a castaway — unfettered, adrift, untethered to whatever had come before.

She smiled at the thought that she had been literally marooned, waking to blank-slate consciousness on a real island; her isolation truly not a metaphor.

And although she'd wanted to stay in her insular state, happily aloof, she realized that if she continued to keep to herself, and remained a mystery around town, people would make it their business to know hers.

And so she let a few people in, cautiously, carefully: at first, Sandy, who'd rented her a room; then Addie (dear Addie); and, happily, lovingly, at last, Rebecca, her relative, her aunt — the two of them brought together on this island of dreams.

She'd never have imagined such a thing, even if she'd let her mind wander, which she did not: she consciously steered clear of rumination — too much thought might arouse the shuttered past.

In the end, when the past did pour back in, she realized it was the death of her husband, and his tragic fall from atop the eroding bluff at Sankaty Head, that most likely had triggered her journey into blissful oblivion. There was a price for forgetting: when the memories returned she grieved all over again.

But she had her friends to help her through these trials; friends who gave her comfort, and space, and time.

For a few short months, life had been a dream. But, as Verona could now attest, dreams, no matter how real, are sometimes fragile, and delicate as a butterfly's wing.

She came with Addie to the beach now and then, more often than not, but he wasn't as enraptured by the stars as she, and, being one to follow her compulsions, she stargazed frequently, with or without Addie.

Cassiopeia climbed in the sky, while the Big Dipper seemed to be moving downward. Andromeda journeyed eastward, waiting for Perseus to save her from Cetus, the approaching Whale. Verona was learning the constellations, slowly, but she was in no hurry — the stars may move in the sky but they didn't change.

When twilight finally ebbed and receded, she got her bearings by finding not the easily recognizable and sparkling stars of the Dipper, but a smaller and fainter constellation, the Pleiades, or the Seven Sisters. Its dimness made it difficult to find, particularly on nights that weren't cloudless, but it was that difficulty that made it precious, a gem, hers.

It had been the first constellation she was drawn to (perhaps because of its wispish qualities), and for that reason she identified it as her own.

Soon after she had first met Addie, they had seen a shooting star arc over the water. "Make a wish," Addie had told her.

She wished she would never find out who she was.

But she had.

Nevertheless she was happy.

In the last days of summer, whales were seen along the south shore of the island, attracting scores of the curious who patiently scanned the horizon through binoculars awaiting the telltale blow of water or splash of tail. Pods of whales were somewhat close to shore at first, but they gradually moved farther offshore, in search of plankton and krill, their favorite food source.

The irony wasn't lost on anyone that these were Right Whales, which were once plentiful in these waters until whalers decimated their populations, hunting them for their oil, which, before kerosene, and later, gas, was the main illuminant for lamps around the world. So ruthlessly were these whales hunted almost three hundred years before that they were nearly killed to extinction; they remained an endangered species with an estimated worldwide population of under 400.

With whales back in island waters, Nantucketers were compelled to find them, to spot them, to scout the different areas where sightings had been reported.

They couldn't help themselves.

Just after sunset, at that magical moment before nightfall fully envelops the sky, Verona turns to the horizon as the darkness absorbs the afterglow. One by one the first white stars blink above her. She lies down on her blanket and looks skyward. The night is calm; the waves fall gently on the shore.

A faint sound catches her ear, almost like a foghorn. She sits up and listens. Is it the wind? But there is no wind tonight, not even a whisper. She hears it again — a long, low moan. From where is it coming? She can't tell. But when it sounds again, louder, more insistent, a call in the gloaming, its origin becomes clear.

It was coming from the ocean.

Chapter Five

SANDY BRONSON didn't know how she was going to tell Ken she was quitting. She had been his stalwart, the one he could count on when the college kids, after putting in their one-or-two-year stints, began quitting earlier and earlier in the season, and were becoming more and more unreliable and uncaring. Unlike the cadre of undergrads who'd looked at the job as a challenge, and who goaded each other into who could do the most trips in a day, the newer crop was habitually late — if they showed up at all — took no pride in the quality of their tours, and, worst of all, refused to relate with the customers. The best thing the old college kids did was engage the passengers — they weren't stupid, they knew where the tips came from. Ken ultimately made the switch to retirees, most of whom were as old as Sandy is now, but who seemed so much older to her at the time. And, like the college kids, the retirees, too, were phased out by Ken, but for different reasons.

Like the time one driver's foot slipped off the brake and the bus almost went off the dock; or the other time when a driver thought he was taking a shortcut across an old parking lot, but he didn't see the metal pole at the end of the chain link fence sticking out at an odd angle and it plowed right through one of the side windows and across two passengers' laps — thank goodness no one got impaled.

So now they were back to an amalgam of veteran drivers, like Sandy and Addie, and a couple of younger kids, and a couple of retirees who worked part-time and were done before noon.

Who was going to train the new drivers? Sandy had been teaching the new recruits for years. Addie? Maybe. He'd gotten a lot more reliable since he'd started going out with Verona.

Verona. It seemed as though she'd dropped to Nantucket from another planet. When Sandy first met Verona, when she'd rented her a room in her house, she'd thought, frankly, that she was pretty weird.

But, without telling Sandy, without telling anyone, Verona was suffering through some type of amnesia. That took strength, Sandy had to admit. And she was glad their friendship had grown.

Sandy didn't want to be like the other retirees; she didn't want to start repeating herself; she didn't want to look so bloody tired all the time; she didn't want to start ambling to her bus looking at her shoes because her back was crooked and she couldn't stand up straight anymore.

Above all, she didn't want to wreck her perfect driving record.

She should have quit with that crazy bastard Chuck Finley. Things just weren't the same without him and his whacked-out sense of humor. Oh, she'd been angry with him the day he left the island, mostly because of how he'd frightened Verona, unwittingly, as it turned out. But still, he should have known better than to nod in her direction in the courtroom, sending Verona into a tizzy and a tear-filled dash out the door. That was Chuck, though: to act on whatever entered his mind with no consideration at all of how it might affect anyone else. She remembered Chuck's words vividly:

"So I told the judge I was with the FBI, and that I was undercover investigating this woman who was stealing people's credit cards and Social Security numbers. It was the first thing that popped into my head. I'd just seen a story about it on TV."

"I can't forgive what you did to Verona," Sandy had told him.

"Verona?"

"When you pointed her out in the courtroom."

And she couldn't forget Chuck's very Chuck-like response:

"I wasn't pointing at Verona. I was looking at you."

She wondered where Chuck was now. The last postcard he'd sent was from somewhere in Mexico. Why was she thinking *last* postcard, it had been the *only* postcard. There were no other tour bus drivers before or since like Chuck, that was for sure.

Which was probably for the best.

Every fall, when the kids went back to school, the tours were filled with old people —senior citizens — whatever you wanted to call them. Sandy and Ken had a name for this older crowd: Blue Hairs. "Here come the Blue Hairs," they'd laugh, because the Blue Hairs never tipped, and after the tour was over never left the wharf. They'd have lunch at the Tavern, an ice cream cone at Straight Wharf Fish Market, and sit on the benches until it was time to get back on the boat, a three or four hour wait, depending on which tour group they were in.

Sandy would exhort them to at least walk off the wharf and see Main Street. "No, we're fine right here," they'd say. But after a while, they tired of watching the yachts and pleasure boats tie up, and of sitting in the sun, and of looking at each other and, inevitably ended up in the office, asking what time their boat would be leaving.

And now Sandy was as old as the Blue Hairs. And she was having a hard time with it.

She had wanted to talk with Rebecca about it on one of her now daily visits to the Homestead, where Rebecca resided, but the timing never seemed right. How do you talk about getting old to an old person, especially when the old person in question is at least thirty years older than you? How did you talk about it without seeming conceited, or uncaring, or patronizing?

How, at 64, do you look for whatever it is you're looking for from someone in her mid-90s — was it advice; compassion; some untold secret — and not have her thinking about her own age and the time she had left to her?

How selfish could she be?

Was it selfishness that compelled her to tell the lie, Rebecca wondered? She'd put it out of her head, mostly, but at night sometimes, two or three times a week, the thought would wake her with a start, and she'd lie in bed wondering if she'd done the right thing.

It had all happened so quickly: Verona — so earnest in her desire to know the truth — producing the letter Rebecca had written to her daughter decades before; the daughter she'd held too briefly, only once, at birth.

And Rebecca had intended on telling her the truth: how Verona *was* her daughter, there could be no doubting it; there were just too many coincidences for it not to be true.

But what really left no doubt was the feeling Rebecca had, the certain knowledge that her daughter had found her — and she *was* real, and asking her questions, and wanting to know the truth.

But the truth would have helped no one — that was her sincere thought at the time. What good would have been served to admit that, yes, she was the mother who'd put her baby up for adoption, who had vowed to stay out of her life, save for the anonymous gift of money on her twenty-first birthday that brought Verona to Nantucket in the first place? It would have been selfish to ignore the promise she'd made to herself and Verona's adoptive parents to stay out of her life.

To claim title at this late stage, simply because her daughter had unknowingly entered her life, would benefit whom? Why complicate things. It was enough to now have her daughter as her friend. Who knows, being friends might lead to a better relationship; she knew of some daughters and mothers who never spoke to one another.

And yet, as time passed, Rebecca began to harbor doubts about her decision. She yearned in her bones to be able to tell Verona how wonderful it had been to carry her for nine months, to have her living inside her, sheltered, as close as two humans can be. She wanted to explain that because she was in her late forties she had assumed she was too old to have a baby; that she would have been a single mother and the couple chosen as her adoptive parents was better able to support her, to nurture her. She needed to tell Verona how much she'd missed her every day, every single millisecond of every day, and how, through the years, she'd had to stop herself from wondering what kind of person her baby was becoming — wondering what she looked like, what she sounded like, and, most of all, if she was happy.

Yes, Rebecca was comforted, extremely so, just being in Verona's company, getting to know her bit by bit; trying not to need so much; accepting the pleasure of Verona's presence as the greatest gift of her life.

But parents shouldn't lie to their children, and she had, and she didn't know how to reconcile that — with Verona, or with herself.

Chapter Six

As THE long summer waned, Digit prepared his gear for scalloping, unfolding his chain netting, checking and replacing the wood bracing that defined each dredge. He still had to haul his boat to get her ready. He had to change the name of the boat, too. She remained the "*ClarMar,*" a combination of his first name (Clarence) and Marsha's, the name all his boats had had ever since they'd first started going steady. It had seemed too abrupt to paint it over when Marsha first divorced him — he had become as accustomed to the name as he had been to living with Marsha — but what was it now? Two years? Time to change the name.

To what, exactly, would come to him in time. First things first. Paint it over, *then* come up with a name.

He loved the ocean — loved being out on it, part of it. When life on land became intolerable, Digit knew he could escape to the sea. He was lucky he had grown up on the water: he'd accompanied his father and grandfather so much their knowledge practically slid off their oilers. He remembered being a toddler and waiting for his grandfather to return home in the late morning/early afternoon with his daily limit of scallops. He'd watch through the lower half of the glassed-in storm door for the old man's pickup loaded down with boxes of the ridge-shelled beauties.

He stood on tiptoes as his grandfather unloaded his catch — lifting each large plastic milk crate-type box off the back of the pickup, hauling it into the shanty, and summarily upending it onto the long, table-like workbench where the unpacked scallops spilled out. Digit knew to wait until all the boxes had been transferred. Then, with his mother's permission, he'd don his child's coat, and his child's-sized rubber fishing boots, and head out to the shanty, where his grandfather picked him up, and deposited him on the bench. Then he'd watch his grandfather slip the cords of a black rubber apron over his head, grab a stainless-steel bowl and his opener's knife and, one by one, open each scallop and deposit its sweet-tasting muscle into the bowl.

The first scallops, however, had to be sampled by his grandfather, the muscle still pulsing as he popped it straight from his knife to his mouth. Digit knew to be ready. After a quick snack of several scallops and with a steady hand and unerring aim, his grandfather flicked scallops straight into Digit's mouth, Digit anticipating each flying scallop as naturally as a gull.

From her house window just beyond the shanty, Digit's mother took pleasure in witnessing these moments every day. After his grandfather had popped a dozen or so scallops into Digit's gullet, she knew he'd soon be hoisted down from the bench and sent home.

Digit still preferred fresh, raw scallops to fresh, cooked scallops. And there were no better scallops than on Nantucket.

But, like his grandfather, he only ate a few, if any, while he was opening. When he scalloped for a living, he seldom had them for supper.

That would be cutting into his profits.

Chapter Seven

HE HAD forgotten what the island looked like from the air, like a pork chop, tossed boomerang-like from somewhere on the Cape. He hadn't flown much to and from the island, anyway, so seeing the island come into view after such a long absence was both surprising and nostalgic. Hard to believe Nantucket really looked like it did on the plastic placemats they used to sell at Robinson's Five and Ten.

Seeing the island come into view at all was a relief.

If he'd known how foggy it was on the island, he wouldn't have gotten on the plane in Hyannis. Almost as soon as the plane took off, they went from bright, late summer sun into a cloud that seemed to swallow the plane whole. The sensation inside the fog/cloud is of the plane speeding up, not exactly the sensation he wants. And while the passengers around him stare calmly and vacantly ahead, he grips the seat in front of him and looks at his feet, not wanting to reveal his terror, but, at the same time, desperately wanting to talk to someone, to ask if anyone on the plane is as frightened as he is.

Then the plane takes a sharp descent, and he wants to get

up and GET OFF, but instead he sits, looking up now, focusing on the side air vents, consciously breathing in, breathing out while the plane, nose down, seems to pick up speed, and there is no way they are going to make it, and if this goes on any longer he'll have to stifle a scream, and . . .

They break through. They're level; they're right side up.

As the plane approaches through the mist, the town rises out of the ocean, like a child's pop-up book, as fairy tale looking as always. The plane seems to follow the line of the jetties, and he can see the moors, and Sankaty, and Sesachacha (although he'd forgotten its name), and now the roads are clearly defined, and is that a tour bus? But he loses perspective as the plane descends and the runway comes up to meet them and the wheels touch down and he is back.

After twenty years away, he is back.

He was not back for a visit, but to live — for a while, anyway. He couldn't believe it when he got the opportunity to oversee the study and possible excavation of a Wampanoag burial site. A developer had bought the land eyeing the possibility of 140 house lots, with one quarter of them set aside as "affordable" for islanders. But, the abutters protested, that land had always been regarded as unbuildable, sacred land. When the Wampanoag tribe from Aquinnah, on Martha's Vineyard, lent its voice to the protest, the Commonwealth of Massachusetts moved in, halting any groundbreaking until the matter was settled.

That no one in his Boston office jumped at the chance to relocate to Nantucket for several months, or even up to a year, wasn't surprising. It was September. No one wanted to move to Nantucket in the off-season.

But he did. To him, it was the best time of year, a time beyond the busy-ness of summer.

And to get to move back to the island now — to be here legitimately — was like a gift. He wondered how much the island had changed, if anybody he knew was still around.

With any luck, no one would remember him.

Chapter Eight

IT HAD been great living with Digit — the house was big enough that Addie and Verona practically had their own apartment within it — but it was time to move on. He and Verona needed their own space, not that Verona would ever say anything, but he knew she was ready.

Fortunately, Digit knew it, too.

"You know, it won't hurt me if you two wanted to move out," he'd said as Addie helped him clean out his shanty.

"And what's that supposed to mean?"

"It doesn't mean anything. But it's been a few years. Verona would probably like a place of her own. And I know you — if you're not shoved, you're not moving."

"So, you want us to go, is that it?"

Digit took a seat on the high stool in the corner. "Of course not. But it's not like you're in your twenties anymore. It's been great having you here, and stay as long as you want, seriously. But don't you think Verona would like to have her own place?"

"Of course I do, you know that. But how am I going to afford a place?"

"You've lived on this island long enough. They're planning some affordable houses near here. You'd qualify."

"That project's on hold. They think it's an Indian burial ground."

"It probably is. Oh, well. So much for that idea."

"No, you're right, Digit. I've been thinking it'd be nice for Verona to have a place of her own. I didn't want to hurt your feelings by saying I thought it was time to move."

"And you let me go through all that . . ."

"What are friends for?"

And so it was that Addie found himself at the offices of *The Island Looking Glass,* taking out a classified ad for a winter rental.

Although he had lived on the island for nearly two decades, he had never before set foot inside the newspaper office. The girl who greeted him was friendly, and helped him fill in the form, reminding him that they charged by the word.

He looked around, everyone typing away, everyone busy. They all seemed friendly enough, but how could he tell? The only one who'd acknowledged him was the girl behind the desk.

They were writing in here; they were what? — purveyors of words. He chuckled to himself at his little turn of phrase. The girl was looking at him. "Everything fine?" she asked.

"She thinks I'm nuts," he thought.

Under "Wanted to Rent" he wrote:

Long-time island couple seeks year-round or winter rental. We're clean, and we don't have any pets.

He wanted to add: *And we're not nuts.*

Chapter Nine

FROM A bluff above the beach a pair of eyes, through binoculars, scans the far shore, seeking a particular reference point. The eyes follow the point down to a spot in the harbor where, in conjunction with a point on the opposite shore, a triangle is formed, with the spot in the harbor being the triangle's vertex. It was perfect, if you knew what you were looking for. The spot could be plotted on a map of the harbor, if need be.

To anyone unaware of these particular coordinates, there would be nothing — no tree, no house, no pattern — that would stand out as a clue.

The binoculars now follow a solitary rower who has been in the vicinity the past couple of weeks. It seems as if the rower is merely being repetitive in an exercise regime, but even though the rower isn't predictable in adhering to a regular schedule, the movements are too precise — stopping each time, for a rest, presumably, at the exact same location — for it to be mere exercise. No, something is afoot.

And after following the rower's movements for a third time it becomes clear just what the rower is up to, and what the rower is thinking: it has to be buried here. There is no other explanation.

Addie McDaniel handed over the classified advertisement he'd just filled out. After the girl looked it over and said it was fine — although maybe he'd like to change "*Long-time*" to "*established?*", to which he agreed — and that it would be in that Friday's edition of the newspaper, he looked at her and said, without a hint of forethought:

"I was wondering if you might have any employment opportunities available . . . "

"Excuse me?"

What? What did he just say? So he didn't look like a total idiot, he cleared his throat and repeated: "Do you have any employment opportunities?"

"You know, I think they are looking for someone. There's the editor's desk over there. Go over and talk to her."

But before he could say, "Maybe some other time . . . " she called out:

"Merle. He's here looking for a job."

Chapter Ten

DIGIT GUNNED the outboard. The waters were shallow in this spot, but the way the tide was running he knew he'd get over the shoal without getting hung up.

He had an intuitive sense on the water. On another day, he would have remained in deeper water, skirting the shoal until he was able to go around it. His father and grandfather had taught him, letting him take the wheel or the tiller for short stints, talking to him all the while, having him study the waters without his realizing it. But he had a feel for a boat from the start, not oversteering, knowing the wind, how to navigate through chop. He knew the harbor better than he knew his own backyard.

He instinctively avoided the waters just ahead, because it was extremely shallow there, even at high tide. At low tide, it became a small island that housed congregating gulls, and cormorants, and sometimes a seal or two. To him, it was nothing extraordinary, just a tidal occurrence, as normal as the side streets he passed in his truck: he was aware of them, but took no special notice.

There were other places in the waters around Nantucket

where it became extremely shallow at low tide, where you could anchor and walk on the revealed sandbar. Some of these shoals shifted through the years, but others remained where they were from season to season. To know which ones shifted and which didn't, you had to be on the water quite a bit.

In fact, you probably had to make your living on it.

He had heard the reports of whales along the south shore, so after tying up his boat at the town pier, Digit headed out in his pickup to Surfside. There were a few people with binoculars but no whales to be seen.

Because he was out and about anyway, he headed to the Milestone Road and over to Maddequecham. Ever since he was a kid he'd always loved this valley, with its abundance of native wildflowers and grasses that led to a pristine beach. He followed the dirt road that skirted the valley and parked at the beach.

He had a bathing suit in the truck. There was no one around and, using the driver's side door as a shield, he wriggled into it quickly. Like others who made their living on the water, Digit seldom went for a swim, but when he did he wasn't cautious about it. As soon as his toes hit the water he dove in.

Nirvana. The water was invigorating. He lolled in the surf, floating up and down the incoming waves before they crashed on the shore. God bless Nantucket. It took a while for the ocean to heat up in the spring, but you made up for it in the fall when the waters surrounding the island slowly relinquished summer's warm embrace. He had to do this more often.

He sat on the beach to dry off a bit. The late-morning sun made everything bright, alive; even the sandy bluffs sparkled.

Leaving the beach, his vision is awash with colors: the vibrant sky, the vivid greens and yellows in the valley. The colors surround him so that he senses everything from all angles:

to the left, right, overhead, behind him. In a good way, it is as though his consciousness is being swallowed by the verdancy, and he senses its pristine and unsullied beauty through the ages, as though he is part of some long ago experience that is also part of the present, that the now is connected to the past, and at this moment, in this place, he is one with the history of Nantucket. He knows that this valley has always looked the same, just as it does now, that if one of his ancestors was walking beside him right now, he would feel right at home.

In his diary, James Hathaway reflects on the whale's tooth he keeps on his desk.

> *. . . it is a remembrance, a souvenir, given me by one of the crew, Owen Otis. On it he has scrimshawed: Capt. J. Hathaway, Home from the Whaling Grounds, 1829. It is a handsome tooth. Some of the men are quite adept at scrimshaw, decorating teeth large and small with inks made from gunpowder or soot mixed with whale oil. They keep them as remembrances themselves, I suppose, or give them to their wives as a record of what was accomplished on a voyage, as some of these pieces can be quite complicated, etched with a sail maker's needle, or, sometimes, a knife.*
>
> *Ivory has its place, and its uses: as piano keys, or handles of walking sticks, or as corset stays, I ask you! On my voyages, I was only interested in the oil, particularly the spermaceti, the finest lubricant ever discovered. The sperm whale who owned this tooth was a fine specimen, if I recall correctly, delivering 50 barrels of oil, with each barrel holding 35 gallons! That was when a typical voyage of three to four years reaped 2,000 barrels of oil from forty or more whales. Now, twenty years later, it is considered a successful voyage if one-third that number is found.*

I have spoken to present-day captains and ship owners who say we should explore further, that there are vast uncharted waters still, the so-called Northwest Passage among them. They are so mule-headed in their beliefs that I do not bother to tell them there is nothing left to explore, that all the world's seas of consequence have long been charted by us, by Nantucketers. Others speak of quotas, that by limiting our haul, over time the whales will return. Still others say whales are an infinite resource, that their stocks will never diminish, we need only sail south, to Antarctica.

I look to history, to the facts of our industry. That at first, whales were plentiful in the waters surrounding Nantucket. They haven't returned, no matter that we long ago began seeking our fortunes in the far reaches of the fierce Atlantic. And when we were rounding the Horn, and naming great areas of the Pacific "the Nantucket Ocean" the whales didn't come back to us.

At one time Nantucket "lit the lamps of the world." No more. While there are growing numbers of lamps to be lit, with each succeeding year there are fewer and fewer whales to supply those lamps with oil. Still, no one speaks of solutions, only that we must continue to hunt whales as if it is our birthright, as if there is no other alternative. They will not be satisfied until all the whales have been slaughtered.

And who will light the lamps then?

Chapter Eleven

SMALL, FEISTY Merle Eastham motioned Addie to her desk. Not one for small talk, she said: "We do have a reporter's job open. Have you written before?"

"Some poetry," Addie said softly. "I wrote book and music reviews for my college paper."

"That'll do. I get these kids in here from journalism school — you can't teach them anything. Better to have somebody like you that we can train. We're an island: reporting on things is different here. Monday's Labor Day. You can start Tuesday, eight a.m. My name's Merle. I'm the editor. Also the copy editor, ad proofer, and 'Sconset delivery person."

It was sinking in that Addie had been offered a job he had no intention of taking but it was too late to back out now. He'd feel like a fool asking for a job and not taking it. He offered his hand. "I'm Addie McDaniel."

"I don't care what your name is — you're hired."

They shook, and that was that.

Addie walked into Ken's office not sure if he was happy about his new position or not. Ken was smoking, as usual.

"Uh, Ken? I don't think I'll be able to stay on to Columbus Day this year."

Ken was unfazed. "Going on a trip?"

"Going to a new job."

Ken swiveled in his chair to face Addie. "Oh? Doing what?"

"A reporter."

"For the Looking Glass?"

"Uh-huh."

Ken swiveled around to do what he was doing before. "That'll screw up your unemployment," he said without looking up.

"No kidding," Addie said.

Verona was letting her hair grow. During the time of her amnesia, she had cut it as a way to confirm her new identity; since she had rediscovered herself, however, she wanted it to grow out as an outward sign of her renewal. It was grey and auburn but she did not color it, and over time it cascaded over her shoulders and framed her face. When she put it up, she preferred the old-fashioned combs. For Christmas Addie had given her an antique pair he'd found in a jewelry shop downtown.

She had it up now as she sat on the bench with the old fisherman, Wilson. He knew a lot about Nantucket history: about the Old North Cemetery where she still liked to wander; about the history of the houses on Main Street; about the lighthouses, which no longer carried the same interest for her they once had, but seen through Wilson's eyes brought a new lens of appreciation.

Mainly she enjoyed listening to Wilson's voice as he told his stories, his Nantucket accent with the dropped r's and the "yes-suhs", and how his voice blended with the noises of the sidewalk and the street — the separate conversations of passersby; the opening and closing of car doors; the birds in the trees overhead — and the rhythms of all these sounds soothed her like a lullaby.

Wilson was telling her today about hardtack, the biscuit whalers were provisioned for their long voyages. "And it *was* hard," he was saying. "Like a rock. You'd have to soak it in something for a long time to even get your teeth into it."

"Why was it so hard?" Verona wanted to know.

"So it would *last*. Can you imagine how wet things got on those ships? Hardtack was purposely made to be impervious to just about anything. They'd even cook it in boiling whale oil to soften it up."

Verona liked hearing Wilson's stories about food, about chowder, about steaming clams, about the proper way to boil a lobster ("Stroke his back before putting him in the boiling water — you'll *mesmerize* him.") She and her late husband had owned a restaurant in San Francisco, and she was preparing to start a catering business the following summer with her friends Sandy and Irene.

She supposed she'd have to cut her hair again when she got back in the food business, but until that time she'd continue to let it grow.

Sometimes when she'd pass a mirror, the interwoven grey in her hair reminded her that she was older than Addie, a thought that never entered her mind when she'd had amnesia. Age was not a concern during that time, especially among her small circle of friends. Everyone seemed the same to her, except Rebecca, of course, whom she recognized as older, but only in a way that "older" meant "wiser." And in the foggy days that followed her return of memory, she wondered if she was closer in age to Sandy than to Addie, and if it would make a difference in their relationship.

But Addie never brought it up — not once — and since it didn't matter to him, she let it go.

Besides, it wasn't like they were married. They were friends.

Well, more than friends. And it was good.

Ken asked Sandy if she'd train a new hire. "She drove a school bus, so she has experience and, most important, her bus license. You mainly need to take her with you for a couple of days, work up to letting her drive while you give the tour, let her do a solo with you as passenger, and then she'll be good to go — with your approval, of course."

"It's kind of late in the season, isn't it?"

"Well, she became available and she says she'll be here next summer, so I didn't think I could pass her up. Besides, Addie's quit."

What?

"What?" she said out loud. Addie couldn't quit — *she* was supposed to be the one who was quitting. Sandy looked out the window at the lineup of buses, walked around the room, finally sat down on a bench facing Ken. "When did he tell you this?"

"Today."

Today? Had Verona told Addie that Sandy was going to quit? No, Verona wouldn't do that. If there was one thing Sandy was sure of, Verona knew how to keep a secret. Addie must have guessed it. He knew Verona was about to start a catering business, and of course Sandy would be joining her — they regularly cooked together, tried out new cuisines, loved refashioning old recipes. And who was the usual beneficiary of all this yummy goodness? Addie, of course. Addie, the backstabber. Sandy looked at Ken and couldn't speak.

"Don't look so tongue-tied, Sandy. He got a job at the *Looking Glass.*"

"The *Looking Glass?*"

"He's going to be a reporter. You want to hear something funny?"

"Try me."

"The new girl . . . well, she's not really a girl, our new hire was a reporter at the *Looking Glass.*"

"Oh, yeah. When did she work there?"

"She quit today."

Addie was pulling in as Sandy left the office. "Thank you, thank you very much," he said as each exiting customer tipped him. He was counting his money when Sandy approached his opened door.

"Have a good tour?" she asked.

"Forty bucks," he said.

"Good for you, asshole."

Addie froze in his seat. "What . . . "

"Don't talk," Sandy interrupted. "Ken told me about the little stunt you pulled."

"Wha . . . "

"Don't talk!" She walked onto his bus, sat in the seat opposite him. "How could you?"

"What did I do?"

"You quit, that's what you did, Mr. Jerk. You could've told me before telling Ken. I thought we were friends."

"We were. I mean, we are. Listen, Sandy, it happened so fast."

"Spare me. Please."

"Hey, wait a minute. Why should you care if I quit? The

season's just about over, anyway."

"Because I'm going to quit! Or I was."

"Oh . . . " Addie slumped in his seat.

"Yeah, oh!" she said. "Well, guess what? That new job you've taken can't be all that great."

"Why not?"

"Because Ken just hired a new driver, and guess what? She just quit her job at the *Looking Glass* to come here. How about that?"

Addie tapped the steering wheel and looked out the windshield. "Yeah. How about that."

Chapter Twelve

"YOU'VE GOT to develop a nose for news, get to know where to start digging. Eventually, it'll become second nature, like the fishermen who know where to drop their dredges." These were the words of Hal Humphries, who wrote the "I Cover the Waterfront" column for the *Looking Glass*. They were words that addled Addie's brain.

It was his first day on the job, and he was freaking out. He didn't know the first thing about reporting. A nose for news? What's that supposed to mean? Wouldn't that be prying?

The night before he'd stayed up with Verona, lying on a blanket at the beach, looking up at the stars, voicing his trepidations.

"Why did I ask if they 'had any employment opportunities'? What have I gotten myself into this time? I'm not going to be able to do this job."

"You'll do fine, Addie," Verona said, looking for the Northern Crown constellation. "It's good to take chances sometimes."

"Not if you're not qualified. I haven't got the first idea how to do this job." Following Verona's lead, he scanned the heavens and grounded himself by finding the Big Dipper, the only star grouping he really knew.

"Which might be good," Verona said, letting her gaze wander to the Swan, with its impressive array of stars. The night was black, the stars shone white. "You won't go in with a head full of ideas, which is a good thing."

"You're right," he said, turning to her, watching the starlight in her eyes. "I should treat this like an adventure. It's about time I got off my ass and got a real job."

Verona didn't answer. She was miles away, floating amid the constellations.

"Why do the stars comfort you so much?" Addie asked her.

"They give me hope," she told him.

"Hope?"

"That there's more to life than this."

Also looking skyward was Digit Hathaway, on his boat, clearing his mind. Although he usually used his boat only for work (gas wasn't cheap) sometimes it was good just to get out on the water.

He'd meant to get back to shore by dark, but nightfall was occurring earlier and earlier and, as usual at summer's end, it snuck up on him.

The sunset was royal blue and deep orange. He dropped anchor and admired it as it morphed into a pink *rosa rugosa* glow. He thought of taking a picture with his cellphone, but it was tucked away in a waterproof bag and turned off. Nantucket was nicer without cellphones.

That's when the island really started to change: when the first cellphones arrived. Before then, when you were on Nantucket you really *were* removed from the mainland: there was no instant contact with the world; no checking for texts or news updates; no glow at the movies from a hundred tiny screens; no families or couples locked into their own devices while out to dinner; no people driving through people's yards because *GPS told them to!*; nobody walking like zombies up Main Street incessantly talking, talking, talking; and nobody driving around the island with a phone permanently attached to one ear, as if the newest requirement for operating an automobile was to "insert key, start engine, engage mouth." And where were the cellphone towers located? In the spires and steeples of the churches downtown, the highest buildings on the island. Even the divine had acquiesced to inevitable progress, it seemed.

He sat on his boat's bottom and let his mind drift as the sky turned from rose to deep blue to navy to black. In the blueness, the stars began to appear. It was calm, unusual for Nantucket, for even when there was no wind, there was wind, as Digit could tell you each and every day of scallop season. Floating in the stillness, with the stars as canopy, he was removed from the world, from history, from the present.

He thought of the mariners who used to navigate by the stars. How lucky you could still see the stars on Nantucket. He and Marsha used to go out on star-watching adventures, either from his boat or his four-wheel-drive. They particularly liked going to Coatue (by boat) and Great Point (by four-wheel-drive). He couldn't tell you how many times they'd made love under the stars. Who said there was nothing to do on Nantucket? He and Marsha had a lot of laughs over that one.

Funny how he didn't mind thinking of her now, even though she'd left him, run off with that home-wrecker whose name he refused to remember. He kept himself busy; what else could he do?

He and Marsha used to have their favorite stars to look at — he searched the sky for different stars now.

Chapter Thirteen

EXCERPT *from the diary of Capt. James Hathaway*

They are leaving now, more each day, not that I walk the wharves for head counts, but with every stroll through town it's more and more noticeable.

Those from the south seas are gone, among them the tattooed harpooneers. The impressive men of Africa are fewer now, as are our neighbors from Martha's Vineyard, the Indians, along with those from Cape Cod who taught us to whale to begin with. Many are off to New Bedford, I hear, seeking to ship out once more, ironic since it was we Nantucketers who began the industry in that now burgeoning city.

The Portuguese remain, as do some of the men from Norway and Scandinavia, having forsaken whaling, they are now chasers of the cornucopian cod.

How glorious it was when the docks teemed with those from around the world, and with every step a different language was heard (assuming that the cadences and clucks were languages), a symphonic polyglot as the island's music.

How Nantucket once represented the world, how she

was the center of it! And now that the different cultures are abandoning ship the island will be the poorer for it.

We value money above all: so much so that we are drowning in it; we build our homes to glorify our riches rather than taking comfort in the richness of our relationships.

Chapter Fourteen

He saw him out of the corner of his eye, Cy, driving his pick-up truck up Main Street.

But it couldn't have been Cy, because Cy was dead.

The funeral took place the November before. Digit peeked from the vestry through a crack in the door. The pews were packed. He didn't know how he was going to do this.

But he had to.

Cy was dead and Digit was about to deliver the eulogy.

Digit could see Addie and Verona in the back of the church: Addie because he'd once worked with Cy, Verona because she and Addie were together now, a couple. You seldom saw one without the other these days. Sandy Bronson sat behind them, with Rebecca, an old Nantucketer who was probably related to Cy somehow.

As was Digit, which was why he was chosen to give the eulogy. Cy's sons wouldn't do it, so he, Digit, their cousin and closest relative, was asked.

"But I didn't know him that well," he protested. "Addie McDaniel probably knew him better than I did: he worked with him."

"Addie's not family. You are. Just a few words."

And so, as Digit stood at the lectern of the Congregational Church, whose original vestry was built in 1725, the oldest church on the island, he tried not to think about where he was. Breathing deeply, he began:

"Cy is probably wondering why we're here, in church, I mean. I think the last time he was here was when he got married." Silence. Digit could feel three hundred pairs of eyes on him. He took another breath, and continued. "We're here to celebrate Cy, to remember his life and what he meant to all of us." The stares subsided.

"For me, Cy was the embodiment of what it means to be a Nantucketer. He was gruff, but you always knew where he stood; he didn't hide his opinion, be it bad, as it usually was, or good, which he doled out like drops of gold. You felt better about yourself if Cy praised an effort, for, no matter what, you knew that he knew what he was talking about. In this specialized world, Cy was a throwback, the one you'd call on for help with anything: carpentry, plumbing, mechanics, fishing. And when the job was done, you were glad you did call on him.

"He was of the island: born here, raised here, married here, brought up his family here. I think the longest time Cy ever spent off-island was two weeks for vacation. I remember him saying, 'The mainland's a nice place to visit, but you wouldn't want to live there.' He was a true islander.

"Cy was protective of the island — especially its water supply and the waters of the harbor, causes he championed by serving for years on the Harbor and Shellfish Advisory Board — but he never lamented the changes. 'This island's been changing since I've been alive,' he'd say. 'You're not going to stop it.' But he did wish the town did more to house its native sons and daughters. 'People born and raised here should be able to live here,' he said as well.

"Cy enjoyed the company of the summer people, called many of them friends, and looked forward to seeing them each year, particularly those who valued the island, and its way of life, as much as he did. Although some of them were rich, he was never impressed by money, and those he called his friends admired him for this. Cy was impressed more by those who worked hard for their money: an honest day's pay for an honest day's work, a trait imbedded in Nantucket's Quaker roots.

"So, what is a Nantucketer? One who sees things as they are; who doesn't embellish his own accomplishments, but who is quick to acknowledge a job well done; a person who is accepting of all, provided they are forthright, and reliable (and hard workers, don't ever forget that); one who is comfortable in the company of laborers, or executives, and who doesn't hold either in greater esteem; one who enjoys the diversity of the world, but who knows that, in time, the world will eventually come to him.

"And that was Cy. May there be many more of his likes to come."

When the service had ended, Digit's cousins thanked him, saying: "We knew you were the right person for the job. You always were smart in school. Neither one of us could have said what you said.

"By the way, we thought you said you barely knew our father?"

"I guess I knew him better than I thought."

"You sure as hell did."

Chapter Fifteen

THERE WERE others, like Cy, that Digit would almost wave to, but then realize they were dead. Once he thought he saw Mrs. Rayburn, his fifth grade teacher, in the checkout line at the A & P one summer, and taking a second look he realized there was a resemblance, slight, but it couldn't have been Mrs. Rayburn because she, like Cy, was also dead. It was in Mrs. Rayburn's class that he acquired the nickname, 'Digit,' when a new boy in school, an off-islander, a 'coof' if ever there was one, thought he saw him counting on his fingers. "Look at Clarence," the boy remarked, "can't even count without using his fingers. Hey, Clarence, take off your shoes and then you can use all your digits." And the name 'Digit' stuck. Over time the label lost its meaning and even became an endearment, especially when he played defensive end in football and his fellow teammates would taunt the opposition: "Oh, yeah, single digits for you when Digit's in the house." Digit never told anyone, not even Marsha, that he was daydreaming when the misnomer was first directed at him, using his fingers, for sure, but not for a simple arithmetic problem: he was ticking off the Periodic Table of Elements, a memorization exercise he had assigned himself.

So now, as he turned onto Main Street from Union Street, Digit thought he saw Dirk Caspian walking across the cobblestones toward the Nobby Shop. But it couldn't be: he was seeing people again. Dirk Caspian hadn't been on the island in twenty years. Digit almost pulled over but kept going up the Main Street cobblestones. Was he crazy, thinking he'd seen Dirk Caspian? Forget about it: he had nets to mend.

Dirk Caspian. Now there was a blast from the past. He hadn't thought of him in years, neither consciously nor subconsciously. Wow. And they had been friends, too. Best friends.

Too bad it had ended so badly — and quickly.

The last time Digit had seen Dirk Caspian was in court.

"All rise."

Addie was in the Nantucket District courtroom, standing in the first row in seats reserved for the press. He was nervous. The only other time he'd been in the courtroom was for the trial of his former fellow bus driver Chuck Finley, which ended with Verona frantically running out of the room, but weirdly led to their living together.

"Just write down everything you hear," Merle had told him, "and I'll help you sort it out when you get back. It's after Labor Day, so there shouldn't be much happening."

Next to him was a girl/woman scribbling frantically in her notebook. What was she writing? Nothing seemed to be happening other than the judge entering the courtroom. Addie hesitantly introduced himself.

"Hi," she said, still scribbling. Then, stopping, she turned to him. "You're new. I'm Ellen," offering her hand. "I'm a stringer for the *Cape Cod Advocate*."

Stringer? What the heck was that? He wasn't about to ask

and sound stupid, and the proceedings were about to begin.

A man sitting at a table facing the judge's bench stood up and said: "If your honor please, our first case is an arraignment but we were hoping we could dispose of this matter today."

"And what is the charge?" the judge responded.

"Jacking deer, your honor."

"Excuse me?" The judge raised an eyebrow.

"Poaching, your honor. Luring deer into his yard by feeding them, and then freezing them in their tracks by shining a flashlight in their eyes, and then shooting them out of season."

The judge put his head in his hands. "And who is the accused?"

The man at the table turned and motioned for a man to stand. "One Isaac Coffin, your honor."

"Ike Coffin?" the judge bellowed.

"Yes, your honor," the defendant said quietly.

"Stand up! You know better than that. Weren't you in here for scalloping out of season?"

"Yes, your honor," Isaac Coffin said, half standing, supporting his weight with one hand resting on the table.

"I should throw you in jail." The courtroom went quiet. "Well, Mr. Prosecutor, what's your recommendation?"

"A fine, your honor. I believe it's $500."

"Done." The judge rapped his gavel. "And I'm putting you on six months' probation, with a six months' suspended sentence. Do you know what that means?"

"Yes, your honor," Isaac Coffin said softly.

The judge continued as though he hadn't heard him. "It means that if you get into any trouble within that time," his voice rising, "you'll be going to jail for six months. Do you understand that?"

Isaac Coffin nodded.

The judge spoke quite loudly now. "Answer me! Do you

understand!"

"Yes, your honor."

"Good." The judge pulled at the sleeves of his robe. "Now, pay your fine and behave yourself."

Addie was scribbling furiously, but Ellen barely wrote down anything. Man, he was never going to get this right.

After a few more cases, the judge called for a brief recess. *Whew!* Addie turned to Ellen. "I'm not getting any of this."

"I'll help you," she said comfortingly. "This is your first day. It can be confusing. But this is good experience for you. Before you know it, you'll know more than a first-year law student."

Addie couldn't imagine *that* ever happening. He was a poet. He wasn't interested in the law.

The last case of the day was called. The defendant admitted to facts, which was that he had stolen a moped.

"What would your parents say?" the judge asked the boy, a Nantucketer, who was barely eighteen. "You're an adult now, at least in the eyes of the law." The boy hung his head. "For your sentence," the judge said, "I want you to write a 500-word essay on why stealing is wrong. Do you understand that?"

"Yes, your honor," the boy replied.

"Good," said the judge. Then, beginning to rise he raised his voice, "And DON'T SAY IT'S BECAUSE YOU MIGHT GET CAUGHT!!"

And with that, court was over.

"He used to banish them," Ellen said to Addie after the courtroom had emptied out.

"What?"

"If someone wasn't from the island, and stole something, or

was found guilty of assault and battery, he'd tell them to get on the next boat . . . "

… "and don't come back." Digit remembered well the judge's words. Like so many others, Dirk Caspian was ordered off the island.

And even though their friendship had once flourished, Digit never saw or heard from Dirk Caspian again.

Which was why he couldn't have seen him on Main Street — once Dirk Caspian was thrown off the island he never returned.

Digit always thought it had been a trumped-up charge anyway. Dirk Caspian had been accused of hitting a kid with a pool cue at the annual "See you later, Alligator" party on Labor Day weekend. The cops hauled him away to spend the weekend in jail and appear in court first thing the following week.

Maybe if Digit had been at the bar that day things might have turned out differently. But he wasn't.

When the judge banished Dirk from the island, Digit assumed he'd just wait a year and then come back. Lots of people did who'd received the same sentence.

But he never did.

And he never called or, to Digit's knowledge, ever tried to get in touch with his old friend.

And though they'd been tight, real tight, talking 'til dawn tight, Digit and Marsha got closer and closer until he didn't particularly care if Dirk Caspian came back to the island or not — if he didn't care about Digit, why should Digit care about him?

Chapter Sixteen

Dirk Caspian could've sworn that was Digit Hathaway driving up Main Street. Although it had been years, Digit, or who he presumed to be Digit, still looked the same. Could it be Digit's kid? No, he looked older than that. Whatever. It was a small island; he knew he'd eventually have to run into Digit sooner or later.

When that happened, he hoped Digit wouldn't want to reminisce. If they were to resume their friendship (fat chance of that), he'd prefer to start fresh, with no talk of the past.

And he did like the way Digit talked, with that accent peculiar to Nantucket; that New Englandy, clipped way of speaking that he hadn't yet heard this time around: "Pow-ah boat;" "Hey, Cap;" or "Finest Kind."

The Nantucket accent was fading, he could tell just in the short time he'd been back. Sitting at the bar at The Atlantic Café he listened to the conversations around him while pretending to be immersed in his phone. The guy to his right, who talked to his companion about coming to Nantucket to get a break from the Hamptons, was clearly not a native. The man to his left, however, had the weathered face of an islander. He was lamenting the cost of a new outboard engine.

"It was time, I guess," he was saying to the person on *his* left. "I put who knows how many hours on it, and I bought it *used*."

"Can't be helped," said the other. "Outboards are pretty expensive."

From his past experience hanging out with Digit, Dirk Caspian knew that a Nantucketer would have used the modifier "some" instead of "pretty," as in "some expensive, Cap." Not that he cared. He hadn't returned because of some deluded and nostalgic yearning to reimmerse himself in the 'Nantucket Way.' And he certainly hadn't returned to re-establish former friendships.

Was he sorry he and Digit hadn't remained friends? For a couple of years they were close, as thick as two people could be; sharing their fears, their insecurities, their family secrets. All those late-night conversations in the dark, at the beach, or at Digit's house, whispering on the front porch or in Digit's living room (the parlor, "pah-la," as Digit's mother had pronounced it), Digit on the couch, he lying on the floor, until they had either talked themselves out or fallen asleep.

No, he had to leave the island when he did, for a variety of reasons.

Not the least of which being that had he stuck around, Digit would have no other option but to hate him.

Chapter Seventeen

LIKE A twisted rubber band wound tighter and tighter, summer was about to snap.

Traffic was at its worst, the worst anyone could remember. Cars, piloted by drivers distracted by their cell phones, bounced off curbing. There were tie-ups and traffic jams at every corner; pedestrians walking into traffic without looking; lines of bicyclists of all abilities zig-zagging this way, then that. By mid-August, it was almost better to just stay inside.

And then someone honked. Digit couldn't believe it. He was stuck in traffic heading towards the Rotary when someone behind him leaned on his horn — with emphasis! What did this person think, that traffic would somehow move because he used his horn? Nobody beeped on Nantucket. Digit could see the driver in front of him looking back at him through *his* rear-view mirror. Digit threw his hands up, intending them to say, "It wasn't me — I didn't beep," but he suspected this gesticulation was misconstrued, that the driver in front of him now thought that Digit *did* beep, and that somehow he wanted him to get moving. "*Great,*" Digit thought, "*that's all I need, an altercation because some idiot behind me beeped.*" He exhaled deeply and thought of the old saying: "I should have stood in bed."

But then, miraculously, Labor Day arrived, the tension eased, and fall was in the air, you could almost smell it. Relief rose like air escaping from an over-inflated balloon while the humidity seemed to drop with each departing visitor.

Even though few bothered anymore, Digit began giving the wave with frequency right after Labor Day.

The wave.

It was a carryover from the maritime tradition of waving hello to passing boaters, Digit figured. Whenever you passed someone you knew while driving, you gave a little wave, a gesture of recognition to a fellow Nantucketer. It was a sign of survival in the summer, a signal of comradeship in the winter. It meant you were from the island, and a wave was only proffered if you were recognized as such.

Living on the island year-round didn't necessarily merit a wave. You had to belong, you had to be of the island; you had to *get* it.

Coast Guard Chief Sally Nancy got it, but the chief after her didn't and nobody gave the wave to him. Addie got it, and even gave the wave from his tour bus. Sandy didn't care, but people waved to her anyway.

Sometimes you'd give a wave by taking one hand off the steering wheel, but that was rare. Most of the time, Digit gave the wave by lifting the four fingers of each hand off the wheel and steering with his thumbs.

Others had refined the practice to an upturned index finger or two. Frank Marks had it down to lifting his head back slowly and opening his mouth in a silent "hi."

When someone gave you the wave, it was customary to wave back. Most of the time waves were given simultaneously, as islanders who still practiced it knew each other's cars. If someone bought a new vehicle, of course, it took seeing it a time or two before the waves recommenced.

It used to be that you'd feel badly if you passed someone without giving a wave. "Shoot, that was Ben Cartwright. When did he change trucks?" The Fire Chief solved that problem: he didn't wait to see if he knew the person or not: he just waved at everyone he passed, using the four fingers off the steering wheel method.

Time has a way of eroding traditions, however. The fire department once sounded an air horn to alert volunteers, and all islanders, to a fire call. The number and pattern of blows on the horn represented different neighborhoods. When it snowed, three single blows meant no school, a welcome sound in Digit's youth. The fire horn was dismantled years ago, leaving the island's school children without the expectant yearning of listening for freedom's call on a snowy morning.

There was also the aforementioned issue of beeping. It mainly occurred during the summer, but lately people were laying on their horns in the off-season as well. As far as Digit was concerned, you only used your horn on the island in an emergency, or, more likely, to toot hello or good-bye. A friendly beep was sometimes used in conjunction with the wave.

Digit also wondered how many people remained on Nantucket who knew why the Town Clock's bell sounded fifty-two times after ringing the hours of 7 a.m., noon, and nine at night. In 1849, the island's selectmen decided that the bell would toll additionally at those hours to signal the times to get up and go to work, eat lunch (or "dinner" as it was then called), and observe curfew, or get off the streets.

Fewer still probably realized the significance of the number 52. It wasn't the number of weeks in the year, nor was it the number of whaling ships lost at sea, as Digit had heard erroneously over the years. According to Jay H. Gibbs, the town's last bell ringer before the bell was electrified in 1957, 52 was the right number of pulls required for the full three minutes decreed by the Selectmen in 1849; a revelation discovered, apparently, by a long-ago bell ringer reluctant to shed his gloves on a frosty morning to consult his pocket watch.

At least you could still get a frappe at the drugstore soda fountain; there was some solace in that.

As September's days poured out, and the island's moors adopted their maroon velvet hue, Verona bade the season farewell at Surfside. As she swept the sky, a fingernail of crescent moon hung high in front of her, a watercolor peach prevailed to the west, while, behind her, to the north, a faded-jeans blue washed the last day of summer twilight. Watching the horizon as the pink-hued sunset faded into navy blue, she heard the sound again. It seemed to travel across the surface of the ocean to her ears: the same low moan she'd heard before, almost as if it were calling to her, almost as if it were a cry for help.

Chapter Eighteen

DIGIT COULDN'T remember who'd told him about the whale, but he wasted no time in biking to the beach to see it.

It was early October, and he was in the fifth grade. Word spread as it does among school children, and Digit was off to the north shore without hanging around to learn if it was true or not: a whale was on the beach.

When he got there a bunch of people were gathered around something, he couldn't tell what, but then he'd never seen a whale before. He ran to the shoreline and whatever it was, it was huge. But there to the right was what looked to be a giant tail. A man in waders walked up to the creature and then climbed right up onto it. More kids began showing up and they gathered round and watched as the man in waders sank into the blubber and seemed to bounce with each step he took.

That was all that Ed Stackpole needed to see. Off came his shoes, up went the cuffs of his pants, and onto the whale he climbed. It took him a second to get his bearings, but he soon got comfortable walking on the whale's rubbery white belly. And then he started to jump. It was like he was on an enormous trampoline. The kids on the beach looked at each other. Junior Ramos was next, and soon he and Ed Stackpole were jumping and laughing in the yellow autumn sunshine.

Digit had already rolled his cuffs. He didn't need to wait for an invitation. The whale was slippery, but Junior and Ed lent a hand and hauled him up. And Digit jumped, cautiously at first, but his feet felt the buoyancy of the whale and despite the slipperiness he let go, jumping higher and higher and whooping with joy. It truly was the most fun he'd ever had. A girl in one of the lower grades was trying to climb up. As Junior and Ed had done for him, Digit offered his hand and pulled her aboard. She tried a couple of jumps, but what seemed to be a good idea from the beach became unsettling when she felt the skin of the dead animal against her toes and she climbed down.

Her unspoken trepidations seemed to silently signal to the boys that the jumping jamboree was over and they climbed down as well. Trudging up the beach to his bike, Digit looked back briefly at the washed up whale and was glad no one else was clambering onto it for a ride. He could see now that the whale looked out of place on its side on the beach; marooned in a foreign atmosphere; vulnerable despite its massive size.

Still, he *had* had a blast.

When he got home, his mother shooed him out of the house and made him take off his clothes outside. "You stink to high heaven," she said. "Where have you been?"

"Jumping on a whale."

Of course he was, she thought. Why wouldn't he be?

The next day, Digit's father took his clothes to the dump along with the rest of that week's rubbish.

Digit and his classmates later learned in school that the whale was a Finback, second in size only to the Blue Whale.

Its skeleton was later displayed as an exhibit at the Whaling Museum.

For reasons unthought of and never discussed, neither Digit, nor Ed Stackpole, nor Junior Ramos ever mentioned their whale-jumping adventure again.

Chapter Nineteen

IN TIME, Addie grew more accustomed to his job at the newspaper, learning not to agonize over court or police write-ups, but to bang them out and not have them hanging over his head. He liked starting each week with a clean slate. "Don't try to learn everything all at once," Merle advised him. "You'll catch on." After the paper came out on Friday, there was time to hang around the office and learn what he could about newspapering from Merle.

"It was my job to meet each boat in the summer and see who was back for the season," she told him. "I also went to the hotels and guest houses every week and get a list of the people staying there; and then we'd print it in the paper, as a service, so people would know who was here and who wasn't. Couldn't do that now, of course; they'd say we were violating some kind of privacy law, no doubt. Whenever there was a fire, my father, who owned the paper then, would wake me up and I'd go cover the fire with him."

Merle made sure Hal Humphries' exuberance didn't overwhelm her new hire. After she'd heard Hal tell Addie, "Wait'll you get your first banner headline, kid," she'd taken Addie aside. "Don't worry about Hal," she said. "He can seem pretty aggressive but that's just his style. After you get used to him you can learn quite a bit about journalism, if you want to."

Ellen was also a help to Addie. They developed a routine where they'd meet for coffee Friday afternoon and go over their respective newspapers. She helped him with his note-taking.

"Addie, you can't write down everything people say in long hand. You need to develop a shorthand system."

"What do you mean?"

"Use a 'plus' sign for 'and', for example; use the number 2 instead of 'to' or 'too'; shorten words when you can. Just make sure you can decipher it afterwards. And don't ever be afraid to have someone repeat something. Nobody minds. They want you to get it right."

"So, what's a stringer?" Addie asked her.

"It means I'm not quite a staff writer. But if I do a decent job covering Nantucket, they'll put me on the regular staff over on the Cape. I'm working on a story now that might get me noticed."

"What story's that?"

Ellen smiled, as an elementary school teacher might kindly smile at a student who isn't quite getting it. "I can't tell you. It's a pretty good story, though."

"Is it something I should know about?"

"You tell me after it's printed." She paused. "It's not something your paper would be interested in, so don't think about it. You should be finding your own stories to write about."

"They say the thieves tossed the whole thing overboard."

It was from C. C. Dennison that Addie first heard about the robbery.

"It's a mystery," Dennison said, putting his arms behind his head and leaning back in his chair. "Never been solved. Close to twenty years ago now."

C. C. Dennison was two chiefs removed from revered Chief Sally Nancy at Coast Guard Station Brant Point, where the second lighthouse in the American colonies was built in 1746, and where, after being moved or rebuilt nine times (more than any other lighthouse in the country), the current light was built in 1901. Addie checked in with the chief once a week to see if there was any Coast Guard news. In the lull between early autumn and winter not much was going on.

"What was it?"

"A safe. An old safe. Taken from the old town building behind Main Street. Some people claimed the sea chest inside it had $500,000 in cash, and thousands more in ivory and scrimshaw. Some thought the safe itself was waterproof. The thing is, if they'd just dumped it overboard, how did they think they'd ever retrieve it? Some parts of the harbor are pretty deep."

"Maybe they dumped it outside of the harbor," Addie suggested.

"Oh, that was explored, you bet. But the idea was quickly abandoned. Anything dumped outside the harbor, on either the north or south shores, would be next to impossible to fetch. Besides, the equipment needed to run that kind of salvage operation would call a little bit of attention to itself, don't you think? Well, anyway, that's all moot because anybody can go after it now."

"What do you mean?" Addie asked.

"The statute of limitations. It's expired. It's the same now as if it'd been lost at sea, taking into consideration that it ever landed in the sea."

Addie looked lost, Dennison could tell.

He stood up, got a cup of coffee. "Let's assume they buried it somewhere in the harbor, or in Madaket harbor. This was twenty years ago. Don't you think by now someone's scallop dredge would've caught on it? Don't you think some diver, beyond all the divers sent out back then, would've come across it by now? And yet," he said, sitting back down with his coffee, "people still believe it's got to be in the water because the safe has never been found on land. And the island was scoured, believe me."

"So what do you think?" Addie asked C. C. Dennison.

"Well," he said, inhaling slowly through his teeth, "here's what I figure . . . . "

Chapter Twenty

REBECCA HAD heard about the robbery. It made it into all the papers, and being from Nantucket, she was curious and read about the theories and lack of progress in catching the thieves in *The Brockton Enterprise*. By the time she returned to the island, no one was talking about the robbery anymore. People were talking instead about too many houses, and a supposed need for traffic lights (heresy!), and how the island culture was eroding.

She had forgotten to change her calendar to October. Her aged fingers had difficulty gripping the page and she inadvertently flipped ahead to November. Veteran's Day. She thought of her fiancé, Gerald, and of his fate during World War II, lost at sea, his ship sunk by a Nazi torpedo. There weren't many of her generation left, a fact that seemed to drain her more with each passing year.

She was 95 now, one of the few on Nantucket who could even remember World War II. Soon, they would all be gone, relics, with no one to remember those years or what it had been like to live through them.

In another time this might have wearied her, lamenting what was lost. Everyone she had known on Nantucket was no longer around, the island on which she had grown up only a memory. She easily could have slipped into melancholy, were it not for Verona.

Verona. Her daughter. She had to remember not to think of it too often, lest it slip when Verona came to visit.

But with each visit she could see the familial resemblance, hear the inherence of generations past in her voice. Best of all she could touch her, if only to reach for her arm when Verona bent down to kiss her forehead.

As she felt when she gave birth to her, Verona was a gift, a gift who had been lost, but who had endured her own share of hardships and crossed Nantucket Sound to return to her, herself an island refugee who had eventually found her way home.

It was hard to stand after sitting for so long, but Rebecca forced herself out of her chair and shuffled to her bureau. Holding her mirror, she saw traces of her daughter in the corner of her eyes, in the curve of her mouth.

Verona's hair was turning grey. Would it eventually become all white, as Rebecca's own hair had done? White, like snow. Just thinking of snow made her shiver. Winter was coming on, she could feel it in her bones.

As a child she didn't mind the winters, particularly when it snowed. If it snowed enough to call off school, she'd follow her friends over to Main Street, where police blocked off cars for the day so the kids could sled from the Town Clock on Orange Street all the way to the fountain at the bottom of Main Street, if conditions were favorable.

During a freeze-up, there was skating on the ponds, and if it got cold enough, and the harbor froze in, they'd even skate on the ocean near Children's Beach.

The reliving was almost like skating again, and she made

her way back to her chair, worn out from the memories.

When Verona came, she'd have to tell her all about it.

Verona sashayed toward the Homestead, lightly dancing up the sidewalk. She wasn't young, but she moved at a youthful pace. "What a crazy life," she thought, swinging her now shoulder-length hair from side to side, relishing the feeling and the movement. When she'd first heard about Nantucket she'd never imagined that not only would she end up living here, but that she'd have found a relative here as well.

But that's how Nantucket was — an island of untold treasures.

She seemed to grow closer to Rebecca each time she saw her. There was an ease in their relationship, unlike anything she'd known before, not even with her husband.

She visited Rebecca every day, sometimes taking her for walks among the old houses near the Homestead, sometimes venturing down North Liberty Street to Lily Street and over to the Lily Pond. That was a long walk, however. Lately, they'd just hang out in Rebecca's room and Rebecca would reminisce.

Verona didn't want to tell her aunt about the feelings she had, that she felt more and more as if they'd known each other before. But that would be crazy because they couldn't have; Verona had grown up on the mainland, after all.

It was chilly today, so Rebecca probably wouldn't want to venture outside. As she walked through the front door, Betty, one of the staff, greeted her.

"How is she today?" Verona asked.

"Oh, she's been quiet today, she's not so steady on her feet these days, but I'm sure she'll perk up when she sees you."

And as Verona gracefully took the stairs to Rebecca's room, Betty paused for a moment; out of the corner of her eye, she thought for a minute that Verona was Rebecca, just in the way she turned her head before taking the stairs.

Chapter Twenty-One

BACK AT the *Looking Glass*, Addie asked "I Cover the Waterfront" columnist Hal Humphries if he knew about the robbery.

"Know about it? I covered it, for this paper and as a stringer for the *New York Times*. First robbery in a hundred years — got everyone's attention real quick. Still unsolved, although nobody really cares about it anymore. At the time, though, people wanted it cleared up quickly, so quickly that rumors were flying everywhere, and every rumor, it seemed, was explored. Someone suggested that the safe was water-proof and that it must have been dumped in the harbor. Well, they sent divers down in the deep spots, spent maybe a week or two doing that, but they found nothing.

"Here's what makes it interesting: the robbery was discovered about three in the morning by a passerby, which gave the police and State Police plenty of time to search every car and truck heading off on the first boat. They went to the airport, too, just in case, but of course no one was about to take a safe onto a plane. But they inspected every box being shipped off, and every oversized piece of luggage for a week or so.

"At the boat, the inspections kept up for a week, which was a major undertaking because it happened right around Labor Day. Oh, people were complaining like crazy. Every boat was delayed.

"What I came to realize was that it wasn't the size of the robbery, the value of whatever was in that safe, but the gall of the robbers that ticked everybody off. No robbery in a hundred years. That's a pretty good record. The islanders took it personally. I wrote about it for weeks; the story had legs, as they say.

"But opinion turned. All of a sudden it took on the notoriety of a folk crime, a legend. People were secretly hoping the thieves would never get caught, that it would remain the great unsolved crime.

"And it has, I suppose. The safe has never been found. Inside it was a wooden chest. People took to calling it a pirate chest, but it was really just an old sea chest. What was in *that* has been disputed everywhere from the Pacific Club to the Maddequet Admiralty Club."

"So what was in it?" Addie asked.

"Ah, now that's the conundrum," Humphries said. "If you ask me, the whole thing was suspicious right from the start. Understand that this wouldn't be such a big deal if it happened on the mainland, but this being an island magnifies every occurrence, kindles romantic notions of isolation and days of yore, if you will.

"This wasn't an armed robbery, or a holdup, but a robbery all the same," Humphries continued. "The chest was going to be opened the very next day, with great speculation as to what was inside. This newspaper sponsored contests for kids, both islanders and summer children, asking them to guess.

"It had been found in the basement of The Pacific National Bank, so named for the ocean where Nantucketers' fortunes were made. With great fanfare, the safe had been put on a dolly one July Fourth and hauled up from the cellar by members of the Nantucket High School Whalers football team. The safe was on display that whole day in a special case made by the high school woodworking class, complete with red, white, and blue bunting.

"At ten the next morning, the dolly was put on a horse-drawn cart and driven down Main Street to the old town building — where the football team once again performed the ceremonial task of lifting the safe from the cart and placing it in the old town clerk's office, which was then an exhibit of sorts run by the Nantucket Historical Association.

"The safe wasn't overly large, but it wasn't what you'd call 'small' either. The combination had been found in an old ledger and still worked. Inside were outdated deeds, old maps, ship's logs — and the chest, what the old-timers might have called a 'ditty box.' It was sturdy, though, complete with padlock.

"What was in the chest? The whole island was captivated by it, it seemed. School children drew crayon pictures of the treasure chest and the gold they thought it contained. Everyone on the street was eager to talk about it, how it was good publicity for the island, and didn't it capture the history of the island, that ship traffic in these waters was once phenomenal, and now here was a real relic of that time? It could only be good for business; shop owners played up the treasure aspect, running advertisements claiming that their stores carried the 'best treasures' or the 'finest kind of finds.' I particularly remember that one.

"But after the robbery? You may as well have rolled up the sidewalks, as they used to say. You could almost feel the energy drain from the island. Shops closed down right after Labor Day, just like the old days, the real old days. The anticipated business boost from treasure curious shoulder season visitors didn't happen.

"Not that anyone expected the chest to actually contain

anything of value; it was the *idea* of the island's vaunted history come to life that fired people's imaginations, the sense of island pride in its rich past that spurred celebration. It was like an island-wide carnival and then, poof, it was gone.

"Don't get me wrong, nobody cried over it — well, maybe a couple of school kids did. Within a week, everyone stopped talking about it. Cheering on the high school football team helped. That fall you knew where everybody on the island was on Saturday afternoons — at the football field. Pretty good team that year, too, despite being the smallest school in the state; they won the league title.

"People realized what they'd known all along — the real treasure was in each other. And that's the beauty of Nantucket, its storied past, sure, its natural glory, but it's in sharing the joys of being on this island together that really counts. And if from time to time we need the diversion of sunken ships or buried treasure to remind us of what's really important, then so be it." Hal cleared his throat, seemed to be collecting his thoughts.

"You got me going there, kid. Didn't mean to bore you with my proselytizing, but if you can remember that in your reporting, that you're not just covering meetings, you're really writing about people, then you'll do just fine."

Chapter Twenty-Two

LATE OCTOBER, and the subtle overtones of fall painted the golden afternoon: the apple-red leaves on a few trees downtown; the yellowish-grey/green groundcover at Surfside; the purplish hue of the late afternoon autumn sky. It was Digit's time of year.

And not soon enough. On his way to the south shore to check out the sky before heading home a guy hauling lumber in the bed of his pickup fishtailed onto Bear Street from Orange Street, in the kind of hurry-up expected on the mainland. There were a lot of people on the island who were only here chasing a buck, Digit thought. He supposed you had to be pretty fast to catch it.

Time to get back on the water, away from the money chasers, away from the madness.

He remembered a real off-season, when the people left right after Labor Day. You could almost feel the island rise out of the water, as if relieved. There was never any traffic to speak of, and you knew everybody you passed. The pace immediately got slower, more relaxed. It seemed that everyone who wasn't a shopkeeper, or teacher, or worked for the town was out on the water in those days, scalloping — and some of those people went scalloping after work. It was a tradition that kept people tied to the sea, to an industry that was ingrained in the island's identity, and kept the idea going that the island was at its heart a fishing village. Why, there had even been talk at one point of revamping the town docks into a commercial pier, with the notion of reviving the island as a fishing port, getting back to its roots. Fishermen from New Bedford could off-load their catch on Nantucket and be back at Georges Bank in no time.

Well you know what happened to that idea, Digit thought. He didn't want to think that Nantucket's transformation into a full-blown, high-priced resort was inescapable, but as more and more came to chase the dollar, he supposed it was. The days of Nantucket as a fishing port were long over; like whaling, lost to history.

He wondered how many would be fishing this year. The scalloping had been good the year before, maybe more would try their hand at it.

But Digit knew that was unlikely, what with the unpredictability of the season, and the sheer expense of outfitting a boat for scalloping. Why a new outboard motor alone could set you back close to $15,000, never mind the cost of a boat.

And that was the catch: not only was scalloping a fragile resource, there were no young people coming on.

And wouldn't that be ironic, that if the thing to end scalloping wasn't that there weren't any scallops left, but no one left to fish them?

At least there was Lance Willoughby — maybe he'd get some of the younger guys interested.

Even though he'd only been scalloping about ten years or so, Lance Willoughby was one of the best fishermen Digit knew. He went about his business with a calm confidence, not like some of the guys who thought they knew everything, guys who had more years than Lance but nowhere near his know-how. "Look, I've been out here twenty years," they'd tell Digit.

"Hell, twenty years is just getting started," Digit would reply.

But Lance would never boast; it wasn't in his nature. If anything, he could be too deferential.

"I notice you haven't moved to Madaket yet," he'd said to Digit last season when the scallops were getting scarce around town.

"You think it's time?"

"I do, but I've been waiting for you."

"Waiting for me? Why?"

"Well, you know more than I do about these waters . . . "

"The hell I do," Digit told him. "Don't wait for me. You could be waiting all year if you wait for me. Just do what you feel."

While Digit worked odd jobs in the summer — caretaking, carpentry, a little landscaping — Lance was mate on a charter fishing boat. He was never off the water.

Yes, Digit thought, when it came to fishing, Lance Willoughby had a nose for it.

He looked forward to seeing him when the season started.

Chapter Twenty-Three

On Halloween, Verona walked by her old haunts — the Lily Pond and Old North Cemetery — and continued on towards Main Street. The afternoon was warm, the sun dappled the remaining orangey foliage, inviting further explorations. As she approached upper Main Street, her eye was drawn to an expanse of grass, a field bordered by a split-rail fence that she had bypassed many times before. It was at the beginning of the bike path to Madaket, and although her mode of transport was a bicycle, her previous travels had mainly taken her in the other direction, to 'Sconset. "Quaker Cemetery" was carved into a boulder at the corner of the lot facing her.

A couple of small gravestones were near the boulder, and a few rows of perhaps ten in each row were clustered near one periphery, but for an open area so large there were hardly any tombstones to be found. "Curious," thought Verona. This was nothing like the North Cemetery, where there were scores of old grave markers. Were only a few people buried here?

The lot was hilly for Nantucket. As she walked amid its miniature valleys and rises, Verona sensed a calm about the place. She wished Addie was with her: he'd know at least a little something about this old graveyard.

That night, as Verona and Addie huddled in a blanket watching the stars at Surfside, a figure crept through the old Quaker burial ground and appeared to kneel at one of the few gravestones.

There was nobody else around, no one near, no one to question what the kneeling figure was up to.

The day after Halloween, Digit Hathaway rises at 4, pulls his wool pants on over his long johns and two pairs of socks, slips on a light sweater, then a heavier one over his long-sleeved T-shirt, fills his Thermos with coffee, and goes scalloping.

It was the first morning of the new season, and Digit was excited. Even though he couldn't drop his nets until 6:30, he was too antsy to hang around his house; he was at the dock on Straight Wharf before 5:30.

While his father and his grandfather before him had moored off Children's Beach, which meant they had to row a skiff to their boat every morning, Digit liked the convenience of being on Straight Wharf, where he could pull his truck right up to his boat. Docking in one of these spots in summer was cost prohibitive, but, fortunately, docking rates in the off-season were significantly reduced for scallopers. Even though it was more money than having a mooring at Children's Beach, the time and effort saved was worth it to Digit, especially now that he was getting older.

He brings his coffee on board and then returns to his truck to don his foul weather gear: boots, rain jacket, rain pants. Even though skies are clear, baby blue, scalloping is a wet business.

His boat glides across the water as he leaves the dock, but as he exits the boat basin and adds throttle he sends spray along his bow and a watery rooster tail off his stern. After reaching his preferred spot, he calms his boat and throws his dredges overboard — four from the port side, and four from starboard. Back behind the wheel, he nudges the throttle and drags his dredges across the harbor bottom until he can feel the nets getting full. (A good deal of scalloping is predicated upon *feel.*) Each dredge will be threaded through an A-framed, metal brace that stands securely in the center of the boat's console, and hauled up from the bottom by means of a small "donkey" engine. Once out of the water, the dripping net is pulled over to the culling board and, upended, its contents spill onto the board like a freed piñata. Quickly, the bounty is sorted through, with adult scallops tossed into metal baskets, immature scallops tossed back overboard, along with the occasional crab and flopping, undersized flounder. Quahogs are set aside on the board or flipped into their own basket, with the attendant eelgrass, small fish, and empty conch shells swept over the side. Down goes that dredge, back into the water, while another is power-lifted out of the ocean. And all the while, he is steering the boat, keeping a watchful eye out for other boats, retaining his bearings in the harbor waters and remaining steady on his feet. Although his boat rests on top of the water, he is working *in* water, perpetually baptized.

On this first day of the new season, when the scallops are relatively plentiful and the weather is mild, he remembers stories from his father and grandfather about how they used to hand-haul their nets in the days before donkey engines became standard equipment. They would reminisce, too, of the scallopers who came before them, who fished without outboard engines but under sail, the harbor filled with catboats: single-masted, shallow draft wooden sailboats, all towing dredges. Ah, those were the days, but not really. Digit had had his days of pulling his dredges by hand when his donkey engine failed. He could do it if he had to, but why do it if you didn't have to?

Digit gets his limit by 8:30 and is back at his shanty by 9:30. *His* shanty, even though it is not at his house but at his mother's, the house in which he grew up. His grandfather had built it less than ten yards from the back door sixty years ago, and his father had modified it — rebuilt it really — when Digit was a boy. A quarterboard on the outside proclaimed it "Hell's Half Acre," made by Digit in high school wood shop as a joke gift for his father one Christmas, and proudly nailed to the side of the shanty by his father that spring.

Digit dumps his scallops on the bench, a built-in table that runs the length of an inside wall, the same table he sat on as a child, a baby really, when his grandfather popped one scallop after another into his waiting mouth.

Everything from the ground up inside the shanty is painted white: the ceiling, the walls, the bench. The cement floor slopes gradually to the middle, to the drain. After all the scallops are opened and dumped into white buckets that are carried out to the bed of his pickup for transport to the fish market, the shanty will be hosed down, and the door latched open to air it out.

His opener will be there shortly. As the season progresses, and Digit gets back to the dock later as the scallops are fished down, opening will generally commence after lunch. Today, however, opening day, Roland Hussey will be by as soon as he catches wind of the first fishermen coming in. Digit wouldn't be surprised if Roland is on his way to the shanty already — word quickly traveling from the docks through town in the opening day buzz; everyone hoping the scallopers get their limits early, portending, perhaps, a good season.

There were openers, and there were openers, and there were

those like Roland Hussey, who, if not exactly born an opener, was certainly bred to it. His parents still opened, as did his older sister, who still opened with Bettina Cartwright, as she had now for over twenty years. Scallopers and their openers were extremely loyal to each other. Roland was Digit's opener, and would remain so until either Digit quit scalloping, or Roland quit opening — and neither of them was about to do either.

Digit sheds his scalloping gear in the mudroom and waits inside at his mother's kitchen table for Roland to show up. They'd be standing for a few hours once they began opening, so the tradition was for each of them to have a cup of coffee — sitting down — on the first day of the season.

Roland walks in without speaking and Digit pours the coffee in silence as well.

"Good day?" Roland asks after his first sip.

"Not bad."

Roland nods. He won't ask Digit where he fished, or what the prospects looked like for the season. They drink without talking until Roland says:

"Well, might as well get to it."

"Yup," Digit agrees.

In the shanty, they step into knee-high rubber boots and don black rubber aprons. Digit tunes into whichever FM station gets the best reception, and they commence.

Now Digit is a fast opener, but Roland is quicker. To open a scallop, you must first have a scallop knife, which is not sharp or spiked like an oyster knife, but blunt and rounded. Slide the knife in at the top of the scallop by the hinge and, drawing the blade towards you, scrape the top of the shell with your knife so that the muscle separates from the shell. Now, flip that top half of the shell off and into the barrel at your feet. Go back in with your knife and, working along the bottom half of the shell, remove the guts of the scallop, lifting them as a mass over the top of the still quivering muscle. Cut along the bottom of the shell, freeing the muscle, or the 'eye' (which is the meat of the scallop) and, with a flick of the thumb, send it flying into the stainless steel bowl in front of you.

The idea is to keep a scallop in the air at all times, meaning that if you were good, you were picking up and opening a scallop cleanly in pretty much one motion, and taking only a couple of seconds to open each one. Roland made it seem effortless, perpetually flicking scallops through the air like a juggler.

A good opener left nothing behind in the shell. Digit remembered his grandfather looking through the barrel of opened shells whenever he had a new opener. Even a fingernail-thick residue of scallop on the bottom of a shell would draw his ire. "You're cutting into my profits," he'd admonish the culprit, which is where Digit picked up the phrase.

A scalloper lived on the margins, with every essential of the job a drain on whatever the day's take was from the wholesaler, from the investment in a sturdy boat and engine, to the price of gas, to the donkey engine that hoisted the dredges, to the cost of the dredges themselves. If the fish markets were paying a good price, say $20 a pound, then a reasonably good living could be made over the winter.

There was a time when a scalloper could live off one season's profits for the whole year, make a comfortable but by no means extravagant living, but not anymore. Rather than being a main source of income, if you scalloped you had to do something else: Nantucket had become too expensive for scallopers to survive by fishing alone.

On the second day of scallop season, high-powered binoculars scan the water from a porch overlooking the upper harbor. The rower hadn't been spied in more than a week now. Had it been an exercise regime after all?

No, the movements had been too deliberate to dismiss them as coincidence. The rower was looking for something. It couldn't be coincidence, either, that the rower suddenly materialized during the time frame agreed upon all those years ago.

If the rower was playing games that was fine — he'd been patient this long. He could wait.

It wouldn't be long before he'd be able to flush him out.

Chapter Twenty-Four

LANCE WILLOUGHBY was working the area near the Horseshed off Coatue and having a little luck, but not much. He found it somewhat amusing when other scallopers followed him, since many of them had been fishing much longer than he had. He had to admit it felt good to have the reputation as one of the best fishermen out there, a natural.

He ought to be, he thought, he'd practically lived on the water ever since he moved to the island.

Or, to be more precise, moved back.

When he first arrived he was seventeen, had just graduated high school and didn't know a soul on Nantucket, but he'd heard it was a fun place to spend the summer from a classmate whose older sister had driven a tour bus.

Fresh off the boat, and alone because he couldn't talk any of his friends into joining him, he followed the day-trippers off the wharf. In town, he discovered the Hub bulletin board, not sure what he was looking for, when a kid about his age asked if he was looking for a place to stay.

"How'd you guess?"

"The backpack and goofy expression gave it away. If you want, come with me. The place I'm staying has a bed open. You share the room, but it's only a hundred bucks a week."

"A hundred bucks?!"

"Find something cheaper. And if you do, you'll be sharing a toilet with ten other people, if the place even *has* a toilet. This place is clean. Besides, you'll easily make a hundred bucks a day working on Nantucket in the summer."

He went with him, saw that it was clean, and agreed to the hundred dollar a week terms. The same day he found a job bussing tables and dishwashing, where he did make the promised hundred dollars a day.

He worked six days a week that summer, going to the beach on mornings it didn't rain, and all day on his day off. He was shy, and didn't really make any friends at work, but he enjoyed making the money and one day off a week was enough for him. He was young; he had plenty of energy.

The only people he really got to know were his roommates: the boy who'd told him about the spare bed, and one other guy, who was a few years older. The three of them didn't really hang out until near the end of summer when, for a few weeks, they were inseparable.

And, because of this friendship, when he left the island after that summer he wasn't sure if he'd ever return.

Chapter Twenty-Five

As the season moved into its third week, the scallops were getting scarce. What took two hours in the early going last year now took four, or five. "The gravy boys will soon be giving it up," Digit thought as he finally headed back to the dock, four and a half hours after he started. He noticed that Lance Willoughby was still at it, which didn't bode well for the rest of the season.

A storm was predicted for later in the week. Might be good, Digit told himself as he pulled into his slip. We could use a good blow to shake things up.

As one bumper sticker succinctly put it: *No eelgrass, no scallops.* Scallop seed thrive in clean eelgrass and cling to it in order to evade predators. Lately, however, the eelgrass was dotted with algae and was dying out in places. A storm might conceivably clean out some of the dead eelgrass and push the scallops around.

Not that scallops need the wind to move. Unlike oysters, which are moved only by ocean currents, or by scallop rakes or dredges, scallops scoot across the ocean floor in a zig-zag motion through jet propulsion by opening and closing, or "clapping," their shells.

The Nantucket Bay Scallop *(Argopectan irradians irradians)*, pronounced *scal-lop,* with the same *a*, as in 'ball,' or 'call,' has a life span of one to two years, and generally spawns once in its lifetime. Its appearance is similar to that of the Shell gas station sign. A scientific report of the U.S. government rates its "overall vulnerability" and "biological sensitivity" as "very high." The Nantucket fishery is closely monitored with respect to the scallop's sensitivity, with strict limits on catch sizes and an insistence that only "adult" scallops, that is, those with an identifiable growth ring on the shell, can be harvested. Fishing is prohibited if the air temperature falls below freezing, and overpacking, or "crowning" scallop boxes is punished by forfeiting that day's catch combined with the further prohibition of another day's fishing. The fragility of both the scallop and the scallop industry are taken quite seriously. Scallops are treated with such regard that if a heavy storm blows the spat, or "seed," ashore, there is an immediate response by islanders, who collect the seed from the beaches and take them in their boats back out into the harbor where they are gently reintroduced. Taking scallops out of season is taboo. To those who scallop, protecting the resource is akin to protecting the island itself.

Chapter Twenty-Six

When Rebecca agreed to put Verona up for adoption, she never thought she'd see her again — that was the agreement, and those were the terms.

There was only one condition: when the baby turned twenty-one her adoptive parents agreed that Rebecca could send, through their attorney, an anonymous letter to the daughter she never knew. In it, she bequeathed a sum of money to her unknown daughter, revealing only that it came from a relative on Nantucket Island. It was never Rebecca's intent to meet her daughter, or to have her daughter ever find her because of that letter.

But it happened.

And Rebecca could sense Verona's questionings. The baby she never thought she'd see again was wondering how Rebecca fit into her life. She could understand that; it was only natural.

But because she had lied, and told her daughter she was her aunt, how could she now betray her trust by telling her the truth?

She had only lied to protect her, to shield her.

She stood and looked at herself in her dresser mirror. Surely there was a resemblance between them, anyone could see it, except for her hair, grey to Verona's salt and pepper. But Rebecca's hair could no longer be called grey — it had grown white, as white as the snow, as white as the lie she'd told her daughter.

Chapter Twenty-Seven

THE PRESSES were rolling. Although they were loud, the insistent ka-ching, ka-ching, was like a lullaby.

The presses were located within the *Looking Glass* building, on the other side of the wall from the newspaper's main offices. As soon as the presses started up, Addie went through the door and into the press room.

As the huge spools of paper unwound over rollers that inked the paper and moved it along to be mechanically folded and cut, aproned pressmen snatched the first issues off the conveyor belt before moving here and there around the press, adjusting the tuning peg-like dials that controlled the flow of ink. Addie watched with wonderment.

Addie hadn't read the paper much when he was driving the tour bus, although Ken always made sure to pick up a copy. Digit, he knew, also needed his fix of the weekly paper. Now, seeing his stories in print, even though they were merely the court and Coast Guard write-ups, he felt a slight rush, as though he were a real writer now.

"Something, isn't it? Always gives me a thrill to hear the

presses rolling." It was Merle, standing right beside him. He hadn't noticed her arrival. Merle grabbed a paper as it came off the press, held it open in front of her, scanned the front page satisfactorily, and made her way back into the inner offices.

Chapter Twenty-Eight

ADDIE HADN'T seen Digit since the start of the season, but because it was mid-afternoon, he knew where to find him.

Having lived with Digit for several years, Addie was well acquainted with the shanty; he had, in fact, opened for Digit on numerous occasions, especially those times when Roland couldn't make it for one reason or another and Digit was desperate. It was how Addie got to meet a bunch of Nantucketers — there was always somebody hanging around the shanty, either looking to buy scallops, or to borrow some tool or equipment that only Digit would have, or to shoot the breeze, or all three. What with all the scallops flying through the air, and the radio going, and the steady talk, shanties were lively places.

Addie was there early; although the day's catch had been duly deposited on the bench, neither Digit nor Roland was around. Digit must have gotten in earlier than anticipated and was out running errands until Roland showed up.

As soon as Addie opened the door, the scallops announced their presence through the clacking made by the opening and closing of their shells. Addie remembered the first time he had seen mounds of scallops on this bench, and how daunting the task of opening them seemed. But he learned, through Digit, not to consider the whole, but to tackle one scallop at a time.

"In the time you've spent thinking about it, the job would've been done," Digit had told him.

Looking at the scallops now, Addie noticed their different colors and shapes: how most had a greyish tinge to them, while others had a grey top and a white bottom. Some were all white; some were white and brown streaked. They were all pretty much the same size, two-and-a-half to three inches in diameter, while a handful leaned closer to three-and-a-half inches. The shells were all slightly convex, although some had a distinct bump, and some were definitely rounder than others. Seeing them as a group, they were all scallops, although few looked exactly alike. "Just like people," Addie thought. "But why do we focus on our differences, and not our similarities?"

He didn't hear Digit come in. "Well, grab a knife and get opening. Don't just stand there with your mouth open."

"Jesus, Digit. Don't scare me like that."

"What were you doing, counting them?"

"Yeah, something like that."

Digit tied his apron around his waist, placed a stainless-steel bowl amidst the scallops and started to open. "So, you going to open or not?"

"I thought I'd buy a pound to take to Verona."

"Buy a pound? There's an apron, there's a knife, there's a bowl. You can open your own pound."

Addie knew Digit wasn't kidding. Although he hadn't opened in a couple of years, the motions came back to him automatically. He wasn't fast, but he didn't cut into Digit's profits, either.

Roland entered. "Oh, Christ, time's must be desperate," he said.

"Nice to see you, too, Roland," Addie said.

"Step aside and leave the opening to the natives." Roland took up his usual spot at the end of the bench. Immediately, the scallops were flying.

They opened in silence. Roland already had at least a pound in his bowl, while Addie, who'd started well before, had maybe a quarter of that. "You guys ever hear about the robbery?" Addie said matter of factly.

"What robbery?" Digit said.

"If there's been a robbery, I'd've heard about it," Roland chipped in.

"No, this one happened years ago," Addie said. "It was a treasure chest of some sort, locked in an old safe."

"The one the school kids were trying to figure out what was in it?" Roland asked. "I remember that. They all thought it had pirate gold in it. What about it?"

"Nothing. I just thought it was interesting."

"You going to write about it?" Digit asked.

"Write about it?" Roland said as his hands continued their non-stop motion. "You writing a book report or something? I thought you drove a tour bus."

"He works for the paper now, Roland," Digit said.

"Oh, Jesus," Roland said. "Better be careful what I say. I ain't never been in that paper, and I never intend to."

"Why not?" Addie asked. Roland's comment took him aback, and he wasn't sure why.

"I don't need nobody twisting my words around."

"What makes you so sure anybody'd want to talk to you, anyway?" Digit said good-naturedly.

Roland stopped opening for a moment. "Remember that girl from the Cape paper came in here a year ago, looking to write up something about scalloping?" He recommenced opening, as though he couldn't talk without working. "I think it was opening day or something. You'd gone out with George and had a double limit and he was in here with us. I think Jimmy Caldwell was in here too."

"Oh, yeah," Digit said, reaching for a scallop. "She came by when we were unloading; I think George told her she could come by the shanty."

"He probably wanted to ask her out, or something," Roland said. "Well, she came in here asking her questions, and I wouldn't say a peep. She tried taking a picture, too. That's when I went out and emptied my barrel."

"Was her name Ellen?" Addie asked.

"How in hell should I know?" Roland said. "Why, you want to ask her out, too?"

"I've got a girlfriend, remember?"

Roland snorted, continued opening in a way that said the conversation wasn't worth his while.

"Anyway," Addie exhaled, "I guess they never caught whoever did it."

"I'd forgotten all about that," Digit said. "Didn't seem that important." He stopped and thought for a second. "I do know this: it was right around the time Dirk Caspian got arrested. Maybe that's why I didn't take much notice of it."

"Who?" Addie asked.

"Oh, nobody you'd know. An old friend." He paused, his scallop knife still in the shell but unmoving. "Well, he used to be a friend."

"Will you two stop yapping," Roland said. "You're taking all the fun out of this job."

"Sorry, Roland," Addie said as he put down his knife. "I think I've got a pound here. As soon as I weigh these babies up, I'll be on my way."

"Just take them," Digit said. "No need to weigh them."

Addie emptied his scallops into a plastic baggie and rinsed

off his apron. "Thanks, Digit. Good to see you, Roland."

"I'd say good-bye, but you'd probably put that in the paper, so I won't say anything."

Chapter Twenty-Nine

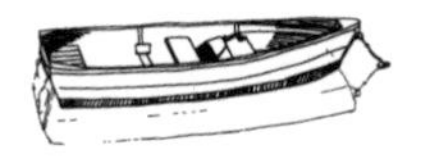

Although Verona liked living in Digit's big old house, she was happy she and Addie had found a place of their own. They'd had plenty of space at Digit's, to be sure, but after all that had happened to her, it was nice to be alone with Addie, somewhere she could call home.

Home. She'd been on the move so much it seemed, tossed from one situation to another, all of it without setting foot off Nantucket. She'd roomed with Irene, the first person to befriend her on the island, before moving in with Sandy, whose house harbored its own special history, and then on to Digit's, where she not only explored the many rooms and the layers of Hathaway heritage they contained, but where she and Addie had room to nurture their new relationship, learning to come together while retaining their individual spheres of identity. When they had achieved their own delicate balance of coupling, she knew it was time to move on and find a place of their own.

Addie's classified ad bore fruit in the form of a small, cozy cottage. It was all they needed now that they truly were a couple. Oh, they still had their own lives, and separate interests, but it was better to be together and share their interests. They liked learning from each other. The cottage was outside of town, but very much within walking distance of Main Street, and if Verona wasn't biking, she was walking.

When she walked she observed, and listened. She enjoyed the sweet birdsong, the clarion call of departing boats, the wind that never seemed to whisper on Nantucket, but whistled, sang, shouted, and showed its strength in scudding clouds, dancing tree tops, blown away birds, and its gentle and not so gentle shoves as you either moved against it, or with it.

On this day, however, she remained inside the cottage, rearranging what little furniture they had, seeking placements that pleased her and she hoped would please Addie.

Did Addie complete her? She'd pondered it the night before, sitting by herself on the cottage's tiny deck, tugged outside by the full November moon, the Beaver Moon, or Frost Moon, so named by the Algonquin tribes and adopted by the early colonists. In her study of the stars, she'd learned a little about the moon, its effect on tides, its gravitational push and pull in conjunction with the sun, creating higher than normal tides (spring tides) and lower than normal tides (neap tides). How fitting to contemplate the moon on Nantucket, she thought, where the rise and fall of the ocean was so important, so integral to the natural rhythms of the island.

An insightful moon child herself, born on the waning crescent moon, she had allowed her own rhythms to intertwine with her feelings toward Addie. With time, and familiarity, abandoning her at first instinctive reluctance, she allowed Addie into her sphere, if not fully into her heart.

Her life included Addie now, with all the impulsiveness and unpredictability that included. Life with him was more interesting than life without him.

And, right on time, Addie arrived, with his welcoming

smile and a pound of scallops.

The idea was that she and Sandy were going to start their own catering business. As Addie and Sandy knew, Verona was an excellent cook, and with this batch of succulent bays fresh from the harbor, she wanted to try a new recipe.

Verona's Bay Scallops

Preheat oven to 375 degrees
In a bowl:
Beat 1 egg
Add 1 lb. rinsed scallops and toss
Measure about ½ cup flavored breadcrumbs and add to mixture, leaving a little bit in measuring cup
Toss lightly to coat scallops with breadcrumbs
Turn out in single layer into baking dish
Sprinkle top with remaining breadcrumbs
Melt ⅓ cup unsalted butter and drizzle over top
Bake 20 minutes
Serve with lemon wedges

Two evenings later, Verona and Addie went down to Surfside. It was quite cool at night now, but nothing a blanket or two couldn't fix. As fall took hold, and the full moon waned, there were new stars to look at, new constellations to ponder.

She had taken with her a book she'd found at the library, one that pinpointed the constellations at different times of year. It was by H. A. Rey, the same author who'd created the *Curious George* books. Huddled in their blanket, scanning the sky, then finding the corresponding stars in the book by flashlight, Verona identifies the constellation that's recently appeared in the night sky.

"It's right here, Addie, see? Next to Aquarius." She traces the outline of the constellation with her finger.

"Cetus?" Addie asks.

"Cetus," Verona agrees. "The whale."

And then, out of the quiet darkness, a low moaning from the ocean.

Chapter Thirty

Making his rounds the next day, Addie stopped by the Town Clerk's office to say hello. Ellen had introduced him to Susan Clark Coffin right after he had started newspapering. The Town Clerk knew everyone on the island, it seemed, and would help Addie with names and familial relations of the people he'd just encountered in court. On this day, before he could say hello, she said, "Sit down. I've got something to show you."

She took a paper off her desk. "This is a notice of a hearing to be held tomorrow night," she said quietly. "It's the regular Conservation Commission hearing, but there's a little addendum that just came in from the state. Now usually they give a month, or two weeks' notice of what's going to appear on the agenda. For some reason, this is being rushed through."

Addie looked at her quizzically.

"Obviously, the state wants as few people to know about this as possible. You ought to be there."

"What is it?" Addie had already had plans to watch the sunset with Verona the next night. It was paper day, which meant the paper was put to bed for the week and he had the night off.

"It's a notice that there's to be an excavation of some kind in the marshes off Bear Street."

"So?"

"So, the Conservation Commission is charged with protecting wetlands. And this isn't a request from the state — it reads more or less like an order."

"Well, if the state wants to do something . . . "

"Then you ought to be there to find out why. This isn't usual." She lowered her voice and leaned closer. "Look, it probably isn't coincidental that this little addition to the agenda is on the same day the paper comes out. For some reason, they don't want any reporters there. You should go."

"What am I looking for?"

"Go, and find out."

"I should tell Ellen."

"That's up to you. I'm telling you because I figured you could use a little help with what could be a pretty good story. It's about time your paper did some digging."

"What are you doing here?" It was Ellen.

"Susan Coffin told me about it."

"Oh, did she?" Ellen flipped through her reporter's notebook as if looking for something important. Addie could tell she was irritated. Maybe he should have told her about this meeting. But then she was here, so maybe she should have told *him*.

He looked around the room. There were a few people who worked for the town, a couple of others he'd met in the course of his reportorial duties. There was no one he didn't recognize.

The Conservation Commission members entered, took their seats. They accepted the minutes of the last meeting, announced that night's agenda. Addie knew most items on the agenda were routine, and the people in the audience exited, one by one, as their concerns were addressed or explained. Through it all, Ellen scribbled furiously and never spoke or looked once at Addie.

"Well, that's about it," the chairman announced, "except for this addition from the state. Is there anyone here to speak on this topic?" Besides Addie and Ellen, there was no one else in the room.

But then the door opened, and a thin man in a white suit and black tie with his hair pulled back in a ponytail entered the room. "Sorry for the intrusion," he said. "I hope I'm not late."

"Are you here from the Commonwealth?" the chairman asked.

"I am, Mr. Chairman."

"Well, I have here an Emergency Certification Form for town-owned land in the vicinity of Bear and Orange Streets."

"That's correct," the man said. Ellen stopped scribbling and eyed the man intently.

"And the necessity for this order?" the chairman asked.

"If I may," the man said. "This is for the excavation of certain wetlands . . . "

"Now, hold it right there," the chairman said. "There's not supposed to be any excavating of any wetlands . . . "

"This project is necessary to protect the health of the citizens of Nantucket, Mr. Chairman. Besides, there is a major commercial development that already encroaches on much of that wetland . . . "

"Two wrongs don't make a right, Mister . . . Mister . . . "

"Caspian, sir. Dirk Caspian."

"Mister . . . Caspian. We're not aware of any possible health issues connected to that particular wetland. What's the state's interest in this?"

Hearing the name Caspian got Addie's attention. Where had he heard it before? Pay attention, he told himself; he could figure it out later.

"Mr. Chairman, it's come to the attention of the Commonwealth, through surveys and extensive research, that harmful chemicals may be leaching into the groundwater in that wetland and immediate action is required."

The chairman's eyebrows arched; Ellen's head snapped up.

Caspian continued. "We are also of the firm belief that an artifact of great historic value may be the cause of this toxicity."

Ellen started writing like mad. Even Addie knew this was important.

The chairman shook the Emergency Certification Form at Caspian. "Just what are you driving at, Mister, Mister . . . . "

"Again, sir, Caspian. Dirk Caspian. Mr. Chairman, it's the Commonwealth's contention that the engine named *'Dionis'* is buried in the wetland. We intend to dig, er, bring her up!"

"You mean the engine from the old Nantucket Railroad?" the chairman asked. "Preposterous! We've all heard that story, that it supposedly went off the rails there. That's nothing but a myth, a fable. Besides, what kind of shape would she be in if she *were* buried there?"

"Bogs have a way of preserving things, Mr. Chairman. I'm sure you're familiar with *Tollund Man.*" A couple of board members turned to each other and nodded knowingly, although neither had the faintest idea what he was talking about. Caspian continued, "It's the belief of the Commonwealth that hazardous materials used in the construction of the engine *Dionis*, including heavy metals, are entering the groundwater at that location, constituting a serious threat to health, safety, and the environment."

"Hence the emergency."

"Yes, sir. Our job will be to locate the locomotive, excavate it, and rid the site of dangerous pollutants. With the approval of this board, of course."

"I've got a feeling the state's going to go ahead with or without the approval of this board." Ellen was really writing now.

"This board's approval would mean agreement with the state's findings."

"A formality."

"We like to think of it as a compact, sir."

"Like the Pilgrims."

"Looking at it from a historical perspective."

"And the state's got history, and everything else, on its side."

Dirk Caspian didn't answer. When put to a voice vote, the board assented, with the chairman voting no. "I'm assuming the vote doesn't need to be unanimous," the chairman said.

"No, sir, it doesn't. As you yourself said, a vote wasn't really necessary."

With that, the meeting ended. Ellen rushed after Dirk Caspian, who beat a hasty exit out the door. Addie approached the chairman.

"Don't go looking for a quote from me, young man," he said. "I've got nothing to say about this."

"But you did vote 'no,' " Addie said.

"Look," the chairman said, "they're already digging up too much of this island as it is, and I always thought the wetlands were sacrosanct. Now, to have this railroaded through by the state . . . "

"Pun intended, sir?"

"Awww, go away, will you? And everything I just said's off the record. If you print it, I'll deny it."

"Just one more thing," Addie interjected quickly. "This person from the state . . . ," he flipped through his notebook pages, ". . . Mr. Caspian. Is he from Nantucket as well?"

"Never seen or heard of him before."

Ellen caught up to Dirk Caspian outside the building. "A reporter, huh?" he said. "Everything I wanted to say I said in there." Ellen, pencil poised, didn't move, waiting for the quote she knew was going to come.

"But I'm hungry. Are you? Maybe we could discuss this over dinner?"

Chapter Thirty-One

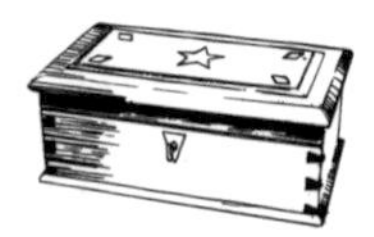

Ellen's story appeared on page one of that Sunday's edition of the *Cape Cod Advocate*. Addie had the rest of the week to get his version in the *Looking Glass*. During court that Monday, Ellen asked Addie if he'd like to go for coffee afterward.

"I thought you were mad at me."

"I was. But I had no right to want that for myself. Now you know what I've been working on for a couple of months."

Over coffee, she elaborated.

"I've got a friend who works in the state house, up in Boston. He got wind of some special order regarding Nantucket, tracked it down, and let me know about it. I'd been doing background on it, waiting for that meeting last week."

"Your story was thorough," Addie said. "Why didn't you write it up before the meeting?"

"It wouldn't have been as dramatic. What if the Conservation Commission said no? If they had listened to the chairman, they would have. Now *that* would have been a story: *'Island doesn't dig state mandate.'* "

"That chairman's pretty feisty."

"Oh, he's that, all right." Ellen flipped through her court notes. "That Caspian guy asked me to go to dinner with him that night," she said without looking up. "Told me he'd tell me all about it."

"Did you go?"

"Of course not! That would have compromised my whole story. I think he's a creep, anyway."

"Would you mind if I talked with him? I've still got mine to write."

"Go ahead. He's supposedly working on some other state project over by Miacomet," Ellen said as she looked back through her notes.

"No," Addie said after thinking about it, "this is *your* story, Ellen. Everyone knows about it now, anyway. For my write-up I'll follow up with the chairman, take a different angle. Besides, I've got my own story I'm working on."

"What about?" Ellen was smiling, but interested, Addie could tell.

"None of your business. You'll find out."

Still smiling, Ellen closed her notebook and hit Addie on the arm with it — hard.

Chapter Thirty-Two

So Caspian *was* back: Digit hadn't been seeing things when he saw him on Main Street. Digit didn't ordinarily read the *Cape Cod Advocate,* but after Addie stopped by the shanty and told him how this guy named Dirk Caspian wanted to dig up an old railroad engine, he couldn't believe it. He had to see it for himself.

After he read the story, he didn't know what to feel: whether to be furious, or curious as to why his old friend was back on island.

Old friend. Now that was a laugh. They hadn't parted as friends, that was for sure. Still, twenty years had passed. Why hadn't Caspian looked him up? If he'd had the gall to come back to the island, you'd think he'd at least say hello to the person who'd bailed him out of jail. Yes, Digit said to himself, you'd think. Well, he wouldn't let himself think about it. If he thought about it, he'd be hurt, and he'd been through enough hurt lately with Marsha.

To hell with Dirk Caspian. That was then, this was now. He had better things to think about.

It had been easy for Dirk Caspian to secure state approval for the project. Working his way up from one state agency to another, with each job bringing a little more responsibility, and a lot more familiarity with who actually got things done, he'd learned how to use the bureaucracy against itself.

It had been perfect. Because it was on Nantucket — separate, removed, a county unto itself — and because he had done his homework and filed the proper paperwork with the right people, and in the right order, his emergency authorization was rubber-stamped, no questions asked.

Back when he'd first lived on the island, he'd heard a rumor about an old engine named *Dionis* going off the track in some marshland. In fact, it had been Digit who'd told him about it, and who'd told him all about the Nantucket Railroad.

After years of planning, the Nantucket Central Railroad made its initial run, to much fanfare and celebration, on July 4, 1881. Starting at Steamboat Wharf, where disembarking boat passengers boarded its small, inviting cars, the narrow-gauge train made its way down Easy Street and out along the Creeks to Monomoy. From there, it chugged past what today is the island's main traffic rotary and through the woods out to Surfside, where there was a small train station and, later, a hotel. After Surfside, it followed the shoreline past Nobadeer, Maddequecham and Tom Nevers' Head and rolled out to 'Sconset before chugging its way back to town. The little train was popular among summer visitors and year-round residents, as island by-laws of the time forbade the operation of new-fangled automobiles, or what many islanders referred to as *machines,* on the roadways of Nantucket.

Leading the procession of railroad cars was the proud locomotive *Dionis,* named after the bride of Tristram Coffin, one of the island's first settlers of English descent.

Caspian chuckled to himself. If he did find *Dionis*, it would be the find of the century.

But he wasn't looking for *Dionis*. The Conservation Commission chairman was right: even if the engine *had* fallen into the bog, there was probably nothing left of it.

Was he surprised that no one contacted him after the article about the project appeared in the *Cape Cod Advocate?* He supposed not.

But once that backhoe got going, he was sure he'd be hearing from somebody.

When Lance Willoughby read about Dirk Caspian's planned project in the paper, he spit out his coffee.

So, he's returned.

He hadn't seen Dirk Caspian around, but then Lance spent most of his time out on the water or in the shanty. He didn't socialize, other than to have the occasional beer with other fishermen, and that was always at the Anglers' Club, which was private. And even if he did bump into him, Lance was certain Dirk Caspian wouldn't recognize him.

Studies have shown that a person not seen in ten years, particularly a teenager, would be unrecognizable to people who hadn't known him well. Facial features change dramatically in that time, and if the person were a passing acquaintance — or an innocuous kid washing dishes — there'd be slim chance of knowing who he was if he passed you on the street.

Especially if the years had darkened his blonde hair to brown, and if the clean-shaven, pimply face, was now deeply tanned and framed by a full beard.

And that's how Lance Willoughby returned to the island, ten years after he'd gone. He'd been back ten more years since then. There were only two people who might recognize him from twenty years ago: the one who'd rented him the room, and Dirk Caspian. But the first one had gone off (Was it to college? He couldn't remember), and Lance didn't know where he'd gone after that. He knew the kid wasn't an islander, and was pretty sure he didn't have any family on Nantucket.

Lance wasn't sure if he'd even recognize *him* if they bumped into each other. Over the years, not thinking of him, never trying to recall his name, he had forgotten what his name was. And though he probably could retrieve it from the folds of memory if he thought hard enough, he wasn't about to.

He'd recognize Dirk Caspian, though. He'd never forget that face, or his name, no matter how many years had elapsed.

He knew one thing for certain: no one would ever expect to run into Lance Willoughby, aka Nate Powell, for that was his name when he was washing dishes. No, as far as anyone knew, Nate Powell was dead.

And that's the way Lance Willoughby liked it.

Chapter Thirty-Three

C. C. Dennison was working on his second pot of coffee when Addie stopped by for the weekly Coast Guard report.

"Cup of coffee?" he asked Addie.

"Sure, Chief, why not? Last time I was here, you were about to tell me more about that robbery."

"Which robbery?"

"The one from about twenty years ago."

"Let's see," Dennison said, holding his mug, eyeing the ceiling. "Oh, yes . . . Where were we? Right. After you left last time, I remembered that some time after the robbery, maybe a month or two later, this station responded to a call about a distressed motorboat. This was late at night, maybe near midnight. The 41-footer was dispatched (the Chief couldn't help but talk in Coast Guard-speak) to an area up harbor, near Abrams Point. There was a Boston Whaler going in circles — the outboard was cut hard to starboard — and when the crew got closer, it was determined there was no one aboard. The crew was able to secure her, boarded her, and, yup, no one aboard.

"So," the chief ruminated, "was it an accident, a suicide, a felony of some kind?"

"Wait a minute, Chief. How was this connected to the robbery?"

"Glad you asked. Well, you see . . . "

And just then Ellen walked in.

C. C. Dennison stopped talking, Addie looked down at his notebook.

"Hello, you two," Ellen said. "Am I interrupting something?"

"Just getting the Coast Guard report," Addie said matter-of-factly.

"Cup of coffee, Ellen?" the Chief asked.

"No, thanks. So, anything newsworthy, Chief?"

"Nope, been pretty quiet. Addie and I were just talking about an old robbery . . ."

"Really? Not too many robberies on Nantucket."

"You're right," the Chief said, "there aren't, are there? Anyway, this one happened about twenty years ago."

"Save it, Chief. Not interested."

"Whew," Addie thought. But why was Ellen here? She never bothered with the Coast Guard report. "So what brings you here, Ellen?"

"Dirk Caspian, that's who," the Chief said.

"Chief!" Ellen said. "You think maybe we could have a private conversation? Sorry, Addie, but this is between the Chief and me."

"Oh, I don't mind," Addie said. "I'll just sit here and be quiet. You two go ahead. Sounds interesting."

"Addie!" Ellen said. "I'll come back another time, Chief." As she stood, Addie said: "That's okay, Ellen, I'll go. Catch you later, Chief."

"Meet me for coffee in an hour?" Ellen asked him.

"May as well. Didn't get to finish the one the Chief just poured me."

Ellen stared him out of the room.

The coffee shop was pretty empty, which was good, because Ellen didn't want to be overheard. "You want to tell me about the robbery?"

"You want to tell me about Dirk Caspian?"

"Touché. So here's the deal. I've known Chief Dennison since he was stationed on the Cape. That was right before he was transferred to Brant Point. Naturally, when I got the job over here for the *Advocate* the first person I got in touch with was the Chief. He's been a pretty good source."

"And for me as well." Addie liked that he could throw that in; made him feel like a real reporter.

"Although one thing the chief isn't is discreet. He treats everyone the way he treats his crew: everything's on the table; no secrets." She looked around to make sure no one was eavesdropping. "I don't want to play games with you, Addie," Ellen said seriously. "You've got a story you're working on; I've got a story I'm working on. Instead of trying to avoid each other, let's make a deal."

"I'm listening."

"I won't touch your story, and you don't touch mine. That way, when you're talking to Chief Dennison and he inadvertently lets slip something about Dirk Caspian, or he mentions your robbery to me, which he will, we'll both let it go. How's that sound?"

Boy, Ellen sure was an operator. Addie had never met anyone like her before.

Who was he kidding? He wasn't a reporter. It seemed like he was always prying, writing about things that seemed like none of his business. Ellen, on the other hand, loved sticking her nose into other people's business. Her mind was always on the go. Still, he wasn't so sure about this deal she was presenting.

Ellen looked at him quizzically. "What's going on in that brain of yours?" she asked him. "Stop furrowing your brow. Look, this isn't like I'm telling you *not* to write about something. The chief's helping me with some background, that's all. If he hadn't slipped up today, we wouldn't be having this conversation at all. You'd be blissfully unaware that I was speaking to the chief about anything."

"This is just for this one thing, right?"

"You've got it, Addie. Look, if it makes you feel any better, I'll tell you what I'm looking into. The chief's not happy with whatever it is Dirk Caspian's up to, and neither am I. Caspian was sent down here for something completely different: to research whether there was a Wampanoag burial ground on the proposed site of a public housing project. That's it. Now, suddenly, he's got a permit to dig up a wetland? He's just a minor bureaucrat. This is way beyond his job description. The chief knows some people in Boston, and they're checking into Caspian's background. That's all. It may go nowhere, but if it does it could land me on the newspaper staff. This is an enterprise story, one I'm looking into on my own. With any luck the editors will recognize my initiative. Now don't get me wrong, but I'll bet you weren't even thinking about looking into Caspian, were you?"

She was right. It hadn't occurred to him at all. Damn it. Who was he kidding? He didn't know how to be a reporter. While Ellen, boy, it was like she was born to it.

"So, have we got a deal?"

"Sure, why not?"

"Don't look so glum. This way I can bounce ideas off you, let you in on what I find. Look, if it turns out to be something of importance, something *newsworthy*, I'll share it with you. Only my story runs first. *Capisce?*"

"Yeah, I get it."

"And Addie, your robbery story. If it happened twenty years ago, it's old news. Have fun with it."

Thanks, Ellen, he thought.

Chapter Thirty-Four

SHE VISITED him again last night. They were lying together, talking softly.

"Don't you want to know about my husband?" she asked him.

"Wouldn't he mind that we were together?"

"Not when I'm with you."

And then Digit woke up.

"Whoa." He bolted upright. It had been so real, as though she was really visiting him, but she couldn't have: he hadn't seen her in over twenty years.

It was the year before he'd started dating Marsha; he was seventeen. She was a summer person. He'd met her while he was diving off the wharf for pennies thrown by passengers on the Steamship. She was blonde, pretty, and standing with her mother. "Hi," he'd said after a particularly deep dive. "This is for you," and he held out the penny he'd just retrieved. The mother, ignoring the offer, pretending he didn't exist, pulled her daughter away.

But the girl was back on the dock the next day, alone, and

she accepted his penny. Digit asked if he could buy her an ice cream cone, and she said yes.

Her name was Cordelia and she lived in one of the majestic summer houses along Brant Point that Digit had seen only from the outside. "The Gold Coast," islanders called it. Some of the houses were adorned with authentic ship's figureheads. Soon after they'd met she'd told him matter of factly, without bragging, that she was descended from a whaling captain. He didn't tell her that he, too, had a whaling captain for an ancestor; he didn't want her to think he was making it up to impress her.

They'd meet at Jetties Beach. She was reading "Cheaper by the Dozen" and telling him about the little lighthouses the Gilbreth family occupied nearby, the former "bug lights" employed by the Coast Guard at Brant Point as aids to navigation. "They're right over there," she pointed out. "The father thought it was healthy for the kids to take baths in the ocean all summer."

Sometimes they'd walk by the house, noting the name of one lighthouse, *Cyc,* and the cottage, *The Shoe.*

"You know, like the old woman who lived in a shoe," she said.

As with everything Cordelia said, Digit mainly nodded and smiled. Although he never went to her house, and they probably only got together about ten times, she was everything good about summer.

Riding their bikes together after supper, feeling the warm breeze on his face, looking over at Cordelia as she pedaled to get ahead of him, laughing, he was as happy as he'd ever been, or ever hoped to be.

And when she was leaving, they exchanged addresses, and he wrote, but she never wrote back.

And he looked for her the next year on the docks, but she never came. And he'd go to the Jetties on the days they'd used to meet, but she wasn't there.

And he didn't see her the rest of that summer.

But that didn't mean he hadn't loved her.

As the years went by he sometimes thought he'd caught a glimpse of her as he walked up Main Street. Once, when he happened to be on Jetties Beach, meeting a friend or something, he was sure he saw her, so certain that he walked up to her blanket, and stopped, and said hello, and she said hello back, but he knew from her response, and the angle at which she held her head, that it wasn't she.

"Sorry, I mistook you for someone else," he apologized.

She pulled her sunglasses partway down her nose and replied, "No problem," and turned back to her magazine.

Now, since his divorce from Marsha, she came to him in dreams and talked as though they'd known each other all their lives. She still looked the same; she hadn't aged. He couldn't remember most of these dream conversations, but he awoke with a pleasant feeling.

The thing is, it seemed so real, and he didn't know why he'd wake with a pleasant feeling at all.

And now that Caspian was back, he wished she'd leave his dreams alone.

Chapter Thirty-Five

WHEN YOU aren't thinking about it, twenty years goes by more quickly than you'd imagine. Time speeds up as you age, perhaps, or maybe it's that you simply get distracted by other things — by life itself, with all its unplanned unknowns and lessons to be learned. For Dirk Caspian, however, the two decades that had elapsed since he'd last been on Nantucket had seemed an eternity.

He'd thought about it every day, sometimes every minute of every day, waiting for the time he could return. Twenty years! That he had been the one to set that future date was even more infuriating.

But at last, at long, long last, the time had come, the day finally neared when his reward would be realized, and the interminable and maddening wait would end.

And it had been maddening. There were moments when just the *idea* of it almost made his head explode. But he couldn't get his mind off it, and as the years went by, its importance to him grew and expanded and magnified so that it was not the *value* of it that mattered, but its possession that nearly overwhelmed his senses. It was his, his to have. He had been patient; he deserved it; he was owed it; he *needed* it.

To think it had started out so — there was no other word for it — innocently.

That everything had been unplanned was what made it so indefectible, and it all came together so wonderfully, so seamlessly.

At first, anyway.

It was the summer of his senior year in college. It had been a lousy one: lousy job, lousy apartment, lousy roommates. He had started the summer in a lousy state of mind as well —no thanks to Digit Hathaway. They had been great friends once, but before that summer had even begun he'd wished he'd never met him.

He had been coming out to the island all through college, doing various jobs, getting plenty of beach time in. He'd met Digit that first summer at a beach party. Even though Digit was younger, still in high school at the time, they enjoyed doing the same things: tossing a Frisbee on the beach, playing pickup basketball, fishing, talking about girls. Both looked forward to seeing the other in subsequent years.

His last summer, however, Dirk Caspian avoided Digit; in fact, he almost hadn't returned to the island, but he had a good job lined up with the Department of Public Works (thanks to Digit's help), and he needed the money, so he came and rented a cheap room with a couple of kids he couldn't stand at first, but that was okay, he didn't feel like socializing anyway.

But Digit finally tracked down Dirk Caspian that July when he saw him picking up trash barrels on Main Street, and smiled broadly when he saw him.

"Hey, Dirk, where've you been? Man, you've been making

yourself scarce lately."

Caspian didn't have much to say. "Yeah, I guess I've been pretty busy." He seemed different to Digit. It was okay with him if Caspian wanted to be aloof, but he seemed more aloof than he should have been.

"So," Digit said, "you want to go fishing sometime?"

"Yeah, sure." He didn't even look at his old friend. "No, you know what? I don't think I'll be going fishing this summer." He looked at Digit then, all right, with a look that said, "Leave me alone, kid."

What Dirk Caspian didn't want to tell Digit was that he had stolen his girlfriend.

He had heard all about Digit's blossoming romance the summer before. She was a summer girl, and as the season progressed so did Digit's and her friendship. Digit shared with his older friend all his feelings about her, how he couldn't wait to see her, how the days that he didn't see her dragged on and on, and even though she was going back to school soon, they had promised to stay in touch throughout the winter, and next summer, well, who knew? "Wait'll you meet her," Digit said.

And Dirk Caspian did meet her, right before she left for the summer.

And how was he to know that her high school was in the same town where he went to college? And that soon after arriving on campus, he'd see her in a coffee shop downtown? And of course he'd go up and say hello, and she being friendly, especially to someone who knew Digit, she invited him to sit down. And he did. And he started going to the coffee shop more frequently because she said she and her friends hung out there pretty much every day after school, and soon he was meeting her there alone, and soon after that he asked her out on a date, and he was charming, and older, and before long she'd forgotten that she was going to write to Digit back on Nantucket, and she couldn't remember what she'd done with his address anyway.

After a couple of months she and Dirk Caspian were an item. Oh, her parents didn't approve ("He's a senior in *college,* for God's sake"), but that only made him more attractive.

And when they made love, in the front seat of his pickup, Digit Hathaway was officially in her past.

They dated throughout the school year, but before the summer began, she broke up with him, deciding that he was, in fact, too old.

And if she hadn't met Digit Hathaway, she'd never have met Dirk Caspian.

And so, in his mind, Dirk Caspian blamed Digit.

It took the whole summer to even begin getting over her. Fortunately, Digit got the message and stayed away from him. Digit was just a kid, anyway.

As were his roommates, who were, in fact, younger than Digit. But he arrived on Nantucket in such a funk, and so wrapped up in his own misery, that they were easy to ignore, and he used the room simply to sleep. He didn't even notice that they were hardly around either.

One rainy Sunday, however, about a month before Labor Day, the three of them had nothing to do and were all in the apartment together. They lay on their beds and stared at the ceiling, none of them saying a word. "Let's go to breakfast," Caspian finally suggested, so they went late, over to The Dory on India Street, when most of the breakfast crowd had already eaten. From there, they went to the Rose and Crown because one of them had heard a pretty good acoustic band, Poland Strings, had an afternoon session. Two of them, underage, nursed iced teas, secretly admiring Caspian's ability to order beer, which he surreptitiously snuck them from time to time, elevating their esteem.

For the next few weeks they hung out together at every opportunity. They went to the beach when they could, drank beers Caspian bought, and talked long into the night in their shared room about their plans for the future, what they were doing after Labor Day, and that they were definitely going to room together next summer —maybe find a beach cottage so they could just hang and not have to sneak beers at bars.

And then, just before Labor Day, they went out for a last fling together.

He would never admit it to them, but his roommates, through their interest, revitalized Caspian. They were so enthralled by his stories, so eager to hear his opinions, so *captivated* by him that Caspian reveled in his newfound celebrity. Whatever he wanted to do, wherever he wanted to go, was fine by them. At first, he was put off by their adulation (he just wanted to have a good time before the end of summer and utilize their company) but he came to view their fascination as an outgrowth of some kind of natural magnetism that he emanated. Rather than merely share ideas and feelings, as he had with Digit, he could have a real influence on these two, mold them, lead them.

Because he was a natural leader; he just needed circumstance to draw it out. And it seemed that circumstance was now.

The three roommates capped off the summer with a bar crawl, abetted by the fake IDs Caspian provided. As they headed back to their room, they walked by the old town building where an ancient safe was on display. They stopped.

"Everybody's been trying to guess what's inside," one of them said.

"Probably nothing," said the other.

But Dirk Caspian, during his summers on the island, had heard about the *Susan's* Teeth, scrimshawed ivory from the whaleship *Susan* that were supposed to be worth a bundle — if any of them ever turned up. He didn't know why he was thinking of that now, but he seized on the idea. Ivory — what else would be in an old Nantucket safe? It sounded exotic, it sounded valuable.

"They're going to open it tomorrow," one of them said, turning the doorknob on the old town building just for the heck of it.

And the door opened. They looked at each other, and, as the one who opened the door was about to close it, Dirk Caspian said: "They can't open it if it's not there."

"What do you mean?"

"I mean, let's take it."

"Are you kidding? Are you crazy?"

"Wait here," Caspian said. "I'll go get my truck."

The two of them tried acting nonchalant, hanging across the street as if they were waiting for a ride, which, of course, they were. "I'm not so sure about this," one of them said to the other. "Maybe we should just leave."

"No, let's wait," the other insisted. "Dirk knows what he's doing."

When Dirk Caspian returned with his truck, both of them hoped he'd tell them to hop in, that he was, indeed, just kidding. But it wasn't to be. "Come on, you two," Caspian said, "get moving. Get that thing over here."

Even though the safe weighed close to 200 pounds, they found it wasn't as heavy as they thought, and they later realized it was probably their fear of getting caught that provided the needed strength. As hurriedly as they could, they crab-walked the safe to the back of the pickup, where Caspian finally helped them heave the old artifact into the bed of his truck and on top of an old blanket he'd retrieved from behind his seat. They scrambled into the cab and slowly pulled away.

"I think I forgot to close the door," one of them said.

"Too late now," Caspian said. "Did you at least remember to wipe off the doorknob?" And he started laughing.

None of them saw Cy, who had just turned the corner from Main Street.

They headed out to the moors, Caspian laughing, the other two justifiably nervous.

"Let's just ditch it out there, and pretend nothing happened."

"Yeah, Dirk, this is nuts. We could get in a whole lot of trouble."

"Just calm down," Caspian said. "There could be nothing in there."

"It doesn't matter; we stole it. We could go to jail."

"Relax, nobody's going to jail."

And as he turned off the Polpis Road and drove out past Altar Rock to Sauls Hills, Dirk Caspian formulated his plan.

Chapter Thirty-Six

HE TOLD them what he knew about the *Susan's* Teeth.

"That's fine, but what if that's not what's in there?"

"It's got to be something good," Caspian said. "Why else would it have been hanging around all those years inside the bank?"

"Because nobody wanted it. Could be just a bunch of papers."

"Think again. It's the sea chest inside the safe that has what we need. It has to be a treasure chest."

"What an imagination! What, you think there are gold doubloons in there?"

"Could be."

"Well, let's open it and find out."

"No. Now this is where we have to be careful. The whole island is going to be looking for this safe. If we open it now, where are we going to hide what's inside? We don't have time to divide things up. And we wouldn't be able to sell any of it anyway. Opening it now is just asking to get caught. No, we're just going to have to be patient."

"Let's dump the whole thing somewhere out here — hey, let's throw it in Gibb's Pond!"

"And why did we bother stealing it? Let's figure this out later. Look, I drove out here because I know a perfect place to ditch this until we do figure it out. Nobody will find it there. Digit and I discovered it a couple of years ago and we used to hide our hooch in it."

"Who?"

"Digit Hathaway . . . oh, forget it. You don't know him. He was a friend of mine."

"Maybe he'll come out here looking for it."

"Not a chance."

Not turning on his lights, or applying his brakes, Caspian slowly rolled down the hill. Nearby, he pulled into a copse of scrub oak, and instructed the other two to follow him. They carried the safe through the small trees, branches scratching their arms, pawing their ankles, reaching for their faces.

"Ouch."

"Be quiet, you idiots."

"We can't see."

"Shhhh. Just follow my lead."

"We can't see *you.*"

"Shut up and move."

Finally, they reached a small clearing. "It's right around here," Caspian said. "It's perfect."

And it was. Behind a tiny tree were some bushes, and in the middle of the bushes was a hole, almost as if something had been excavated there, or a creature had burrowed it out. The safe fit perfectly. "Careful, don't turn the handle. We don't have the combination."

"Man, I'd forgotten all about that. The joke would be on us then, wouldn't it?"

"I'm not laughing," Caspian said.

Just in case, they checked to ensure the safe was still open. It was. They carefully covered it with leaves and branches. Still keeping his headlights off, Dirk Caspian drove the long way through the moors, not keeping to any particular path. It was late summer in the very early morning. No one else was on the moors that night.

Chapter Thirty-Seven

"Where'd you get those scratches on your arms?" Cy asked Dirk Caspian the next morning.

They were in the DPW truck, once again emptying the trash barrels on Main Street. Caspian looked at his arms. Man. Should have worn a long-sleeved shirt.

"Oh, I was helping someone clear some brush from their yard. Didn't realize I got a bit scratched up."

"Oh yeah, who?"

"Who, what?"

"Who were you helping out?"

Without thinking, Dirk Caspian blurted out: "Digit Hathaway."

Cy nodded his head slowly. "I'm related to him."

Caspian looked out the window. "Of course he is," he thought. "Who isn't related on this island?"

That night the three of them rendezvoused back at their room. Each was bleary-eyed from lack of sleep, and two of them were even more haggard-looking from worry.

"What are we going to do now?"

"Do you think anyone saw us last night?"

"What about fingerprints?"

The town was buzzing with news of the robbery. Everyone wanted the thieves caught *now,* and to have the book thrown at them. It was a matter of island pride: there hadn't been a robbery on Nantucket in well over a hundred years.

"We sit tight," Caspian said, "until this blows over."

"I don't think it's going to blow over. Everyone's saying this is the first robbery in over a hundred years."

"It's not really a robbery," Caspian said. "It's not like we robbed a bank or something."

"It's got the name of the bank right on the safe. It sure is like we robbed a bank."

"Relax," Caspian said. "Can you see now why we didn't divide things up? You two would be jumping out of your skin. We'd be caught for sure. Just keep your mouths shut. I'll figure something out."

Two nights later, with no early morning knocks on the door, with the cops not yet coming to get them, they were all a bit calmer. They agreed the best thing to do was wait.

"But we've got to get that safe out of that spot," Caspian said. "I've thought about this, and I think this is the best way to go."

And, as they listened, he outlined his plan:

"We'll take out the chest and ditch the safe; throw it overboard, somewhere deep, somewhere out on the ocean. Then, we'll bury the chest and leave it until things quiet down."

"Bury it?"

"Yeah, just like real treasure."

"But how are we going to bury it? Someone will see us."

"That's why we're going to wait."

"How long?"

"Not long. Now the way I see it, Nate is the least known of all of us; he just got here this summer, and he really doesn't hang out with anybody but us. So, Nate, first you're going to use my truck and take the chest out of the safe. You'll have to do this late at night, and remember to kill your headlights when you get near the spot."

"Okay, then what am I supposed to do?" Nate's voice betrayed his reluctance. He wasn't too certain of Caspian's plan.

"Bring the chest back here."

"Are you crazy? Look, this is getting way out of hand."

"Who comes here?" Caspian asked. "Nobody, that's who. None of us has had a single soul come to visit us this summer. And the chest won't be here long, a day or two at most."

"What are we going to do with it?"

"As I told you, we're going to bury it. But only one of us is going to know where it is."

"What?!" they both said at once.

"The less each of us knows, the better. If we don't know where it is, we can't tell anybody, right?"

"Yeah, but one of us will know."

"We're just going to have to trust one of us. So, tomorrow night we'll meet back here. Before then, each of us is going to write down where he thinks the chest should be buried. Don't tell anyone what you've written on the paper, not even each other. Well, that's it."

"That's what?"

"That's it for now."

The next night, sitting on the floor of their room, Caspian continued with his plan. The only light came from a candle in the middle of the floor.

"What's up with the candle?"

"I thought it added the right atmosphere," Caspian said as he unfolded a small manila envelope. "Did you write it down?" He looked at their faces made ghoulish by the candlelight. They nodded. "Good. Now here's the deal: we're going to put each of our papers in this envelope, then we'll draw straws. The short straw gets the envelope, gets to choose the location from the papers inside, and gets to bury it."

"Shouldn't it be the long straw that gets to do all that?"

"Does it make a difference? Okay, the long straw." Which is what Dirk Caspian hoped they would say.

Because he was going to get the long straw.

He had plucked the straws from a broom being sold downtown at Hardy's Hardware. All the attention in the store was being paid to the flags being sold: the Nantucket flag, the state flag, the "Don't Give Up the Ship" flag, and to Bingo, the store's pet parrot, who escaped from the store so much he was chained to his perch. Caspian selected two fat straws and a thin one. At first, he was going to have the thin one be the longest one, figuring the other two would go for the thicker, and obviously taller, straws. But he noticed one of the thicker straws had a slight crook to it: that's the one he'd make the longest. Surely the other two would believe the crook would make it the shortest.

They agreed that since Nate was the one charged with retrieving the chest, he should hold the straws. "Close your eyes, you two," Caspian said, and he put the straws in Nate's hand, who closed his fist around them. Caspian patted the tops of the straws down gently so they were even.

"Now, just to make it fair, I'll choose last," he said.

"No, Dirk, since I'm holding them, it's only right that I get the last straw," Nate said.

"That's right, Dirk," the other one said. "That seems fair."

"Okay," Caspian said, "I'll choose second." This was working out better than he could have imagined.

The first straw selected was the skinny one, just as Caspian had hoped. Now, it was Caspian's turn; he couldn't lose. The candle threw weird shadows onto Nate's hand. He couldn't tell which was the crooked one. Did he put the straws into Nate's hand upside down? No, he was sure he hadn't. Was that the crooked one, or this one?

"Come on, Dirk, what are you waiting for? Looking for something?" the other one said.

So he chose — the wrong straw.

Nate pulled the final straw from his fist, looked at it, looked at the others. "I guess I win." He wasn't excited.

"Congratulations," the other one said, relieved to be out of it.

"Yeah, congrats," Caspian said. How could he have been so stupid? Drawing straws. His real plan, of course, was to cut the other two out, bury the chest, dig it up in a year or two when the heat was off, and take it off-island. He'd figure out what the statute of limitations was and sell the ivory then, for he was certain that's what the safe contained.

Now, he had no choice but to trust Nate Powell. He had to think quickly.

"You know what to do, Nate. Take the chest, bury it in one of those spots, and ditch the safe. Forget about bringing the chest back here; I've changed my mind — too chancy. Now, here's the second part of the plan: in about a year, you, Nate, will send us by certified mail the location of the chest. Then we wait. I figure twenty years ought to do it."

"Twenty years!" the other two said together.

"Any sort of statute of limitations will be over by then, and nobody will care about what was in the safe. We'll be able to open it in the middle of Main Street if we wanted to. And, this is the best part, whatever's in there will have appreciated even more by that time."

"Yeah, but twenty years!" they both said again.

"Look, we'll only be in our forties; Nate, you won't even be forty. And you know what they say, 'Life begins at forty.' "

"What if Nate decides to dig it up before then?"

"He won't. If either of us finds out, which we will, then we go right to the cops."

"And then we'll all be in trouble."

"Possession's nine-tenths of the law. Who are they going to believe? Us, who are doing our duty as good citizens, or Nate, who'll have the goods?

"So," Caspian said, "we'll meet up, the three of us, no matter what we're doing, in twenty years at Altar Rock. Agreed?"

"Twenty years from today?"

"No, let's make it a date we can all remember. How about . . . March 31. Rain or shine.

"March 31?" the other two said in unison.

"Last day of scallop season. And remember, not a word of this to anybody. Ever."

And they shook on it.

And went their separate ways.

Chapter Thirty-Eight

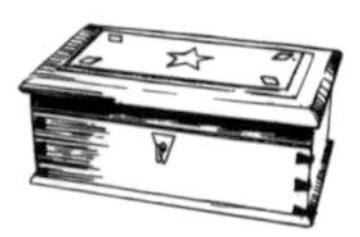

DIRK CASPIAN was furious. He just wanted to go out and grab the safe then and there.

But the island was crawling with additional cops and state troopers called in to comb the island, never mind the volunteers. They were all over the moors. But they wouldn't find it, not where they'd hidden it; they couldn't.

And if they did, what then? Maybe it would be better.

As long as the other two kept their mouths shut.

But no matter what, they'd all have to keep their mouths shut or risk going to jail, so may as well hope the plan works. He'd just have to trust them, especially Nate, who now knew where the others had planned to bury it. He was in charge now, not Dirk Caspian.

Dammit! His was such a perfect location, too; nobody would ever have found it there.

Twenty years! Who was he kidding? He had blurted out the number, hoping the other two would abide by it, and he could figure out how to get the treasure before then.

He wanted so badly to talk to *her* about this — she who

had let him down, dumped him! All because of Digit Hathaway. If Digit hadn't introduced him to her . . . oh, it was no use. He couldn't talk to her; he couldn't talk to anybody.

Nate decided to wait before retrieving the safe from the moors, that the best course of action was to take no action. If the spot was as great as Caspian said it was, then leave it alone. He'd have to get in that mindset, anyway, to leave things alone once he'd buried the chest. Twenty years. Could he wait that long?

He supposed it didn't matter much: he was in charge now.

With responsibility came confidence. Neither he nor the other roommate had wanted to go along with Caspian's scheme, but they had, so there was no other choice but to see it through to the end.

He also knew this — their mutual friendship had come to an end as well.

All that talk about living together next summer was over. Stealing the safe sucked the joy from their relationship. Where before everything was carefree, they now had a secret, something to be hidden.

But if that's the way it had to be, that's the way it had to be.

And all because of Dirk Caspian, their fearless leader. Oh, they had followed along with the scheme; what else could they do? They had stolen the safe, and they were in it as deep as they could go. But once Caspian started in with his plans, with no discussion, with no thought to ask them their ideas, their dynamic changed. Oh, he made them *think* they were contributing, but they weren't really. They were scared, and Caspian was a smooth talker. And if things had gone Caspian's way, no doubt it wouldn't have hit them until months later what Caspian's plan had really been.

As soon as Dirk Caspian pulled that short straw, Nate knew,

he could read it in his face: Caspian was going to double cross them. He knew which was the long straw, and he blew it.

Now Nate held the cards. All of them.

What a dumb plan.

And then Dirk Caspian got arrested.

Chapter Thirty-Nine

THE "SEE You Later, Alligator" party was a Labor Day tradition. Some islanders, who'd had enough summer, enough traffic, enough people, and enough preppies, got together at one bar or another to kiss them all goodbye. It was often rowdy, and the rowdiness usually spilled out to the street.

Dirk Caspian showed up at the Chicken Box already drunk. The energy in the bar lifted him along, and he got swept up in the moment. He had a shot and a beer, then another, and maybe another, he wasn't keeping track. He stumbled over to the pool tables, his momentum carrying him more than his legs. As if he were going to play, he approached the cue rack. In the corner was a guy wearing an alligator shirt. "See you later, alligator," Caspian thought, and, as if he had a license to do so, he swung the butt end of the cue at the alligator, missing the alligator entirely but hitting the guy squarely in the face.

And that's the last Dirk Caspian remembered until he woke up in a jail cell the next morning. It was Sunday. A cop hollered at him to wake up.

"Get up," the cop said. "Tomorrow's Labor Day, court's not

’til Tuesday. We want you out of here, but we can’t release you on your own recognizance. You got anybody you can call?”

Caspian looked at the cop through bleary eyes but didn’t understand.

“Look, you’re going to have to call someone. We can’t have you staying here for two nights. Do you understand?”

He didn’t, but before the cop recited the same thing again, Caspian told him to call Digit Hathaway.

He just wanted the cop to shut up. Digit was the only person he could think of to call — his was the only number he knew.

Chapter Forty

"HEY, DIGIT?"

"Yeah."

"This is Dick Preston, down at the police station."

"Hi Sarge, what can I do you for?" Sergeant Preston had been a high school classmate.

"Got a package for you down at the station, one Dirk Caspian."

"Oh yeah? Well, you can just keep him."

"Come on, Digit. We've already kept him overnight. Chief says he's got to go until his court appearance Tuesday morning."

"Court appearance? What'd he do?"

"Clobbered Fred Rutherford in the face with a pool cue."

"Why'd he do that?"

"Beats me. You can ask him when you pick him up."

"Dick, I already said . . . "

"We've already done the paperwork. We're releasing him into your custody. Just make sure he stays out of trouble."

Dirk Caspian shuffled from his cell with downcast eyes. Without acknowledging the police or Digit, he followed Digit out of the police station to Digit's waiting pickup.

"You want to talk about it?" Digit asked as he hopped into the cab of his truck. The unkempt Caspian stared straight ahead.

"Fine. Have it your way. But you might as well get used to it because I'm supposed to take you home with me."

"No," Caspian said softly.

"What did you say? I thought you said, 'No,' and that's not going to wash. You're my responsibility now."

"Just take me to my place," Caspian said.

"No can do. I've got to keep an eye on you, not that I want to."

"So take me home."

Home. Maybe not such a bad idea. Digit drove to his mother's house.

Digit's mother, Katharine, rented out a couple of rooms to college students each summer, and Digit knew her boarders had already gone for the season. He didn't want to burden her, but he didn't know what else to do with his onetime friend. If she couldn't help him out, she'd at least have an idea.

Caspian still said nothing as Digit pulled into the driveway of his mother's home. Even though Caspian knew the house well, had spent many nights there, he remained stone-faced. Digit kept an eye on his passenger as he walked over to greet his mother who came to the door when she heard his truck pull up.

"To what do I owe the honor . . . " she began before looking at Digit's truck. "Is that who I think it is? Haven't seen him all summer. Hello, Dirk."

"Don't bother, Ma, he won't answer."

"Oh?"

"He's in some kind of trouble, nothing serious, but he's let me know he wants nothing to do with me. I hate asking . . . "

"But you're asking anyway. So how can I help?"

"Can he stay here for a couple of nights? I hate to do this to you, but . . . "

"Of course he can stay here. Dirk," she said, turning to the pickup, "I know you know where the spare bedrooms are; take your pick. There are clean towels and sheets on the bed."

Caspian didn't budge. Digit leaned against the driver's side door and spoke through the rolled-down window to his former friend. "Look, I don't know what's up with you, but this is the best offer you're going to get. If I take you back to the police station they'll either fine you or send you to the prison over in Barnstable. I don't think you want either of those things. You look like hell. Go take a shower and go to bed." Caspian left the truck without talking or looking at Digit. He walked past Digit's mother into the house, the same house where he and Digit had huddled and laughed and made plans. Those days seemed now like they had never existed.

"And, by the way," Digit called after him, "you're welcome for getting you that job."

After showering, Caspian slept the rest of the day and all that night. Digit's mother looked in on him and let him sleep. The next morning, he woke with a smile. His plan was working. With any luck he'd get thrown off the island.

He had rationalized the disappointment of not getting the long straw pretty quickly. The disposal of the safe and hiding the chest was now Nate's problem; if anyone was going to get caught it would be Nate. He let his head sink into the pillow and smiled. If he had thought things through more fully this would have been the plan to devise. Let someone else do all the dirty work. It was perfect, a happy accident that now worked in his favor.

He knew whom he was hitting with that pool cue, all right. He wasn't as drunk as he appeared. It was risky, especially since the guy's friends would have sent him to the hospital if the cops hadn't shown up, but it had been worth it. Assaulting the court clerk's son would definitely get him thrown off the island, it had to.

Because then the other two would think he was out of the picture, believing he'd never be able to return to the island. And if he couldn't return, he'd wouldn't be able to claim his share of the treasure.

But he'd bide his time, and wait, and one day he'd be back.

And he'd have a plan. The treasure was going to be his. He had twenty years to figure it out.

Caspian woke before sunrise that Tuesday morning and quietly left Digit's mother's house. He walked to his rented room; neither of his roommates were there. Good. He knew one had gone off to college pretty much the day after they'd drawn straws; Nate, he knew, liked going out for a pre-dawn run. He packed everything he needed into a backpack — the rest of his stuff was now Nate's to deal with, including his truck. He was going to start over, make a plan for the next twenty years, and the fewer possessions he had the better. He walked into town, sat on a bench, and waited for court to begin.

It had been a busy Labor Day weekend and Caspian sat with the other defendants in the front rows of the courtroom. Because he had hit the court clerk's son, his was to be the last case called: the prosecutor wanted to make sure the judge would be fully exasperated by the time he was to dispose of Dirk Caspian.

Just before he was to face the judge, Caspian looked around the courtroom. Sitting near the back was Digit. Caspian smiled. Was Digit there out of friendship? How touching — loyal to the end. The prosecutor grabbed his elbow; his case had been called.

He watched the judge's face turn red as he read the complaint and looked down at Caspian with disdain. "Assault? With a pool cue? On a respected member of the community? How do you plead?"

Caspian didn't hesitate. "Guilty, your honor."

"Guilty. So you admit it?" The judge paused as if to carefully consider his verdict. Caspian waited, hoping for the worst. "I don't know who you think you are," the judge began, "but you don't seem to care about the island, or its people. Your actions, which you *admit* to, only serve to underscore this. Are you sorry for what you did?" Caspian said nothing. "Well, *are you?*" Caspian looked at the judge with a stare that froze the jurist, with a glower that literally gave him the chills. In all his years on the bench he'd never been on the receiving end of anything quite like it. The judge composed himself. "I can only hope some day you find the compassion you appear to be lacking. You leave me no choice." The judge leaned forward as his voice rose: "You're to be escorted to the next boat where a one-way ticket off-island will be provided. And don't come back!! If you do you'll be arrested and sent to jail."

Caspian tried to hold his glee but his smirk didn't sit well with the judge. "Get him out of here!" the judge shouted. Two police officers took Caspian from the courtroom. Digit couldn't even say good-bye to his old friend.

Not that he was sure he even wanted to.

Chapter Forty-One

BY THE time Nate decided it was time to retrieve the safe, the novelty of the robbery had faded somewhat around the island: the loud rumors about who did it and where the safe was stashed had diminished to a low murmur. The additional state cops were back on the mainland; the volunteers who'd scoured the island for clues had all gone home as well.

The night before Hallowe'en, with a full flotilla of stars in the firmament, Nate drove Caspian's abandoned truck through the moors, taking random roads, making sure no one was following him. Once he was certain he was alone, he made his way to the bottom of Sauls Hills and to the dense thicket of scrub oak. In the deep indentation was the safe, still hidden under the branches and leaves they'd piled over it. His heart pounding, he hoped the safe would still open after all this time. He pulled the handle . . . and it opened! And there was the chest!

He took the chest to the cab of the truck and put it on the passenger seat — although the chest was less than two feet wide, it was still too large to fit on the floor. Moving quickly, he went back to get the safe. Using a hand truck and moving straps he'd brought for the occasion, he secured the safe to the frame and, pulling backwards, extracted the safe from the underbrush and half-wheeled it, half dragged it over to the pickup. Dropping the tailgate, he grabbed two planks from the bed of the pickup and positioned them into a makeshift ramp. He tied a heavy rope around the safe and hand truck, hopped up into the bed of the pickup and, with some effort, hauled the whole works up onto the truck.

Throwing the planks back into the truck bed, he quietly closed the tailgate. He couldn't help but smile — the first part was over.

Now came the tricky part.

Chapter Forty-Two

HE'D THOUGHT of taking the chest with him when he left the island, but the risk was too great — who knew if they had a plainclothes state trooper still hanging around the boats and airport? Caspian was right about that. Better to dump it now and leave it. If all worked out, it'd be worth it.

Of course he was going to bury it in the spot *he'd* selected: the other two had no idea what his location was, although he had to admit they had been pretty creative with their ideas.

But his was genius. The timing couldn't have been better, either. He would bury the chest the next night.

And by the night after that, he'd be off the island.

Unlike Caspian and the other roommate, Nate had no plans for college, nowhere he had to be. With both of them gone, there was no one on Nantucket who knew much about him, or would care if he left the island. The dishwashing job had ended Columbus Day, and nobody there asked him what he was doing next, nor did he volunteer anything.

On the same night he buried the sea chest, he drove Caspian's truck onto the beach near Shimmo. Moored near the shore was a 17-foot Whaler. He'd come by at night several times over the past few weeks — the Whaler hadn't been used once in that time, as far as he could tell. He decided to act now, before either the boat's owner or the owner's caretaker hauled her out for the winter. He only hoped there was enough gas in the engine. He also hoped the scheme he'd devised would work.

He rolled up his pants legs, took off his shoes, waded out to the boat, and slipped aboard. Moving quickly to the stern, he turned to the engine. It had to start, or he was sunk. After a couple of tugs on the starter rope, however, it sputtered to life. He unhooked the mooring line and headed the short distance to the beach.

He pulled in sideways to the shore and anchored. He jumped off the boat and into the pickup. He backed the truck so that the opened tailgate hung over the side of the boat. He took a square of plywood from the back of the truck and placed it on the deck of the Whaler. Crawling up onto the truck bed, he untied the safe, and, using the leverage of the hand truck, dumped the safe into the boat. A corner of the safe smashed through the plywood and put a sizable divot into the deck of the boat. "I guess I'll find out soon enough if these things are unsinkable," he thought.

Steering the boat out into the harbor, his body felt as if it had been pumped with air, and he wanted to let out with a raucous whoop, but he controlled his emotions. All he could do was smile, and he smiled so wide his cheeks hurt.

Chapter Forty-Three

He had checked the charts. He was headed for the deepest water in the harbor. With the summer long over, the only boats moored in the boat basin were scallop boats and a couple of liveaboards; there were no boats in the upper harbor. As he neared the spot, he cut way back on the throttle, and was about to toss out the anchor. But no, he thought, dropping anchor would add another step, might be one move too many. This shouldn't take long.

Taking hold of the rope he'd kept tied around the safe, he pulled the safe close to one side of the boat, the port side, and tried rolling it up and out of the boat. Whether he was drained because of the excitement, or his adrenaline was spent, the safe was now heavier than ever — it weighed a ton. Jerking it towards the gunwale, he pushed up with his arms and legs and gave a great heave.

And he and the safe both went overboard.

Fortunately, the safe went one way and he the other. When he surfaced he realized he must have hit the throttle with his leg or something because the boat was now going in circles. Great!

How was he going to get back on board a runaway boat?

He decided he didn't have to. Slowly, he moved away from the boat and headed to the nearest shore, sometimes swimming, sometimes floating on his back. The boat continued its spiraling path. The water was cold but it wasn't yet too cold and he was only about thirty yards from shore. Stay calm, he told himself. Panicking would only set him up to drown, and wouldn't that be a kick in the ass?

He was freezing when he stepped ashore. He started to shiver. Where was he, on the same side as the truck, he hoped? He looked out at the still circling boat and got his bearings — yes, the truck was only a couple of hundred yards down the beach.

The wet sand stung his bare feet, forcing him to hop-step along as quickly as he could. When he made it to the truck his feet were so numb he couldn't feel the gas pedal. A working heater was never so welcome.

Sufficiently warmed, he drove off the beach and back to his room, quickly changing out of his wet clothes and stuffing them, and the few possessions he had into his backpack. He'd be off on the morning boat.

He tried to sleep but couldn't. He had no plans; he'd figure things out once he got off-island.

But it had worked. It had worked! And no one had seen him!

Around 5:30 the next morning, he picked up his backpack and left the room where the three of them were once so close, closing the door and forgetting the suitcase he'd bought at the Hospital Thrift Shop and stuffed into the closet a month before.

Chapter Forty-Four

"... so, we figured when we got the call of a boat going in circles in the harbor with no one aboard that someone had fallen overboard, or committed suicide." C. C. Dennison was conferring with Addie once again about the robbery. "And when I say, 'we,' you understand, I mean the Coast Guard at the time. I've only been stationed here a couple of years." Addie nodded. "But when the boat's registration numbers were checked, the boat's owner was contacted, who said he hadn't used the boat in over a month and was, in fact, off-island that night. He hadn't authorized anyone to use it either."

"So it was stolen," Addie added.

"So it was stolen," Dennison concurred. "Still, there was an investigation, but no body was ever recovered, no sign of foul play, so the Coast Guard concluded its investigation.

"But," he continued, "I think that it was somehow part of the robbery."

"What makes you think there's a connection?" Addie asked.

"Coffee?" Dennison asked. Addie shook his head. Dennison walked over to his coffee pot, poured a cup, and turned to face Addie. "It just wasn't . . . *right*," he said. "It was too soon after the robbery. Besides, what was a boat doing out in the harbor, at night, on Hallowe'en — and not a scalloping boat either, mind you — going around in circles? Somebody had to drive it out to the middle of the harbor; it didn't start up all by itself." He sat back down at his desk. "And it was stolen. Somebody had taken it for a reason."

"So where did that somebody go?" Addie asked. "As you said, you never found a body."

"Precisely," Dennison said, proud of himself for coming up with the word. He said it again: "Pre-cise-ly. Where did that somebody go?"

Chapter Forty-Five

CHRISTMAS. THE day dawned crisp and bright. No scalloping today. Digit slept in, for him, until seven.

He had no tree. Since Addie and Verona had moved into their own place, and because he was living on his own, he hadn't bothered with a Christmas tree for the first time in as long as he could remember. It was all right. He was getting together that afternoon with Addie, Verona, Sandy and Rebecca at Sandy's house. Sandy had a tree.

Christmas trees also lined both sides of Main Street, a tradition since 1948. But, as his grandfather had told him, the very first lighted community Christmas tree stood in front of the Pacific National Bank in 1915, and was celebrated that Christmas Eve by school children singing carols. May as well stroll downtown and take a look, Digit thought, as he tucked the red mohair scarf his mother had given him for Christmas years before inside his wool jacket.

He hummed carols as he walked to Main Street. As was the custom, the Hub was giving away the morning papers in two plastic buckets placed outside the closed doors. There was no one else around. Not a car or truck on Main Street. Empty. If there ever was a day where Nantucket seemed unchanged, had the same look and feel and atmosphere as it did in the mid-1800s, it was on Christmas.

Excerpt from the diary of Capt. James Hathaway

December 25

At sea once again on this holy day, but there are no celebrations, save for a fruitcake for the crew. It is a work day, just as any other, although we may as well have declared it a holiday, for there are no whales. Tomorrow, perhaps. Inscribing the date only reminds me how much I miss my wife and family, and my home — but my home today is this ship; my congregation, my crew; and my parish, the ocean.

How I once yearned to be at sea, how being on land seemed foreign, and I was not comfortable until my feet trod the deck of a ship and we were underway once more. The movement of a ship comforted me, and I never slept more soundly as I did to its steady rocking. But now, the days at sea grow longer and I look forward instead to our homeward voyage. The whaling is longer and longer. It once was that there was so much work, there was no time for thought. Now, it seems, time is all we have, and we count the hours, and think. At least today the weather is pleasant. I wonder how things are at home. Had there only been another ship in our vicinity, carrying news from home, anchoring next to us for a gam — that would have been pleasant.

How I miss the bustle of Nantucket.

I search the heavens for the stars that remind me of home, but the sky is different here. There is no Big Dipper, no Little Dipper. I search for Perseus, the whale hunter, but am also too far south for that. I know my way around the heav-

ens, but these stars won't lead me home.

How I miss my wife! Being at sea only makes me miss her more, for she came with me on my last voyage, which is customary for Nantucket whalers, that captains' wives sometimes accompany them. It was a relatively short expedition past Greenland toward the arctic and back to the Azores, where we laid in for some repairs. She enjoyed the opportunity to go ashore. We were treated as royalty, sampling the delights of the beautiful island of Sao Miguel, which made her exceedingly happy.

Would that she were with me now, but I know this is not possible, so I must not dwell on it. I have only the motion of the ship to console me, and it is scant consolation indeed.

The Christmas quiet was a welcome respite from the frantic pace of summer. Digit didn't mind not being on the water today. Walking back home from the Hub on the empty Main Street made him think of his heritage, of the connectedness he felt to the island. His grandfather walked these same streets. And so had his grandfather's grandfather. If only his grandfather could be with him today, he thought. How lucky he was to have grown up with him; he missed him and his love. But then, Digit reasoned, maybe his grandfather *is* with him on this day of days.

His contribution to Christmas dinner was going to be easy: bacon-wrapped scallops. He figured about a pound and a half would be plenty for them and any last-minute guests Sandy invited, which she always did, but he was bringing two pounds anyway. The best thing about it was that there was no preparation ahead of time. He brought over the scallops, a pound of bacon, and toothpicks; that was it. At Sandy's there'd be a small assembly line as he and Sandy and Verona got the ingredients together and onto the broiling pan.

Bacon-wrapped Scallops

Rinse scallops in colander (or not)
Cut raw bacon strips into thirds
Wrap bacon around scallop, secure with toothpick
Arrange in single layer on broiler pan
Place broiler pan under broiler
(but not too close to heat or flame)
Turn scallops after 3 to 5 minutes and broil an
additional 3 to 5 minutes until bacon is crispy
Place on serving plate and enjoy after suitable
cool-down period

He'd also bring a couple dozen littlenecks that he'd brought up in his dredges the past few days. Nothing wrong with that — if there was any bacon left over, some clams casino wouldn't hurt.

Clams Casino

Shuck littlenecks, leaving loosened clam meat on
bottom of shell. Do not rinse.
Arrange in single layer on cookie sheet lined
with aluminum foil
Top each clam with small slice (or cube) of
cheddar cheese
Top cheese with strip of raw bacon (cut to fit)
Place under broiler (again, not too close)
Cook 5 or so minutes, or until bacon just begins
to crisp
Garnish with parsley (if you want)
Serve with lemon wedges (also optional)

The day warmed enough by mid-morning for Verona to be on her bicycle; she headed out on the bike path to Madaket. She looked forward to being with Rebecca later that day, to spending time with family.

Family. It was a concept that had been foreign to her most of her life. Oh, she loved the family who adopted her, no doubt about it, but she'd always had a sense of being on her own in this world. Ever since Rebecca had told her she was her aunt, her blood relative, a portal in her heart seemed to open. She instinctively felt close to Rebecca, a bond unlike anything she'd felt before.

But a strange sensation now came over her, making her shiver, and she gripped the handlebars tightly — there was something trying to get out, something she was supposed to know, some revelation.

Oh, she couldn't think about it. If she thought about it too much it would drive her crazy. Whatever it was would come to her in time. She pedaled harder against the wind, for there was always some wind on Nantucket, and the effort helped her forget.

A few evenings before, on the solstice, she and Addie had driven down this road in his old car, seeking the conjunction of Saturn and Jupiter — a phenomenon where the two planets seem to nearly align, and, because it was occurring at nightfall, this was to be its closest observable appearance from Earth in nearly 800 years. They parked at First Bridge facing the southwestern sky, where the two planets were forecast to appear above the horizon shortly after sunset. The moon was bright behind them in the twilight sky, but clouds ribboned the skyline in front of them.

"How long should we wait?" Addie asked her.

"I'm not sure," she answered. "I really don't know what to expect."

She exited the car and looked behind her, towards the North Head of Long Pond. "Clear," she called to Addie. "But I'm not seeing any stars this way either." Suddenly, a murmuration of starlings rose and twisted above her, swelling and circling in a mystic dance before spiraling out of sight. She got back into the car. Addie popped his old cassette of Bob Dylan's *New Morning* into his car's tape player, right at *Winterlude:*

Winterlude, Winterlude, oh darlin'
Winterlude by the road tonight . . .
. . . Oh, I see by the angel beside me
That love has a reason to shine . . .

They looked out the windshield together in silence as the song played on, until Addie concluded: "I guess we missed it. Maybe tomorrow night." Verona snuggled into his arm. Some high clouds parted. Addie noticed two lights in the sky that appeared to be approaching. "There it is," he said with mock excitement. "Too bad it's only an airplane." Verona leaned forward and watched the lights that twinkled clearly between the clouds. "I don't think that plane's moving," she said. They both got out of the car and looked.

It manifested as two bright stars close together: magical headlights in tandem. They watched as airy clouds suggested movement, then slowly concealed the starry phenomenon, as if a heavenly curtain were drawn.

Two planets appearing nearly as one; it gave Verona hope. They drove home happy, and singing:

The moonlight reflects from the window
Where the snowflakes, they cover the sand

Come out tonight, ev'rything will be tight
Winterlude, this dude thinks you're grand

"Perhaps that is what I'm feeling," Verona thought now as she crossed First Bridge on her bicycle. "Like the planets, Addie and I are getting closer." She smiled at the memory of their celestial discovery, happy they witnessed it together, happy that Addie enjoyed life's simple pleasures. Her legs pumping against the wind felt good; exertion and release. Her expectation was that the solstice, signaling change, would bring comfort, not questions. She supposed seeing the conjunction of Saturn and Jupiter offered a kind of cheer. The Sun glared.

"My goodness," she thought. "Look at the time. I'd better get back or I'll miss Christmas."

Rebecca enjoyed visiting Sandy's house, her old house, but she also looked forward to going back to the Homestead at the end of each visit. Her mobility wasn't what it once was, and not being able to move freely from room to room, or even consider using the upstairs bathroom, left her, if not melancholic, wistful, as her body forced her into the role of observer. Sitting on the divan in the front room it seemed as though she'd never spent as much time looking at the walls when she lived here as she did now. Oh, everyone was nice, and did their best to make her comfortable, but she didn't feel that she was part of their conversations unless they were addressing her directly, more out of kindness, she felt, than interest. Is this what her life had come to, that people felt obliged to include her?

But in her heart she knew those were her old, uncomfortable bones talking. She knew how much Sandy cared for her, and Digit, and Addie. And as for Verona, well, how lucky could an old lady get to be spending Christmas Day with her daughter in the house she'd grown up in? In all her life, not even as a wide-eyed child wondering what treasure Santa Claus might bring, had she felt such happiness at Christmas. The tree was lovely, she had to admit, and she lost herself in a near hypnotic haze staring at the colored lights and how they danced and reflected in the tinsel. For a moment she could almost imagine herself traveling back in time, at one with her child self, the promises of days yet to come flowering within her. And there it was, an ornament she recognized, a small silver ball with yellow and green and red stripes. Even the angel atop the tree appeared wonderfully familiar with its tiny porcelain face. They had to be facsimiles; they couldn't be the original ornaments she remembered.

Just then, Sandy entered, extending a drink of some kind. "Eggnog," Sandy said. She had noticed Rebecca staring at the tree. "I've used those same decorations every year since my former husband and I bought this house," she said. "We found them in an old box in the cellar. They were too beautiful to throw away."

"Some of these look just like the ones on our tree when I was a child," Rebecca said, wanting to believe it was true.

"They very well could be," Sandy said. "The box they were in was falling apart. It had to have been in the cellar for years, decades even."

"I can't believe how well they've held up," Rebecca said. "It's so nice to see them again, whether they were mine or not."

"Let's just say they are," Sandy said. "So here you are, reunited at Christmas." And she clinked her cup of eggnog with Rebecca's before returning to the kitchen.

Rebecca's eyes lit up when Verona entered the room and sat next to her on the couch. "Let's open presents," Verona said.

"You haven't even had any eggnog yet," Rebecca told her. "Patience is a virtue."

"Well, I can't wait," Verona said, bounding to the tree and kneeling before it. She reached around back and extracted a present wrapped in plain paper but decorated with different colored star and heart designs. "They're potato prints," Verona said. "This is for you." And she handed Rebecca the package. "Open it," she implored.

"Shouldn't we wait for the others to come in?"

"No, this is between us."

Rebecca carefully unwrapped the gift as Verona watched, her eyes widening as the present was revealed — a painting, a watercolor. It was a winter portrait of the Lily Pond as viewed from the back window of the house they were in, the same scene Rebecca had seen since childhood, with the elegant white spire of the Congregational Church almost shining in the background. There, too, was her old school, Academy Hill, with its stalwart red-brick presence, in her youth a short walk from her back door. The watercolor drew her in with its evocation of winter days gone by, and Verona beamed as Rebecca smiled.

"This is the most thoughtful present I've ever received," Rebecca said truthfully. "I can almost see myself in it."

The others entered and Rebecca held up the painting for them to admire. As they passed the framed picture among themselves, Rebecca said quietly to Verona, "And I have something for you." From her jacket pocket she took a small package wrapped with ribbon and placed it in Verona's hand. Verona carefully unwrapped the delicate tissue paper and found a necklace with a gold chain and a small sperm whale carved from ivory, complete with a tiny carved eye. "I thought you'd like to have something of mine," Rebecca told her. "My father made this for me when I was a little girl."

Verona held the necklace to her chest and kissed Rebecca. "I'll cherish this," she said.

"Don't cherish it, wear it," Rebecca said. "I'd help you with the clasp but I don't think my fingers can manage it. Addie, help your girlfriend, why don't you?"

Verona pulled back her hair and drew it up into a bun. The necklace hung gracefully against her sweater, as though it was meant to be there. "Yes," Rebecca thought, as she wiped away a tear she hoped no one would see, "it's where it's supposed to be."

It was a Christmas dinner that couldn't be beat. As Digit walked home along the quiet streets the aid to navigation horn at the end of the east jetty was heard clearly, bugling its monotoned song in the moist night; the nearby branches, in repose and supplication, bowed in the soft Yuletide breeze, while the moon was partially obscured by the passing clouds of an oncoming front. Through the mist, the Town Clock's Portuguese Bell tolled the hour as it echoed above the cobblestones. Digit, and probably all of Nantucket, hearing through the gentle night: "Stille nacht, heilige nacht — Silent night, holy night." It was how Digit thought about the island. It was home; it was holy.

"Now where else would you conjure that?" he said to himself.

"Nowhere," said Verona. "I'd rather be nowhere but here."

Bundled in a blanket, she sat with Addie a week later on the beach at Surfside. The moon was bright, and its beam shone like a sublime spotlight on the stretch of ocean below. It was New Year's Eve. While most revelers gathered in various venues around town, Addie and Verona reveled in being alone.

"Got a resolution?" Addie playfully asked.

"We all want to change the world," Verona answered. "Isn't that how the song goes?"

"I think you're thinking of *Revolution*," said Addie.

"Like our planet. No revolution, same stars every night."

"Whatever you say."

The champagne stayed cold in the winter night. Addie popped the cork and they toasted each other's love.

"The mothers stay with their babies," Verona said.

The comment came out of nowhere. "What are you saying?" Addie asked her.

"I read about it this morning, in the book you gave me for Christmas about whales. It said mothers and their babies, called calves, have a real relationship. Mothers will stay with their babies for months, or even years in some cases."

Addie pulled the blanket closer around them. "That's interesting," he said, nuzzling her cheek. "What else does the book say?"

"You know what's real interesting?" Verona said, pulling away in her excitement. "In some whale species, sperm whales among them, other females will help the mother at times."

"Like baby-sitting?"

"I suppose so. That's all I've read so far," she said, as she reached inside her coat and caressed the ivory whale Rebecca had given her. She tried to push thoughts of her birth mother from her mind, and, looking to the sky, concentrated on the love that surrounded her now. All her life she had not delved beyond thinking of her adoptive mother as anyone but her mother. To do so, she believed, would be a futile exercise that could only lead to sadness: for her, for her adoptive mother, and, by transference, to her birth mother as well. She had always accepted the life she was born into. She had been raised in a loving, nurturing home and was both thankful and grateful for where fate had placed her.

The feelings she'd had the week before, however, still lingered, still settled in her soul. What was it? What was she supposed to know?

In the dark stillness a rumbling came. It traveled from the vast reaches of the ocean to the far-off horizon and sped towards shore, the lamentation Verona had heard before, only this time it was louder, more insistent, like an oncoming locomotive.

Chapter Forty-Six

On New Year's Day, a sperm whale washed ashore on the beach off 'Sconset. Word spread quickly across the island, and by early afternoon, hundreds had traveled to the east end to see the giant animal for themselves.

It was an eerie sight against the white-grey winter sky. From a distance it seemed a gigantic shapeless thing, almost formless. But as people walked toward it, they could see its eye and make out the blowhole in its massive head. The onlookers spoke in hushed tones, or not at all, as if they were at a wake. The enormity of the beached mammal was almost too much to comprehend; the incongruity of the water-dwelling creature on land underscoring that it did not belong here; that it was truly out of its element. Where in the water it led an existence of grace, land made it grotesque. Rather than a sense of wonder, the whale corpse elicited feelings of something gone wrong.

Verona had been one of the first to arrive that morning in the cold quiet of daybreak. Her dreams had been unsettling: at first she was floating, not in air, not on water, but in some type of benign liquid. She marveled at how sharp her senses were: how easily she could see and hear — the sounds, like ethereal music, drawing her in, taking her deeper, calling to her.

Then the music stopped. And she fell, and was falling, faster and faster, and the lightness she felt before had vanished and she felt heavier and heavier, like a rock, and she was sinking now, deeper and deeper.

She woke up on the floor.

She hadn't awakened Addie. Good. She hurriedly dressed, put on her wool hat, scarf and mittens, and hopped on her bicycle. The sounds she had heard at Surfside the night before were now in her head, urging her on, like a signal.

She took the bike path to 'Sconset, a ride she had taken many times before. The winter air invigorated her.

When she reached the top of the hill at 'Sconset, she instinctively knew to turn left, to head toward the ocean and Low Beach Road.

At that hour, there were only a few people near the hulking carcass of the whale. She biked faster. When she reached the sand, she ran. She ran past the people and up to the whale, and touched it, and cried.

Excerpt from the diary of Capt. James Hathaway

Because it was my business, nay, my duty, I did not see the whale as anything but a commodity when I first went to whaling. The whole enterprise was a spontaneous hysteria, a mania that infested every man aboard, as the whale was hunted in a fury fueled by a single-minded drive: to overtake and overpower the leviathan. There was a saying on board: Death to the living, Long life to the killers, Success to Sailor's Wives and Greasy Luck to Whalers.

On calm nights, when not even our sails were bothered by the wind, we could all hear the calls across the ocean, as if the sirens themselves were calling out to us. We knew it was the whales calling out to each other, communicating across vast distances of ocean. Why, even the most callous harpooneer was heard to describe the sound as 'beautiful.'

Why then, when the chase was on, were we so heartless to only consider these great mammals as a thing, with no reason to live but to provide us with oil, great barrels of oil, ships full of oil, enough oil for England, and France, and the Americas, and the world? That was the beast that had to be fed, and we were the beasts to do it. Bloodthirsty was what we were, no better than the madmen written about by Shelley or Poe! In fact, when the whale spouted blood we rejoiced in it, would bathe in it if we could. Enough was never enough. It was not enough until the boat was full, and if we could have, we'd have added more decks to fill with barrels of oil, topped them off, and added some more.

Chapter Forty-Seven

EVEN BEFORE he realized she was gone, Addie knew Verona was in 'Sconset. As soon as Digit called him about the whale, Addie understood she would be there without needing to feel the empty space next to him in bed.

When had he become so intuitive about Verona? Knowing she had gone to the whale came to him instinctively. Did it mean he was finally beginning to think beyond himself? "Right," he told himself as he got dressed. "Stop taking yourself so seriously."

Digit picked him up. By the time the two of them got there, there were maybe fifty people milling about the whale, among them Ellen, notebook in hand.

"Where's your notebook, Addie? Now, *this* is a story. At least you're here. Isn't there a notebook in your car? Go get it. Are you even hearing me?"

Addie scanned the crowd. Everyone was bundled up in scarves and hats; he couldn't tell anyone apart. Was she here? She had to be.

As if in a vacuum he heard Ellen's voice: "What are you looking at? The whale's over there. Come on, there are people from the New England Aquarium who've just arrived. Let's go talk to them." And before she could hurry off, Addie reached for her arm. "I'm looking for Verona."

"She's right over there," Ellen said matter of factly, "talking to the Marine Mammal Stranding Team."

It didn't look like Verona, but then he saw her hair poking out from under her wool hat, and the turn of her head that ensured it was indeed Verona.

He ran to her, and embraced her. She looked at him quizzically. "Verona," he whispered in her ear, "I knew you'd be here." And he hugged her some more.

Verona delighted in Addie's embrace, but he seemed to be overreacting. What was he thinking? But Verona had made up her mind long ago not to concern herself with what other people were thinking.

She hadn't wanted to wake him, that was all. Without knowing why, she had an insistent urge to be here, a calling she couldn't ignore. She didn't know what was pulling her to the ocean until she arrived.

From afar, it looked as if a boat had come ashore. But as she got closer and as her eyes adjusted, she knew.

Dirk Caspian wasn't happy when he got the call from the state, ordering him to get all his digging equipment out to 'Sconset. He thought about mentioning the historic importance of his excavation, but immediately thought twice: what could be of more historic significance on Nantucket than a whale?

A whale about which he couldn't care less.

Chapter Forty-Eight

THE WHALE was dead. What to do with it? Representatives from the New England Aquarium conferred with the state office of Fisheries and Wildlife. Should they tow it out to sea? Dig a hole and push it in?

Finally, someone from the historical association offered an idea: *Look, we've got all the tools from whaling: the flensing knives; the boarding knife; the cutting spade; the bone spade. Why don't we cut up the whale like they did during whaling, and preserve the skeleton for the museum addition we're planning?*

Whatever the decision was, it had to be made quickly: the whale was going to stink pretty badly very soon.

It was decided that, yes, the tools could be used for "cutting in" the whale, for that is the term that was used during whaling. It seemed the most respectful way to deal with it.

They had to consult the old ship's logs and reference works to figure out how to use the tools properly, but the workers caught on quickly, and they attacked the job with reverence and gusto.

The Caspian and robbery stories were put on hold. Ellen and Addie devoured the whale story, each of them working independently but with no competition between them. There was no secrecy about this story, no sources to keep from each other. There was nothing to hide: there was the whale in all its washed-up glory. All that mattered now was how it was written.

Because of this, they shared quotes and interviewed people at the same time. Ellen had a daily deadline to meet, so if there were any press releases to be had, Addie or Ellen scooped up two of them — it's not like different releases were being put out for the Boston and New York newspapers, or the mainland radio, or TV outlets, all of which descended on the island for a day or two.

Until they started cutting up the whale, that is. The mainland media wasn't interested in the gory side of the story; they dispersed before the first cut was made, packing up their cameras and microphones and heading out to the airport.

Addie had to be out there every day, but after that first morning Verona never went back. In her eyes, the whale wasn't there anymore.

Instead, she went out at night to the beach at Surfside, to survey the stars and search for Cetus. She saw the stars but Cetus was gone, off to a different sky in another part of the world.

And the calls coming from the ocean ceased.

Chapter Forty-Nine

THE WHALERS called it "greasy luck." A sperm whale was full of oil. Oil even seeped through its bones, which is why the plan was to put the bones in steel cages and submerge them for a year in an undisclosed location in Nantucket Harbor: for the oil to seep out.

As to why the whale washed ashore? The scientists who oversaw the operation rendered their verdict — it was in some kind of trouble, the reason all whales beach themselves.

Soon after the whale was flensed, the bones carefully numbered and carted away, and the remains buried by Dirk Caspian and crew, temperatures plummeted, and the island was locked in a deep freeze.

There would be no scalloping for a while, and before long there would be no boats coming to the island at all. The ice coated the upper harbor at first and spread, working from the edges of Coatue and Wauwinet and Pocomo, to Abrams Point and Shimmo, then down to Monomoy and the Creeks, and into the boat basin, following the curve of the shoreline, and layer by layer expanding outwards; squeezing, then stilling the harbor currents. The cold continued, and the ice moved out through the jetties and into the Sound, until it stretched the nearly thirty miles to Cape Cod, surrounding the bell buoys and holding them fast, rendering them mute and motionless.

Everywhere was white. The whiteness covered all the waters, and when it snowed, the whiteness touched the land and blanketed the boughs and branches until all was white, as white as Digit had ever seen it, and when the sun was shining it was blinding white.

He had hauled his boat before the freeze-up, but others hadn't gotten around to it in time. Lance Willoughby had; Digit wasn't surprised.

With the deep freeze, and the whiteness, came the wind — the incessant, breathing, living wind that in the winter blew like a banshee that bent and bothered everything in its path.

The island was truly isolated.

Some, like Verona, enjoyed the insularity, as did Addie, Digit, Rebecca, and Sandy, who liked the idea of being cut off from the world. As soon as the weather turned, they knew to stock up on supplies and canned goods. If they started to run low, they also knew they could count on each other.

"*Splendid isola-tion,*" Addie sang, driving down a carless Madaket Road. As he looked out across the open, fallow vista, the island seemed to be in a bubble, embraced by the white afternoon sky.

There were others, however, who felt very uncomfortable with the idea of being cut off, with not being able to leave when they wanted, with no exit from the island; a forced quarantine. These were the people who saw no reason that there shouldn't be a bridge to the mainland.

Like Dirk Caspian, whose life hinged on getaway plans.

And Ellen, who didn't like the feeling of being trapped. It was a strange sort of claustrophobia, in which the perimeter of the island seemed to be steadily shrinking, its edges rapidly eroding. Before long, there'd be nothing to do but drown.

"Now, Addie, I haven't been off-island in six months, so it's not like I don't know how to live on this island. It's just when I can't go if I want to go that I don't particularly care for it."

"Isn't your bathroom working?"

"What?"

"Forget it."

For Dirk Caspian, the freeze-up meant no digging. At least there was still some research and paperwork to be done on the Wampanoag burial ground project; even if the state wanted to call him back to Boston there was no way of getting there.

He was stuck, alone. He could already feel the walls of his rental cottage closing in on him.

Musn't think that way, he told himself. He had wanted to come back to the island, remember?

But it was more than that: he needed to.

In the years since he'd left the island, he'd tried to occupy his mind by working incessantly, climbing the bureaucratic ladder in state government; taking the necessary graduate courses to better his position (and pay grade); working overtime, and weekends; taking required vacation time to read up on ivory in general, and whaling in particular. He discovered, for instance, that the Sperm Whale was the only large whale to have *teeth*. He read so much about Nantucket, he felt like he was there.

He took to wearing white suits; he ate his pasta *al dente*.

With the deep freeze into its second week, Digit was in his attic, sorting through boxes, figuring what he could heave and what he should save.

Because he had inherited the house from his aunt, who'd had no children, there were things of hers he'd put off going through: photos, some old newspapers, house records. Sorting through this kind of stuff was the last thing Digit wanted to do — working on his donkey engine would be more to his liking — but he found that once he got into this project, he enjoyed it.

The old papers, though yellowed, were large broadsheets that would have required the wingspan of a professional basketball player to hold open and read. There were papers old enough to mention reports of a couple of whaleships bound to return; others mentioned Nantucketers fighting in World War II; the most recent were of the time when Digit was just in high school, when the old wharves were being converted into the Boat Basin of today. "Addie might get a kick out of these," he thought.

And there he was at the bottom of the stairs, as though the thought of him had conjured him. "Hey, Digit, you up there?" Addie called.

"Come on up. Had enough whale for a while?"

"Sure have." He reached the top of the stairs. "Oh, no," Addie said, poking his head into the attic. "This just reminds me of all the stuff I still have to go through."

"Some of it's still up here," Digit said. "Take it with you."

"Let's not get too hasty," Addie said. "I'm on my way to the historical association's research library. Maybe some other time. Just stopped by to say hi."

"Hi back," Digit said. "Now get going and let me get back to work."

"Hey, look at these old newspapers."

"I thought you might find these interesting. Take a look, but be careful, they're fragile."

"What is this stuff?"

"My aunt's; her mementos." He rubbed his nose. "Really should be wearing some kind of mask, I suppose, with all the dust I'm uncovering." He looked into a box, almost dreamily. "I read somewhere that all the particles of air ever breathed are still floating around out there," he said. "It's crazy, but if that's the case I'm breathing in air my aunt breathed out."

Addie was incredulous. "You mean I'm breathing the same air as Mozart, or Beethoven?"

"Could be," Digit said. "Feeling especially musical?"

"Only around you."

"Yeah, right." Digit duck-walked over to another carboard box. Inside was a small, intricately detailed wooden box. "Well, look at this," he said, opening the lid. "I'd forgotten all about this."

"What've you got?" Addie asked him.

Digit held a whale's tooth in his hand, large enough to be held almost with two hands. It was decorated with scrimshaw that included a drawing of an unfurled banner bordered in black ink with an inside inscription etched in red. "Take a look," Digit said, holding it out.

Addie carefully took the tooth. "It's beautiful. What is it?"

"It was my great, great, great grandfather's. He was a whaling captain. My aunt used to have it out on the mantel."

Addie tried reading the inscription. "What's the writing? It looks like it's dedicated to him or something."

"It was a gift from his crew. I've heard the story from my aunt, and my grandparents, and other aunts and uncles. They were all very proud of him. Captain James Hathaway. You should ask about him at the historical association since you're going there. I believe they even have a painting of him."

Digit inspected the inscription on the tooth. "I used to know what it said. Kind of faded now. Something looks like it starts with a 'V'. " He put the tooth back inside the box. "What are you looking up, anyway? Still investigating that bogus robbery?"

"How'd you guess?"

"The news must be pretty slow for you to still be bothering

with that."

"No boats, no planes, no court," Addie said. "Besides, it gets me out of the office."

"Since you've got nothing better to do, why don't you take some of your crap with you?"

"Sorry, Digit, got to go," Addie said. "Captain Hathaway, huh? Thanks for the tip."

"Anytime," Digit said. He picked up the box holding the scrimshawed tooth. "Maybe this would make a story, now that you're a whale expert. Why don't you take it with you to the research library, find out what it's worth." He handed Addie the box.

"I don't know, Digit. That's a lot of responsibility. I wouldn't want to lose it."

Digit downplayed Addie's trepidations. "It's just a tooth. I'd forgotten it was even up here. It's probably safer with you than me. Go ahead, take it. I trust you."

"All right," Addie said, descending the stairs. "Who knows? It might make a decent story at that."

Good, Digit thought, one less thing to deal with. Watching out not to hit his head on the rafters, he slowly stood up and arched his back until he felt a satisfying crack. He took in a long breath and wondered if, circling in the air around Nantucket, some essence of Captain Hathaway still existed.

Chapter Fifty

THE RESEARCH librarian was at lunch. While waiting to find out about the tooth, Addie poked around and came across some tapes, oral histories of the island. He flipped through a few cassette boxes and then stopped: Cy had made a recording. Well, how about that? From working with him at the DPW, he remembered Cy as having nothing good to say about anybody. Why would they want that on tape?

Curious, Addie settled in for a listen. What he heard was surprising.

At first, Cy is talking about growing up near town, when outside of town was all wide-open fields, and pine groves and moors, on a sort of farm (pronounced "fahm") with a couple of cows that needed to be milked every morning, and a large chicken coop on family property a block away. As the oldest boy, Cy was expected to do most of the farm chores before and after school. "I always worked," Cy's voice said on the tape. "Never knew anything different. No, I wasn't able to play on the football team, I had to get home to tend to the cows and chickens. My old man was working two jobs himself, baking at the bake shop in the morning and then the night shift at the gas plant. In between he cut lawns."

He described a different island than the one Addie knew: with service stations and garages downtown; with most everybody living in the old town; with an active Navy Base at Tom Nevers and nothing else out there for miles around; with 'Sconset having its own one-room schoolhouse; with a few year-round residents in Madaket, but little summer home development there, or anywhere besides 'Sconset, really.

He talked about people literally living off the land, depending on scallops not only to make a living but for sustenance; on eels as an island staple, along with beach plum and rose hip jelly; with homemade beans and brown bread for supper every Saturday night; of rabbit stew, and pheasant, and deer hunting as a right of passage that he lamented was too quickly disappearing. He talked of being born during the Depression, and of how his father said Nantucket felt the effects of the Depression later than the rest of the country, "but once it hit Nantucket, the island didn't recover until years after everyone else. Those were some lean times. Nobody ever turned down a job, no matter what it was."

He spoke, too, of the island being truly self-sustaining; of dairy farms, and milkmen, and how, if some people's milk deliveries went missing, they knew that the kids down the street had empty bellies and to blame them would only bring shame. So, they quietly came to Cy to ask if he might have a quart to spare from his own cows, saving everyone embarrassment.

Cy was also a scalloper. Like some married couples, he and his wife each had a commercial fishing license, meaning they were allowed a double limit. "I'd get up early and head out to get a jump on things, while my wife got the kids ready for school. I could see by the Town Clock what time to head in, and there'd she be, standing at the end of the town pier, waiting. Then we'd both head out and get our double limit. The scallops would be in the shanty for the kids to open when they got home from school. And we weren't the only couple who did that, neither."

And then he talked about the robbery.

"I'd heard about it, yeah, who hadn't on the island? First big robbery in over a hundred years. I mean they say it was a robbery . . . but . . ." and his voice trailed off.

Addie was startled by a tap on his shoulder. "Find what you were looking for?" It was the research librarian, back from lunch. He was about to say yes when he felt the box at his side.

"Actually," he said, "I wanted to find out more about this."

"Where did you get this?" she asked him, looking over her reading glasses.

"Digit, um, Clarence Hathaway."

"That's all right, I know Digit. And where did he get it?"

"He said it was his great-great-great grandfather's."

The librarian inspected the tooth again. "Wait here, I'll be right back."

Moments later she returned. "Have a seat," and she pointed to the table in the center of the room. "I thought we had a ship's log relating to Captain Hathaway, but I can't yet locate it. It might be filed under a different name. I'll keep looking. In the meantime, would you mind leaving this tooth with me? I promise I'll take good care of it."

"I guess so," Addie said. "If I can't leave it here, where can I leave it?"

"I just wanted to check something out. Have you ever heard about the *Susan's* Teeth?"

"No, should I?"

"I thought you may have done some prior research. The *Susan's* Teeth are quite valuable, and don't pop up very often.

They were the work of a Nantucket sailor who served aboard the whaleship *Susan* in the early 1800s, a sailor by the name of Frederick Myrick. I can't come up with the number of teeth he engraved off the top of my head, but I think it's somewhere in the vicinity of three dozen."

"Wow," Addie said.

"Wow, indeed," she said, mimicking him subtly but caringly. "The engravings are pretty involved, which is remarkable when you consider he reportedly etched all these teeth within the span of ten months or so. If this *is* a *Susan's* Tooth, Digit will probably want to insure it, if he hasn't already."

"I'll let him know. How much do you think?"

"Some have sold for as much as $150,000."

Addie whistled.

"You're still in a library, Addie."

"Whoops."

"That's okay, there's no one else here if you haven't noticed. Would you mind if I showed this tooth to our museum director? I'm sure he'd have some insights."

"Why not?"

"I also want to check to see if Captain Hathaway was ever in command of the *Susan*. That's why I also wanted to look into our ships' logs. I'm sure I'll have some answers for you, or rather, Digit, by tomorrow. We'll lock the tooth in a vault tonight. Would you feel more comfortable calling Digit about this?"

"As I said, if I can't trust you, who can I trust? I'm sure he won't mind."

"All right. Come by tomorrow afternoon."

Addie stood, shook her hand, and was about to leave, when he remembered.

"Digit also said something about a portrait."

"Just a minute, I'll check the database." She went to her desk and typed at her computer. "Here it is, in storage. Do you know where our storage facility is? Here's the address. I'll let them know you're coming."

Chapter Fifty-One

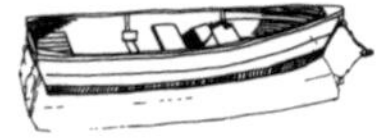

FUNNY HOW things work out. That's what Dirk Caspian was thinking.

Funny that the backhoe broke down working on the whale; funny that the freeze-up prevented any digging anyway; funny that he was back on this island, in the middle of winter, with nothing to do but stew and watch his money dwindle away.

No, it wasn't funny. His teeth ached thinking about it.

On the plus side, because he'd turned it over and over and over in his head during the last twenty years, the one positive thing to consider was that he hadn't gotten the long straw. He definitely would have buried the chest in the marsh. He was so compulsive back then: the marsh would have either absorbed the chest, or eaten it away. So, as he'd been telling himself for two decades, it was a stroke of luck that Nate Powell had gotten the long straw.

Nate *must* have buried the chest. Yes, he was certain of it. For the last ten years he'd checked every maritime auction in the United States and United Kingdom for sales of *Susan's* Teeth, and none was ever put up for auction by Nate Powell. Sure, Nate could have used another name, but he wouldn't have, he couldn't have; he just couldn't.

They authenticate those things, don't they? Besides, he didn't think Nate would risk arrest by selling the teeth anyway.

No, if anyone was going to sell the teeth, it had to be him. He had the brains for that kind of thing. And the *Susan's* Teeth he'd seen offered at auction were commanding over six figures. He got a chill just thinking about it. He'd waited so long. The wait will be worth it, he told himself. His ship *will* be coming in soon.

His ship, not theirs. It was his idea, after all, to take the safe in the first place; his supposition that the chest was probably filled with ivory. Why wouldn't it be? The antique shops all sold ivory for big bucks; he'd even heard that some people bought ivory as an investment. Ivory was almost a commodity on Nantucket, and you couldn't import it anymore, not since the Marine Mammal Protection Act of 1972, making it more valuable; authentic scrimshawed ivory from Nantucket's whaling days was more valuable still.

It was Digit who'd introduced him to ivory, when he'd shown him the tooth from his fireplace mantel. Caspian could still see it: the graceful etching, the depiction of a whaling ship. "Not many people have an original one of these from whaling days," Digit had told him. "Most of them are in museums. We have this because it was my ancestor's; it's been passed down through the generations. I think it could be pretty valuable."

And Caspian checked out the scrimshaw at the whaling museum and stopped into the antique shops downtown and came to the conclusion that ivory was indeed *very* valuable.

Stealing the safe at first was just a lark, a prank fueled by alcohol. But the idea of ivory immediately took hold, took hold of him as they were driving the safe out to the moors, and had only intensified over the years. He drove himself crazy thinking about it, but he had to be patient; yes, he just had to wait until it was time.

And the time had finally come.

He wondered why he hadn't seen the other two around since he returned to the island. There weren't that many people on-island in winter, you'd think you'd run into someone sooner or later.

But he'd been able to avoid Digit, even though he saw him that time driving up Main Street. Maybe the other two were trying to avoid *him.* But certainly they knew he was back. His name had been in the newspapers. They *must* be on the island.

Because the date was drawing near — the agreed upon time when they'd meet up and claim the treasure. They were here; he could feel it in his bones.

This freeze couldn't last forever. The backhoe was being fixed. Soon he'd be able to start digging; that'd draw them out.

Chapter Fifty-Two

WHEN REBECCA fell, the Homestead called Sandy, who'd left her number as emergency contact. Verona didn't have a phone.

Not knowing the seriousness of the situation, Sandy went straight to the Homestead. She was met by her friend, Irene, Irish Irene from Cork, who'd begun working there several months before. Irene saw the concern on Sandy's face and reassured her. "She's in bed. She fell in the bathroom and couldn't get up. She's fine, no broken bones, we don't think, but she needs to be checked out at the hospital."

Rebecca had her eyes closed when Sandy entered her room. Perhaps her perception was formed by the Homestead's call, but Rebecca seemed frail to her, more delicate. Rebecca sensed Sandy's movements and opened her eyes. Sandy sat on the edge of the bed and Rebecca let out a small gasp. Sandy immediately stood up. "How are you feeling, Rebecca?" she said softly.

"I hurt," Rebecca said, trying to force a smile. "I'm not sure what happened."

"You fell," Sandy said. "They think you should go to the

hospital."

"Who does?"

"We do, Rebecca," Irene was in the doorway. "Just to make sure nothing's broken."

Rebecca waved her away. "I'm fine," she said, but as she attempted to sit up she winced in pain.

"That's it, then," Sandy said. "I'm taking you to the hospital." Rebecca weakly shook her head no.

"We've already called for the ambulance," Irene said. "It's just a precaution, Rebecca, but we have to do it."

"Can't I just lie here?"

"Unfortunately, no," Irene said. "Talk to Sandy."

"Do I have to go?" Rebecca asked Sandy.

"As Irene said, it's just a precaution."

"I've only been in the hospital once before in my life."

"When was that?"

"When I had . . . " and she caught herself.

"I'm sorry, when?"

"Oh, I can't remember. I'm old. Don't mind me. Can you help me get into my robe?"

"You already have it on." Sandy smiled at her benignly.

"Right. I was just getting ready for the day." She tried sitting up again, but hesitated.

"Just relax," Sandy said. "Don't try to do too much." Rebecca relented; her frustration palpable.

"Where's Verona?" she asked.

"I'll go get her. We'll meet you at the hospital."

Rebecca smiled. She was too weak to talk.

Hours later, after the X-rays, blood tests and EKG, a nurse beckoned Sandy and Verona to the inner sanctum of the emergency room. There, behind a curtain, Rebecca was in a hospital bed hooked up to a heart machine, an IV on a stand beside her. To Verona, who hadn't seen her at the Homestead, she looked wan, fragile; to Sandy, she looked better. A doctor entered the room, consulting a chart.

"Are you next of kin?" he asked Sandy.

"I guess I am," Verona said quietly. "She's my aunt."

"All the tests are fine, her blood's good, no broken bones," the doctor said. "When she's finished with that IV, we'll release her."

Verona and Sandy looked at each other and smiled.

"Still," the doctor continued, "at her age, and because of her unsteadiness, I'm going to recommend she be released to a long-term care facility, somewhere more equipped for geriatric care than her present situation."

Sandy and Verona looked at each other again. This time they weren't smiling.

"And where would that be?" Sandy asked. "The only place like that on the island is the nursing home."

"Precisely," said the doctor.

"But she's not feeble," Sandy said. "She gets around fine. She's just had this one mishap, a fall. Everyone falls."

"When you're older and fall, it's seldom good," the doctor said. "I know it's hard to accept when a loved one enters the next stage . . . "

Before he could finish, Sandy said, "She's not entering the next stage of anything, and she's not going anywhere. She's coming home, home with me, back to her house. I'll take care of her."

The doctor looked up from his clipboard. "I don't recommend it, but I can't prevent you from taking her home," he said. "Of course, such a thing would have to be approved by her health-care proxy. Does she have one?"

"How about her next of kin?" Sandy asked. "This is her niece, after all."

"I'll release her in her care. It'd be wise to get that health-care proxy taken care of, though."

"Thanks, doctor," they said in unison. "We're on it."

It comforted Verona greatly to have Rebecca move in with Sandy, back into the house Rebecca had grown up in. It seemed that everything was as it should be: Rebecca was home, truly at home. For Verona, who had lived with Sandy just a few years before, it was a homecoming of sorts as well.

Verona could remember all the things that happened during that time when Sandy had taken her in, when she had blotted out her past and couldn't even remember her name. But people had been so kind to her, especially Sandy.

She was glad she and Addie had found each other, but his new job at the paper kept him so busy that they pretty much saw each other now only on weekends. Which was fine, it made things that much sweeter when they were together.

But even her relationship with Addie left her conflicted. Did she love him? Most definitely. Would she marry him?

That she couldn't answer. It had been years, but the pain of losing her first husband lingered still.

For now, it was nice to have this extra time with Rebecca — her aunt, her relative — and share in *their* closeness. She felt she was being granted a gift to be able to help care for her with Sandy.

Rebecca didn't like the idea of moving into her old house, not one bit; it frustrated her to think she was old and needed help. But when she got there, and reacclimated, it was like slipping into an old shoe. Yes, she had to admit, it pleased her to be amidst rooms that brought back memories, as if the house, and her past, were embracing her. It had been decades since she'd last spent a night, and she feared it might be too uncomfortable to be back, but it wasn't; it was good.

Besides, it was Sandy's house now, had been for quite some time. Once somebody else moves into a house it becomes theirs, and Sandy's presence was rightfully everywhere.

The fall had frightened her. It wasn't that she might have broken something, but the loss of control that concerned her. Being in the hospital made her sad, then depressed, because it reminded her that her only other trip to the hospital had been when she'd lived off-island, when she'd had her baby.

The baby who had grown up to be Verona.

And here was Verona now, bringing her a cup of tea, and sitting beside her on the couch, and looking at her lovingly.

Please, Rebecca thinks, please don't ask me how I'm related to your birth mother. Not now, not yet.

Chapter Fifty-Three

"So, HAVE you dug up anything more on Caspian?" C. C. Dennison offered Ellen a cup of coffee, which, as always, she refused.

"I have found something." Ellen pulled out her always-ready notebook. "You probably already know about this, Chief, but Dirk Caspian was arrested for assault and battery and booted off the island."

Dennison leaned forward. "You don't say? When did this happen?"

"Almost twenty years ago. You didn't know this?" Dennison shook his head casually. "You need more?" Ellen asked him.

"Yes, please," he said, "fill me in."

"Well, with some time on my hands I've been looking through old newspapers, and according to the court report at the time, which is where I got this info, Caspian got into a bar fight right around Labor Day, and had the bad fortune of assaulting the district court clerk's son with a pool cue."

"Really. Was there anything more mentioned?"

"Just that he was told to leave the island and 'never come

back,' quote, unquote."

Dennison leaned back in his chair and looked up at the ceiling. "So, he's got a past here, and not a stellar one at that." He exhaled before taking a sip of his coffee. He thought for a while before speaking. "Does the judge know he's back?"

"I'd assume so, Chief. He's appeared before the Conservation Commission; he's had his name in the papers."

"That doesn't mean anything. I don't read the papers. I'll bet the judge doesn't either, especially this time of year. He only lives here in the summer, the rest of the year he commutes." Dennison stood up and walked over to the window. With his back to Ellen, he said:

"You know, somebody ought to put a stop to him digging up that wetland. It's terrible how these people from off-island are allowed to ruin the natural habitat."

"*You're* from off-island, Chief." Ellen was never one to let a fact pass unnoticed.

He turned to face her. "But I'm serving the public, not destroying the island's beauty. He shouldn't be allowed to dig. Period."

"He says he's going to uncover a revered artifact."

"My eye. There's no railroad train in that marsh."

"I thought you didn't read the papers."

"I've got friends in Boston, remember?" He walked back behind his desk. "I knew there was something about Caspian. You know what you should do? You ought to tell the judge."

"What good would that do? The judge doesn't exile people anymore."

"Maybe, just maybe, he'd be interested to know one of his exiles has returned. From what I hear, the judge has quite a temper."

"Only if you've broken the law."

"Exactly," Dennison said, satisfied. "Ex-act-ly."

"I'll think about it, Chief," Ellen said, putting her notebook back in her purse. "Speaking of your friends in Boston, anything I ought to know about?"

"We pulled another Whaler off the jetties."

Ellen turned towards the door. "Tell Addie about it. He might be interested." And she left.

That Ellen, Dennison thought. She sure acts like a tough reporter.

Let's see if she talks to the judge.

Chapter Fifty-Four

THE HISTORICAL association's storage facility was a large, barn-like building out by the golf course. Addie was greeted by an amenable historic collections staffer. "Wait over there by that table, I'll be right back with it."

He returned carrying a large rectangular something covered by a protective cloth. "Well, here he is," said the worker, holding it up on the table, and he removed the covering, revealing the painting of a man with a Captain Ahab-type beard, wearing a blue, high-collared jacket and the type of tie fashionable in the early-1800s. He wasn't smiling, but his expression wasn't dour, as Addie had noticed in other portraits he'd seen from the same period. He had a full head of hair, but something else drew Addie in: whoever painted this portrait captured his eyes. He had kind eyes.

"Funny you asked for this one," the worker said. "We're getting ready to do an exhibition on whaling captains of Nantucket, so this was on our list anyway."

"Was this painted by a famous artist?" Addie asked.

"Not sure, but what is kind of unusual is that this portrait includes his hands, and isn't a bust like most of them."

"What's so unusual about that?"

"It's just a bit different." He leaned in closer to the painting. "Interesting."

"What's interesting?"

"Oh, nothing, just that he's wearing a ring. What was his name again?"

"Hathaway."

"Look." And Addie looked. "Doesn't that look like a 'V'? It's certainly not an 'H.' "

"Maybe it's a Masonic ring, or something," Addie ventured.

"No, I'm a Mason, and a Masonic ring would have the letter 'G,' for God, or geometry. Oh, well. Not important."

"Could it be a maritime thing?" Addie asked.

"Could be, but doubtful. Never run across a ring like that in our collection. Anyway, seen enough?"

"Yeah, thanks." And as Addie inspected the portrait one more time he backed up a bit, and it became clearer to him.

No doubt about it, once you got past the beard, it could have been a portrait of Digit.

It seemed somehow fitting to Rebecca that she would once again be in her house during a frigid winter, with memories of long ago rekindled. In her mind's eye she could see herself resting her cheek in her hand as she gazed out her schoolroom window and daydreamed. She remembered the whiteness of the snow, looking out from the second floor of the Academy Hill School, admiring how it blanketed the fields and meadows all the way to the horizon with a storybook purity.

She'd gotten less wobbly, more sure-footed since moving

in with Sandy, and more comfortable moving around her old house on her own. At night sometimes, when Sandy was asleep upstairs, Rebecca would explore her downstairs domain, shuffling carefully between the adjoining rooms but with the confidence of *knowing* each room's shape, every room's threshold. This had been her house, after all, the dimensions were the same as they'd always been even if the furniture was different.

There were still some relics from her girlhood that remained: the mahogany dining room table; a bookcase in the front parlor; even an old painting or two. During the day, she'd run a finger down the spines of the books that had never been replaced by subsequent inhabitants: Macy's *History of Nantucket; The Ashley Book of Knots;* Chapelle's *The History of American Sailing Ships; Great Sea Stories.* She touched a candlestick holder on an end table, its familiar brass feel awaking memories of power outages and wintry shadows, of conversations and card games by candlelight.

She shuddered, not because there was a chill (Sandy kept the thermostat raised for her, God bless her) but because she did not want these memories to die with her. There was no one left from when she was a girl; not one of her classmates survived to reminisce about the snowy view from Academy Hill. She supposed she was thinking this way because she was among younger people now, people who still had experiences to encounter, and to share.

There were so many things she had forgotten about that the walls of her old house brought back to her. How she wanted to pour out these recollections to Verona, but in so doing would she let her guard down, let slip more than she wanted Verona to know?

She couldn't have it both ways. Either she relinquished the fable that she was Verona's aunt, or she kept her treasured history to herself. She didn't want to share anything anymore that wasn't the truth.

All this thinking was making her tired. She'd decide things later. She had to be absolutely certain that Verona wouldn't be hurt if she decided on the truth.

"That tooth of your grandfather's could be pretty valuable," Addie said to Digit.

"Great-great-great grandfather to you. How do you know that?"

"The librarian at the research library told me."

"Libby?"

"Who?"

"Libby. She's the head research librarian. She knows as much about Nantucket as anybody, probably more. There's even a bench outside the library dedicated to her: 'The Seat of all Wisdom.' "

"So you don't mind that I let her keep the tooth?"

"Keep it?"

" 'Til tomorrow. She wants to do a background check on it."

"It's a tooth, not a person, Addie. I mean I know scrimshaw can be valuable, but how valuable?"

"She said it could be over a hundred thousand . . . if it's the right tooth."

"Well, whaddaya know?" As usual, Digit didn't seem too impressed. "Okay, let me know what Libby says."

"Will do. I also saw that portrait you told me about. Have you ever seen it? It's very interesting."

"I think once at the whaling museum. My father took me to see it. I don't think it's hanging there anymore."

"They're going to be putting it back out for a new exhibition. You should take another look, now that you're older." Addie snapped his fingers. "Do you know anything about the ring he's wearing?"

"I haven't seen the painting since I was a kid. What ring?"

"He's wearing a ring with the letter 'V' inscribed. Mean anything to you?"

"Not a thing. Could be the number of whaling voyages he took in Roman numerals; maybe something the artist added."

"I'll bet that's it. Well, you're busy here, I should get back to the paper." He was halfway down the attic steps when he ran back up.

"You never told me your friend was kicked off the island."

"What are you going on about now? What friend?"

"What's his name, you know, Dirk somebody."

"Dirk Caspian. Again?"

"No, twenty years ago. Ellen told me."

"Yeah, he was." Digit stopped, looked wistful. "I'll tell you about it some other time."

"Sure, Digit. You don't have to tell me at all."

"Thanks, Addie. You are a friend. Come here."

Digit stood and gave Addie a bear hug.

"Is this how we greet each other now?" Even though Addie was kidding, he thought he saw a glisten of moisture in his friend's kind eyes.

Before leaving, Addie said, "When they put up that new exhibition in the whaling museum, I want to go with you. I have to see your reaction."

After Addie left, Digit sat on the attic floor and enfolded his legs with his arms. Caspian. They had been so close; he thought they'd be friends for life.

But Caspian had found new friends. Seemed like one couldn't do anything without the other two. For a month or so there, the three of them did everything together. It was ridiculous. People were even starting to talk about them.

But when Caspian got arrested, whom did he call? Digit didn't even think about it at the time, but where were the other two when their friend got hauled into court, and kicked off the island?

Yes, where were they?

He hadn't known the other two's names, but he vaguely remembered their faces. He stood up.

And was off to talk to Lance Willoughby.

Chapter Fifty-Five

LIBBY HANDED the tooth back to Addie. "Sorry to say it's not a *Susan's* Tooth," she said. "This tooth is unsigned; Myrick signed all his work. And Captain Hathaway never served aboard the *Susan*."

"That's okay," Addie said. "Do you know which whaleship he did serve on?"

"I only checked what we have on the *Susan*. I could help you research ships' logs and see what we can find. It shouldn't be too difficult to find Captain Hathaway's history. He took several voyages, if I remember correctly. Get comfortable over at that computer, and search for 'Hathaway' and 'ships' logs' as a start. I'll be over when I can."

Besides "Hathaway" and "ships' logs," Addie also searched for the letter "V." Couldn't hurt, he thought. Before he was able to read the first page of results, Libby was at his elbow.

"Will you be listening to any more tapes?"

Tapes? Addie looked at her inquisitively.

"You were listening to oral histories last time you were here. I wasn't sure if you were finished."

Cy. He'd forgotten about Cy. He wasn't finished, but for now he was more curious about Captain Hathaway and 'V.' "Boy, Libby, once you start researching, it takes you down all kinds of paths and alleyways."

"Now you know why I love my job," Libby said with a soft smile. "There's always more to learn."

For some reason, those last words resonated with Addie. He needed to learn more about something.

But what? What was that something?

With no scalloping, Digit wasn't sure where to look for Lance Willoughby. He knew that in the summer Lance worked on the charter fishing boats, but he'd never considered what Lance might do in the winter, other than scallop. He'd find him, though, there were still no boats going to and from the mainland; he had to be on island.

Unless he took a plane off-island, but that was a chance he'd have to take.

Digit had a hunch. He wasn't sure why, but the image that flashed in his memory reminded him somehow of Lance. Maybe Lance had an older brother who'd hung out with Caspian and those other two guys. Not that he cared much, but it bugged him, and he wanted to get it off his mind.

He could have tracked down Caspian, he supposed, but he really didn't feel like talking to Caspian at all; once Digit wrote somebody off, they were written off for good.

Besides, he liked Lance. Lance would be easier to talk to.

Lance couldn't believe twenty years had passed already.

So, the other two *had* shown up.

Caspian was here, that much was obvious, with his phony

story about looking for *Dionis*. What did he think, that Nate Powell wouldn't know why he was digging at that particular location, that he didn't know where Caspian had wanted to bury the chest? Twenty years hadn't changed Caspian much; he was predictable as ever. He could kick himself for ever looking up to that guy.

And the other one? Oh, he was here all right. And as far as Lance could tell, neither of them knew that *he* was here.

March 31, the last day of scallop season. You never know how your mind works, how the unconscious truly guides you; perhaps that's why he chose scalloping when he came back to the island. The thing was, scalloping had gotten into his bones; it fulfilled him more than anything else ever had. That he had a natural bent for it made it that much sweeter, as sweet as the scallops he harvested.

Funny how things work out. He really didn't care about the chest, or if there was any treasure in it. He had found his treasure fishing.

Until recently he had pushed the sea chest and the whole stupid robbery out of his mind, let it loll in the recesses of memory. True, he had come back to the island intending to dig up the chest and leave, but he'd wanted to be careful, not act hastily and get arrested, or whatever the penalty would be. The chest was safe: of that he was absolutely certain. And so he moved slowly, working first on a fishing boat and then sliding into scalloping. He discovered that being on the water was where he was meant to be. The treasure could stay where it was: his fulfillment came from doing what he was doing.

He was convinced that if he had sought out a livelihood — be it business, or banking, or whatever — it would have seemed forced, contrived, and he'd always be searching for something better. That he chanced upon scalloping by accident was fate, he was sure of it. His fate. He was supposed to be here, not like

Caspian and that other guy.

He wondered what Digit would think if he ever found out they hid the safe in his hiding place in the moors. That was Caspian, always using somebody else's ideas, always wanting things the easy way.

So why did he care about the treasure now? Because the agreed upon time was almost here. Because he knew how much the other two wanted it.

But they weren't going to get it.

It was getting near time to put his plan into play. May as well have some fun.

Chapter Fifty-Six

VERONA WATCHED as Rebecca slept. It warmed her that Rebecca felt comfortable enough to fall asleep in her presence. With her glasses off she looked old, but Verona saw the beauty in her age. Her hair was wonderfully white and wavy, and her small mouth reminded her of a child. Funny how age brings us back to childhood, Verona thought.

She rose carefully so as not to disturb her aunt and collected both teacups to take back to the kitchen. On the way she passed the hall mirror, and stopped. Something in her reflection caught her eye. She put the teacups down on the side table and looked closely. What was it? She pulled her hair off her forehead. She could see it now in her own face: Rebecca's nose, her forehead, even the set of her eyes. She wanted to go back and look at Rebecca when Sandy approached her in the hallway.

"How's Rebecca?" Sandy said, snapping Verona's reverie.

"She's fine; she's sleeping."

"Let's not wake her. I'm making a dump run. Can you help? We'll leave Rebecca a note. It'd probably be good to have the house quiet. I've already loaded the car."

Verona enjoyed going to the dump. It was one of the few social situations where she felt relaxed, and on Nantucket, going to the dump *was* a social situation.

Digit had told her of the days when men would gather on Sunday mornings to shoot rats. Anybody running for public office on the island made sure to campaign at the dump, standing at the entrance waving, holding a sign, because you were sure to see pretty much everybody there.

Even after the shooting of rats was prohibited, and the old dump transformed into a recycling center, everybody still called it the dump and still congregated there: tossing their refuse down the chutes dedicated to plastic, tin, and cardboard, watching children smash bottles into the glass dumpster, helping a neighbor toss an old filing cabinet into the metal bin, and visiting the expanded Take it or Leave it shed— the dump's main attraction.

"Can we stop by the Take it or Leave it?" Verona asked Sandy on the drive out to Madaket.

"Verona, how well do we know each other? You'd think I'd ask you to come and *not* visit the Take it or Leave it?"

It was a bonus that it was a weekday afternoon, so they wouldn't have to negotiate the phalanx that crowded the entrance to the Take it or Leave it every weekend. There were treasures to be had, and the pickings for furniture, appliances, sporting equipment, books, games, and yes, clothes, were usually pretty good. Many of Verona's clothes— including cashmere sweaters, designer dresses, and even brand new blue jeans — had come from the dump. She was always amazed at the compliments received on items found at the Take it or Leave it.

Sandy looked through the books, while Verona browsed the various tables. She thought of the stories attached to everything, as a woman held up a sweater by its arm for inspection and frowned. Somebody may have loved that sweater once, Verona thought. Were the old board games and kids toys brought here because there were no longer any kids in the house, or had they simply outlived their usefulness? She supposed she'd never have any kids herself, no family of her own.

Family. It wasn't something she'd ever given much thought to until she'd met Rebecca. Yes, she'd been married before, but hardly long enough to think of themselves as anything other than a couple still in the process of pairing.

A feeling had grown since she'd met Rebecca, a yearning to know about her biological family, her heritage. So much of Nantucket was about history, a history she was fascinated by. She'd learned so much about the whalers, and the stories behind the whaling mansions on Main Street. And lately, Addie had told her about the inspiration Nantucket had had on the poet Robert Lowell.

Her discovery of the Quaker Cemetery took her to the library, where she absorbed stories about the resilience of the Quaker women who ran the town while their husbands were away at sea. The women of Nantucket were leaders in suffrage, independence, and education. And to think her aunt, Rebecca, was part of that tradition by birthright.

Did her birth mother have the same connections?

Stop it, she reminded herself. Live in the present. Her birth mother had given her up for adoption. She had Rebecca, and Rebecca was in her nineties. Be with her, she told herself. Be with her while you can.

She was so lost in her thoughts, she hadn't realized she had rested her hand on an old suitcase that the woman who had scorned the sweater was eyeing intently. "Excuse me," the woman said, startling her. "Would you mind?" And Verona lifted her hand and absent-mindedly rummaged through the nearby clothes pile, as the woman looked inside the suitcase, and decided that it, too, was not up to standard.

"Any finds?" Sandy, holding a cookbook, walked over.

"Just this," and Verona lifted the suitcase and walked back to the car with Sandy.

Chapter Fifty-Seven

REBECCA WAS awake when Verona and Sandy returned. She saw that Sandy had a book while Verona had a suitcase.

"Back from the dump?"

"That's right," Verona said. "Not much to pick from today."

"But you've got a suitcase."

"It spoke to me."

"I won't ask what it said. Anything in it?"

"I don't know, I haven't opened it."

"Well, let's see," Sandy said.

"Let's go in the living room. I'll open it on the floor in there. Probably better than opening this old thing on the kitchen table."

It was a worn, leather suitcase, almost a relic. Rebecca and Sandy sat on the couch together as Verona undid the one clasp that still worked. "Well, here goes," Verona said, as she opened the top.

"Nothing," Sandy answered, and indeed there was nothing inside. "Well, so much for that excitement," she said, patting both knees and starting to rise.

"Look," Rebecca said, "there's a compartment inside the lid." And Verona undid the two snaps and scouted with her hand, coming out with an envelope. "Empty," she said, but it had an address on it. "Nate Powell, general delivery, Nantucket." There was no return address. "Any of you know a Nate Powell?" Both Sandy and Rebecca shook their heads.

A zipper ran alongside one edge of the bottom. Verona unzipped it and pulled out folded over papers, three of them. Folding one back, she said, "Look, it's a map."

"Now this is getting a little more interesting," said Sandy. "Bring them up here, onto the coffee table so we can have some fun."

The map was written on lined paper, and appeared to have been torn from a notebook. It was a real map, all right, complete with an 'X'. "I'm not sure where this is," Sandy said. "I can make out 'Orange Street' on the bottom, but is that a side street? And what's all this scribbling in the middle? It's got an arrow from the 'X' into the middle of it. This is nuts."

"Let me see," said Rebecca, and she studied the makeshift map for a while. "You know where this is? This is the marsh over by Bear Street. See, where Orange meets Bear. That has to be it."

"So, all that scribbling is the marsh. What's the 'X' mean?" Sandy asked.

"I'm not sure," said Rebecca, sitting back. "This is probably something drawn by kids while they were here on vacation. What's on the other papers?"

Verona unfolded a second paper, this one written on the back of an old menu from some place called "The Lamp Post." It was a much more intricate map, with compass points indicated. It appeared to be a map of a shoreline, with numbers written at various points in the middle of the map and, as with the last one, an 'X' clearly marked. But this time the 'X' appeared to be off by its own with no land around it. There were also two lines drawn from asterisk-type dots at the top that came together in a 'V' and intersected at the 'X.'

"These kids must have been reading 'Treasure Island,' " Sandy said. "What's with all the numbers?"

"They look like soundings," Rebecca said. The other two looked inquisitively at her. "Like on a nautical chart, water depth."

"Wow, pretty involved," said Sandy. "But what about those two dots and the lines coming from them?"

"Those are stars," Verona said. "And if I'm guessing right, stars that are visible in early spring." Now Rebecca and Sandy looked flummoxed.

"All right," Rebecca said, "may as well see the third one."

But when Verona unfolded the paper, it had just one word on it:

Cemetery.

"I guess you never know what you're going to find at the dump," Rebecca said as Verona latched the one clasp on the suitcase that worked. "I wonder if kids still draw treasure maps like that."

"Did you, Rebecca?" Verona asked.

"Oh, sure I did, when I was little. I'd heard all the talk about the shipwrecks around Nantucket. With a little imagination pirate treasure could be anywhere." She looked down at the two maps on the coffee table. "You know something?" she said, picking up the less detailed of the two, "there were stories of the *Dionis* falling off the rails by Orange Street and being buried in the marsh. That's what this is, I'll bet, some kid putting his Nantucket history to work."

"*Dionis?*" Verona asked.

"It was one of the engines of the old Nantucket Railroad," Rebecca said. "Used to take passengers from the steamship to 'Sconset. But the railroad had ended years before I was born."

"Do you think the engine's still down there?" Verona asked.

"If the story's true? I suppose so. But it's most likely just another Nantucket legend. They'd have dug it up by now if there was any truth to it."

"There's someone trying to dig it up now, Rebecca," Sandy said. "It's been in the paper."

"Doesn't Addie write for the paper now?"

"Sure does."

"Well, give him this map. Maybe he can print it in the paper, help that fellow out."

And they all laughed.

Chapter Fifty-Eight

THE DEEP freeze had ended; the Steamship resumed its trips from Hyannis. Although there was still ice in the harbor, it was beginning to break up. The rest of scallop season might be able to be salvaged after all.

Digit blasts music in his truck on his way down to the docks, chewing gum like crazy, getting fired up, psyching himself up for the cold. At least the air temperature was above freezing for a change. "Downright balmy," he joked aloud. How many tows would he need to get his limit?

Lance Willoughby would be out on the water today, he was sure of it. He never did find him the day he'd gone looking for him. After he'd driven down to the docks, and to the shanty where he knew Lance opened (on the outside chance that Lance might be doing some kind of inside work there), Digit stopped by the houses of some fellow scallopers in hopes they might know where Lance lived. None of them knew, and none of them seemed to care. Typical, Digit thought, his mission very much not accomplished — they were either jealous that Lance was a better scalloper, or they still considered him an off-islander, even though he'd been living on the island for over ten years now.

Had he been here ten years? Digit wasn't sure. He really didn't know much of anything about Lance Willoughby. No matter; he'd run into him sometime.

But as the weather warmed and the water began to thaw, Digit put Lance Willoughby, and Dirk Caspian, and whatever he felt about the past, behind him.

As he gets underway, Digit scans the harbor. From a lifetime of being on the water, he knows the contours and intricacies of the harbor floor: he can *see* it. He knows where the drop-offs are, where the bottom unfurls, and where it is flat. He can see the shallows, and the depths; where there is eelgrass, and where there is none.

After the freeze-up and all the wind, Digit senses the harbor bottom has changed. Motoring into today's blow he decides to head up harbor, a little past Monomoy and over near Shimmo. Stealing a quick glance at Brant Point he notices the small craft advisory pennant flown by the Coast Guard; gale warning flags would probably be hoisted later. There was nobody else around, no doubt deterred by the weather forecast. Too bad for them. Every day lost is another day that has to be made up.

He tosses all his dredges overboard and cruises slowly near shore. When he feels his dredges full he hauls them on board and dumps their contents onto his culling board. Some quahogs, a couple of crabs, but mostly scallops, and not many nubs. A full basket. Not bad for a first tow. He drops his dredges again and heads away from shore this time, into deeper water. This would be a good tow too, he could tell. Pretty good start for just getting back out on the water.

When, bam!, his dredge catches something that almost jerks him overboard.

Even though scalloping was done near shore for the most part, you at all times had to be alert, especially when you were fishing in winter, when hypothermia would set in quickly. One slip on your deck, one unexpected roll of your boat could be fatal. You didn't think about it, but it was there. With his dredges out, Digit wasn't moving too quickly, but whatever it was he got caught up on brought his boat to a sudden, and quite unexpected, stop. He pitched backward with a quick lurch —as if someone had recklessly yanked the hood of his sweatshirt — and was able to keep his footing only because he never let go of his wheel.

It took him a few seconds to get his bearings and cut his throttle. Whatever he got caught up on wasn't moving, that was for sure, and his boat sure as hell wasn't going anywhere as long as his dredges were snagged on it. In all his years scalloping, he'd never felt anything like that, like his boat was going to split in two. What the hell was down there? It felt like he'd snagged a boat.

Could be a boat. He knew of some old Nantucketers who'd simply abandoned their workboats if there was too much baling, or if they'd sunk during a storm.

He could think about that later: right now he had to get unsnagged. He figured he'd back her off slowly for a start, hope his lines and dredges might slip off. He was able to back up a bit before he felt his lines pull. Damn! The wind out of the northeast pushed at his boat, meaning he had to fool with his throttle just to stay stationary. He tried backing off again. No good. He went forward a bit, just to see if he'd jogged his lines free. He felt the tug almost immediately. One more time backing up, but he sensed less slack in his lines than before. The hell with it. He revved his engine wide open and threw the throttle forward. His dredges caught again with a jerk, but even though he had a hard time keeping his footing, he was prepared for it. He tried for more throttle. His lines strained against his boat, tightening but not yielding. The engine whined horribly. He felt like the side of his boat was going to rip right off. Dammit! He cut the engine. Only thing he could do was lose his lines and dredges.

With his boat dead in the water, the cold came in fast. He had trouble freeing his line with his fingers going numb.

What did he lose? Three? Three dredges? Could have been worse, he supposed. Fortunately, the lines were nylon and floated. He tied a life preserver to one line and got back to scalloping. He'd come back to rescue his lines later.

One thing was for certain: he would avoid that spot in the future. And he couldn't help but think:

What was down there?

Chapter Fifty-Nine

THE BINOCULARS scan the spot yet again, eyeing the rower performing the same maneuvers as before the freeze-up, at the same time, on the same day of the week.

"It's almost like he wants to get found out," Lance said to himself as he put his binoculars back in the case. "Low tide, there he is, same as he has been for months." He chuckled to himself. "If you didn't know any better, you'd have to say he was obsessed." He whistled happily as he walked away. "Well, old friend, obsess no more." And he laughed out loud.

Lance had discovered the rower quite by accident months before. He had taken his boat, his Sea Ox, out for a spin up harbor in the warmth and sunshine of late spring. He had anchored in a secluded inlet to enjoy the weather and do a little bird watching.

Following the low, graceful flight of an egret, he spied through branches something moving on the water. He focused in and noticed a rower not acting like a normal rower. Instead of moving toward a particular target, this one seemed to be going in circles in a wide, deliberate path. He wished the branch wasn't in the way so he could get a better view. The rower stopped suddenly. Did he see him? Lance put his binoculars away and hunched down.

When he looked back at the spot, the rower was gone.

Lance was caretaker of a couple of summer people's houses, and the next week he began the task of opening up one of them for the summer. Coincidentally, it was near the inlet where he'd stopped in his boat the week before. He paused on the porch to admire the upper harbor when he saw a rowboat making its way from shore. He grabbed his binoculars from his truck and knelt behind the porch railing, using the railing to steady his elbows. This was a much better perspective than the week before, affording a better focus on the boat, and a clearer view of the rower.

The rower again made the same circular movements, but this time Lance could see what was being circumscribed: a sandbar, an island in miniature. He tried focusing in more closely, but the shadow cast by the brim of the rower's baseball cap obscured his face.

No matter, the rower would be back. And he now had the perfect vantage point.

And if the rower didn't come back? Well, life didn't always go as planned.

But the rower did come back: again, and again, and again. Just a few more sightings, Lance thought, and he'd have his man.

Chapter Sixty

C. C. Dennison leaned back in his chair and gazed at the wall chart of Nantucket. He'd been stationed here, what, two years? Man, the time had gone quickly, a lot quicker than the previous eighteen of his Coast Guard hitch.

He hadn't intended on joining the Coast Guard, had never thought he'd make a career on the water, even though he was a lifeguard his sophomore and junior years in college. His plan after college was to go into business, or real estate.

But the office job he'd found after graduation bored him. One lunch hour, looking out over San Francisco Bay, he noticed a Coast Guard boat skipping across the water. It looked so freeing, so fun. On impulse, he enlisted. They were glad to have him.

He was assigned to San Diego at first, and the busy-ness of the port, and the always-perfect weather, made the job that much more appealing. He enjoyed working with his hands, literally learning the ropes. He also took to the strict maritime aspects of being a sailor: piloting a boat; learning charts; plotting a course. He moved rapidly from Seaman Apprentice to Boatswain's Mate, to Petty Officer, to Chief Petty Officer, being deployed to stations in Texas, Florida, and then Cape Cod.

He hadn't planned on coming to Nantucket, but when the opportunity arose he let it be known that he'd accept the transfer. Being highly regarded by his superiors, the transfer was put through and he arrived as the new chief of Brant Point Station.

Although he wasn't new to the island. He'd been on Nantucket before; many years before.

"Addie, C. C. Dennison isn't what he appears to be."

Ellen was more fired up than usual, which for Ellen was pretty fired up.

"I thought you knew him from the Cape, that you and he were old friends."

"I never said we were old friends."

"So, who is he really?"

"For one thing, his real name isn't Dennison, at least that wasn't his name at birth. He changed it."

"How do you know? And does it matter?"

"I checked in with one of the guys who worked with him on the Cape. Something didn't sit right: him telling me to talk to the judge; being a little too interested in Caspian's projects. It got me thinking . . . "

"No one needs to get you thinking, Ellen."

"Stop interrupting. Anyway, I know a couple of guys from Chatham, and this one said he'd been in Dennison's office one day while he was going through his mail. One of the letters was addressed to a Conrad Chase, and Dennison opened it like it was his. When this guy questioned him about it, Dennison got all defensive and told him he was crazy, that there was no mail addressed to 'Conrad Chase' and to stop being so nosy and to get his eyes checked.

"Well, he did forget all about it, until he was talking on the phone to a friend who had served with Dennison in Texas. This guy, apparently, didn't know Dennison had been assigned to the Cape and asked my guy who his new chief was. 'You ought to know,' my man said, 'you served with him: C. C. Dennison.'

" 'You mean Conrad Chase,' the other one said. 'Oh, I forgot; he changed his name.' "

"Changed his name?" Addie said.

"For some reason he took his wife's name when he got married," Ellen said. "And when they got divorced, he kept it."

"But what does that prove?," Addie said. "So, he changed his name."

"After you hear the rest of it you tell *me* if it means anything: I followed him."

Chapter Sixty-One

"YOU FOLLOWED him?" Addie was incredulous. "Why?"

"The situation presented itself and I took it. I happened to be at Brant Point, near the lighthouse, taking a walk, clearing my head. I couldn't stop thinking about Dennison: why had he changed his name? Why did I have this feeling about him?

"As I was walking back to my car, I noticed the Coast Guard truck leaving the station, with Dennison behind the wheel."

"Did he see you?"

"No, and if he had he wouldn't have recognized me in my walking outfit: baseball cap, hooded sweatshirt, a scarf. He's only ever seen me wearing a skirt, and certainly never in a hat. I don't know what compelled me, but I was near enough to my car to follow him.

"He drove out of town, to Monomoy, and then onto the dirt road to Shimmo. I kept my distance, which was pretty easy, because he was flying. He drove to the beach. Fortunately, it's winter, and I parked in the driveway of a summer house. I watched from a distance as he pulled a skiff into the water and started rowing."

"So you lost him."

"Au contraire. As I said, he was rowing, which gave me time to make my way towards the water. I followed as far from the shore as possible, climbing over bulkheads, sometimes cutting across people's lawns, but he wasn't looking toward shore, not at all. He kept looking over his shoulder towards the middle of the harbor. I have to say, for a big guy he glided across the water.

"Finally, he slowed, then stopped. I was able to get up to higher ground and hide behind a tree. You won't believe what I saw.

"From that perspective, I saw what looked like a tiny island, a rounded mound of sand rising gradually from the water. You'd never notice it unless you were looking for it."

"What did he do then?"

"He just stopped and looked at it, that's all. Then he rowed back, kind of in a jigsaw pattern."

"And then what happened?"

"Nothing."

"Nothing?"

"Nothing. He dragged the boat back onto the beach, got into his truck, and drove away."

"He's a Coast Guardsman, isn't he? He was probably just getting exercise. It sounds like the kind of exercise a Coastie would do."

"It wasn't exercise, Addie. If you'd seen him, you'd know he was up to something.

"But what?"

"Damned if I know. But I'm going to find out."

Chapter Sixty-Two

ADDIE MET up with Verona at Sandy's house. It was Saturday, and they had all agreed to have supper together: Verona, Sandy, Addie, Rebecca, and Digit. "It smells delicious," Addie said as he entered the house.

"It's Rebecca's recipe," Verona said. "Baked beans."

"She said she hadn't had homemade baked beans in years," Sandy added.

"Great. What else is on the menu?"

"Hot dogs," Verona said.

"Hot dogs?" Addie's voice rose. "You hardly eat meat!"

"She's kidding," Sandy said. "Rebecca said she grew up eating baked beans and frankfurters most every Saturday night. Instead of the franks we're substituting another Saturday night staple: codfish cakes."

"My recipe," Digit said, strolling into the kitchen. "Well, my father's. One of his specialties; the other was kale soup."

There was time before supper, and they all joined Rebecca in the living room, or as Sandy and Verona now referred to it, per Rebecca's preference, the front parlor.

"How's the newspaper business?" Rebecca asked Addie. "Finding any interesting tales to tell?"

"Oh, you know, this and that. Not much going on this week, other than a Whaler running aground on the east jetty."

"Verona's got something that might interest you, or interest that fella who's trying to dig up the Nantucket Railroad," Rebecca said.

That got Digit's attention. He cocked his head at the mention of Caspian. Could he be anywhere these days without being reminded of him?

"What's that, Verona?" Addie asked. "Got something good?"

"Oh, just some old things in a suitcase."

"Treasure maps," Rebecca teased. "Go ahead, Verona, and show him. May as well have some fun with it."

Verona brought out the suitcase and took the papers from their respective compartments. Upon second viewing, they seemed even more like childish scribbles. Addie and Digit took a look.

"See there?" Rebecca said about the paper Digit held. "See where it is? It's that marsh over by Bear Street. See where Orange Street and Bear Street are written in?"

"That could be where it is, all right," Digit said.

"Where's that?" Addie asked.

"Where that guy wants to dig up the Nantucket Railroad," Sandy said.

Digit burned inside. "Just a coincidence," he said. "Looks like some kid drew this."

"It's got some detail for a child to have drawn it," Rebecca said.

"If you want detail," Addie said, "look at this one," and he showed the paper he was holding, the one with the compass marks, and all the numbers, and what looked like lines of latitude. "I can't make it out, except for the 'X.'"

Verona sat beside him. "Those lines appear to connect to stars," she told him.

"Is that why 'Venus' is penciled in there?"

"I don't see it."

"It's very faint." Addie inspected the paper more closely. "And look here," he said, pointing to one edge of the paper. "It's been erased, but I can just make it out, 'something Point.' Wonder what that means?"

"Let me see," Digit said, eager to have something to take his mind off Caspian. He looked at the paper closely, held it at arm's length, inspected it again. "Do you have a magnifying glass?" he asked Sandy.

She went into the kitchen and came back with a magnifying glass in miniature, the kind people once used to read small print. Digit looked at her with a slight frown. "Can you afford it?"

"Ha, ha," she said.

Digit scanned the paper with the magnifying glass, nodding his head. "Got it," he said. "I know exactly where this is." He showed Addie and Verona the paper. "See that? It's an 'A,' and the 'X' is beyond that. I almost had it with the configuration, but the depth markings really give it away. All I needed was to see the 'A' for 'Abrams Point' to be sure."

They all leaned in.

"It's not that big a deal," Digit said. "We all stay clear of this area, or else we'd run aground. See that 'X'? Well, that's a sandbar, a pretty big sandbar, that shows itself at low tide. Don't know what the 'X' means, other than it's a place to be avoided. That's it," he said, snapping his fingers. "I'll bet this was drawn by a kid learning to navigate the upper harbor. He certainly wouldn't want to run his boat aground, probably his father's boat, at that.

"Yessir," he said, sitting back. "The only way to get to that 'X' would be by canoe, kayak, or rowboat; you'd never take a power boat in there."

Addie perked up. "Did you say rowboat?"

"Yes. What about it?"

Addie smiled. "Nothing really. Just that Ellen was telling me a story about a rower. A coincidence." He looked in the suitcase. "What's this letter?"

"It's not a letter, just an envelope," Sandy said. Addie picked it up. "Who's Nate Powell?"

"Never heard of him," Sandy said. Addie raised his eyebrows at Digit. "Nope," was all he said.

"Well, if we're done playing games," Verona said, standing up and heading to the kitchen.

"Better go with her, Addie," Digit thought. "And don't mention Ellen anymore."

Rebecca's Baked Beans

as handed down by her mother

Soak a cup and a half navy beans overnight in cold water, making sure you use enough water because beans double in size

Next morning: *drain and add fresh water*

Low boil until skins loosen (takes about ½ hour — to test, place bean on tip of spoon and blow on it: skin will burst if cooked enough)

Drain beans, reserving the liquid

Rinse a 6 to 8 oz. piece of salt pork and make a few cuts in rind, about an inch deep. Cut a small (¼-inch) slice and put in bottom of beanpot

Add the drained, cooked beans to beanpot

In 1 cup of the reserved liquid,

Add *½ teaspoon each:*
Ground mustard and salt
Along with:
2 tablespoons molasses
2 tablespoons brown sugar
Stir mixture and add to beans
Fill pot to top with more reserved liquid
Place remaining fat salt pork, rind up, on top
Cover beanpot and bake all day (7 to 8 hours) in
250 degree oven, adding water when needed
Uncover for last hour of baking.

Chapter Sixty-Three

So Caspian's here, but where's Powell? C. C. Dennison feared the worst. Powell would have been back on the island by now, if he were still alive.

He thought feeding stories to Ellen and Addie might draw Powell out, but nothing so far. He was lucky to get the call from Woods Hole Command to check out the planned wetland excavation, just to ensure it wouldn't impact the harbor or any coastal areas; otherwise he may have missed that Caspian was back on the island. What he'd told Ellen was right: he didn't read the papers.

He was taking a chance, he knew, talking to Addie about the robbery, but he figured there was little risk involved. Addie was so eager to get things right that he could tell him anything and Addie would believe him. Well, that's Addie's problem if he trusts him.

Just like he once trusted Caspian. What an idiot he'd been. "Live and learn, Addie," he thought. "I had to."

He'd left the island before Caspian or Powell that summer, and he was happy to go. Overjoyed. With all the police and all the talk and all the conjecture and rumors, it was a relief to get away and back to college, far away, in California.

He'd never heard from the other two, and that was fine with him: no news was good news, right? More than recovering any treasure, he'd been more concerned with getting caught.

Especially when he joined the Coast Guard. How would he explain the robbery away, how could he? He couldn't, of course. If he were found out, they'd probably kick him out of the service.

Which would destroy him. He loved the Coast Guard, loved being on the water, loved the camaraderie. It wasn't the career he'd envisioned for himself when he was younger, but it fit, it made him happy.

And he didn't want to lose it. Which was why he'd changed his name.

Before he got married, he remembered from years before someone on Nantucket telling him that when you apply for a marriage license it's one time when you can legally change your name; most likely a rule to accommodate a woman adopting her husband's name. But, he was told, either party can change names, and it could be any name, even Bozo.

And so he adopted his wife's name, further distancing himself from his past, he hoped. Conrad Chase became C. C. Dennison and stayed that way, even after the divorce.

Why had he listened to Caspian? Oh, he was young and impressionable, but that was no excuse. If only they'd dumped the whole thing overboard that night.

Which was why, when he returned to the island and heard about the boat going in circles, he figured that's exactly what had happened.

Why had he come back? Getting stationed on the Cape had been as close as he'd wanted to get. Still, when the opening was posted for Brant Point Station he'd put in for it. Eighteen years had elapsed, after all, and he was curious if people were still talking about it; deeply interested to know if the other two had ever returned, or had ever even left the island.

Soon after he'd arrived at Brant Point Station, an old Coastie who'd served at the station and retired on the island came by to welcome him. After the usual pleasantries, and the comments about how the station really hadn't changed at all, Dennison offered his guest coffee and asked about the scuttlebutt on the island.

"Well, the island's grown, population-wise," the retired Coastie said. "Had to triple the size of the supermarket." Then he asked Dennison if he'd been to the island before.

"When I was a kid," he replied, purposefully vague. "Don't really remember much, besides going to the beach."

"Well, you might not get much beach time now," the visitor said. "Not that you'd want to; you'll be out on the water enough."

"I've been reading up on Nantucket history," Dennison said, which was true. "I find it fascinating that the first lighthouse here at Brant Point was only the second one built in the colonies, after Boston Light."

"Oh, you'll find a lot of firsts if you keep on studying Nantucket history. One thing you won't find are a lot of robberies."

"Oh?" Dennison couldn't believe it. Just what he'd wanted to hear, and it came up without prompting. "More coffee?"

"I usually only have two cups, but why not? Just a half."

"Have there been any robberies lately? I mean, should I get in the habit of locking the door of my truck?"

"Leave the keys in it. Where are they going to take it?" the man laughed. "No," he continued, accepting the coffee, "the last robbery was about twenty years ago; still unsolved."

Dennison's heart flipped. "You don't say? Was it a big robbery?"

"Nah. Some small safe. Broke a lot of kids' hearts, though."

Dennison found he had to sit down. "Why's that?"

"Oh, you know, the kids all thought it was pirate treasure. You see, it had been found in the basement of the Pacific Bank — that's the one at the top of Main Street — and the bank was holding a promotion to guess what was inside. It was stolen the night before the opening. All the kids thought it was filled with gold doubloons."

"Was it?"

"Don't know, never been found." The visitor paused to take a sip of coffee. "I was working here at the time. Oh, they had us on patrol, checking boats and the like. Now wait a minute, I'd forgotten about this." Dennison tried to appear nonchalant and not let his expression reveal his interest. "About two months later, we responded to a call about a boat going in circles near the upper harbor. Figured someone might have fallen overboard. It didn't take us long to get there, and sure enough, it was a Whaler spinning around in wide circles. No operator. We were able to stop the boat and mounted a big search and rescue effort, beginning that night, and lasting into the next day, and the day after that. We never found a body."

Dennison's mind was racing. He looked right through his visitor, who was finishing his coffee and didn't notice. "One thing we do know: it wasn't the boat owner. We traced the boat's serial number and located him. Off-island. Evidently, the boat had been stolen."

"I thought you said there weren't any robberies on Nantucket," Dennison said, reaching out to shake his visitor's hand. He hoped he appeared normal.

"Well, not usually," the visitor said, standing up to leave. "Thanks for the coffee, Chief. Hope you don't find any boats going around in circles. At least not tonight, anyway."

They both chuckled, although Dennison wasn't laughing inside.

Where do some feelings come from? From where does a gut instinct originate?

Dennison was positive it was Nate Powell who'd been on that boat. He went back through the station files and read the report. Even the officer in charge at the time thought something was fishy, Dennison could tell by the way the report was written; a seasoned officer in charge knew how to write, and read, between the lines.

The timing made sense: October 31st, Hallowe'en. That was 'round about the date they'd agreed Nate should dump the safe. Did he dump the whole thing overboard; did he go overboard with it? If it was an outgoing tide it could have carried him out to sea.

Or had Nate buried the chest before getting rid of the safe? If he had, and if he'd drowned, neither Dennison nor Caspian would ever know where it was buried: none of them knew what the others' plans were, another brilliant idea of Caspian's.

But he had a good idea now where Caspian had wanted it buried.

He had to stop him, which was why he'd been siccing Ellen on him. He knew from his experience with her on the Cape that Ellen was tenacious in her reporting. He'd hoped her original story would have set the island against Caspian, but then the whale washed ashore, and the harbor froze, and enough time had elapsed that people had forgotten about Caspian and his plans.

But maybe Ellen *would* talk to the judge. It might work. If not, he'd think of something.

Caspian had to go. With no Powell and no Caspian, he could dig at the spot he'd selected without any interference.

Now that he was back on island, back at the scene of the crime, his proximity had a way of erasing his fears of getting caught; just the *idea* of the treasure filled his mind. He'd been back two years — nobody was talking about the robbery anymore. With the other two out of the way, nobody would ever have to know of his involvement.

And his spot *was* the perfect spot.

Powell *must* have buried it there. He wouldn't have tossed it overboard, not after all the trouble they'd been through.

Was Powell dead? For two years Dennison had been thinking about it. One, a letter from him never came. Two, in the time he'd been back on-island he hadn't seen or heard about Powell, which was why he'd gotten Addie involved, hoping *he'd* find him.

But Addie wasn't the reporter Ellen was: maybe he should have given Ellen *both* stories.

No, he couldn't get overly enthusiastic about it; Ellen might have gotten suspicious. She'd have realized the robbery wasn't really a Coast Guard story, so why would he push it on her?

Besides, Addie kept asking *him* about the robbery, another fortunate coincidence, just like that old retired guy bringing it up.

Anyway, Powell was dead, as dead as a doornail. He was as certain of it as he was of the next high tide.

Chapter Sixty-Four

Addie sensed something was going on with Verona Saturday night: she was quiet, more quiet than usual. Something was bugging her, he could tell.

But he could get nothing out of her, so he did his best to give her space. And she gave him space: she stayed at Sandy's house for the weekend, saying she had private things to discuss with Rebecca. She was sure Addie could entertain himself for a couple of nights, she told him after their Saturday night supper. "You could work on whatever story it is you're working on," she said to him. "Now that I've given you new clues, maybe Ellen could help you."

"Ellen?"

And she closed the door. In his face.

Alone at his and Verona's cottage, the rain and dreariness matched Addie's mood. Verona was usually so even-tempered, so matter of fact. True, the paper kept him busy, but he was still learning the job, and there was a lot to absorb. He plopped on the couch, exhaled, and popped up again, pacing the small living room. What was that about Ellen? He didn't care about Ellen. Well, he liked her okay; she was helpful, but she wasn't a friend, really, not like Digit; no, certainly not like Digit, and not even like Sandy.

Why was it okay to like Sandy?

"Because you're not meeting her for coffee every Friday; you're not calling her to see if you've got your facts straight," he said out loud. "What a dope."

And then it hit him: Ellen was a young, attractive blonde; younger than Addie, much younger than Verona. It had never occurred to him that maybe he was a little too enthusiastic in recounting his and Ellen's conversations. Verona could have taken his enthusiasm for excitement.

But Ellen didn't excite him, his new job did. And neither stirred his emotions — didn't even come close — like Verona.

He'd make it up to Verona, take her out to dinner. No, she wasn't exactly a fan of going out. He'd have a picnic at the beach! No, too cold. He'd figure something out.

It was good to think things through. In a way, he was lucky Verona was angry: he had planned to tell Ellen about the map after court Monday morning, and how Digit said you could only get there by rowboat. Whew! He wasn't going to say anything to anybody now. Better to keep it to himself, especially since it was Verona who'd *found* the maps.

He sat down and thought about it. *Why* was he going to tell Ellen? Because it was pretty obvious it was the place where C. C. Dennison, or whatever his name was, was rowing to the day Ellen had followed him. Okay, so Dennison happened to be rowing to a spot that some kid had sketched out on a map. So what? As Digit had said, the map was probably drawn to *avoid* the spot. It had to be a coincidence.

He grabbed his notebook and lay back down on the couch.

Doodling helped him think. Ellen had said Dennison seemed pretty interested in the sandbar. Hmmm. Then there was the other map, the one that Rebecca and Digit seemed to agree was where Caspian planned on digging up the old railroad engine.

Curiouser and curiouser, as Verona liked to say. Oh, Verona. He thought of her face, how he loved looking at her while she slept. He wished he could kiss her now. If he could draw a map of her face, he'd put an 'X' right on her lips.

Map. Two maps. Why two maps in one suitcase?

His notebook dropped to the floor. He fell asleep and dreamed of Verona.

Addie didn't go for coffee with Ellen after court Monday. He went to the library instead.

The library; the Atheneum; the first public building constructed after the Great Fire of 1846; the meeting place of ideas. He'd spent Sunday putting together everything he'd learned about the robbery of twenty years before. He thought about his conversations with Hal Humphries, the "I Cover the Waterfront" reporter; his talks with Dennison. Addie knew that the safe had been stolen from the old Town Building, and that no one had ever found it, or the culprits. As Ellen had told him, it was "old news."

So why was Dennison so eager to talk to him about it, and why was he so sure that the boat going in circles was connected to it? And why did Dennison care? Was it just something to talk about after he gave Addie the weekly Coast Guard report? Dennison wasn't even on Nantucket during the robbery, or so he said.

And that's why Addie decided to inspect the old newspaper files at the library. He had a hunch.

Maybe he was turning into a reporter after all.

Chapter Sixty-Five

VERONA REALLY did want to be with Rebecca that weekend; it wasn't a ruse.

Although she felt as well that a little separation from Addie was good for both of them. She hadn't liked the hint of jealousy creeping into her mind. Addie was adjusting to his new job, a new routine, she knew that. She also knew that Addie probably looked up to Ellen as someone who could teach him as he learned about reporting.

Lately, however, she'd had enough of hearing about Ellen. It generated feelings she didn't know she had; feelings of uncomfortableness, of questioning. They were feelings she'd never felt before, not even with her husband. She needed to talk to Rebecca, not necessarily about these unwanted emotions, but to seek solace from a person to whom she felt more and more connected.

What was once the sewing room, on the first floor of the house, had been reimagined by Sandy as Rebecca's room. It was small, but cozy. Digit had long before converted a double window in the room into a window seat; Rebecca enjoyed sitting there, where she could lean back into large pillows and enjoy the view of the Lily Pond, a place so familiar to her since childhood. Verona sat by Rebecca, saying nothing, smiling demurely.

How Rebecca thrilled at having these moments, sitting with her daughter; a daughter who thought she was her aunt. "What's troubling you, Verona?"

Verona stared out the window. "Nothing. I just enjoy being here with you."

"No, something's on your mind." Should she tell her? Verona had been hurt so much, she didn't want to needlessly hurt her again. How could she explain why she'd lied, that she'd thought it best? Or was she afraid that Verona would reject her, blame her for giving her up for adoption, for not even trying to be a mother to her.

How could she ever explain that she'd never have had the resources Verona's adoptive parents had, that it seemed like a good idea to let her baby be adopted when she first discovered she was pregnant, that the doctor had told her of a worthy family who would be loving parents, and that the papers had been finalized long before she'd been born, but at birth, when Rebecca gazed upon her newborn daughter, however fleetingly, she realized that she'd made a mistake, one that she would rue for the rest of her life?

Wasn't it enough that they had each other now?

At least that's what Rebecca had been telling herself. She must have furrowed her brow unconsciously because Verona said:

"What's troubling you?"

"Me? Oh, I was just thinking."

"What were you thinking about?"

"First you tell me what's on your mind, then I'll tell you."

Verona looked away and said quietly. "Lately, I feel that there's something about me I don't know." She could see Rebecca was concerned. "Oh, it isn't anything unsettling, it's just, oh, how do I put it?" And she sat back to face Rebecca and said:

"Remember when I first remembered?" she said, referring to the amnesia that had blocked all knowledge of her past. Rebecca looked at her sympathetically. Verona continued. "And it all came back, I thought, my name, that I'd been married, why I came to Nantucket . . . and I was sure that that was it, that it was all there. Well, I'm not so sure anymore," she said with a melancholy that made Rebecca's heart ache, but Rebecca knew not to talk, not yet.

"It happened around Christmas. It came over me suddenly, that there were things about me I still didn't know. Oh, I don't know, Rebecca, maybe I'm imagining things."

"Listen to your heart, child," Rebecca said. "From what I know of you, your instincts are true." And she waited for Verona to ask her: ask her who her birth mother was. But Verona didn't. Instead, she said:

"It's like there's something missing. Something right in front of me that I'm not getting." And then she paused, and smiled. "Have you ever felt that way, Rebecca?"

And Rebecca wanted to tell her how she thought every day of the baby she never knew, about the years a vital part of her was missing. But before she could speak, Verona said:

"Remember last night, after we were looking at those silly maps, and I got up to go to the kitchen? I had a feeling that Addie thought I was mad at him, but that wasn't it at all."

"To be honest, Verona, I thought that, too, especially when he mentioned that girl, Ellen. You looked hurt."

"No, I wasn't hurt; I was confused. You see, there was something about the paper they didn't look at that bothered me. It was as if I should know something about it, and it's been troubling me ever since."

"And what paper was that, Verona? We looked at all of

them, didn't we?"

"No. It's the one that only has one word on it: 'cemetery.' It's as if I should know something about it. That's why I wanted to talk to you, Rebecca. I can't talk to Addie about these things; he wouldn't understand."

"Don't be so sure about that, Verona."

"Okay, enough about me. Your turn. What were you going to tell me?"

Rebecca was so engrossed with Verona's bewilderment, she'd almost forgotten. But she answered her truthfully:

"I was going to ask when you were going to marry Addie."

Verona's jaw dropped. Rebecca laughed. "Don't look at me that way, Verona, you know you love him. And he'd love you back if you let him know it."

"But I'm older than he is."

"And that makes a difference?"

"It could. Oh, I don't know, it's so confusing."

"Come closer," Rebecca said, reaching out to hold Verona's hands in hers. "I can see the love Addie has for you. That's all that matters to him, and that's all that should matter to you. If Addie thinks at all about your difference in ages it's only that it adds to your mystery, which is a good thing."

"It is?" Verona asked softly.

"A mysterious woman is a rare treasure. Addie's lucky to have you."

Verona's face shone.

"You're a keeper, Verona." And although Rebecca smiled broadly, it belied the pang she felt saying those words aloud.

Chapter Sixty-Six

ADDIE WAS scanning the newspapers from twenty years before, searching for anything that might pull everything together. He knew the robbery happened around Labor Day, so he began with the edition of the week before. The only thing in the paper that week was a small item on the front page: " 'Treasure' Chest to be Opened Next Week," the headline read:

'School children across the island are anxiously awaiting the opening of the ship's chest that was discovered earlier this summer in the basement of The Pacific National Bank.

'The sea chest is believed to have come from a whaler that returned to the island over 160 years ago. The contents of the chest have been the subject of much lighthearted speculation on Nantucket these past weeks, with guesses ranging from pirate gold to bills of lading to pots and pans. The bank's board of directors said the contents will be donated to the Nantucket Historical Association, no matter what they may be.

'A contest sponsored by the bank and this newspaper invites all children aged 6 to 13 to guess what's inside, with drop-off boxes at the bank and at this office. Island residents and summer visitors alike are included, which is why the chest is to be opened before Labor Day. The child with the most accurate guess will be awarded a $50 savings bond.

'The chest will be opened at noon next Thursday by Nantucket's Junior Miss, attended by bank officers and the board of selectmen.'

Stories in the next week's edition were not as lighthearted.

'Thieves Steal Whaling Chest,' the headline read. 'Safe taken in daring robbery.'

The accompanying story described how the safe was found missing by an employee of the historical association (which had already been awarded custody of the safe), and that there was no sign of forced entry, leaving the police chief to speculate that the safe was taken as some kind of prank. The article quoted the chief as saying that if it was taken as a prank, or a publicity stunt, then charges would be filed.

The next week's paper, however, told a different story.

'Robbery Still Unsolved; police comb island for culprits.' A subhead read:

'Steamboat Wharf, airport under surveillance.'

Accompanying the article was a photograph of a young boy with visible tears on his cheeks.

Addie scanned the write-ups but found nothing he didn't already know. The next week's headline about the robbery was on the bottom half of the paper, 'below the fold,' as Addie had learned, which meant its importance had diminished. Looking ahead, the robbery moved to page two, then four, and then became part of the usual police reporting, a footnote after the listing of stolen bicycles and noise complaints. Just as Hal Humphries had told him, the island seemed to have lost interest.

Then a headline next to the police report caught his eye: 'College student banned from island.' Addie read the lead:

'A visiting college student charged with assault and battery was exiled from the island in district court action Monday.

'Dirk Caspian, 22, address unknown, was ordered to get on the next boat and never return, a verdict that was once a usual practice but has been employed sparingly in recent years. "There's been too many shenanigans going on," District Court Judge G. C. Flanagan said, referring to the recent, and still unsolved, robbery of a whaling chest.'

"So there it is," Addie thought, "he *was* banished." Addie had seen enough for one sitting, but quickly looked back through that summer's editions to see if anything popped out at him. He stopped to look at photos of July Fourth festivities, which included a picture of the safe on display outside the Pacific National Bank. On the opposite page, there was a photo of that year's crop of lifeguards. He was about to leave the library when a name in the caption caught his eye. He read the caption carefully, reading through every name, when he saw it — 'Conrad Chase.' He looked back at the photo and matched the name with the lifeguard, front row, seated. There was no mustache, and the lifeguard was a lot thinner, but there was no mistaking C. C. Dennison.

"Wow," Addie said as quietly as he could.

There was only one thing to figure out: what did it mean?

Chapter Sixty-Seven

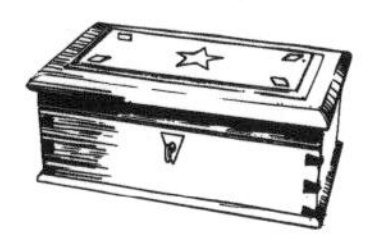

WHAT NEITHER Lance Willoughby nor C. C. Dennison realized was that they had seen each other numerous times since Dennison's return.

Willoughby noticed the Coast Guard vessels in and around the harbor, but regarded them as he would any other boat — he never considered who might be on them. He and Dennison even waved to each other a few times when Dennison was at the helm.

But in the winter, both were covered up pretty well, with Lance wearing a watch cap and hooded sweatshirt, and Dennison in his heavy coat with the collar turned up and his cap pulled down low.

They'd even been at the Anglers' Club at the same time. Dennison had his usual seat at the bar, while Willoughby always sat away from the bar huddled with another fisherman or two, not wanting to draw attention to himself.

He'd heard people he was sitting with call out to Dennison, but the name meant nothing to him, so he took no notice.

Strange how you can be looking right at someone and not even see him.

Lance had to be certain who the rower was. He was sure it was Chase because the rower's interest in that particular spot was too coincidental. He couldn't get a good look at his face through his binoculars from the perspective of his caretaking job, so he scouted out locations that would be closer, yet still hidden. When he found the right vantage point he visited it at low tide every afternoon, waiting for the rower to reappear.

He was there when the rower returned. "*Gotcha,*" he thought.

But when he fixed his binoculars on the rower, it wasn't Chase.

It was Digit.

He hadn't noticed Addie in the boat because Digit's dinghy had only one seat for a rower. Addie was sitting on a life preserver on the boat's bottom. Willoughby was so intent on seeing the rower that he missed that there were two people in the boat instead of one.

Not wanting Digit to see him, he quickly left his hiding place and headed back to the house he was caretaking. He had no idea why Digit would be rowing in that area, but he knew Digit wasn't looking for any buried treasure.

But he was wrong — Digit was.

"I don't know why I let you talk me into these things," Digit said to Addie as they approached the sandbar.

"As I told you before, I'm following my hunches," Addie said. "And my hunch tells me that this is where the thieves buried that sea chest."

"And tell me again, oh, wise one, how you arrived at that

hunch?"

"It hit me after I saw C. C. Dennison, I mean Conrad Chase, in that old paper. I woke in the middle of the night wondering if it meant anything. Dennison had been lying to me about never being on Nantucket before; and if he was lying to me about that, what else would he lie about? He'd changed his name, hadn't he?

"And then I thought of how Dennison kept bringing up the robbery. Well, if he's Conrad Chase, which he is, then he was here at the same time as the robbery."

"So what if he was?" Digit said.

"Like I said, I've got a hunch. We know that Caspian wants to dig in the same spot as one of the maps, why not check out this one?"

Digit shivered at the mention of Caspian's name. He stopped rowing. "I don't ever want to hear that name again," he said under his breath. Addie knew to keep quiet. Now that they were stopped, he could feel the cold. Where the rush of discovery had warmed him, the whole plan seemed stupid to him now. On top of it, he'd upset Digit, who didn't hesitate when Addie asked if he'd row them out to the sandbar. Digit never even asked why.

Finally, Digit said: "Might as well finish what we started. Let's see what's there." And he started rowing again.

When they reached the sandbar, Digit said: "Let me get out and anchor this thing, and then I'll help you out. No sense in you capsizing this boat."

But before Digit could step onto the sandbar, he noticed someone rowing furiously towards them. "We've got company," he said.

Addie looked. He couldn't believe it. C. C. Dennison was coming right at them.

And he was angry.

Chapter Sixty-Eight

"WHAT'S GOING on here?" Dennison bellowed. He hadn't noticed Addie.

"Hiya Chief," Addie said. "Fancy meeting you here."

Dennison looked at him with an expression of disbelief. He sat with his oars crossed across his lap before saying: "What do you think you're doing?"

"Quahogging," Digit said.

Dennison peered into Digit's dinghy. "With a shovel?"

"I forgot my rake."

Normally, Digit would have addressed anyone from the Coast Guard with deference, but what did this guy care? And why was he out here in a rowboat? Something wasn't right.

And when Digit stepped into the shallow water and onto the sandbar, he sank beyond his ankles. The sandbar was quick-sand-like. No wonder all the old timers always steered clear of this area. "Addie, hold out the handle of that shovel so I can grab onto something — and hold tight."

Using the handle as leverage, Digit was able to extricate one foot, then the other and fall onto the bow of the dinghy. He rolled back into his boat, happy he hadn't lost both of his boots. As he pushed off with one of his oars, he asked Addie: "Where's that Coast Guard guy?"

"Over there," Addie said, as Dennison rowed away as quickly as he came.

Dennison didn't need an outboard — an internal flight response propelled him back to shore. He'd never expected someone to sink like that. He'd always assumed the sandbar was more solid. What an idiot!

He'd discovered the sandbar back in his lifeguarding days, when he'd been out for a joyride in a friend's boat. As they sped past, the little island intrigued him. "What's that?" he asked.

"Just a shoal that pops up at low tide. If you went anywhere near it in a motorboat you'd run aground."

And it was on that scanty bit of information that he'd decided it would be a perfect place to bury the sea chest. As his friend had told him, everybody avoided it. Now he knew why.

As he drove back to town in the Coast Guard pickup, he wondered if Nate Powell *had* tried to bury the chest there. There was no way. If Nate sank into the sand like that, he'd have dropped the chest. And what would he have buried it in: water?

Dream done, he told himself, exhaling slowly and accepting that it was all a crazy idea anyway. He should have known better. Time to grow up. Nate Powell was dead and Caspian could dig all he wanted in that marsh. Wherever Nate buried the chest, they'd never find it, not unless they dug up the whole island.

But what about Addie? After all his prodding to have him look into the robbery, wouldn't Addie think it suspicious that he was out there this afternoon, practically yelling at them and asking what they thought they were up to?

Relax, he told himself. As Coast Guard chief, it was none

of their business why he was out there. They probably *were* just quahogging. If Addie asked him about it, he'd change the subject, tell him he was kidding around, or tell him he'd simply wanted to see their shellfishing licenses.

After all, Addie couldn't possibly know that he had any connection to the robbery and that the sandbar was where he'd wanted it buried. How could he?

There was nothing to think about. He even started to whistle.

Something, call it a premonition, told him to return to his hiding spot, and he was glad he had.

Lance was curious as to why Digit would row all the way out to that sandbar. It seemed unlike him, especially since it was still scallop season — the last thing Digit would want to do in the early afternoon was go out for a row. So he went back for a look and couldn't believe it when he saw the other rower approaching. It was *his* rower all right — with all the spying he'd done, he knew how he moved. This time, he could hear him clearly and, more important, get a good look at his face. Oh, he'd aged a bit, but who hadn't? And the mustache threw him at first, but there was no mistaking who was behind the mustache.

Yep, good old Conrad Chase. Pretty good trick, joining the Coast Guard, Conrad, but now I've got you, and Caspian.

Chapter Sixty-Nine

A MAN in a trench coat waited outside C. C. Dennison's office.

"What does he want?" Dennison asked his boatswain's mate.

"He said it was personal, Chief."

When the man entered his office, Dennison invited him to sit.

"I won't be here long," the man said. "Conrad Chase, I presume."

What was this, some kind of joke? "C. C. Dennison," Dennison said.

"A.k.a. Conrad Chase. I know who you are." And without saying another word he dropped a large manila envelope on his desk and left.

Dirk Caspian was happy. The weather had warmed, his front-end loader was fixed, and he was ready to get going. As he staked out the area, a man in a trench coat approached.

"Dirk Caspian?"

"Yes."

He handed Caspian a large manila envelope and walked away.

Dennison opened his envelope figuring it must be communication from his ex-wife. Sure enough, it was something from an attorney's office, all right, but it wasn't from his wife.

His hands grew cold touching the document.

Dirk Caspian tore open the envelope expecting a stop work order. He scanned past the legal greetings, reading the paper quickly. Then he leaned against the wheel of his backhoe and read it through carefully.

He couldn't believe it was real.

Chapter Seventy

PHASE ONE of his plan was accomplished. Getting the man in the trench coat was easy. Lance asked one of the guys he opened scallops with if he'd help him out with a little pre-April Fool's Day joke, a harmless prank. All he had to do was wear a suit and act like a lawyer and drop off a couple of envelopes. He'd pay him a hundred dollars for his trouble. That the guy owned a trench coat was even better.

Neither Dennison nor Caspian even noticed the guy was wearing sneakers.

During the time he was living off-island, Lance worked for a while as a paralegal. One of the things he learned was drawing up official documents. Using his computer he conjured a legal looking letterhead, using the name of a Nantucket lawyer who'd been dead the past ten years.

He came up with the scheme after a trip to the dump. He'd found an old ream of unlined typing paper at the Take it or Leave it. It had just the right aged look, and, along with the typewriter he found at the Hospital Thrift Shop, made his documents look old: twenty years old to be exact.

Dirk Caspian read the letter again:

'Dear Mr. Caspian, The estate of Nate Powell has directed that you are to receive this document with this message: May what you find bring happiness.'

Enclosed was an envelope with a riddle:

'Seek the gourd and skyward find
'Alone, a P
'Still
'A Pole to follow.
'Below's a Pearl,
'By wisdom's hall,
'A period marks the spot.
'From India, then,
'to Egypt, where
'legend says
'a spoon
'let out
'in the vicinity of a smoky charm
'usually rightside up, but upside down
'the Sunset.
'From there, carry the Weight,
'and follow one who catches in the fog,
'from west to east, past healthy cottages three.
'Navigate to center,
'til larboard bound and broadside,
'locate the candlemaker,
'wherein scratched works of white
'appear
'not the standard eighty-eight,
'but toothsome treasures all the same:

'the substance of a quest?
'Follow, if you will, on a southerly sea to the mighty
'Main
'Starboard now
'Towards the great ocean's
'Locker, not of Davy Jones,
'But heed the sign of Jones's good-natured mate.
'Westward ho!
'Approach the obelisk,
'Where cobble meets brick,
'Seek "the end of the whaleroad and the whale"
'A seven-stanzaed plea
'Is an elegy:
' "(W)here the bones
'Cry out in the long night for the hurt beast
'Bobbing by Ahab's whaleboats in the East."
'Will you find surcease?
' "What it cost
' "Them is their secret." '

The document was dated twenty years before, on October 31. There was one other message: 'You are to receive this letter twenty years after the demise of Nate Powell.'

The first thing Caspian was going to do was find that lawyer's office and get to the bottom of things. "The estate of Nate Powell," he said to himself. "What a bunch of …."

So Powell *was* dead. C. C. Dennison looked at the letter in his hands. Did Powell go to this much trouble just in case something happened to him? It didn't seem like something Powell would do, but how well did Dennison really know him? To see a lawyer, though? How would he know to do that? Powell was just a kid.

But maybe Powell came from a rich family. He didn't really know anything about him. Rich people always had lawyers.

And what was up with the stupid riddle? Why didn't he just draw a map?

He folded the letter and put it in the top drawer of his desk. The first thing he was going to do was go and see that lawyer.

Chapter Seventy-One

C. C. Dennison walked to the Broad Street address printed on the letter, looking for the law office of Robert F. O'Donohue. It was a little bit of a hike from Brant Point, but he seldom had business in town, so it was a good excuse to get out. When he got to Broad Street, however, he couldn't find the lawyer's office. He walked up and down both sides of the street, checking the address on the letter, but the address had to have been wrong because it wasn't a law office but a restaurant. He examined the other buildings for Robert F. O'Donohue's name, but nothing. He was so intent on auditing addresses that he bumped into a passerby.

"I'm sorry," he said and stopped. "You!!"

"Excuse me?" Dirk Caspian asked before he, too, stopped, then stared. Was it? Of course it was. Funny how you don't recognize people at first when they get older. "So you're here," he said. "I shouldn't say I'm surprised. Nice mustache."

Dennison noticed the letter in Caspian's hands. So he got one, too. He was about to walk away when Caspian spoke:

"Maybe he moved."

"What?" Dennison didn't even want to acknowledge Caspian's existence.

"O'Donohue. He must have moved."

Dennison stared at him. If there was one person he never wanted to see again, it was Dirk Caspian. The restaurant door opened and a man descended the steps. Caspian spoke to him: "Hi. Do you know where the law offices of Robert O'Donohue are located now?"

"What?"

"Robert F. O'Donohue, the lawyer?"

"His office used to be here," the man said.

"I gathered that," Caspian said. "Do you know where he moved?"

"Yes, I do," the man answered, "to the cemetery."

"The cemetery?"

"He's dead." And the man walked away.*

Sitting on a bench outside the Nantucket Town and County Building, Lance Willoughby, in baseball cap and sunglasses, pretended to read that week's edition of *The Looking Glass.* "So there they both are," he thought, watching Caspian and Chase — who now called himself Dennison for some reason — gesticulate at each other. Judging by their expressions and their conversation with the man on the sidewalk they must realize that they won't be asking any questions of Robert F. O'Donohue. Now isn't that just too bad.

He watched as they stormed off in different directions. Good luck trying to find someone to decipher those letters, he thought, or who it was who sent the man in the trench coat. He smiled at his deviousness. He'd love to be there when they got back together — because they would, he knew they would. After each tried to figure out that riddle on his own, and failed, he'd be forced to turn to the other for help. Lance laughed out loud knowing they wouldn't be able to ask anybody else because that would give them away. No, they'd have to depend on each other, just as they had vowed twenty years before. Brilliant. Was it justice — or sweet revenge?

He put the paper down and basked in his contentment. He'd had a lot of fun putting that riddle together. Maybe they'd learn something from it. Doubtful. Across the street, a few people were entering the Whaling Museum; behind him, others were coming and going from the town building. He could sit here all day, but he wouldn't.

Scallop season was coming to a close. It was almost time for phase two of his plan.

Chapter Seventy-Two

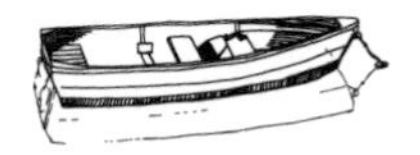

ADDIE WALKED into Brant Point Station on his usual day of the week, and at his usual time. As usual, Chief C. C. Dennison was at his desk nursing a cup of coffee. He had the Coast Guard report in front of him, ready to go.

Neither mentioned that they had seen each other on the water the week before, nor did either one make small talk. For the first time since Addie had started coming to the station, Dennison did not offer him a cup of coffee.

As Addie walked past Dennison's window on the way to his car he noticed Dennison inspecting a piece of paper and shaking his head slowly. It looked important. Was he holding out on him? That's all Addie would need, to read about a rescue at sea in *The Advocate*. Should he go back in? No, that would be too weird.

When he got back to his car, his phone was ringing. It was Ellen.

"You won't believe who just called me," she said. "Dennison."

So he *was* holding out on him. But if there was a story, why would Ellen call him? "What did he want?" Addie asked, pulling out of the Coast Guard parking lot. He didn't know why, but he didn't want Dennison to see him on the phone.

"Said he wants to see me; wouldn't say why. It seems real suspicious to me, kind of creeped me out. Any idea why he'd call?"

"No idea," Addie said. "I just came from there."

"So you'd know. Is there anything going on? Did an oil tanker run aground off Nantucket?"

"Not according to what he gave me, which was the usual Coast Guard report." Addie was getting nervous. He didn't want to miss a big story. He hadn't talked to Ellen in a while, other than to see her in court.

"You all right, Addie?" Ellen asked. "You don't seem like yourself."

"I'm fine," which meant he wasn't. In Ellen's experience, whenever people said they were fine, they weren't. "Have you seen Dennison lately?"

"Not since I followed him, which is why I'm suspicious. Did he say anything to you?"

"About you? No." But Addie hadn't told Ellen either about his and Digit's little adventure with Dennison. He didn't like holding out on her, but the robbery *was* his story. Besides, she had told him he could have it.

Ellen could tell she wasn't going to get anywhere talking with Addie. "Well, I guess I'll go over there. To be honest, I kind of wish you'd be there. I'm not so sure about going to see him alone."

Addie paused a second, then said: "Can you meet me for a cup of coffee? When? Now. Now would be good."

Before she went off to see Dennison, Addie decided to tell Ellen what had happened. He thought of abandoning the robbery story anyway; may as well tell her what he knew. Better to come from him than Dennison.

Fortunately, there was no one in the coffee shop. Addie sat at a corner table by the window. Ellen breezed in, said, "What's up?" and sat down.

And Addie told her about the crude map found in the old suitcase, and how Digit had pinpointed the location to the spot where Ellen had seen Dennison rowing, and how he and Digit rowed to the spot with a shovel just to see if there was anything buried there.

"And was there?" Ellen asked, looking into her coffee cup.

"It was like quicksand," Addie told her. "Digit almost sank to his knees."

"So, that's that," Ellen said.

"No, that isn't it. Guess who showed up right as we got there, in a rowboat?"

Ellen perked up. "No."

"Oh, yes." Addie looked out the window. He thought he'd feel better telling her, but he didn't. He felt as though he'd been keeping a secret from her. "Damn it, Ellen. I'm sorry I didn't tell you this sooner."

Ellen smiled. "Why would you tell me? This is *your* story, remember? You don't owe me a thing.

"In fact, I'm proud of you," she continued. "That took some digging, pardon the pun." She sipped her coffee, thought for a second, and brightened. "This only proves he's up to something. Good work, Addie."

"What does it prove? I can't figure it out."

Ellen stood up. "I'm off to talk to Dennison. Thanks, Addie. I'm glad you told me that before I went there." She saw the look on Addie's face.

"Don't worry," she said, "I'm not going to mention a word of what you just told me. Why would I?

"No," she said as she slung her bag over her shoulder, "I want to hear what *he's* got to say."

Chapter Seventy-Three

C. C. Dennison didn't expect Ellen to arrive so abruptly. He stood up when she entered his office.

"So formal, Chief. You don't usually stand for me."

"Have a seat, Ellen. Coffee?"

"You know it's no. She pulled out her notebook. "You have something for me?"

Dennison closed his desk drawer and locked it. "You in a hurry?"

"I'm on deadline."

"Well, if you're on deadline, this can wait."

"I can stretch the deadline a bit. I guess this isn't something timely?"

"Oh, it's timely, all right," Dennison said. He leaned back in his chair, put his hands behind his head, and looked Ellen in the eye. The look frightened her a bit, but she kept her composure. She flipped her notebook open and sat with pen poised.

Dennison looked out the window and began, "It's come to my attention that a certain Dirk Caspian . . . "

Ellen almost put her pen down. Caspian, again?

"... that Mr. Caspian received a communiqué from one ..." and he leaned forward and consulted a scrap of paper on his desk, "... from the office of a certain attorney, Robert F. O'Donohue. You ever heard of him?"

Ellen said she had not.

"Oh," Dennison said, again looking her in the eye. ('Cut it out, creep,' she wanted to say.) "I figured since you covered the court, you may have. Anyway, he's deceased."

"Caspian?"

He wished. "No, Ellen, Mr. O'Donohue, Esquire. My contact in Boston thinks the information contained therein ... "

"In the communiqué," Ellen said.

"Precisely, pre-cise-ly, may involve other wetlands on this island."

"And if it does, Chief, he'd have to go back before the Conservation Commission." She flipped her notebook closed. "Let me know when you find that out."

"All I want to know is, check that, all we want to know is, who is handling this Robert F. O'Donohue's affairs? He must have made provisions."

Ellen stood up. "I'm on it, Chief. Is that it?"

"That's it for now. You have that name written down, right, Robert F. O'Donohue?"

"As I said, Chief," Ellen said walking to the door. "I'm on it."

Ellen called Addie. "He had nothing for me; another so-called lead on Dirk Caspian's activities. He's got it in for that guy, and I wish I could figure out why."

Addie was relieved a tanker wasn't spewing oil into Nantucket Sound. He didn't much care about Dirk Caspian — that was Ellen's story. "I guess that's it, then," he said.

"No, it isn't," Ellen said excitedly. "I don't think he realizes

I saw this, but when I entered his office he quickly shoved some kind of paper into his top desk drawer. He stood up as soon as he saw me, which is a giveaway if ever I saw one. And then, he tried to sneakily lock the drawer when he thought I was looking down at my notebook. He's hiding something."

Now Addie was excited. "I saw him, too, looking at some sheet of paper. It really seemed to bother him."

"We've got to get our hands on that paper, Addie."

Ellen, always ready to investigate. How did she expect to do that? Dennison wasn't just going to hand it over to them. Besides, how would they even know he was giving them the right paper? "What's your plan, Ellen?" Ellen always had a plan.

"I'll think of something. And Addie . . . ?"

"Yes, Ellen?"

"Let's work on this together."

"Caspian's your story, Ellen. Thanks for the offer, though."

"I don't think this is about Caspian, Addie. I really think we should pool our resources. Two heads, and all that."

Oh, why not? "Why not?" Addie said. "Keep me informed, and let me know what you need from me."

"Oh, I will," Ellen said."

In a way, Addie hoped Ellen didn't come up with anything; he didn't want to upset Verona.

But if Ellen did come up with something . . . . a rush went up his spine. He couldn't wait to get back on this story.

Chapter Seventy-Four

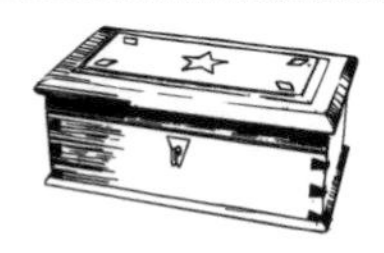

C. C. Dennison had no idea what help, if any, Ellen could give him, but he figured it was worth a try. He could call every lawyer on Nantucket asking who took on Robert F. O'Donohue's clients, but he didn't want to draw attention to himself.

Robert F. O'Donohue was real, that much he knew from checking out a phone book from twenty years ago at the library. He fingered the letter again. The paper was old, there was no doubting that.

Damn. Of all the people to bump into — Caspian. He had to admit he looked good; he hadn't changed much in twenty years. Couldn't say the same for himself.

Funny how that guy in the trench coat knew where to find him. He supposed a little legwork would have dug up that Conrad Chase was now C. C. Dennison. There were people he worked with who knew him under both names. No mystery there, really.

And that riddle! What was that supposed to mean? It more or less proved, though, that Nate Powell had written it. He had known Powell better than he had Caspian, and Powell was into that sort of stuff: word games, figuring out maps. It was because of Powell that he had drawn such an elaborate map, guessing that Powell would do the same.

The map: it was almost as if Addie had used his map that afternoon. In all his days of surveilling the sandbar, no one else had even come near. Why would Addie be out there in a rowboat?

"Chief." It was one of the mates, calling from outside his office door.

"What is it?"

"Chief, there's another Whaler run aground on the jetties."

What was up with these Whalers? Anyone buying a Whaler should be required to take a safe boating course.

"It's your turn at the helm, Chief."

"Coming." And he put the paper inside his top desk drawer, but forgot to lock it.

"The hell with the lawyers," Dirk Caspian said to himself. What did he need to find a lawyer for? Who cares how he got the letter? The important thing is that he *had* the letter. And if it were true, that Powell was dead and that there were only two of them now, so much the better.

Man, Conrad Chase looked different. But the main thing is, he's here, just as they all agreed twenty years ago.

Caspian took that as a good omen. Things were coming together. The *Susan's* Teeth would soon be his. All he had to do was figure out that riddle before Chase did.

And for the next two days, he did nothing but try to decipher it. This *had* to be it. Powell was the one with the responsibility to hide the treasure, and — it was almost too much for him to handle — Powell *came through!*

Upon his return from the rescue mission, C. C. Dennison made a fresh pot of coffee to warm up. A couple of high school kids not paying attention drifted right into the east jetty. He was probably a little rougher on them than he should have been: the wind had come up suddenly, it could have happened to an experienced boater. Let's hope that's it for today, he thought. He wanted to get back to the letter.

But when he opened his top drawer, the letter was gone.

Chapter Seventy-Five

It took Ellen about two minutes to come up with her first strategy. You cultivate sources in order to call on them when needed, and this was one of those times.

Dennison wasn't her only contact at Station Brant Point. She had built a rapport with one of the few women at the station, Boatswain's Mate Mary Mahoney, who served as Dennison's de facto secretary. On the occasions when Ellen had had to wait for Dennison, the two of them had become friendly, friendly enough to exchange phone numbers.

Ellen's timing couldn't have been better: she called just after Dennison had gone on the rescue mission.

"I wonder if you can do me a small favor," Ellen asked. "It doesn't have to be now, whenever is good for you."

"As long as it doesn't involve anything to do on the water; it's cold out there today."

"No, it's inside."

"Fire away."

"When I was there a little while ago, the Chief was inspecting a document that looked pretty important, but he didn't want to talk to me about it."

"Sounds like our beloved leader."

"I'd love to have a look at it. The only thing is he locked it in the top drawer of his desk."

"And you'd like me to steal it."

"No, just make a copy of it, if you can. I'd owe you one big time."

"Not too sure what you can do for me, but I'll take a look. If it's anything classified . . . "

"I understand; I don't need to see it."

"What do you think I'm looking for?"

"I'm not sure, but if there's anything with an attorney's letter-head," she checked her notes, "an attorney Robert F. O'Donohue, that might be it."

"I'll call you back."

"You're in luck. The Chief's out pulling a boat off the east jetty, and if his top desk drawer wasn't unlocked, I wasn't going to search for a key. I believe I found the document you want, something about a will. I made a copy. Don't pick it up here. I'll drop it by your office when I'm off duty."

Ellen's office was her apartment. "Just put it on the front seat of my car. Thank you so much. I'll treat you to dinner."

"The food's too good here. Buy me a drink at the Anglers' Club sometime."

"Deal."

It was unlike her, but Ellen did a little dance around her apartment. She hadn't been this excited since the whale washed ashore.

C. C. Dennison was in a panic. He was sure he'd put that

letter back in his top drawer. He opened every drawer in his desk and frantically looked through every paper on top of it. "Mahoney!" he yelled. "Mahoney, get in here."

"Yes, Chief," the mate said calmly. "Need help with something."

"My top drawer was unlocked when I got back here. Have you been going through my desk?"

"Now, Chief, why would I do that? You've given me enough paperwork to keep me busy for a week. Can I help you find something?"

"I don't know how you can help me; I've looked through everything."

"What is it that you're looking for, Chief?"

"A document, a legal document. I swear I put it in this drawer," and he opened it.

"Let me look, Chief," she said, walking over. She had made the mistake of refolding the letter once she'd copied it. She pulled out the drawer, lifted a few papers, and took the letter from the very back of the drawer. She placed all the papers on top of his desk, unfolding the letter as she did so. "Are any of these it, Chief?"

Dennison's eyes bulged as he picked up the letter from O'Donohue. "Must have overlooked it," he mumbled without gratitude.

When she closed the door, Mahoney wiped a bead of sweat from her brow. "That was a close one," she thought.

Fortunately, the Chief misplaced things all the time. It wasn't out of the ordinary for her to help him find something.

Just the same, she was through doing favors for a while.

"I know I locked that desk," Dennison said under his breath. But there it was, in the top drawer where he'd left it. Why would he even think Mahoney would go through his things; she saw everything of importance that came in. Besides, he had the only key to his desk. He had been in a hurry when he left — maybe he hadn't locked it.

He had to stop obsessing. He was getting paranoid. Why would Mahoney care about a letter from a lawyer? Get a grip, he told himself.

He paced his office. He needed to do something to stop thinking about that letter. He went to his window and looked out at the harbor. It was beautiful on Nantucket, he thought, and he was in a job he loved. Was it worth it to care so much about something that happened twenty years ago?

But the time had come, it was now, not two decades before, and he had the key to the treasure. He couldn't give up on it now and leave it all to Caspian. The only problem was he couldn't make hide nor hair of Powell's riddle. He went back to his desk, sat down, and it came to him.

They'd have to do it together. As much as it pained him, he'd have to join forces with Dirk Caspian.

Chapter Seventy-Six

"ADDIE — unbelievable! Great news. I've got to see you; can we meet for coffee?" Ellen couldn't contain herself.

It was Saturday. Addie was home with Verona. He was excited, too, but he didn't want to rush off to Ellen. Verona was worth more to him than any story.

Oh, he was sure Verona would understand, she knew what he'd been working on. "Why don't you meet me here?" he asked Ellen.

"Where?"

"My cottage. We can have coffee here."

"Is Verona with you?"

"As always. We can talk in front of Verona, she can keep a secret better than anyone I know.

"Besides," he continued, "this is kind of her story, too. If she hadn't found that suitcase, we wouldn't even be talking about this."

"Be right over."

Ellen wasn't in the door when she exclaimed: "I've got it! I've got the document he was looking at."

"*How?*", he thought, but he knew by her look not to ask. "Well, let's see it."

Ellen had made a copy for Addie. They sat around the coffee table, puzzled by the poem. "What does it mean?" Ellen said aloud. "Now I know why Dennison had that look on his face: he was trying to figure it out."

Addie knew what it was. "It's a clue to where the treasure is buried. Do we know if Caspian got one of these?"

"Why would he have one?" asked Ellen.

"If he did, it would finally tie them together, Chase and Caspian." The two of them *were* in on it, Addie could sense it.

"What are you so smiley about?" Ellen asked him.

"This is beautiful; we've got them." Ellen looked at him quizzically. "Don't you see?" Addie said. "This confirms that Dennison was involved in something. And that Caspian is digging in the exact same spot as the other map can't be a coincidence."

"Can I see the other map?"

Addie brought over the suitcase and showed Ellen both maps. As she was examining them, Addie said, "The only thing is, who's this Nate Powell?"

"Don't you remember, Addie?" Verona said. And she handed him the envelope from inside the suitcase, the one addressed to Nate Powell.

Addie fell back into the couch cushions. "Bingo," he said, and he kissed Verona.

"Bingo, nothing," Ellen said. "We can't tie them to the robbery until we find the treasure, if there is a treasure. It may tie Dennison and Caspian together — *if* Caspian also got a letter — but together in what? A couple of maps with X's on them don't mean a thing."

"Think about it," Addie said. "The maps pinpointing exactly where these two have a great interest, *more* than a great interest, an obsession, combined with the name Nate Powell — and all of it found in the same suitcase. It's beyond coincidence. You have to admit that."

"All right, I will. It still doesn't tell us who this Nate Powell is."

"I wonder which one of them this suitcase belonged to?" Addie continued. "Well, if these clues do lead to that old sea chest, we'll just have to get there first."

They all read the riddle again. "This is just gibberish," Ellen offered.

"Wait, I think I'm getting it," and he read aloud:

'from west to east . . . Navigate to center . . .

' . . . til larboard bound and broadside, locate the candle-maker . . . '

"These sound like nautical terms," he said. " 'From west to east' is obviously a direction. Not sure what 'larboard bound' means, though." He thought for a while, and brightened. "But I've got a good idea who might."

"Who?" asked Ellen.

"Libby. I'm going to show her this."

Ellen looked concerned. "The research librarian? Will she keep it under wraps?"

"Libby? If you can't trust Libby, who can you trust? She's precisely who we need to confide in."

"Now you're sounding like Dennison," Ellen laughed.

"You're right," Addie said. "Pre-cise-ly."

Chapter Seventy-Seven

DIRK CASPIAN hadn't been near his excavation site for a week. There was no need to go there, anyway; there was nothing buried there. A thought struck him: wouldn't it be something if *Dionis* really *was* buried there?

Let somebody else dig her up: he had other treasure to find.

But no matter how many ways he looked at the clues, no matter how he read them — top to bottom, bottom to top — none of it made sense to him. 'Seek the gourd?' What was that? A pumpkin? And what did India and Egypt have to do with it?

A knock on the door. No, he must be hearing things. He hadn't befriended anyone since returning to the island. No one had ever been to his place. That's why he took a rental in 'Sconset, to be as far as he could get from people.

Knocking again. Was it the wind? He opened the door.

"About time you came to the door," C. C. Dennison said. "We need to talk."

With scallop season nearing an end, the number of scallopers started to drop as the fishing became scarce and the amount of adult, or catchable, scallops dwindled. Only the diehards remained, fishing their own territories, not wanting to crowd each other with only a handful on the water. Nobody was getting his limit; most fished for several hours before heading back.

As Digit pulled into the dock, Lance Willoughby was unloading his catch onto the finger pier. Digit tied up his boat and walked over. He hadn't seen Lance at all lately, and he wanted to catch up.

Lance didn't acknowledge Digit's approach, but there was something in the way he turned his head that made Digit stop, something familiar in his profile. He remembered that he'd wanted to talk to Lance about Dirk Caspian, that perhaps he had an older brother who knew him. He hadn't thought about Caspian's friends in years, but Lance brought back a sense of recognition. He tried to conjure a picture of Caspian and his two buddies. For a while there they were inseparable, a three-headed alliance. Everybody talked about it, the people with nothing better to do, anyway. But it was no use — he couldn't quite picture the trio.

And if he wanted to be done opening before supper, he'd better unload his catch.

He couldn't put it off any longer — the time had come for Lance Willoughby to move.

The way Digit Hathaway looked at him that morning unsettled him. He looked like he knew something.

After he'd returned to the island, and after he'd been scalloping for a couple of years and gotten to know Digit, he remembered seeing him in the days when he and Caspian and Chase were hanging around together. Digit and Caspian had spoken a couple of times, but nothing more than terse 'hellos' when they bumped into each other on the street. It wasn't until they were originally ditching the safe that Caspian even spoke of his friendship with Digit.

In all the years he'd been back, Lance was positive Digit hadn't recognized him from those days. But that look today . . . yes, the time had come.

This time there wouldn't be any missteps, or accidents, like falling overboard. No, every step was going to be deliberate.

He wondered if the other two were having fun with his little riddle.

Caspian eyed Dennison warily. This was *his* treasure, dammit. He didn't need his onetime roommate poking around like a puppy dog looking for a bone. The way Dennison stood in the doorway, however, let him know he wasn't going to go away. "Come in," he said to his former co-conspirator.

"Don't mind if I do," Dennison said. "You could at least offer me a cup of coffee."

"What do you have in mind?"

"Oh, just black."

"No, you idiot. Why are you here?"

Let's see who the idiot is, Dennison thought. "Figured out that riddle yet?" he said.

Had *he?* Caspian thought. What was he trying to pull?

"Well, have you?" Dennison continued. He looked intently at Caspian. "Right. Didn't think so."

Caspian didn't want to show his hand. He tried looking as noncommittal as possible. "Do you really think Powell's dead?"

"I've known that for a while. Oh, I forgot, you weren't here when he met his demise." Dennison was getting comfortable now. "Surprised you even came back to the island, being exiled and all."

Caspian sat in the chair opposite him. "How did you know about that? You'd already gone."

"Oh, I have my ways," Dennison said. "You're pretty bold these days, getting written up in the papers . . . . Not exactly keeping a low profile."

"It wasn't supposed to be in the papers," Caspian said under his breath. "It was all supposed to take place in executive session, but somebody tipped off the reporters."

"I wonder who that could have been?" Dennison said casually. Caspian scowled. "Don't look at me. I'm just a Coast Guard guy."

Caspian wanted Dennison gone. "Just what do you want, anyway?" he said. "You didn't come here to catch up."

Dennison leaned forward just a bit. "We need to team up."

Caspian stood up quickly. He leaned over Dennison. "No way."

Twenty years ago he might have been intimidated, but Dennison knew he had him. He waited before he said: "You know and I know we're not going to figure out that puzzle without help. If you had, you wouldn't have been here poring over it when I arrived. Don't deny it. I saw the letter on the table when I came in.

"If we put our heads together," he continued, "we'll get it sooner rather than later. That's what it's all about, isn't it? Finding where Powell hid it?" Dennison knew he had him. He studied his old friend calmly before getting in a little dig. "You really didn't think Powell would have buried it in the marsh, did you? I have to admit, that was pretty ingenious, getting the state *and* the locals to sign off on that excavation project."

"It could be there," Caspian said, defeated.

"Tell you what, if it *is,* you can have it. If these clues bring us to your swamp, it's all yours."

Dennison walked over to the table and leaned over the letter. "So, what do you say, old friend," he said sarcastically. "Should we get started?"

Chapter Seventy-Eight

LIBBY INSPECTED the copy of the letter Addie had given her. "Yes, I knew Robert F. O'Donohue," she told Addie. "A good man, smart, too. Went to MIT, I believe, before going to law school. Is he what you wanted to ask me about?"

"Well, that, but I was mainly interested in the poem, or riddle."

"May I ask where you got this? It's addressed to a Conrad Chase."

Addie gave her a look that said, 'please, don't.' He opened his mouth, but before he could say anything Libby nodded her head sagely. "It appears to be twenty years old, anyway," she said, "and Mr. O'Donohue's dead. I don't think we're treading in unwise territory. Let's see . . . " She read the opening lines of the riddle. " 'Seek the gourd and skyward find alone, a P. . . . ' Skyward. Might be some kind of astronomical riddle, although I don't know what India and Egypt would have to do with that. A lot of the constellations are based on Greek mythology; I'm not familiar with any based on legends of India or Egypt."

"Well, thanks, Libby. I thought you might find it interesting."

"Has it got anything to do with a story?"

Addie was coy. "Maybe."

"Maybe, huh? Let's make a copy and I'll take a closer look this week."

Addie tried his best to act cool, but couldn't help blurting out, "Great! I mean, thanks, Libby."

"Are you still looking into James Hathaway?"

"Who?"

Libby looked at him impatiently. "Digit Hathaway's ancestor. You were very interested a couple of weeks ago. Any more finds out in storage?"

"Not lately. Did I tell you about the painting?"

"No, you didn't." Libby sat down at her desk. "Tell me about it."

"Just that the worker out there said it was unusual for the portrait to go to his waist, and not just his head and shoulders."

"Or what you in the newspaper business would call a 'head shot.' "

"What?"

"Never mind. Yes, from what I know that is unusual."

"He was wearing a ring, in the painting."

"Oh?"

"Yes, inscribed with the letter 'V'. We figured it might be the number of whaling voyages he took, in Roman numerals."

Libby nodded her head. "Not an improbable conjecture. Has Digit found any more scrimshaw among his souvenirs?"

"I'm not sure. Nothing he's told me about, anyway."

"Let me know if he does. You never know when a *Susan's* Tooth will show up."

"Right. Oh, Libby, what does larboard mean?"

"It's an old nautical term, meaning the left-hand side of a boat facing forward, opposite starboard. It's called 'port' now. Why?"

"You'll see it; it's in the riddle."

"Think of the riddle later — haven't you got a paper to put out?"

C. C. Dennison, née Conrad Chase, knew that 'larboard' meant 'port,' and that it stopped being used on boats because it was too confusing; if you're on deck in a storm, 'starboard' and 'larboard' can sound too similar. Snap decisions based on hearing the wrong command were dangerous. 'Port,' or left, the side of the boat that was typically tied to the dock, came into favor in the mid-1800s when the English Navy adopted the term.

The rest of the riddle meant nothing to him, and to Caspian.

"Maybe we can get those reporters to help us," Caspian said to Dennison.

"Are you crazy? We may as well just tell them that we committed the robbery. If we show them this letter . . . "

"No, you idiot, we just show them the riddle, I mean *you* show them the riddle. Tell them you came across it in an old file. I'm assuming you see them pretty regularly. I read the Coast Guard report in the paper every week."

"*You read* the paper every week? Didn't know you cared that much about Nantucket."

"I started reading it to make sure the Conservation Commission posted its emergency certification for my little project — I didn't need any nosy natives snooping around asking questions. Now I mostly look through the legal notices for entertainment."

"Some entertainment," Dennison thought, but said, "I'm not sure about showing them the riddle. Won't it look fishy?"

"Why? Present it as history. I'll bet you like chatting up that woman reporter anyway."

"You know her?"

"Only because she was asking me a lot of questions after that

Conservation Commission meeting. I asked her out to dinner."

Dennison didn't want to ask what Ellen's response had been. He'd been wanting to ask her out ever since he'd first met her on the Cape. He wasn't so sure about this idea of Caspian's, either. Ellen, especially, might get suspicious. "I'm not feeling this one," he told Caspian.

"Look, we're getting nowhere with this; I bet we could look at it for a year and still not get it. Why not let those two figure it out for us?"

"And what if they find the treasure first? Right? Didn't think of that one, did you?"

"So we keep our eye on them. Make it so they have to report back to you, appeal to their sense of patriotism. That's it, present it as though it would be a big favor to the Coast Guard.

"And then you could ask that woman reporter out to dinner. She wouldn't go with me."

Ellen walked by Mate Mary Mahoney and held out the paper Dennison had just handed her. Ellen mimed, "What the heck?" to Mahoney and Mahoney mimed back, "I know," and shrugged her shoulders.

Dennison had sounded serious over the phone when he'd asked her to come down to the station. She got there as quickly as she could, hoping she hadn't gotten Mahoney into any trouble.

But Mahoney only raised an eyebrow when Ellen arrived and didn't seem upset. Dennison was smiling when Ellen entered his office. This time he didn't even offer her coffee.

"I was hoping you could do us a favor," he said, "and by us, I do mean the United States Coast Guard."

Ellen looked at him quizzically. What could she possibly do for the Coast Guard, besides enlist?

"I can see you're intrigued," Dennison continued. "I came

across something in the files that's had several previous chiefs before me stumped. I figure with your knowledge of Nantucket — you know a lot more than I do, to be sure, and none of the crew are from the island — that with your knowledge you might be able to help us."

Ellen *was* intrigued. "Be glad to help if I can. Not sure what it is you'd like me to do."

Dennison walked over to a file cabinet, pulled out a piece of paper. "No heavy lifting involved," he said, chuckling. "From the notes on this, it seems it might lead to an original artifact concerning this station. One former chief even speculated it might point to the foundation of the original lighthouse. Now *that* would be something we could affix a plaque to; wouldn't you like to know that *you* helped put it there?

"If you could help us decipher this . . . " and he placed the paper on his desk in front of her.

Ellen almost choked. Was this some kind of a trap? She looked up at Dennison, who didn't seem to notice her reaction. "What is this?" she managed to say.

"We're not sure," Dennison said. "Just something folks here at the station have been puzzling over for some time."

Ellen stared at the paper. "Oh, that isn't the original," Dennison said. "I had Mahoney type the pertinent information from what was in the files. Doesn't seem to make sense, I know."

"This is, was, a Coast Guard document?"

"Yes, ma'am. Look, if you're too busy, or not interested, perhaps Addie . . . "

"Oh, no, I'm interested, Chief," Ellen said, not too eagerly, she hoped. "Do you mind if I take this?"

"That's what it's there for," Dennison said. "You know what?" he said, as if he'd just come up with the idea, "show it to Addie if you want. Maybe the two of you together could figure it out."

Ellen wanted to get out of there before Dennison read anything into her expression or body language. She stood up to leave. "Any rush on this? There wouldn't seem to be if it's been languishing in the files all these years. How many years old did you say this was?"

"Could be a hundred, two hundred years old. Not sure if the original even exists anymore. As I said, this was from notes found in an old folder."

"All right, Chief, I'll have a look."

"Fan-tas-tic," Dennison said, before adding, "oh, Ellen, one more thing."

Ellen had her hand on the doorknob. "Yes, Chief?" she said.

"Care to have dinner sometime?"

Did she just hear him correctly? "I'll think about it, Chief."

Dennison smiled to himself after she closed the door. "Better than the answer Caspian got," he thought.

Chapter Seventy-Nine

"TWO HUNDRED years old," that's what he told me. "Can you believe that?"

Addie looked at the photocopy Ellen had handed him. It was just the riddle: no Attorney O'Donohue, no address, no mention of Nate Powell. "What do you think he wants?"

"He wants us to solve this puzzle for him. I never realized he was so stupid."

"Do you think he's on to us? I mean, he saw Digit and me checking out his hiding place."

"He's on to nothing. He even asked me to show this to you. He's desperate, that's all."

"Maybe it's a trap."

"Trap, schmap. That's what I thought too — at first. Who's he going to trap? Us? He has no idea what we know." She thought for a while, then smiled at Addie. "This is so much *fun*. I've never been involved in something like this in my life. And I owe it all to you, Addie. To think I told you this was old news."

"It was you who found out all that stuff about Caspian."

"But you figured out the robbery connection. Without that

. . . well," and she leaned over and kissed him on the cheek.

Blushing, Addie said, "So what happens if we do solve the riddle?"

"Not if, Addie, when. And when we do, we lead him as far from the treasure as possible." She took from her purse the original copy. "Gotten anywhere on this yet?"

"Libby said she'd take a look and get back to me. I can't figure it out."

"I'm going to the library. Maybe I'll find something in one of the old papers. Oh, hi, Verona."

Verona had been on a bike ride. She said hello and goodbye to Ellen as they crossed in the doorway and found Addie at the kitchen table, peering intently at the letter. "Still working on the robbery?" she asked him.

Addie looked up as if emerging from underwater. Verona was moving toward the bedroom, but Addie told her to wait. He wanted to look at her, at her radiance. He stood up and hugged her. "Hey," he said, looking into her eyes, "want to help me?"

Verona wasn't sure what he meant.

"Help me figure out this riddle."

"Oh, Addie, I don't think . . . "

"I should have asked you earlier," he said. "You've got a unique way of looking at things; you're very intuitive."

"Such a big word," she said, smiling.

"Maybe we can look at this later," he said, and they walked to the bedroom together.

Addie and Verona sat side by side on the couch. "Now what is it you want me to look at?" she asked, and he pointed to the riddle.

Verona read it through, not thinking, letting the words flow freely in her mind:

'Seek the gourd and skyward find
'Alone, a P
'Still
'A Pole to follow.
'Below's a Pearl,
'By wisdom's hall,
'A period marks the spot.
'From India, then,
'to Egypt, where
'legend says
'a spoon
'let out
'in the vicinity of a smoky charm
'usually rightside up, but upside down
'the Sunset
'From there, carry the Weight,
'and follow one who catches in the fog,
'from west to east, past healthy cottages three.
'Navigate to center,
'til larboard bound and broadside,
'locate the candlemaker,
'wherein scratched works of white
'appear
'not the standard eighty-eight,
'but toothsome treasures all the same:
'the substance of a quest?
'Follow, if you will, on a southerly sea to the mighty
'Main
'Starboard now
'Towards the great ocean's
'Locker, not of Davy Jones,
'But heed the sign of Jones's good-natured mate.
'Westward ho!

'Approach the obelisk,
'Where cobble meets brick,
'Seek "the end of the whaleroad and the whale"
'A seven-stanzaed plea
'Is an elegy
' "(W)here the bones
'Cry out in the long night for the hurt beast
'Bobbing by Ahab's whaleboats in the East."
'Will you find surcease?
' "What it cost
' "Them is their secret." '

She sat silently for a while. She read the top line again. 'Skyward.' Had to have something to do with the stars, she thought. 'Seek the gourd,' threw her, but 'Alone, a P,' seemed somehow familiar. Maybe . . .

"I've got it," she said to Addie. He quickly sat upright. He knew asking Verona was a good idea.

"The whole thing?"

"No, just part of the beginning. 'Alone, a P/Still/A Pole to follow.' 'A Pole to follow,' from my understanding, usually refers to the polestar, so the 'P' must be Polaris, the North Star. It's a small, faint star but it sits alone in the sky and is 'Still.' "

"What does that mean, 'Still?' " Addie asked. "I don't get it."

" 'Still' means Polaris doesn't move like the rest of the stars. It's right above the North Pole, so all the stars move around *it.*"

"All right," Addie said, "it's a start. Great." He got out his notebook. "What's the name of that star?"

"Oh, am I being interviewed now?"

"Yes, madam. How do you find Nantucket?"

"I didn't find Nantucket — it found me."

"So did I, fortunately. What's the name of that star?"

"Polaris. According to this, it's something to follow. Like

you?"

He put his notebook down. Did she have doubts? Oh, he hoped not.

"Yes, Verona, like me." He put his arms around her. "That's enough work for today. Let's go for a walk."

"I just came from a bike ride."

"Yes, but not with me. I'll buy you lunch at the drugstore."

"You're such a romantic, Addie." But she meant it.

Truly.

Chapter Eighty

ELLEN WASN'T sure what she'd uncover at the Atheneum, but it would keep her mind occupied. Looking at that riddle had her brain going in circles. She needed a break.

She came across the story when the 167-year-old Great Point Lighthouse crumbled in 1984 during a fierce, late March nor'easter, another occasion when there were no boats or planes for three days. She got absorbed with an article about three crazy reporters who waded across the Galls — a narrow section of beach about a mile from the light — to be the first journalists to get to the light on foot. They had to wade across because the storm had washed out the Galls and transformed it into two hundred yards or so of open ocean. They got as far as they could in a borrowed four-wheel drive, donned waders at the ocean break to slog to the other side, hustled the mile to the fallen light with their cameras, crawled over the toppled and ancient rubblestone, ran back to the Galls, re-donned the waders and, cameras held high with the tide rising and a strong, sea-going current pulling at them, trudged back across.

"What some people will do to get a story," Ellen thought, as she looked at the photos, which, she had to admit, were pretty spectacular.

"Finding anything interesting?" She literally jumped in her chair. Who . . . ?

She looked up into the grinning visage of Dirk Caspian. "Hope I didn't startle you," he said. "Must be a good story. You were obviously entranced."

"If it was so obvious, why did you sneak up on me?" she thought, but said nothing. He walked away, still smiling.

Ellen felt chilled after the encounter. "Why does that guy make my skin crawl?" she thought.

It again crossed her mind how Dennison (or Chase or whatever his name was) was so eager to get dirt on Caspian, and how he'd recently urged her to set the judge against him.

"Of course," she said to herself as she stood up to leave. "He wants him gone."

Walking down the library steps, she thought: "With Caspian gone, he'd have the treasure to himself."

Which made her all the more determined to figure out that riddle and send Dennison and Caspian as far from the treasure as possible.

C. C. Dennison wasn't pleased when Dirk Caspian waltzed unannounced into his office. "What the . . . "

"Don't look so surprised. I simply told your secretary I was here on official state business," he said. He took the chair opposite Dennison. "Powell's not dead."

Dennison wasn't sure he'd heard him correctly. He didn't have a secretary, he had a *mate.* Caspian didn't know shit. "Who's not dead?"

"You know who: Powell."

Of course Powell was dead; they had the document to

prove it.

"I thought about what I'd told you," Caspian continued, "about checking the paper for legal notices. I did a little research at the library just now and guess what? There was no notice of Powell's death in the newspaper twenty years ago, or nineteen years ago, or even eighteen."

"What does that prove?" Dennison was tired of Caspian and his know-it-all attitude. Why did he ever think they could work together?

"Because there has to be notice whenever a will is being probated. And, according to that phony letter we received, Powell supposedly left a will." Dennison looked at Caspian but said nothing.

"He's playing with us," Caspian said.

Chapter Eighty-One

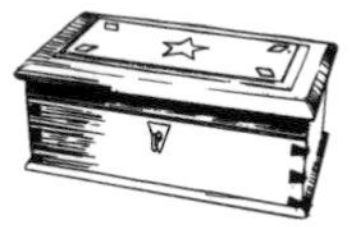

"I BELIEVE I've got it — a good part of it, anyway."

Addie sat across the table from Libby at the research library. "Once I got the first part, which was a little tricky, the rest of it fell into place, although there are a few places where, I have to admit, I'm stumped. But we'll get to them later. Are you ready?"

Addie got out his notebook. He was ready, all right.

"Let's take it line by line. First, it says, 'Seek the gourd and skyward find, alone, a P.' That one came to me as I was brushing my teeth. And Libby began to sing, softly, because they were, after all, in a library. "Follow the Drinking Gourd, follow the drinking gourd." She had a beautiful voice. "It was a song sung by slaves in the mid-1800s. They followed the Drinking Gourd to freedom."

Addie looked at her with a puzzled expression.

"We call it the Big Dipper," she said. "Nantucket was an abolitionist stronghold, and very pro union. Did you know Frederick Douglass, the former slave turned orator, gave his very first public speech right here at the Atheneum in 1841? Nantucket was also part of the Underground Railroad, so I've done a bit of research into the island's strong anti-slavery sentiments. Funny how the document we're looking at came from the office of Bob O'Donohue: he would happily recall the Memorial Day parades of his childhood, watching the last remaining Civil War veterans proudly march up Main Street. But I digress. I had forgotten about 'Follow the Drinking Gourd' until you gave me this."

A nice story, thought Addie, but . . .

"How does this fit in with the puzzle?" Libby said, as though reading his mind. "If you follow the outer stars of the Drinking Gourd, or Big Dipper, they point to the North Star, or Polaris."

Just like Verona said, Addie thought. "Are you following *me?*" Libby asked, noticing Addie's wandering gaze. "Let's continue," she said.

"The riddle then directs: 'Below's a Pearl, by wisdom's hall, a period marks the spot. From India, then, to Egypt.' This was a little trickier, but not much. India was the real clue here."

"That's what's had me stumped," Addie admitted. "I couldn't figure out how India and Egypt had anything to do with Nantucket."

"It's not India, the country, but India *Street,* which used to be called *Pearl* Street. And which hall of wisdom is on India Street? None other than our renowned Atheneum, which, as you'll notice next time you're there, has a period at the end of its name on the façade of the building. To back up a bit, the Atheneum, indeed the town itself, is situated in the northern part of the island, so someone could, conceivably follow the North Star and find a *Pearl.*"

"So is there an Egypt street as well?"

"What do you think?" Libby asked as though Addie was her pupil.

"I'm guessing the answer is, 'No.'"

"And you'd be guessing correctly. Back to our little riddle.

If we reverse direction on India Street and follow it to the end, we're close to North Liberty Street and a section of the island that was once referred to as 'Egypt,' ostensibly because it was out of town; 'Egypt' implying remote or mysterious. Our riddle continues: 'where legend says a spoon let out in the vicinity of a smoky charm, usually rightside up, but upside down.' This was also a bit of fun. If I'm right about this part, and I have no reason to believe I'm not, our writer is going a bit afield in his island geography, but not much.

"The first keys are the words, 'a spoon let out.' The Lily Pond could be called within the bounds of Nantucket's 'Egypt.' The Lily Pond was originally a large pond, complete with a water-powered mill. As the story goes, one day in the early 1700s, a little girl, Love Paddack, was playing at the edge of the Lily Pond with a spoon." Libby paused. "Not to change the subject, but have you ever seen Hummock Pond or Sesachacha Pond opened to the ocean?"

"You mean when they take a bulldozer and dig a ditch through the beach from the pond to the ocean? Yes, I have."

"And what happens?" Libby again being the schoolteacher.

"Some of the pond drains into the ocean . . . "

". . . Lowering the level of the pond and invigorating it with the intrusion of salt water. It was a practice taught to the settlers by the Wampanoags, the island's original inhabitants."

Addie didn't want to ask, but Libby anticipated his question.

"What's that got to do with the Lily Pond?" she asked rhetorically. "You don't need a bulldozer to open the floodgates, so to speak. The Indians certainly didn't have bulldozers. More recently, some eager beavers have made the cut with a shovel. The point being that even a small ditch will quickly expand from the force of the escaping water. Our little girl in the 1700s had opened a gully through the banks of the Lily Pond. What was only a fascinating trickle when she was called to supper, became a torrent overnight.

"In the morning, the first person to see the damage allegedly called out: 'Someone has let out the Lily Pond.' It wasn't until seventy years later that the little girl, now an old woman, confessed to the deed on her deathbed. The poor thing, carrying that all those years. Do you need me to slow down?" Addie was furiously scribbling away. Libby waited until he looked up from his notebook.

" 'In the vicinity of a smoky charm, usually rightside up, but upside down.' Again, once you think about it, it becomes obvious. Nearby the Lily Pond, near enough for our purposes, anyway, you will find a 'charm' of sorts, a horseshoe."

"On somebody's house, on an old barn?" Addie asked eagerly.

"Let's not get ahead of ourselves. Let me ask you, Addie, in which direction is a horseshoe usually attached to a house, rightside up or upside down?"

"Rightside up, so the luck won't drain out."

"Just like the Lily Pond."

"I don't follow . . . "

"Never mind, Addie. Anyway, near enough to the Lily Pond is the Oldest House, where you'll find on its chimney a large horseshoe design crafted in the bricks." She took out an old painted postcard from a folder. "Notice anything about the horseshoe on the Oldest House?"

"It's upside down. Libby, you're brilliant."

"I'm not sure I could be described as brilliant; learned, perhaps," but she smiled at the compliment.

"What's next?"

"That's it."

"But there's more to the riddle. Come on, Libby, I'm chomping at the bit here."

"That's *champing* at the bit. If you're going to say it, at least get it right." Libby tapped her folder on the desk. "That's as far as I've gotten. For the life of me I can't figure out the lines: 'From there, carry the Weight, and follow one who catches in the fog.' Haven't the foggiest clue about that, if you'll pardon the pun.

"Isn't that enough for one day?" she said pleasantly. "I believe I've gotten you pretty far along."

"You're right, Libby. I can't thank you enough for this."

"As I told you, it was fun. Now, show me the kind of researcher you are and figure out the rest of it."

Chapter Eighty-Two

Addie practically skipped out of the research library. "What a beautiful day," he thought, as he walked to his car. He could smell Spring, and the scent was invigorating. His phone rang. "Ellen," he said, looking at his screen. "Wait 'til she hears about this."

But when he answered the call, Ellen was crying.

"Addie," she said. "I've been reassigned. They're calling me back to the Cape." Addie was too surprised to say anything. "Addie, can you hear me?"

"Yes, I can hear you. When do you have to leave?"

"Tomorrow." She said nothing for a while. Addie didn't know what to say.

"I know," Ellen continued, "it's what I wanted, to be put on staff, but man, Addie, to leave right when we're on *this* story."

Addie wanted to say, "There'll be other stories, Ellen," but thought better of it. Instead, he said, "Why don't you tell your editor about it? Maybe then you could hang around until it's finished."

Ellen regained her composure. "No, I have to go. They're

moving people all over the place. That's why they called — the Provincetown bureau opened up and they're giving it to me." She laughed. "I guess they figure if I can last out here I'm perfect for P-town.

"And if I did tell my editor about this story, she'd insist that I not share it with you. I'd never do that to you, Addie."

"But you *were* working on it with me. What were you going to do if we finished it?"

"*When* we finished it, you mean. It would already be done, and they'd run it, believe me, they'd run it. Addie, you've got to finish that story. Promise me."

"All right, Ellen, I promise."

"At least I won't have to deal with Dennison or that creep Caspian anymore. And now you've got to promise me one more thing."

"Which is?"

"That when you do find the treasure, you make sure you lead those two in the opposite direction. Send them scuba diving if you have to."

Addie wasn't sure how he'd accomplish that, but he agreed. Ellen wasn't finished.

"There's just one more thing you have to absolutely promise to do, okay?"

"Okay."

"Marry Verona. And invite me to the wedding."

Addie and Verona were at the Atheneum, looking up at the gold-leaf period that punctuated the building's name. The night before they were on their porch, looking up at the Big Dipper.

"See those stars?" Verona said, pointing to the two at the far right of the Dipper's ladle. "Now follow them straight up," and she pointed to a faint star that was alone in the sky. "That's

Polaris," she said. "It will lead you north."

Addie gauged where the North Star was in relation to the island. From what he could envision, it would lead to town. "Follow the Drinking Gourd," he whispered.

"What's that?" asked Verona.

"Another name for the Big Dipper. It's also the name of a song."

"Sing it for me."

Addie tried, but he couldn't remember the melody. So he sang it to the tune of 'Frere Jacques:'

'Follow, follow
'Follow, follow
'The Drinking Gourd
'The Drinking Gourd.
'Follow, follow, follow
'Follow, follow, follow
'The Drinking Gourd,
'The Drinking Gourd.'

"Is that right?" Verona asked. "It doesn't sound like it would be."

"What, you don't like my rendition?"

"I like you better," she said, pulling him toward her for a kiss.

"Come with me tomorrow," Addie said. "I want to see where the map leads us."

From the Atheneum Addie and Verona walked across Federal Street and up India Street. On the way, Addie told Verona about Ellen's new assignment in Provincetown.

"That's too bad," Verona said. "She was a friend of yours."

"Well, it's good for Ellen," Addie said. "It's sort of a promotion."

"But you had a good working relationship. Will they send another reporter over here?"

"Hadn't thought about that. I suppose so."

Verona wouldn't say it, but if someone was sent over, she hoped it wasn't a woman.

"She made me promise to finish this story."

"Weren't you going to do that anyway?"

"Yes, especially now that you're helping me."

He didn't tell her about the third thing Ellen made him promise.

At the end of India Street, they turned right and walked down Liberty Street toward the Lily Pond. "It really was a pond at one time," Addie told Verona. "It even had a working grist mill. The story goes that a little girl playing with a spoon let all the water out."

"How did she do that?"

"I guess she dug a little trench and that was enough to do it. Gravity took over or something."

They passed Sandy's house, where Rebecca was now staying. They'd be back in a bit. Sandy was cleaning out the basement, and she'd asked Verona and Addie to come by to see if there was anything they might want for their cottage.

A short distance away, Sunset Hill beckoned, home to the Oldest House. Although the original chimney had been destroyed by lightning in 1987 (along with half the roof), it had been meticulously restored. "There it is," Addie said. "The upside down horseshoe."

Although she'd visited the house several times, she'd never noticed the horseshoe before. Funny how you can be looking right at something and never see it, she thought.

As Addie and Verona walked toward the house, neither took notice of the man casually strolling by on Sunset Hill, a man who'd been following them since he spotted them outside the Atheneum. Fortunately for Dirk Caspian, they'd been absorbed in conversation most of the time. Still, he kept his distance.

"Well, that's it," Addie said. "That's as far as I've gotten."

"I thought we were going on a real walk," Verona kidded him.

"Far enough for me," he said. "May as well head back to Sandy's. That will add some steps for you."

As they approached Sandy's front door, Dirk Caspian crossed the street and headed back to town in the opposite direction. Maybe they weren't following Powell's letter; maybe they were just out for a walk. It was worth a shot anyway.

Before opening the door, Verona asked how much of the riddle was left to solve. Addie took the letter from his back pocket, and read:

" 'in the vicinity of a smoky charm
'usually rightside up, but upside down
'the Sunset
'From there, carry the Weight,
'and follow one who catches in the fog,
'from west to east, past healthy cottages three.
'Navigate to center,
'til larboard bound and broadside,
'locate the candlemaker,
'wherein scratched works of white
'appear,
'not the standard eighty-eight,
'but toothsome treasures all the same:'
'The substance of a quest?' "

He stopped there. "Might take a while just to figure this part out," Addie said. "I've tried, but . . . hey, where are you going?"

Verona was off at a quick pace. "To the Oldest House," she said over her shoulder. "Are you coming?"

This time there was no one following them. Back at the Oldest House Verona said, "Read that first part again."

Addie pulled the paper from his back pocket. "(I)n the vicinity of a smoky charm, usually rightside up, but upside down, the Sunset. From there, carry the Weight, and follow one who catches in the fog?"

And Verona began to sing:

" 'Crazy Chester followed me, and he caught me in the fog.' You played that song for me when we started going out. We'd sing it together if it came on the radio. Remember? It's 'The Weight,' by The Band. I'm surprised you didn't think of it."

"I'd never have thought it could be that simple. But what does it mean?"

"Chester is the one who catches in the fog. It says to follow him."

"So where is Chester?"

"Let's walk to the end of the road and see what we find."

The road from the Oldest House curved downwards to another road. Addie smacked his forehead with his hand. " 'Down the sunset.' Of course, Verona — the Oldest House is on *Sunset Hill!*" He looked up at the street sign at the bottom of the hill. "West Chester Street. And here's 'Chester.' We follow it," and he took the paper from his back pocket, " 'from west to east.' " He looked to the right. "Madaket's that way, which is west, so we go this way." He kept reading. " 'West to east, past healthy cottages three.' Wonder what that means?"

Verona stood with Addie at the street sign. She thought

back to the time Addie had taken her on his bus tour: he had driven down this street. "What did you say when you drove down this street, when you were on your tours?"

Addie had to think for a moment to get to this part of his tour, as if his mind had to fast-forward through a mental tape. "And before we get to the Oldest House," he said to himself, "we pass the three houses in a row that were the *original Cottage Hospital!!* That's it, Verona." He took her arm and walked a ways. "And here they are! The 'healthy cottages three.' We're on the right track!"

West Chester Street ended at a crossroads. Verona this time noticed the street sign: 'Centre Street.' " 'Navigate to center,' " she said. "Away we go."

They walked up Centre Street as Addie read: " 'Til larboard bound and broadside, locate the candlemaker, wherein scratched works of white appear.' We're almost there." He couldn't stop smiling. He was overjoyed to be sharing this with Verona, no offense to Ellen. He reached for her hand as they approached the First Congregational Church, and stopped. Step Lane was on his left.

"According to Libby, larboard means left," he said. "Do we go left here?"

"Up ahead it looks like there are a couple more streets on the left," Verona said. "Can you read the riddle again?"

" 'Navigate to center, til larboard bound and broadside, locate the candlemaker . . . .' "

"I think we should follow this street until it turns left. What do you think?"

"Verona, I'd follow you anywhere. Lead the way."

At the Jared Coffin House, Broad Street, a wide, bustling thoroughfare, intersected Centre Street in a graceful turn to the left.

"Broad Street, 'Broadside?' This is our left, wouldn't you

say?" Addie noted, to which Verona nodded and said, "All we have to do now is 'locate the candlemaker,' whatever that means."

They walked down Broad Street, passing BookWorks and The Brotherhood, and continued their stroll, looking for something, anything, to do with candles, or a candle. All they noticed were restaurants, none of them having a name even remotely connected to candles, or candlesticks, or wicks, or wax, and the Town and County Building, which had a court, but no candle. Finally, they reached the Whaling Museum, where Broad Street became Steamboat Wharf. Addie walked back and forth, not knowing what to do. "Do we continue down Steamboat Wharf?" he asked Verona. She motioned to a bench outside the Whaling Museum.

"Let's sit down and think this through," she said.

Addie was frustrated, but happy. "We're so close," he said.

"We are," Verona agreed. "But we've gotten pretty far."

"Thanks to you. I was about to give up for the day."

Which reminded Verona of where they were supposed to be. "We need to get back to Sandy's," she said, standing up quickly. "She's probably wondering where we've been.

"Besides," she continued, "maybe she and Rebecca can help us."

Chapter Eighty-Three

When Verona and Addie arrived at Sandy's house, the door was unlocked but nobody seemed to be at home. Rebecca wasn't in the living room, or the kitchen, nor was she in her downstairs bedroom. Verona hoped everything was all right, that Sandy didn't have to take Rebecca back to the hospital.

"Hello," Addie said. "Anybody home?"

"We're down here," came Sandy's voice through the open cellar door.

"Guess we should have checked the cellar before yelling," Addie said to Verona as they descended the stairs.

Although Verona once lived in this house with Sandy, she hadn't been in the cellar much, only to do her laundry. A lightbulb lit the way on the stairs, but only a couple more illuminated the cellar. Sandy was examining something in the far corner with Digit and Rebecca.

Verona was concerned. Rebecca had already fallen once. What was she doing going down the cellar stairs? Sandy knew what Verona was thinking by the look on her face, and took her aside.

"She insisted," Sandy said. "I told her, 'no way,' but she seemed so sad. She said she didn't want to be stuck upstairs alone. Since you two weren't here, I called Digit on the sly. I figured with the two of us helping her, we'd get her down and, more importantly, back up."

Verona knew how insistent Rebecca could be, and how trapped she must feel not being able to do simple things like walking down stairs.

Digit and Rebecca were huddled together, with Rebecca leaning on Digit's arm. "What are they looking at?" Verona asked Sandy.

"There are a couple of old chairs that used to be upstairs when Rebecca lived here," she said. "The owner before me — who Rebecca sold this house to — must have brought them down here and stored them in one of the old coal stalls. I haven't nosed around here much, as much as I should have, I suppose. But now I'm glad Rebecca came down because if you two didn't want them, I may have heaved them. Now I think Digit's interested."

"You say these originally belonged to your grandfather?" Digit was asking Rebecca.

"My great-uncle," Rebecca said, holding onto his arm a little tighter. "They were around the kitchen table."

"And you're sure you don't mind if I take them?"

"As long as Sandy doesn't mind. They are hers, you know; she owns the house now." Rebecca's head rested against Digit's shoulder. "If you don't mind," she said in a whisper, "it's time for me to go upstairs, or I'll be sleeping down here tonight."

Digit gingerly led Rebecca to the cellar bannister. Sandy held Rebecca's arm and walked beside her, step by step, while Digit was right behind, ready to catch either of them. When at last they reached the top step, Rebecca sank into the first available chair. They all gathered nearby in the living room.

"Took you long enough to get here," Digit said to Addie as

they both sat on the couch. "Not that I'm complaining — if you were here, you might have snagged those chairs. They must be over a hundred and fifty years old. Oh, well, you snooze, you lose."

"I think they're older than that." Rebecca made her way into the living room, slowly. Addie and Digit stood up, but she waved them back down. "I may be old, but I'm not feeble yet." When she sat down, and got her breath, Digit asked her about the chairs. "They were made by my great-great-uncle after he retired," she said. "He was a whaling captain." She looked at Digit. "Your ancestor too, I believe. Captain Hathaway."

Addie looked at Digit incredulously. Digit had never told him that both he and Rebecca were related to Captain Hathaway. Digit couldn't recall whether he knew about the connection or not, and the look on his face confirmed it.

"I thought I'd mentioned it to you when we first met," Rebecca said. "All us old Nantucketers are related in one way or another."

Digit stood up and kissed Rebecca lightly on the forehead. "Now don't get overly sentimental about it," she told him, "it's a pretty distant relation."

Addie wasn't sure he wanted to interrupt. "I've been doing a little research into Captain Hathaway," he said anyway.

"That's right," Digit said. "He's even seen the painting of him." Rebecca raised an eyebrow. "At the historical association," Digit continued.

"They're going to include it in a new exhibition at the Whaling Museum," Addie said.

"I don't believe I've seen that painting," Rebecca said. "But then, I've never been to the Whaling Museum."

"We'll fix that," Digit said. "I'll take you."

"You're sweet," Rebecca told him.

"What's going on in here?" asked Sandy. "Everybody getting all lovey-dovey?"

"Digit and Rebecca are related," Addie said.

"Distantly," Rebecca noted. "Not that I mind. In fact, I'm glad to be related to Digit."

"What's that?" said Verona as she walked into the room. She sat next to Rebecca. "Does that mean I'm related to Digit? You're my aunt."

Rebecca thought she felt her heart skip. This was not the way she expected this conversation to lead. She wasn't ready to confront questions about Verona's lineage, not yet. "Could I ask you for a glass of water, dear?" she said to Verona. Fortunately, nobody else offered to get it. When Verona returned with the water, Rebecca took a long, slow sip, and changed the subject.

"So what were you two up to today?" Rebecca asked Verona. "Sandy was expecting you much earlier."

"We were at the Oldest House," Addie volunteered.

"That's nice," Rebecca said, then added, looking at Verona, "Looking at possible venues? Didn't I just read in the *Looking Glass* that someone had a wedding reception there?"

Verona smiled at Rebecca, and gave Addie a reassuring look. "No, Rebecca," she said, "Addie and I were figuring out that riddle." Rebecca wasn't sure what Verona was talking about, but she didn't care: the subject was successfully changed.

"We got pretty far with it, too," Addie said. "Thanks to Verona." He told the group where the riddle had taken them, pulling out the paper to illustrate, explaining that they'd gotten as far as the Whaling Museum where they got stumped.

"What's the next line?" Sandy asked.

Addie read from the paper: " 'Locate the candlemaker, wherein scratched works of white appear.' We looked up and down both sides of the street; no mention of a candle, or a candle shop anywhere."

"Not these days," Sandy said, "but, Addie, I'm surprised you couldn't figure it out. All those years as a tour bus driver, too."

"Come on, Sandy, what are you driving at?" Digit said, to which they all groaned.

"If you hadn't veered from the official tour monologue so much, you would have remembered," Sandy said. "The Whaling Museum was originally a candle factory. That's the candlemaker."

Addie put his head in his hands. Of course. He remembered the tour script now: "And on your right," he was supposed to say before he turned from Steamboat Wharf onto South Water Street, "is the Whaling Museum, the former Hadwen and Barney Oil and Candle Factory, where they once made spermaceti candles from whale oil." He hadn't taken the bus down Steamboat Wharf in so long he'd forgotten the spiel. He stood up. "Let's go."

"Go where?" Sandy asked.

"To the Whaling Museum. Maybe if we all go, we can figure out the rest."

"Hold your horses, Sherlock, the Whaling Museum's closed for the day," Sandy said. "How much is left of that stupid riddle? Maybe we can figure it out here."

"Good idea," Addie said, sitting back down. "Here it is: 'locate the candlemaker, wherein scratched works of white appear, not the standard eighty-eight, but toothsome treasures all the same: the substance of a quest?' "

"Hold it there," Digit said. "It's a museum. Does that mean what they're looking for is inside? And what's eighty-eight got to do with it?"

"And aren't we supposed to be searching for an old sea chest, anyway?" Addie added.

"Maybe it *is* inside the museum," Sandy offered. "Maybe somebody brought it back."

"It would have been in the paper," Addie said. "That would have been too big a story to overlook: 'Mystery solved! Treasure chest dropped on doorstep of Whaling Museum.' Besides, they wouldn't still be looking for the treasure, they would have been caught."

"Not if it was given anonymously," Sandy said. "One of them could have given it back without telling the other."

"It still would have been in the paper," Addie said. "And, as I said, Caspian and Dennison are still looking for it; Dennison is, anyway. No, something's not right."

"There's still the end of the riddle," Verona said. "That might help. Let's take it a little at a time. 'Not the standard eighty-eight, but toothsome treasures all the same.' " She looked up. "Any ideas?"

"I'm out of ideas," Sandy said. "I'm going back down cellar, make sure we turned out the lights. Digit, do you want those chairs now? It'd be a help; I really am trying to clean out." They both left the room.

Rebecca, who'd been quiet to that point, and even appeared to be dozing, said this to Verona: "Walk over to the piano, Verona, and sit at it." Verona did as she was asked and went over to the old upright. When she sat down, Verona said: "I don't know how to play."

"I don't need you to play, dear," Rebecca said, "just count the keys."

"All of them? The white and black?" Rebecca nodded her head.

"Eighty-eight," Verona said. "There are eighty-eight keys."

"And what are the white keys made of?" Rebecca asked.

"Ivory," Addie interjected.

"Toothsome treasures, indeed," Rebecca said.

Digit and Sandy returned to the cellar; they each took a chair. As Sandy reached up to turn out the light, her foot nudged a box tucked away in the corner. She really did need to clean out down here, she thought, as she and Digit walked back upstairs.

Chapter Eighty-Four

"So Ellen's gone," Dennison said to Caspian. "I just heard from one of my former crew that she's back on the Cape."

"So she won't be helping us," Caspian said. "I'm not sure the other one's bright enough to figure it out, although I did follow him the other day."

"Followed him?"

"From the library to the Oldest House. It seemed to me they were following directions, but I think they were just out for a walk."

"They?"

"He and another woman — not Ellen. You had any luck?"

"Other than 'larboard?' No. You say they were at the Oldest House?"

"Not for long. They turned around and went back the way they came."

Dennison rotated around in his chair so that he faced the window. "You sure they weren't trying to lose you?"

"Not a chance. They were so absorbed in each other, they weren't seeing anything."

Dennison pulled open his desk drawer and took out the letter. "You say you followed them from the library?"

"I wouldn't even have noticed them if they weren't pointing at something on the front of the building."

Dennison smoothed out the letter on his desk. "I don't know whether to call you an idiot or to thank you for following them."

Caspian leaned towards Dennison menacingly.

"Now calm down there, Sparky," Dennison said. "It's right here: 'By wisdom's hall, a period marks the spot.' That has to be the library. And now I *will* call you an idiot. Have you ever noticed the lettering on the front? It's one word, but it's got a period at the end. I always thought that was strange."

"But what about all the clues before?"

"Obviously, they figured them out. Who cares? Now look, right after that it mentions India. Well, the library's on India Street, don't ask me why I know that, but I do. And so you followed them to the Oldest House? Did they go straight there, or follow a roundabout route?"

"I wouldn't call it straight, but it wasn't that long a walk."

"I'm looking ahead here, to where it says: 'in the vicinity of a smoky charm, usually rightside up, but upside down.' Did you take a good look at the Oldest House while you were there?"

"Well, no, can't say I did. Like I told you, by then I figured they were out for a walk."

Dennison tapped keys on his computer, and turned his screen so Caspian could see it. "Here's a picture of the Oldest House. Look at the chimney."

"It's got a horseshoe design, so what?"

"If a chimney isn't smoky, I don't know what is. Which direction is the horseshoe."

"It's," Caspian couldn't believe it, "upside down."

"You should have stayed with them, Caspian. They were

leading you right to it."

"You can't blame me. How was I supposed to know? Anyway, we're a lot farther along than we were." He sat back in his chair, crossed his legs. "What now?"

"Get up and get moving. We're going to the Oldest House."

After-hours at the research library, Addie sat with Libby downstairs. He told her how, with Verona's help, they had figured out some of the clues.

"So you got to the Whaling Museum," Libby said. "Nice work. I'd never have gotten that song. Not my era. Isn't it good to do some research on your own?"

Addie agreed with her. "But there's obviously no treasure there."

"That's where you're wrong. The Whaling Museum is filled with treasures, especially its ivory collection, to which this riddle appears to be alluding: 'Scratched works of white.' If that's not scrimshaw, I don't know what is." She paused, said something under her breath.

"What was that, Libby?"

"Oh, nothing. I was just thinking how ironic it was that you recently brought in that scrimshaw that I was hoping was one of the *Susan's* Teeth. We have three of them in our collection; would have been nice to add another. Anyway, that's neither here nor there. Has Digit unearthed any other treasures of his own?"

"He did, but not at his house, a couple of chairs crafted by his ancestor, Captain Hathaway."

"Oh?"

"They were at Sandy's house, well, at Rebecca's old house. Do you know Rebecca?"

"I know of her. She has quite an island pedigree."

"I'll say. Captain Hathaway's her ancestor, too."

"Interesting."

"Digit thought so." Addie pushed back his chair and put his palms on the table. "Back to work, I suppose. Don't think I'll ever figure out the rest of that riddle."

"You should print it in the paper as a scavenger hunt. Have Merle put up some kind of prize for whoever gets it."

"A *Susan's* Tooth, perhaps?"

"Now that *would* be a treasure."

Chapter Eighty-Five

On the last day of scallop season, Digit Hathaway got to the docks early. Even with the deep freeze it hadn't been a bad year. He was encouraged as well by the number of seed scallops — those that hadn't yet matured into adulthood — he was seeing in his nets. There'd be some kind of season to look forward to in the fall.

As he slowly motored out of the boat basin and into the harbor, he kind of hoped he'd see Lance Willoughby. If he could talk to him, he was certain Lance would tell him that, yes, he did have an older brother, or maybe a cousin. That he couldn't quite picture an image of the two who'd hung out with Caspian gnawed at him. With some kind of assurance from Lance, he could let it go.

It wasn't like him to let something bother him so much, and that ate at him, too. Something wasn't sitting right, and he needed to get it resolved.

Lance wasn't among the early scallopers. Digit went to the spot he envisioned in his mind's eye and let out his dredges.

He fished for over four hours and nearly got his limit. Not

bad. Typical that the fishing would be so good on the last day. He remembered a couple of years back when they let them fish past the official end of the season because there were so many adult scallops still around. Once scallops mature, they only live about a year longer: all those scallops would have died off, or been eaten by crabs, before the next season began; no sense letting them go to waste.

He was ready to head in and began hauling his dredges. Lance never showed up. Maybe he was out at the west end, but Digit doubted it: the fishing hadn't been good out there for a while.

Happy with his catch, he put everything else out of his mind and enjoyed the ride back in. It was cool, and still windy, but spring was here.

By the time Lance Willoughby got out on the water, pretty much all the scallopers were back in. It was getting late; the couple of fishermen still out there would be heading in soon.

He'd been at the Anglers' Club the night before, staying longer than usual and drinking way more than usual. At least that's the impression he gave. Each time he wove to the 'buoys' room he brought his beer with him, pouring most of it down the toilet. By the end of the night he'd racked up a dozen beers, of which he'd drunk two.

But he sure acted drunk, enough so that the bartender made him take a cab home (which he'd planned on — he hadn't driven his truck to the club). As he stumbled down the stairs, his arm draped over the shoulder of a helpful patron, C. C. Dennison shook his head and said to the bartender, "Who is that guy? I've seen him in here before."

"A fisherman. He comes in as the guest of a couple of scallopers."

"I didn't think he acted like a member of this place."

"He doesn't usually drink that much," the bartender said, wiping down the counter. "But I know one thing."

"What's that?" Dennison asked.

"He'll be pretty hungover if he's going scalloping tomorrow."

Which is exactly what Lance Willoughby wanted everyone to think.

Lance made several tows while the other scallopers were still out. As they headed in, he headed up harbor and waited for dark.

He tried a few tows before twilight in case anyone happened to notice him from shore. Just his luck that each tow brought up a mess of scallops. What would Digit have said? "Wango!" He remembered from his first year of fishing, scalloping near Digit and hearing Digit call out, "Wango!" when he got a full basket with each tow. There were more days than he could count over the past ten years when he wished it had been so easy. When darkness fell he slowly motored to the widest expanse of the harbor, cut his engine, and waited some more. After about a half hour, he took off his fishing clothes to reveal the wetsuit he was wearing underneath. He put all his clothes into a lightweight gym bag. He dropped his dredges, pushed up the throttle, and turned the boat's wheel. He pulled the hood of his wetsuit onto his head, put on swim flippers, dropped his fishing boots overboard, grabbed the gym bag, and carefully slipped into the water, away from the direction of his boat. A stolen bike was stowed at the summer home he was paid to caretake, a manageable swim away. His truck was parked at the dock, and there it would stay.

This time he wasn't waiting for the six-thirty boat off-island. He had paid good money for a private pilot to fly him to Rhode Island that night, a pilot not from the island; one who cared only about getting paid, and wasn't too particular about the identity of the passenger.

Besides, if the pilot did talk, he'd say that a state contractor needed to leave the island quickly for a family matter, something about his grandfather dying. And if they asked for his passenger's name he'd have no reason to hide that the man he'd flown to Rhode Island was named Dirk Caspian.

And you know, Lance thought, without his beard and with his hair tied back in a ponytail, he could almost be mistaken for Dirk Caspian, especially by someone who didn't know either well.

And if people came to the logical conclusion that a hungover Lance Willoughby, fishing alone on the last day of scallop season, had a horrible accident and fell overboard, well, it was probably the only conclusion to come to.

Goodbye Lance, he thought as he reached shore and headed toward his getaway bike. It was nice being you.

Chapter Eighty-Six

"CHIEF, WE just got a call. There's something happening out on the harbor, an out-of-control boat."

"What time is it?"

"Twenty-three hundred hours, sir."

Eleven o'clock. Who'd be on the harbor at this hour?

Dennison and three crew members boarded the station's 24-foot response boat and raced up harbor. Fortunately, it was still the off-season, no boats were moored in the boat basin. Had it been summer they'd be negotiating through a field of yachts and sailboats.

In the quiet of the harbor the noise from the outboard motor made finding the wayward boat easy. From a distance, Dennison could see it was going in circles in random fashion. He pulled closer, slowed his engines, and observed. "Get the searchlight on it," he told the mate. It was a scallop boat, but Dennison couldn't tell if there was anyone aboard or not. They needed to somehow cut the engine, but the scallop boat was behaving too erratically to chance pulling alongside. He could wait until she ran out of gas, but if there was someone requiring medical assistance, or if the operator had fallen overboard, they needed to move quickly.

Dennison aimed the spotlight in the dark waters surrounding the boat. Nothing. Of course none of these scallopers wore life preservers; with all the foul weather gear they wore, falling overboard wouldn't be hopeful, especially if someone was fishing alone and had no one aboard to even attempt a rescue.

One of his crew was wearing a wetsuit. As Dennison pulled the 24-footer as close as possible to the moving scallop boat, the crewman jumped into the water away from the vessel, swam cautiously towards it, and waited for its bow to swing around. He somehow managed to toss a line onto one of the boat's forward cleats. Pulling himself arm over arm, he slowly hauled himself onto the boat and killed the motor. The engines of the Coast Guard boat seemed to roar in the sudden silence.

The crew member leaned on the gunwale towards the 24-footer and said, "No one here, Chief. A couple of boxes of scallops, though. Must have fallen overboard." He jumped back into the water, and searched under the boat with an underwater flashlight. He surfaced, again shaking his head. He swam to the Coast Guard boat and was helped aboard.

The 24-footer searched the immediate vicinity and surrounding waters. It moved slowly up harbor and back down harbor, and cruised along both shorelines, its searchlight landing on resting seabirds but nothing else. After three hours, Dennison decided it was best to resume the search at first light, and headed back to Brant Point.

By the time the Coast Guard had arrived on the scene, Lance Willoughby was already in the warm, dry clothes he had waiting for him and was en route to his destination. He was glad for the cover of clouds that night. The bicycle had no light, which was good — he didn't want to be seen. He knew it would be hard for cars to see him, but in the waning hours of March 31, he hoped he wouldn't pass any cars. He didn't. Luck was with him.

It would be pitch dark where he was going, but he knew the spot well — he could get to it blindfolded. He leaned the bike against the split rail fence and walked slowly yet deliberately, carrying the small, Army-surplus shovel that had hung from the side of his backpack. It was time.

As C. C. Dennison felt the warm shower water seep into his muscles, he couldn't help but think how strange it was that another riderless boat was found going in circles in the upper harbor, twenty years after that other boat was found doing the same thing; strange, too, that he was now the one responding. He was certain that Nate Powell had drowned back then, but Caspian was convinced Powell was still alive and toying with them. Caspian had said it again the other day when they'd gone to the Oldest House and tried to decipher the rest of the clues.

"This is all crap," Caspian said. "This doesn't mean anything."

"But there's the chimney," Dennison pointed out.

"And?" Caspian said. " 'Find the one who catches in the fog . . . . locate the candlemaker . . . the substance of a quest?' We're wasting our time. We could look at this for a year and never figure it out."

"But Addie . . . "

"Addie, nothing. Like I said, they were out for a walk." He wanted to rip the riddle in two, but stopped himself. He looked at it, shook his head. "He's playing us. He's watching us, I'll bet."

"How? There's no one around here but us. The only vehicle nearby is my truck."

Caspian turned around in circles and began shouting: "Powell. Powell. Where'd you put it, Powell? Come out, Powell! I know you're out there."

"You know what?" Dennison said. "You're nuts." And he walked back toward his truck. "You coming?" he said over his shoulder.

Caspian stood there, not moving, nostrils flaring.

"Suit yourself," Dennison said, and he drove away.

That night Dennison pondered the rest of the clues, skipping over the words he didn't understand, figuring that if he didn't need the first part of the riddle, maybe he could jump ahead. " 'Not the standard eighty-eight,' " he read aloud, " 'but toothsome treasures all the same.' " It came to him right before the call about the runaway boat. He had taken piano lessons as a child. Why hadn't he remembered it before? Eighty-eight keys. He had asked his teacher what the white keys were made of.

"Ivory," she had said.

Caspian's right, he thought, he's taunting us. Yes, sir, that's exactly what he's doing.

Yess-er-ee, Bob.

Chapter Eighty-Seven

"I THOUGHT you were going to put that riddle in the paper. I wanted to be the first one to claim the prize." It was Libby, calling Addie at the *Looking Glass.*

"Oh, Libby, that riddle was driving me nuts. As it is, I shouldn't be spending so much time trying to figure out that stupid robbery."

"So, you're not intrigued by the riddle anymore? That's too bad. I thought you'd like to know where it leads."

"You mean you've figured it out?"

"Didn't I say I was interested in the prize?"

"Wow! Well, as you say, don't keep me in suspense. Tell me."

"I can't go into it over the phone. There's a lot here. Besides, don't you want to understand each line?"

"I suppose so," Addie said impatiently, tapping his pen on his desk. "When can I come by?"

"Why don't you come right before the library closes; we can have another after-hours session. Does that work for you?"

"It sure does. This is great. Can I bring Verona?"

"Verona?"

"I've mentioned her before. My girlfriend. She's been helping me with this. I know she'd like to hear this straight from the horse's mouth."

After a few seconds of silence, Libby said, "I'll take that as a compliment, I suppose. And, yes, please bring your girlfriend. I'd like to meet the woman with the tenacity to put up with you." Another pause; this time it was Addie who was silent. "Oh, one more thing: I really do think there should be a prize," Libby continued. "This is much better than trying to guess what was in that old safe."

Addie kept his car running outside the cottage and ran inside. "Verona," he called before opening the door. "Verona, I hope you're home." She really did need to get a cell phone, he thought. "Verona?"

"Right here," she said calmly, as if expecting him. "You're pretty excited. Did you make a new discovery?"

"Not yet, but we will. Come on, let's go."

"Where are we going?"

"To the library," he almost shouted as he rushed her out the door.

In the car, Verona didn't ask Addie what was going on. He was so worked up she wanted him to focus on his driving. He pulled into the wine store.

"What are you doing? Aren't we going to the library?"

"I need to get Libby a prize."

"Excuse me?"

"I'll explain later."

Addie and Verona arrived at the research library right before closing. "Aren't *we* punctual?" Libby said. "Verona, I assume?" Verona nodded demurely. "Pleased to meet you." Libby checked the time. "Let me lock up and we can get down to business. What's in the bag, Addie?"

"It's your prize," he said, handing her the bottle of wine.

"How do you know I've solved the puzzle correctly?"

"Oh, I'm pretty sure you have. If not, this is the least I can do for all the help you've given me."

Even though she'd never met her before, Verona thought she saw the stalwart Libby blush.

They sat at a large table in the center of the main room. "Addie told me you've been helping him with this riddle," Libby said to Verona.

"A little," Verona said. "Not much, really."

"It shows you know something about Nantucket history."

"Oh, I'm very interested in that," Verona said happily. "I think it's fascinating."

"So do I, so do I." Libby turned to Addie. "Do you know who wrote this riddle?"

"Somebody named Nate Powell. Don't know anything else about him, other than he supposedly died about twenty years ago."

"Supposedly?"

"Everything to do with this robbery's in the 'supposedly' category."

"I see. Well, whoever wrote this knows, excuse me, 'knew,' his history. I meant it when I said it should be in the paper. This would be wonderful for kids to try and figure out."

"Kids?" Addie interjected. "I can't solve the darn thing."

"A little bit of digging and you'd have it," Libby answered. "Yes, some knowledge of island history would be helpful. So let me be your guide. You say you got as far as the Whaling

Museum?"

Verona nodded. "And that the number '88' referred to a piano keyboard."

"And ivory," Addie interjected.

"Yes, I believe we've already discussed that," Libby said. " 'The substance of a quest?' I'll say. Ivory was a 'substance' brought home from every whaling expedition. Any idea where the clues lead from there?"

"None. But to be honest, I've kind of put this on the back burner."

"Kind of? Addie, a researcher needs to be diligent. Let's continue, shall we?" Libby put the riddle on the table and began to read: " 'Follow, if you will, on a southerly sea to the mighty Main.' Sounds like pirate-ese, doesn't it? Our riddler has a pretty good sense of humor."

"I'm not finding the humor in it," Addie said.

"Verona, will you kindly tell your boyfriend to lighten up and not to overthink things? Which street is directly across from the Whaling Museum? South Water Street, our 'southerly sea.' And where does South Water Street end?"

"The Mighty Main," Addie conceded.

"Main Street, correct. 'Starboard,' as you know, means to take a right, and so we head up Main Street 'Towards the great ocean's Locker.' What building is at the top of Main Street?"

"The Pacific National Bank."

"The Pacific National Bank, right again. You see, Addie? You could have done this on your own."

"But it's much easier having you do it for me."

"At least you're honest. Honesty, yes, integrity . . . I'm not so sure. What say you, Verona?"

"Oh, he's a wise guy, all right," she said, looking into Addie's eyes, "but other than that he's okay."

"Because of you, Verona, I'll continue," Libby said. "As we

know, the Pacific Ocean is the 'great ocean,' the largest ocean in the world, and if the Pacific National Bank's not a locker, I don't know what is. It's also where the safe was found in the first place, a little inside joke, I believe, so I'd say we're on the right path. That bit about Davy Jones is merely a lead-in to the next line," and she stood up, "which we'll continue to investigate *in the field.*"

"Are we going somewhere?"

"We're off to solve the riddle, just like a real scavenger hunt."

The Pacific National Bank was a short walk from the research library. Libby had the riddle in her hand. " 'But heed the sign of Jones's good-natured mate.' And what have we here? How interesting." They were facing the bank. Libby led their eyes to a plaque affixed to the left-hand side of the building. "Thomas Turner Square," Libby noted. "If you read the plaque it says he served aboard which vessel?"

"The *Bonhomme Richard,*" Verona read.

"Captained by John Paul Jones during the Revolutionary War," Libby noted. "Thomas Turner, as you can see, was a Nantucketer on that ship, a ship whose name roughly translates as 'good-natured Richard,' an homage from Jones to Benjamin Franklin and his *Poor Richard's Almanack.* Franklin had Nantucket roots as well, but that's a story for another day.

"Getting back to the matter at hand," Libby continued, "what was John Paul Jones's famous quote?"

" 'I have not yet begun to fight,' " Addie answered.

"Westward ho!" Libby said, leading them up Main Street. "What a beautiful day for a late afternoon walk. Addie, you have a copy of the riddle, don't you? What's next?"

" 'Approach the obelisk/Where cobble meets brick.' "

"An 'obelisk,' as you know, is a four-sided pillar topped with a pyramid shape. See any obelisks around?"

Verona laughed. "Not yet, but just ahead we will."

"We will?" Addie asked.

"Tell him, Verona," Libby said.

"It's the Civil War monument," Verona said.

"Of course," Addie said. "You go by it a million times but you don't really look."

"Too true," Libby sighed. "We miss quite a bit, don't we? And what happens right before the Monument, or, to be more precise, The Soldiers and Sailors Monument?"

"Cars go around it? Or try to," Addie said. "People treat it as a traffic rotary, but it isn't, that much I do know."

"The cobblestones end," Verona observed.

"And the street becomes brick," said Libby, "an experiment from the very early 1900s to see how well bricks would hold up as a roadway. As you can see, they've held up pretty well. Unfortunately, Nantucket suffered through an economic downturn and the brick experiment began and ended here. And soon after the bricks end, so does Main Street. What's next?"

" 'Seek "the end of the whaleroad and the whale," ' " Addie read.

"There's more," Libby suggested. And Addie continued:

" 'A seven-stanzaed plea/Is an elegy/"(W)here the bones/Cry out in the long night for the hurt beast/Bobbing by Ahab's whaleboats in the East." ' "

"Now this is where you'd need help," Libby said, "unless you were a fan of Robert Lowell."

"That name sounds familiar," Addie said.

"If you were an English major it should," Libby answered.

"I was."

"You were telling me about him, Addie," Verona said. "Remember?"

"I was?"

"Yes, how Nantucket inspired him?"

"Excellent, Verona," Libby said. "Robert Lowell was a seminal American poet of the last century, the mid-to-late 1900s, who was twice awarded the Pulitzer Prize. In his young adulthood he came to Nantucket with the hope of starting an artist/writer's colony. That idea didn't pan out, but while he was on the island he did write a pretty well-known poem, or a poem that should be better known, particularly here. The lines you just recited are from that seven-stanzaed poem, written as an elegy to his cousin, who died at sea during World War II: '(W)here the bones/Cry out in the long night for the hurt beast/Bobbing by Ahab's whaleboats in the East.' All you need to know now is the name of the poem to realize where this riddle ends," and as they reached the end of Main Street at Caton Circle, Libby looked over to the left. "The name of the poem is 'The Quaker Graveyard in Nantucket.' "

"Cemetery," Verona whispered.

"Cemetery," Addie answered.

Chapter Eighty-Eight

MIDNIGHT. NOT a light to be seen, not even a nightlight from a house window. Clouds obscured the stars; there were no shadows.

It was perfect.

Lance walked confidently toward the location he'd discovered twenty years before. Sometimes when he was out scalloping, he'd think back on it from time to time, how he'd had no idea where he could bury that old chest when Caspian told them to come up with a place and write it down. He'd thought it was the stupidest idea he'd ever heard of, that instead they should have left the chest and the safe hidden out in the moors for a couple of months until everything cooled down — which, in retrospect, it did — and then put it in the trunk of a car and drive it off-island.

But then, by chance, by sheer luck, he happened across the perfect location.

He had been out for a bike ride, trying to figure out if he even wanted to be part of Caspian's machinations anymore — let those two have it, he was thinking; it wasn't worth going to jail over — when he passed by the Quaker Burial Ground.

He'd heard about the old Quaker cemetery when he'd gone to the Whaling Museum shortly after he'd first arrived on the island. His job hadn't started yet, so he thought he'd learn a little about Nantucket. He listened to a short lecture about whaling and, during the question-and-answer period afterwards, someone asked about the Quaker Burial Ground. "There are hundreds of people buried there," he recalled the docent saying, "but only fifty-six gravestones. Those were the upstart Quakers. The original Quaker settlers didn't believe in tombstones — too ostentatious."

The docent was asked if the cemetery was still in use. "Extremely rarely, if ever," was the reply. "I think the last burial there was decades ago."

When Lance rode by that day, however, a group of mourners clustered around a freshly dug grave.

He knew then exactly where he'd bury the treasure. And when Caspian picked the location — which he was sure Caspian was going to rig in his favor — he'd talk him into his idea. No place could have been better. That was why he hadn't even bothered drawing a map, just wrote the word 'cemetery' on a scrap of paper.

As it turned out, he didn't need to convince Caspian of anything. He lucked into the long straw.

The earth was still fairly loose when he returned with the sea chest a couple of months after the robbery. He had strolled through the burial ground many times before, circling by the grave but never too close. What family the deceased had, evidently, didn't live on the island because he never saw anyone visit the grave after the funeral. In the cool darkness of that Hallowe'en night, before throwing the safe and himself overboard, he carved out the topsoil and laid it aside. He then dug down about two feet, carefully placed the chest in the grave, and replaced the grass and topsoil.

He waited in the dunes near Jetties Beach until six, when he walked to the steamship, not to return for ten years.

When he came back, the plan was to hang out on the island for a while, scope things out, blend in, dig up the chest, and leave.

But he found he liked island life. What was the rush? He had to admit, when he'd first visited the grave after his return the hairs rose on the back of his neck, knowing the surprise that was buried there. The ground looked good, undisturbed, the grass the same color and consistency as the grass surrounding it and the grass that covered all the undulating contours of the graveyard's acreage.

The seasons passed. He fished; he was happy. Once he dug up that chest he'd feel compelled to leave, he knew that. And he didn't want to leave. So the treasure stayed where it was — until he happened upon Chase with his routine rowings to his hoped-for spot, and then reading in the *Looking Glass* about Caspian's plans to excavate a marsh in the place he'd selected.

He could have laid low, witnessed their futile efforts from a distance and watched them leave the island when their digging proved fruitless. But that he knew where the treasure was, and they didn't, sparked a new resolve in him to complete what was started two decades before. He hated to admit it, but he wanted to win, to dig up the treasure and have it for himself. They'd roused something in him, greed, he supposed, and greed won out over the good life.

So why wasn't he going to rub it in their faces? Didn't he, in the end, want them to know where he'd hidden the treasure; witness their despair as he bid them farewell?

No, he wanted them to believe he was dead, that the treasure was still out there, theirs for the taking if only they could solve a riddle.

But they'd never solve it. With any luck, it would drive them crazy.

As he neared the grave, he could feel his heart racing. All those years knowing where it was and doing nothing about it, letting it lie there, his little secret, as untold numbers of people walked through the cemetery, let their dogs run free, bent down to read the names on the few gravestones there. How many of them had walked right over it, stood on it, not knowing that treasure was only a couple of feet down? It seemed a shame to have to dig it up.

But he had to.

His small shovel bit into the earth. He worked at first slowly, precisely, gently pushing the point of his shovel into the grassy roots of the turf, as though it were a ritual, as though there was a preordained method to removing the chest. But his precision and care soon gave way to abandon, as he dug down into the dirt, anticipating the moment when his shovel would find the lid of the chest. Time seemed to be expanding. He knew he hadn't been digging long, but he felt like he had been at it for a while. He thrust his shovel at the dirt, digging in with his heel. He felt the ground with his hand. Had he dug down deep enough? It felt like two feet, but his excitement was probably making it seem like he'd worked longer than he had. He threw himself into it now, wishing he had a longer shovel.

He stopped. He'd hit something. This was it! He shoveled lightly now and struck something that felt like a root. He reached in and felt for the chest's wooden top. What he felt was solid, but scattered. Was it the handle? Had it split? He felt around more. There was a lot of it, whatever it was.

He needed to see. With the beam pointed down he turned

on his flashlight and inspected the hole. What was it? Sticks? He held one up to the light. It looked like a bone. Bones! Panic gripped him. He felt nauseous. Was he digging up bones? What was going on? He pushed the dirt away with both hands and shined the light into the grave. More bones.

He sweated. He shook. He was cold. Calm down, he told himself, make yourself breathe. When at last he felt rational, he again shone his flashlight into the hole. They were bones, all right, but what kind of bones? Were they human? Oh, God, please no. His hand trembling, he felt the dirt for a bone and fingered it. Holding the flashlight close, he made himself look at it. Was it an animal of some sort? He again shone his flashlight into the hole. Yes, he could see it, the bones were small, and look, a tail! Thank God, a tail. What was going on? Did somebody bury an animal here? He'd been by here many times — he never saw any kind of group here at night, some cult.

And where was the chest? Had it disintegrated? Had it contained an animal skeleton all this time? Wait a minute. Was this the right grave? He walked around. There was only one other grave nearby, his marker. He shone the flashlight on the grave's inscription. He had it right. He didn't need to look around. This was it. This was it, dammit.

Breathing heavily through his mouth now, he dug to one side of the bones, then the other. He dug underneath the bones and felt for the chest with his hands, then another shovelful down, then another.

Realizing the unescapable truth, he stopped digging. The chest wasn't there! It wouldn't have disintegrated. It was oak, and well made. It was gone.

Chapter Eighty-Nine

BY DAYBREAK, word spread quickly around the island that a scalloper had gone overboard. When the Coast Guard towed the boat into the town pier, the fishermen immediately knew the scalloper was Lance Willoughby.

Digit didn't need to see the boat to know who it was — he already knew.

He had been waiting for Lance to come in that last day of scalloping. He knew Lance had gone out late because he saw his truck parked down by the docks when he drove by in the late afternoon. A couple of hours later, he went to the shanty where Lance opened, but there was no Lance, and no scallops. He went back to the dock, but Lance's truck was still there. He walked to the Anglers' Club, looking for the fishermen Lance usually had beers with.

"I doubt he went out at all today," one of them said. "He had a rough night last night."

"And an even rougher morning, I'll bet," the other fisherman said. They both laughed.

"Well, his truck's here, and his boat's not in its slip," Digit told them. One of them checked his watch. "Nine o'clock. He'd have to be in by now. Are you sure he's scalloping?"

"Like I said, his boat's not in."

They looked at each other, not saying anything, but thinking the same thing. "Call the Coast Guard," Digit said.

Digit drove his four-wheel drive onto the beach at Brant Point and watched the 24-footer zip up the ink dark harbor. He felt compelled to wait, hoping he'd witness the Coast Guard towing Lance's boat back to the dock. If they came back soon, that would be a good sign — engine failure, most likely; embarrassing but not life threatening. After waiting and watching for two hours, Digit drove away from the beach and went home.

He couldn't understand how a good fisherman like Lance could be so careless, going out, alone, late, still fishing after dark. It didn't make sense. Sure, everyone wanted a good haul on the last day of the season, but it just didn't seem right to him. Lance knew better, he kept thinking. Accidents could happen to anyone, but this seemed too much like wanting an accident to happen.

But why? True, Lance wasn't as forthright as he appeared. The afternoon he'd caught a glimpse of him unloading his catch, and the way Lance moved his head, he knew; it was as if he could see right through his beard — Lance didn't have a brother who'd hung out with Caspian, it *was* Lance. But that in itself didn't mean anything; Lance may have wanted to distance himself from Caspian as much as Digit did. All Digit wanted to do was talk to him about Caspian, see if Lance knew anything about the robbery.

As the first light colored the grey April morning, Digit supposed he wouldn't get that chance now, not after Lance's accident.

If it was an accident.

C. C. Dennison checked the scallop boat's registration. Lance Willoughby. Never heard of him. With the search officially called off, Dennison didn't know whom to notify. Addie would be by to get the information at some point. After it was printed in the paper, somebody would come forward.

Lance Willoughby didn't show up at the airport for his departure from the island. His mind was in a whirl. Where was the chest? He had everything planned so perfectly. Now what? Who took it? Who planted those bones there? Who would do such a weird thing? Caspian? Now *he* was being weird. How would Caspian know? How could *anyone* know? It kept repeating in his head like a drumbeat: who took it? He needed to find out. He needed to think.

After smoothing the dirt back over the grave and replacing the grassy sod as best he could, he rode the stolen bicycle back to the house he cared for. He could stay there a month with no one being the wiser; the owners were gone until summer. It would give him time to think.

Chapter Ninety

SANDY CALLED. "Can you give me a hand moving some more stuff out of my cellar? There are a couple of things that are just too heavy for me. Addie said he'd help, too."

The distraction would be good. Digit couldn't stop thinking about Lance. It wouldn't take much for someone to go overboard, one unexpected slip. If Sandy hadn't called, he'd have probably hung around his house all day, alone with his thoughts.

And that, Digit knew, was seldom a good thing.

Sandy had already brought up some ancient tools from the cellar: an old scythe; a post digger; a wood-handled two-man saw. "Going to have a yard sale," she said. "This stuff and some of my own. There's just two large things I need your help with: an old dresser and some kind of box."

Digit and Addie kitty-cornered the dresser, sans drawers, up the narrow cellar steps. "With a little love, that dresser would look just fine," Sandy said. "But I already have a nice one in my room. Would you like to have it, Verona?"

"I'm afraid our cottage is a bit too small."

"I'll take it," Digit said.

"You need a dresser?" Sandy asked him.

"No, but I might someday. Never know when it might be useful."

"You really are a Nantucketer," Rebecca said to Digit as she walked into the room. "Can't stand to see anything go to waste."

"Which is probably why it was put in the cellar in the first place," Sandy said. "Don't forget that other thing down there."

It was lodged in the darkest corner of the old cellar, like it was part of the foundation. "Looks heavy," Digit said. But as he tugged at it, it came away from the wall freely. "Here, grab the other end, Addie. I think it has handles."

Addie and Digit carried the box into the center of the room, where light from the cellar windows could shine onto it. What appeared to be decades worth of dust covered it. Digit looked around, found a rag, but when he began wiping, the dust filled the air. "Let's take it outside and clean it off there."

They went up through the bulkhead and onto the back lawn, where Digit rubbed off the dust. The box was rectangular in shape with hand-beveled edges. Leather clasps in front had worn away, and appeared to be crusted with dirt. A rusted padlock secured the top, however. Digit continued to wipe away the layers of dust. "This is well made," he told Sandy, who, with Verona, had followed them outside. "Dovetail joints, oak plank construction. Those beveled edges are to repel water." He stood up and took a step backwards to look it over.

"I can get rid of that padlock for you," he said. "I've got some old bolt cutters back at my place, what my father used to call his skeleton key — no locked fence or chained gate could stop him. Hey, looks like there's some lettering on the front."

As Digit leaned over and gently worked on the front, the letters began to emerge. "There's a capital letter," he said. "Looks like a 'V.' " He worked with a circular motion then, in an almost caressing fashion. When the rest of the letters were revealed, Digit stepped back. "You're not going to believe this," he said. "Take a look."

Sandy put her hand to her mouth. Addie walked over to the box, and stopped. "It can't be," he said, looking at the lettering. "It says, '*Verona.*' "

And he caught Verona as she fainted.

Chapter Ninety-One

EXCERPT ***from the diary of Capt. James Hathaway***

My wife was enamored of the name. She has read all of the plays of the Bard, and sometimes, to my pleasure, reads them aloud to me. The ship owners had asked me for suggestions for their new whaler, because of my previous greasy luck, I imagine. I had told her I was going to suggest to them her name, but she would have none of it. 'It might bring bad luck,' she had said. 'I would always feel responsible for any failed voyage.' She turned to the volume she was reading. 'Verona, what a pleasant sounding name. Please suggest to the owners Verona.'

She has been a most worthy vessel, and I have been fortunate to have been her captain. Her owners even made me a gift of a gold ring, embossed with the letter 'V.' She is a lucky ship, and I even luckier to have her. May she continue to be so.

I, however, will not be at her helm. A tragedy has befallen me and I must be off on a new journey. Indeed, I shall not rest until she is found.

Her vision foggy, Verona looked into the face of the one who cradled her head. Where was she? In the background she heard someone speaking:

"You think this could be it?"

"Only one way to find out."

"No, don't do it. I think we should wait. If it is, it's not for us to decide."

Verona felt movement, as though she was being gently rocked. Was Addie rocking her for some reason? She looked up again. Addie didn't have a beard. Who was this? She tried to stand, but felt nauseous.

"Careful there," a voice said soothingly. "You hit your head when you fell. Best to stay down."

"Why are you rocking me?" she whispered.

"That's the boat — it's breezing up."

Boat? This couldn't be. Where was she? The voices continued in the background.

"Let's ask the captain." Verona heard footsteps approach. She couldn't keep her eyes open. "Captain," the voice was in front of her now, "was this the chest you wanted?"

"Does it have lettering on it?"

"Aye, Captain. It says . . . "

"Put it back in the hold, that's a personal chest. You want the one without any lettering, that's the one with the rum in it."

"Our mistake, Captain. We thought because it said 'Verona' it had something to do with the ship."

"It does. Put it back."

Verona again tried getting up. This couldn't be happening. How did she get on a ship, and who was this man holding her? She lifted her head, but it felt so heavy. Maybe if she rested she could figure it out, at least stand and see where she was. She should be afraid, she thought, but for some reason she felt secure, enough to sleep. Maybe if she slept she'd be able to stand. She closed her eyes.

"Best to stay awake," the soothing voice advised her. "Open your eyes. Rebecca . . . Rebecca . . . "

"Rebecca, maybe you can revive her. She passed out cold."

Verona was seated on the ground with her head against Addie's chest. "Wet a facecloth with cold water and bring it to me," Rebecca told Sandy, "and bring me a small paper bag." When Sandy returned, Rebecca handed the facecloth to Addie. "Roll this up and place it on the back of her neck." When he did, Rebecca leaned over. "Verona," she said. "Verona, time to wake up." Verona slowly opened her eyes, which had a vacant cast to them. "Addie, try to move her into a sitting position," Rebecca said gently. "Good. Verona, I need you to breathe into this paper bag. Lean forward, put your head down a bit and breathe deeply into the bag." The voice sounded familiar to Verona, as if she'd heard it her whole life. It was a helpful voice, a nurturing voice, and Verona wanted to please it. She did as she was told.

The grey that had clouded her vision lifted; everything was in color again. She made an attempt to move, but her legs were wobbly.

"Careful there," Addie said. "Let me help you." Placing her arm over his shoulder, he walked her into the house. "You need to sit for a while, have some water," he said. As they walked, Verona let her head rest on his shoulder.

"I had the strangest dream," she told him. "I thought I was . . . "

"Shhh," Addie said. "Tell me later."

"I just have one question, Addie. Were you rocking me?"

"I just wanted you to be comfortable."

Chapter Ninety-Two

"YOU KNOW what this is, don't you?" Rebecca sat on the living room couch next to Verona and held an ice pack to the back of her neck. She pointed to the padlocked box they had brought back into the house.

"I have a good idea," Digit offered. "It's a sea chest."

"That's right," Rebecca said. "My father had one he kept next to his bed; belonged to one of his seafaring forebears. Looked just like this one."

"Well," Sandy chipped in, "as we said outside, do we think this is it? Is this the one everyone's looking for?"

"If it is, I know at least two people who'll be awfully disappointed," Addie said.

"Let me go get my bolt cutters," Digit said. "We'll find out soon enough."

"It doesn't feel right," Addie said. "I don't think we should open it — yet. What if it is *the* chest?"

"There are lots of old sea chests on Nantucket," Digit said.

"But no others with the name *Verona* on it," Addie said. "I don't know, there's something about this chest."

Digit took hold of one of the heavy rope handles. "Let's pick it up and shake it, see if anything rattles around."

"I don't know if that's such a good idea," Addie said, helping Digit lift the chest anyway. As he did he looked underneath. "What's this?" he said.

Digit poked his head under the chest. "Something duct taped," he said. "Let's put this back down." And they lowered the chest onto its side. "Sandy, come take a look at this," Digit said. Sandy bent down to inspect it. "Well, this is interesting," she said. Addie didn't know why, but he thought he detected a hint of sarcasm in Sandy's voice. "What do you think it is?" he asked her.

"I know exactly what it is," Sandy said. "A letter. I thought I'd found all of them."

"What do you mean?" Digit asked.

"When I moved into this house, I used to find letters taped everywhere: inside cabinets, under drawers. I even found one inside the fuse box."

"I don't get it," Digit said.

"The owner of the house before me wrote letters explaining how she came into possession of such and such a thing, like a chest of drawers. Most of the time they were things handed down. I thought she'd left the letters for me, but as I discovered more of them, and noticed how old the tape was on most of them, I realized she had written the letters to herself."

"So she wouldn't forget, I suppose," Addie said.

"Oh, it was charming at first," Sandy said. "And I used to read them all. But they kept turning up — everywhere. It turned into a royal pain in the ass. I even saved them to give back to her, but she didn't want them. She looked at me like she didn't know what I was talking about."

"The ingrate," Digit said, kidding.

"I should have figured another one would turn up eventually," Sandy said. "Well, let's see what this one says. I can hardly wait."

"Looks like it's been stuck there for a while," Addie said. "Who knew duct tape could last that long?"

"As with everything, Addie, if you had only asked me, I could have told you."

Digit used the blunt edge of his pocketknife to work the letter free. They all sat around the coffee table as Sandy opened the envelope. "Ready for this?" she said. Inside were several handwritten pages, and she read them aloud, affecting a strong Nantucket accent:

"This chest was found by me and my friend, Eleanor Starbuck, whose aunt had passed away some years before, leaving behind an old dog that Eleanor brought to her home in New Bedford. When the dog died, Eleanor thought it would be a nice gesture to bury the dog with her aunt.

"Eleanor told me, and only me, of her plan, knowing she'd never be granted permission to disturb a grave to bury a pet without a lot of paperwork and probably lawyers. I went with her to the cemetery at night to help her and to lend my support.

"We each brought a trowel to dig a large enough hole for the dog. Fortunately, there was no one around. Just as we were about to finish digging, Eleanor hit something hard with her trowel. At first, she was afraid she'd hit her aunt's coffin, but I assured her we had only dug down a little more than a foot. We don't know why, curiosity, I suppose, but we both dug a little deeper and uncovered this box. Eleanor knew nothing had been buried with her aunt and thought it very strange that a box should be there. We thought it might be heavy, but with a little work we were able to get it out. By this time, the hole was certainly large enough for the dog, so we placed him in, and pushed the ground back over the grave.

"I had parked nearby, and we quietly carried the box to my car and brought it here. Since it was padlocked, Eleanor wanted

to confer with other family members before we figured out how to get it open. She asked if I wouldn't mind storing it here, to which I said yes.

"Sadly, Eleanor herself passed away several months after returning to New Bedford. I have been waiting to hear from her relations as to their wishes concerning this box, but have yet to hear from them. I decided to write this letter while my memories are fresh."

It was signed, "*Mary Worth.*"

"That's who my ex-husband and I bought this house from," Sandy said. "I've got to say this is the best one yet, better even than the one taped inside the lid of the toilet tank."

"What was that one," Addie asked, "instructions on how to use the plunger?"

"It was a reminiscence of her trip to Niagara Falls."

"You're kidding."

"Would I kid you? Anyway, I never took notice of this old chest when we bought the house. When we divorced, he never mentioned it, so it's been sitting there all these years."

"And how many years would that be?" Addie asked.

"Oh, I don't know, but we bought the house about eighteen years ago."

Addie couldn't control himself. "This is it! This is it!" he said. "It has to be. Who else would bury an old sea chest in a cemetery?"

"What are you talking about?" Sandy asked.

"Haven't I told you? I guess I haven't." And Addie told Sandy and Digit and Rebecca how the riddle ended at the Quaker Cemetery. He looked at their faces, sure of his conclusion.

"How do we know which cemetery this chest was buried in?" Sandy asked.

"Oh, come on, Sandy, who goes burying things in

cemeteries?"

"Umm, yeah, sure," Sandy said. "What a crazy place to bury something. Just don't tell the undertaker."

"You know what I mean."

"How do we prove it? That this is the chest from the robbery, I mean," Digit said. "What was the name in that letter, Sandy?"

"Let me look. Eleanor Starbuck."

"Shouldn't we try to track down her relatives first? It couldn't hurt."

"I don't think any relatives would have buried this chest at the grave," Sandy said. "Who'd do such a thing?"

"Well, old Eleanor buried the family pet there."

"True enough," Sandy said.

"Sandy, is Mrs. Worth still alive?" Addie asked.

"Unfortunately, no."

"Well, there goes that angle." Addie thought for a second. "Okay, so if we don't know which cemetery this comes from — but I've got a pretty good idea — we at least have a name to investigate." Addie looked over at his Verona. "You okay?" She nodded her head. "Can't believe I fainted," she said. "It's not like I haven't seen that name before."

Rebecca took her hand. "It had to have been very unsettling," she said. "It hurt to see you on the ground like that." She looked into Verona's ocean-green eyes, and a tear fell from her own. Verona stroked Rebecca's cheek gently, the kindest touch Rebecca had felt since her own mother comforted her as a child.

A silence settled over the group, as each pondered the meaning of the chest. Addie didn't need to ponder — he knew, as did Verona, that this *had* to be the stolen chest. Digit thought back to the suitcase from the Take It or Leave It and the scrap of paper with *cemetery* written on it. Three pieces of paper, three different locations . . . so there *was* a third person involved.

And Digit Hathaway was pretty sure who that third person was.

Chapter Ninety-Three

ADDIE WENT to the office instead of heading down to Brant Point. He was avoiding Dennison as much as he could, but he did need the information on the missing scalloper. Hal Humphries sauntered over to him.

"You haven't been around here much lately," he said to Addie, "which is good. There's no news happening around here; best to be out and about, where you can *hear* things."

Seeing Hal made Addie think of old newspapers. Of course — why hadn't he thought of it sooner: if it was *the* chest, why not check the old newspapers? There'd certainly be some mention, or better yet, a picture, showing the name *Verona*. Taking Hal's advice, Addie was off to the Atheneum, "wisdom's hall," he reminded himself. Like an old song, the riddle kept circling in his head.

"Thanks, Hal," Addie said, hustling past him for the door.

"You're welcome," Hal said, smiling and shaking his head. "You know," he said, turning to Merle who was working on that week's editorial, "I think he's turning into a reporter."

"Well, he'd better hurry up and report on that missing scalloper," she said. "It's nearly deadline."

"He'll get it in," Hal said, hoping he was right.

Addie went through the relevant issues of the newspaper, familiar now with the stories that accompanied the robbery. The photos from the week of the robbery showed the open door to the old town building, with an empty space where the safe once was, along with a photo of the police chief, but no shots of the sea chest. He looked forward through the issues, more pictures of the police chief, and a photo of the safe, but still no chest.

He decided to go in the other direction, to the happy days before the robbery when the safe and chest were initially discovered in the basement of the Pacific National Bank. The first week, there were pictures of the bank executives standing next to the safe, and during the second week a photo of the football team standing next to the safe. In the third week, there was a picture of the open safe with the chest inside, but the photo wasn't clear; it was hard to make out the shape of the chest, never mind if there was any lettering on the front. He kept scanning forward, but no other photo of the sea chest was published.

Now what should he do?

Of course, he'd go from wisdom's hall to the seat of all wisdom.

"Can you help me find anything about a ship named *Verona?*" Addie asked Libby. Libby arched an eyebrow. "Isn't that your lady friend's name? She's lovely, by the way."

"Coincidentally, yes," Addie said. "I mean she *is* lovely. What's coincidental is that it's also the name of a boat."

"You're full of coincidences these days. Meanwhile, I'm up to my neck researching information for the labels needed for the new exhibition."

Addie leaned over her desk and whispered: "We've got the chest."

Libby looked up and said nonchalantly: "Oh?"

With a big smile, Addie said: "It was buried in a cemetery."

And again Libby said, "Oh?" But added softly: "The Quaker Cemetery?"

"That we don't know."

"Oh."

"But we're working on it. Anyway, the sea chest has the name *Verona* on it."

Standing up, Libby said, "Well, keep plugging away. In the meantime, I'll get you started on our database."

Addie had been at it for about an hour when Libby walked over to him. "I don't believe it," she said. "I was checking information I'd gathered on Digit's ancestor, Captain Hathaway, when I came across this: 'Several successful voyages on whaleship *Verona.*' "

Addie could have hugged her. "Libby, you're a genius."

"Some have said so," she said nonchalantly as she walked back to her desk. She turned abruptly. "I forgot to tell you. The storage facility called this morning and wanted me to tell you they've found another portrait you might find interesting."

"Another portrait of Captain Hathaway?"

"No, his wife."

"You wouldn't happen to know her name, would you?"

"Go away. I've helped you enough for one day — enough for a week."

Addie chuckled to himself over Libby's admonishment to 'go away' when he remembered — he had a deadline to meet.

He hadn't been to see Dennison since Ellen left. He had

already gotten what he could about the empty scallop boat and missing scalloper from Sally Nancy, the former chief at Brant Point Station and now the town harbormaster. Everyone still called her "Chief." She told him about the boat going in circles and being towed into the town pier and there being a couple of boxes of scallops aboard, which were opened and donated to the island's Meals on Wheels program.

But she couldn't tell him the identity of the boat owner, or officially confirm that there was anyone on the boat at the time of the incident. "Although the boxes of scallops ought to tell you something," she said, before adding, "but you didn't hear that from me. The official word has to come from the Coast Guard. How's the new guy doing, anyway?"

"You'd know better than I do, Chief. You're still in touch with the crew."

"Only if they come over here. Dennison doesn't like having me around. He made that clear when I first went over there to welcome him. Fine with me, I've got enough to think about over here."

"I'm avoiding him myself these days," Addie said.

Sally Nancy didn't pry. "Yeah, from what I understand, he's an avoiding kind of guy." And she laughed.

Addie pulled into the parking lot at Brant Point Station resolved to get it over with. Ever since he'd encountered Dennison in that rowboat, he'd been wary of him. Dennison knew Addie knew, and Addie didn't want to dance around the subject. He also didn't want to talk to Dennison about the letter, or the riddle, or where it led. Since they'd found the chest, if it was *the* chest, Addie just wanted to steer clear of Dennison until the whole thing was solved.

Addie was about to knock on Dennison's closed door, when

Boatswain's Mate Mahoney stopped him.

"If you're looking for Dennison, he's out," she said. "How can I assist you?"

Man, if he missed deadline he'd be in big trouble with Merle. Why had he put this off for so long?

"Any idea when he'll be back?"

"Not for a while. They're planning on being out there all day." She saw the concern on Addie's face, the same type of look Ellen sometimes had when she needed help on a story. "Just tell me what you need, and maybe I can help you."

"I was here to get the information on that scallop boat," he said.

"I can help you with that," she said. "Have a seat. I'll get the file."

Mahoney went through the entire file with Addie, including — off the record — that the Coast Guard believed there had been a fisherman on board.

"Can you tell me the fisherman's name?" Addie asked.

"Unfortunately, no," Mahoney said, closing the file. "We need to notify next of kin."

"Can I say that?" Addie asked. "That no name is being released pending notification . . . "

"Afraid not," Mahoney said, standing. "The official word right now is there was an empty boat and an investigation is ongoing."

"But wouldn't the boxes of scallops indicate someone was fishing?"

This guy had done some homework, Mahoney thought. Just like Ellen. Mahoney liked when people did some work for themselves and weren't expecting to be spoon-fed everything.

"What if I can find out some other way?"

"As long as you don't mention the Coast Guard, because if you do, Addie, you'll never get anything from me again."

"Understood," Addie said. "And thanks."

Chapter Ninety-Four

TIME WAS moving quickly. Addie had about an hour and a half to get his story in, but he wanted to check out one more source. If he could get back to the paper with at least an hour to write the story, that would be enough.

"Look, Addie, I don't want my name in the paper."

"You'll be an unnamed source. Come on, Digit, I know you know everything that goes on in the scalloping world."

How did Digit tell Addie that he wasn't so sure about the whole thing himself? Lance was too good a fisherman to make a careless mistake. Still, it could happen to the best of them, but it was going to take some convincing for him to believe Lance went overboard.

Even though he was the one who called the Coast Guard, nothing about it seemed right. It just wasn't like Lance to go out so late in the day. Maybe he was in a state of denial. None of the other fishermen on the dock doubted for a minute that Lance had drowned, but they were the ones who were all jealous of him, anyway. But even Chief Sally Nancy told him she thought it had been an accident. She had seen Lance the night before at the Anglers' Club. "He could still have been drunk when he went out," she told Digit. "He really tied one on."

"Doesn't seem like him," Digit had told her. "Especially since it was the last day of the season. If he had gone out drinking the next night, that would make more sense."

"I agree with you, Digit," she said, "but things don't always make sense, especially when people are involved.

"And nobody ever says it, but you know it's true," she continued. "If you go in the water when you're scalloping, you're done."

"The boat belonged to Lance Willoughby," Digit told Addie, "but you didn't hear it from me. Why weren't you down at the dock when they towed the boat in? You could have found this out for yourself."

"How was I supposed to know about it? We didn't hear about it at the paper until later that morning."

"True — but you still could have gone down to the docks. Scallop season was over; nobody had anything better to do than hang around."

"Well . . . maybe if a certain fisherman had thought to call me . . . "

"Okay, okay. Just don't mention my name."

Addie loved writing on deadline; he prided himself on getting in the story without a minute to spare. This time, there wasn't a *second* to spare. Merle didn't have much time to edit Addie's piece. "Lucky for you, your copy's pretty clean," she said. "Still haven't recovered a body?"

"They're out dragging now," Addie told her. "I can call the station."

"No time. This is good to go. We can follow it up next week."

Hal Humphries stopped by Addie's desk. "That's the way to meet a deadline, Addie," he said, not mentioning that he had assured Merle that he would. "Good story, too." He paused. "Funny how the boat was going in circles just like that one twenty years ago. At least then there was nobody aboard, no body, I mean."

"Nobody's so sure there was anybody aboard this time, either," Addie said. He thought of something. "Hey, Hal, you covered that robbery twenty years ago." Hal nodded. "You don't happen to know of any pictures of that old sea chest, do you?"

Hal sat on the edge of Addie's desk. He leaned down and whispered to him: "You're on to something, aren't you, kid?"

"What would make you say that, Hal?" Addie said with a wink.

"Let me check," Hal told him. "I may have an old file, or I may have thrown it out. You want to tell me what you've got?"

"Aren't you the one who told me to keep quiet about things until I was ready to write?"

"Ouch," Hal said. "You don't have to listen to everything I say."

"Don't worry, Hal," Addie said smiling. "I don't."

Asking the captain of the buoy tender to help hadn't been C. C. Dennison's idea. It had been a crew member, a diver, who had suggested it. Since the tender had finished its work and was heading back to Woods Hole the next day, Dennison went along with it.

They had scoured every area near where the scallop boat had been found and, over a three-day period, had widened the search to pretty much everywhere up harbor. On the last day of the recovery mission, the diver surfaced after his third foray in the area. He pulled his mask up and said to C. C. Dennison,

"There's something down there, but I can't get it up by myself — it's half-buried in sand. Might need some kind of winch."

Was the body weighted down? Dennison thought. "What did you find?" he asked.

"Not sure. It's not a body, Chief, but it looks kind of interesting. I figure since we're here . . . "

"We can't waste time hauling stuff off the bottom," Dennison said. "We're still on a recovery mission."

"Okay, Chief, but there's no body down there. There isn't one anywhere around here. Should we look somewhere else?"

No, Dennison thought, if someone had gone overboard, the tide probably took him. "Let's head back," Dennison said. "We'll ask Woods Hole if we should suspend the search."

That's when the diver said, "That buoy tender that's been here would haul that thing off the bottom no problem."

So here they were, the buoy tender's draft allowing it to just clear the shoal water up harbor, its crane being used to raise some mysterious something off the bottom. The diver attached the chains to whatever it was, and the crane did its work.

When it broke the surface, the crane lifted it onto the buoy tender's deck. Before it landed, one of the crew said, "It's got scalloping gear tangled up in it, but it looks like an old safe."

C. C. Dennison staggered backward and nearly fell overboard.

He knew exactly what it was.

While it was being lowered, its door creaked open, but no chest was inside; only a crab that fell to the deck and scuttled across.

Chapter Ninety-Five

In the early morning, before the first light of dawn, Rebecca woke with a start. It had come to her suddenly, when her dreams led her towards consciousness and the realization forced her awake. It was stupid, she thought, but she remembered now: Eleanor Starbuck was a Quaker.

Eleanor was younger, but they were in school at the same time, and while Rebecca didn't know her well, she knew of her, as everyone knew a little something about everyone on Nantucket in those days. Eleanor had moved off-island after high school, but her family remained, including her aunt who almost lived to be a hundred.

What was her aunt's name? Well, that didn't matter. What did matter was that she was almost certainly buried in the Quaker Burial Ground.

She smiled, feeling good that she could contribute something to Addie's quest.

She couldn't wait to tell Verona.

"You all right, Chief?" C. C. Dennison was pale and sweaty. "Why don't you go below?"

"I'll be all right," he said. "Let's head back. I could use a cup of coffee."

"So could I, Chief. Some find, huh? I suppose we should give that old safe to the historical association."

"No." Dennison didn't realize he had yelled; the crew aboard the buoy tender all looked in his direction. "I mean, let's clean it off. We don't have to give it to anyone — rules of salvage, right? Might be a pretty good souvenir for my office."

"Sure, Chief, anything you say."

Excerpt from the diary of Capt. James Hathaway, July 30, 1846

It was on my last voyage that my beloved went missing. I, of course, knew nothing of this until we were homeward bound, exchanging news with a ship off the Carolinas. The captain invited me aboard and into his cabin, assuming I had already gotten word.

"The news of the accident has surely reached you by now," said he. "I'm sorry you need to travel home under these circumstances."

I had no idea what circumstances those were. Having recently gotten word of the fire that ravaged the town and wharves on July 13, and aware of the destruction caused, I could tell by his manner that he had other, grievous news. Had some new calamity befallen the island? I asked him. "No," said he, but his look was dire. "Then you don't know. I must be the one to tell you then. A packet ship from Nantucket to Boston ran into foul weather near Hull and went aground. She was wrecked in the surf. The cargo was lost, but the passengers were saved by the life-saving crew."

I begged him not to tell me what I feared, that my beloved was aboard that ship. I knew she had been planning to visit her sister in Boston, and that she wanted to be back on Nantucket by the time I returned home. But there was hope; he had told me all the passengers were saved.

He then said words I shall never forget, that all the passengers were believed to have been saved, but upon their arrival at the Life-Saving Station one passenger was unaccounted for, my beloved.

I wept. Composing myself, I told him I must be off immediately. Before I took his leave, he told me this: "I know the captain of that packet ship. When he returned to Nantucket, shortly before I was to leave port, he assured me that all passengers had been rescued, and that no one had fallen from the life-saving boats. He said there was some confusion as passengers were taken ashore and crews returned to the wreck, and that the operation took hours. When your wife was discovered missing, they went back to the wreck but found no one. He interviewed every passenger and crew member and was assured she had been in one of the first boats to go ashore.

But she has not been found since?' I asked him. He did not want to answer. "No," he said. "But at least there's hope."

We set sail immediately. If I slept at all I must have done so standing up. The trip home from the Carolinas seemed interminable. As we sailed into Nantucket, I did hope she would be there, and even allowed myself to entertain the thought that she would have spied my ship from our roof walk and rushed to meet me at the dock, but of course she was not there. How could she have been? The North Wharf was gone. There was barely a piling to tie to. There was nothing left of the town from the docks as far as the eye could see. Still, men were already hard at work, rebuilding.

When I later saw our friends and acquaintances I did

not need to ask if they had seen her, their downcast eyes revealed the sad answer. They mourned for me but also for their island. No one is sure if Nantucket will ever recover.

I, however, refuse to give up hope and sail to Boston on the next packet ship. I doubt I will sleep 'til then. I walk the paths on the far outskirts of town, away from the ruins, but on the wind is carried the stench of burnt oil.

With Addie on deadline, Verona rose early to walk the quiet streets of town. It was still dark, there was no one around, and she could hear her footsteps padding on the brick sidewalk. A morning mist emanated from the docks and crept up Main Street, seeming to swirl around the lampposts and over the wooden benches as it journeyed through the old town. Before it spread to upper Main, the dawning sky was clear and Verona spied the morning star. Although it was nearly sunrise, a few streetlights remained on and lent a firefly's glow to the haze that now began to obscure the houses around her and envelop her in its grasp. Verona had walked these streets so often that her pace remained steady, even though the fog thickened.

The murky streetlights seemed to dim as she walked further into the fog. This being early morning, she was confident she wouldn't bump into someone, but then . . .

. . . from the periphery of her eye she sensed a figure. Was it a streetlight? No, it had form and appeared to be moving. The silhouette came closer, approaching her. They crossed paths just under a streetlight, and although the light was like a fading flashlight, she made out what the figure was.

But it couldn't be.

It was a man, about her age, but there was something about him that made him seem ancient. In the fog she couldn't quite tell, but his clothes seemed odd, out of place. Was he walking toward her, or was he a shadow? He seemed to be reaching out to her, but she couldn't see. Should she approach him? Did he need help, or was she seeing shapes that weren't there? She stopped, and reached out, but whatever had been there, if anything, was gone.

"Curious," she said to herself as the fog lifted and she walked home.

Chapter Ninety-Six

When the *Looking Glass* hit the streets that afternoon, pretty much everybody on the island knew about the fishing mishap, including the name of the missing scalloper — those who bought a paper did so only to make sure the reporter had his facts straight.

When there were no calls the next morning, Addie knew he'd gotten it right. Hal Humphries stopped by his desk and dropped a manila envelope onto it. "You might be interested," was all he said and walked away.

Addie looked inside the envelope and pulled out a black and white photo of the sea chest on display in front of the Pacific National Bank. "Merle, is there a magnifying glass around?" Merle took one from her desk's top drawer and handed it to him. There it was, small but clearly legible: '*Verona*.'

"Hal, you're beautiful," Addie called to him. "Where did you get this?"

Hal sauntered over. "I had taken some photos at the time. This one didn't get into the paper. Is that what you were looking for?" Addie nodded.

Hal spoke softly to Addie. "You think you've got a story?"

"I might."

"Maybe it's time for the three of us to take a look at what you've got," Hal said. "You, Merle, and I."

Wearing a baseball cap and sunglasses, Lance Willoughby parked his bicycle outside the offices of the *Looking Glass*, put down exact change for the newspaper, took a copy and walked back outside without talking to anyone. He tucked the paper inside the jacket he had borrowed from his client's closet, and bicycled back to the house he was caretaking.

He went out onto the back porch — the porch that afforded the perfect view of the upper harbor — opened the newspaper, and read Addie's story. "Perfect," he said aloud after he'd finished the story. "This time I'm really dead."

"Are you?" said a voice that startled Lance so much, he just might have had a coronary then and there.

Chapter Ninety-Seven

"SO LANCE, pretty quick resurrection. When's your next miracle?"

Lance was frozen to his seat. It was the last person he expected to see.

"Although without the beard and long hair, I'd say you reverted to your former identity pretty seamlessly, right, Nate?"

"How," Lance was having trouble speaking, "how did you find me?"

"Quite by accident," Digit said as he pulled up a chair. "My friend works at the paper; in fact, he wrote the story about you in this week's paper. Did he get it right?" Digit didn't wait for an answer. "I always park around back with the employees. I was about to walk into the newsroom when I saw you through the door. If you had looked around, you might have seen me, but you were pretty intent on getting out of there without being noticed. That was my first clue. But it was the way you moved that gave you away, that little hitch you have whenever you turn. I used to notice it whenever I was scalloping near you."

Now Lance spoke up. "What are you talking about?"

"Oh, it's not much," Digit said, "nothing to worry about. If I hadn't been working around you the past ten years, it wouldn't even register. Funny, though, isn't it, what you notice about people? There are probably little weird things about me that I'm not aware of, not that I'm saying you're weird, or anything." He looked at Lance, but Lance didn't answer.

"Anyway," Digit continued, "since you were riding that rickety old bicycle it was pretty easy following you out here. I knew you wouldn't be driving your truck, since it's still parked in the town lot; keys are still in it, too, in case you wanted to know. As soon as you hit this driveway, I knew it was you, because I know you take care of this house and that the owners are never here until the end of June." Digit waited for Lance to say something, to deny everything, but he knew there was nothing to deny.

"You know," Digit said, "without the beard it's easy to recognize you now as one of Caspian's old friends: time does have a way of changing people's appearances, don't you agree?"

Lance was silent. He'd never officially been introduced to Digit when he'd lived on the island the first time. Maybe Digit didn't know everything. He started to think of things he could say to cover his actions; tell Digit falling from his boat was such a shock he developed a temporary case of amnesia. That sounded pretty good, actually. Bringing up Caspian was just a lucky guess: Digit couldn't possibly know about his involvement in the robbery.

"Of course, if I hadn't known about the sea chest, I probably wouldn't have figured it out. And even with that, it wasn't until Dennison, or Chase, or whatever his name is, came rowing after us when we were checking out his map that things began to fall into place."

Lance froze, hoping Digit hadn't seen him that day, watching the whole thing through binoculars. He wasn't sure why Digit and his friend were out there that afternoon, but it was a deciding factor in planning his getaway. Digit kept looking at Lance as if he expected a full confession. Well, he wasn't going to get one.

"You know, the whole island believes you're dead," Digit said finally. Lance inadvertently sat up straighter, as if to acknowledge to himself how well his plan had worked. "But," Digit continued, "I never did."

"No?"

"Okay, maybe at first I thought you might have drowned, but after I slept on it I wasn't convinced. You've got Chief Sally Nancy convinced, though, which is a pretty good feat. Yes, I guess you should feel pretty good about that. You may have gotten away with it, too, if I hadn't seen you just now."

"And just what am I supposed to be getting away with?" Lance wanted to ask, but he continued his silent stance. He hoped Digit was nearing the end of his monologue. But he wasn't.

"You see, if I'd believed you were dead, when I saw you at the newspaper office, especially without your beard, I'd have thought I was seeing things, that you were probably somebody else. But you're not dead, and I wasn't seeing things."

Just what did Digit know? Without thinking, he blurted out: "What, you going to turn me in?" As soon as he said it, he wished he hadn't.

"Why would I turn you in? You do something wrong?" He paused for a second. "I wish you had willed me your boat and your truck, though."

"I'll give them to you. Take them. You said the keys were still in my truck. It's yours." Take anything you want, he thought. Just go away.

"Even though you're dead, I think it would still be looked upon as stealing. Speaking of which, you ever find that chest?"

Lance's eyes narrowed. What did Digit know?

"I know this," Digit said, "you didn't find that chest. So let me see if I've got this straight: you, Dennison, and our old friend Dirk Caspian steal the old safe and sea chest. Why, I don't know, but you can tell me when I've finished if you want. For some reason, each of you comes up with a plan to bury it. You make maps. Then, twenty years later, two of you come back to the island to dig up the treasure; *you* didn't come back, of course, because you were already here. Dennison believes the treasure is where he planned to bury it; Caspian goes to great lengths to hide the fact that he believes the chest is buried in the marsh off Bear Street. He should have talked to me: I could have told him that if it was buried there, he'd never find it — the marsh would have swallowed it up long ago."

"What an idiot," Lance thought. "They're both idiots." To Digit, he remained mute.

"And *we* both know that Dennison's preferred spot was a disaster as well. Which leads us to a third spot, a place identified only as 'cemetery' on a scrap of paper."

Lance sat frozen. How did Digit know all this? This couldn't be happening. And when Digit spoke again, Lance thought he was in a nightmare.

"But when you got to the cemetery, the treasure was gone. Am I right?" Lance stared at him, but said nothing. "I just want to know," Digit asked, "what did you think was in that chest that was worth such an elaborate scheme?

"The *lengths* you all went to," Digit continued, "Dennison changing his name; Caspian inventing an archaeological dig; and you, living for ten years under an assumed identity. I have to admit, you were all pretty creative and went to a lot of trouble, but for what? If only all of you had put your brain power to good use."

Lance suddenly seemed smaller. "You were a good scalloper, Lance, you should have stuck with that.

"Of course now you can't even do that, being dead and all."

Chapter Ninety-Eight

THE REASON Digit went to see Addie at the paper was that he couldn't wait to show his friend what he'd uncovered. Continuing to sort through the artifacts in his attic, he found an old leather-bound journal. The leather was worn and cracked in places, but the journal was pretty well preserved. He carefully opened it and found it was the journal of his great-great-great grandfather, Captain James Hathaway. The pages were yellowed in places, but intact. He began reading, and couldn't stop until he had read it all.

What he discovered was fascinating, and emotional. Reading the thoughts of his ancestor was revelatory on so many levels, especially when he realized that the sea chest stolen twenty years ago was Captain Hathaway's, and that it was now, of all places, in Sandy's living room.

But he didn't tell Lance any of this. He did tell him, however, about the suitcase.

"I think it was at the Take it or Leave it," he said. "Anyway, there were these maps inside, sketches really. It didn't take us long to figure out that one of them was the exact spot where

Caspian was doing his digging."

"Us?"

"Oh, yes. We've been having fun with this, sort of a parlor game." He paused, waited to see if Lance wanted to say anything, and when Lance didn't, he continued.

"The other map was more elaborate, with depths delineated, and a compass rose, and, like the other one, a tell-tale 'X.' 'X' marks the spot, right, Lance, although in those two instances, it didn't."

Lance remembered now, the maps. He'd forgotten all about them, hadn't paid much attention to them once he was put in charge of burying the sea chest. What had he done with them? "Where did you say these maps were found?" he asked Digit. Again, once he'd said it, he wished he hadn't.

"An old suitcase, found at the dump. You know, leather, with straps, inside pockets."

The suitcase, the one he'd bought for a dollar at the Hospital Thrift Shop. He thought it might come in handy if he was heading off to college. But that never happened. He could see it, stowed in the back of the closet only to be forgotten. He remembered, too, writing the word 'cemetery' on notebook paper, figuring he'd explain what it meant to Caspian. He'd never have thought that suitcase would turn up twenty years later and ruin everything. How could little scraps of paper have meant anything to Digit?

Digit could almost see the wheels turning in Lance's head. Rather than let him suffer, he continued: "It was the other map, the one with detail, that did it. I knew pretty much where that shoal was. We figured, let's go out there with a shovel and see if there's anything there. We really didn't know what any of it meant. We were convinced at the time it was a coincidence that the first map was exactly where Caspian had set up his little excavation project.

"And if Dennison hadn't come rowing after us, it all would have meant nothing. It would have been one step onto that shoal and out of there, with no way of knowing who drew that map, or why.

"Plus, there was no way of connecting anybody to that little scrap of paper. The other two maps and who drew them became obvious in a hurry, thanks to Dennison, but what did 'cemetery' mean?"

For a moment, Lance had a hopeful look, a look that said Digit couldn't tie him to anything. But the look was fleeting.

"But inside that suitcase was another part to the puzzle that turned out to be the one that eventually pointed to you — and I do mean eventually, because at first it didn't mean anything to me either. It was an envelope, nothing inside, but addressed to a Nate Powell." Lance flinched, but hoped Digit didn't see it.

Digit went on. "Again, Dennison to the rescue. When Addie got a copy of that phony letter from the estate of Nate Powell, I started to remember. The name seemed a little familiar, but I didn't know how. It wasn't until I saw you on the dock, and that little hitch when you turned, that I really remembered: you were one of Caspian's friends twenty years ago. We met once, on the street. Caspian introduced me to you, do you remember? No, I wouldn't have remembered it either except for that hitch. I noticed it then when you walked away with Caspian. Strange how the littlest, insignificant things can be so memorable, although I didn't think of it again until you turned to pick up a box of scallops on the dock that day."

"So what?" Lance said. "I wasn't even here twenty years ago. This guy Caspian probably had loads of friends. My name's Lance Willoughby."

"*And* Nate Powell. What you don't know is that after I met you on the street that day, I was talking to another person I know — he opens scallops for me now, you might know him, Roland

Hussey? but you've never been to my shanty, have you? — and Roland told me that day that he worked with you at the Sail Loft, said you were pretty quiet. Just to make sure, I asked him again last week if he remembered a Nate Powell. He thought about it a while, and he not only remembered your name, he remembered my asking about it twenty years ago. He's got a real good memory for dates, and names."

"You ever think he wasn't talking about me?"

"Come on, Lance, stop pretending. And by the way, Caspian never had loads of friends, he rejects friends as quickly as he makes them. I should know; I was one of them." Lance reflexively nodded his head. "Now where was I?" Digit continued. "Oh, yes, that scrap of paper with 'cemetery' on it. Means nothing on its own, but put together with the two maps — three pieces of paper, three different people. That's Caspian, Dennison . . . and you."

Lance began to say something. "Don't even try, Lance," Digit said. "Faking your own demise kind of pulls everything together — if you're dead, you don't have to share anything with anybody. But I have to ask again: just what did you think was in that chest that was so important, or more likely, so valuable?"

It all seemed so pointless now. Digit was right, he went to an extraordinary amount of effort — for what? His voice hoarse, he said quietly: "I don't know what we thought we'd find. I suppose that's what made it seem like such an adventure, the not knowing. Caspian thought it contained ivory."

Digit tried not to laugh. He felt sorry for Lance. He exhaled through pursed lips, and said, "I know what's inside that chest, Lance, and it's not ivory."

"You say you have the chest?" Lance said.

"I never said that," Digit responded. "All I said was I know what's inside it."

"And are you going to tell me? After all this?"

"I believe you can read all about it in next week's newspaper," Digit said, rising to leave, and adding, "If you're still here, of course."

Chapter Ninety-Nine

MERLE DIDN'T generally meet reporters in her office unless it was something important. Addie had only been called in once before, when he got the verdict wrong in one of his first court reports, writing that someone had been found guilty, when the judge had continued the case *without a finding* for one year. Merle had helped Addie with the correction — and the phone call to the aggrieved — which cemented to him that he needed to pay attention and get his facts straight, particularly when people were involved. When Addie wrote his first obituary, Merle was firm: "Double check you've got the name spelled correctly. For most people, the only time they appear in the paper is when they're born, get married, and die. The least we can do is get their names right." Walking back towards Merle's door, Addie felt as if he was going to the principal's office.

The door was open. Merle sat behind her desk. Hal was seated to her right. "Come in, Addie," Merle said. "Close the door. To what do I owe the pleasure of this tête-à-tête?"

Addie hesitated before speaking. He hadn't yet told Merle of his interest in the robbery. He was glad Hal was there. "I've talked to Hal about it . . . . " Hal raised a bushy eyebrow. "It's about the robbery."

"Robbery?"

"The one from twenty years ago," Hal Humphries told her. "I gave him some background."

"I've been working on it on my own time," he assured Merle, "after deadline, on weekends."

Merle gave him a serious look. "There are certainly other stories that are far more important than an old robbery if you are looking to spend extra time: our sewer system is outdated; will our water supply support the amount of development going on; at what point will we need an additional power cable from the mainland?"

Hal helped him out. "He hasn't been spending a lot of time on it. I've been his sounding board. In fact, since the whale washed up he hasn't even mentioned it."

"Some things just recently fell into my lap," Addie said.

"Oh?" Merle said. "Now that you have my interest, tell me more."

Addie told Merle how C. C. Dennison kept talking about the robbery when he went around for the weekly Coast Guard report; about the suitcase with the maps, and how Dennison seemed more interested than he should have been in a location that coincided with one of the maps; how he and Digit were intercepted by Dennison — in a rowboat — when they went out to see if the treasure was in fact buried in that location; how Dennison's real name is Conrad Chase, and that he had a copy of a letter sent to Chase, giving clues as to the location of the stolen sea chest. That got Merle's attention.

"Do you have that copy with you?" Merle asked.

"No, but it's here. I can get it for you." He waited.

"Well, go get it," Merle said.

Addie returned with the letter and all his notes. "So this is the letter?" Addie nodded. "And Dennison, er, Chase gave it to you?"

"Not directly." Merle raised both eyebrows. "He gave a copy of the riddle to Ellen, after Ellen gave me a copy of the letter you have now."

"Ellen?" she asked. "Ellen who works for the *Advocate?* She's our competition. I don't know about this . . ."

Hal jumped in again. "Blame me, Merle. I got Addie interested in this. I thought it would be a good way to hone his research skills, learn how to search back issues of the paper, develop interview smarts. It was an old, old story. He'd get to know a bit of the history of the island, I figured. Never thought it'd be pertinent again. And, Merle, it wouldn't be if Addie hadn't done some damn good, nose-to-the-ground background work.

"Besides," he continued, "you know and I know it's good to have a rapport with other reporters, build up a friendly competition. Keeps you on your toes. Anyway, the *Advocate* won't be interested in this story. They barely cover the island anymore; all their stories are current. They don't really care about island history."

"And anyway," Addie said, "Ellen's gone."

"Gone?"

"Gone. To P-town; she got reassigned."

"Probably for the best, for you," Merle said. "Addie, it's okay to fraternize with other reporters — as Hal said, it's good to develop a rapport — but don't share sources, or research. Why would advertisers bother with us if they can find the same articles in the *Advocate*, which has a far larger distribution?" Addie looked down at his notes. "Enough with the lecture," Merle said. "What else have you got?"

Addie told her everything, from figuring out the riddle to finding the chest.

"Hal just gave me the piece I was looking for," he said, looking at Hal. Hal's expression remained deadpan. "It's definitely the chest. We have it."

"We?" Merle asked, looking over the rim of her glasses.

"It was in the basement of Sandy's house. It was left there by a friend of the former owner."

"How do you know it's *the* chest?" Merle asked.

"Because of this," and he showed Merle the photo Hal had just given him. "Oh," Addie continued, "you'll need this," and he handed her back her magnifying glass. "Look at the lettering on the front of the chest."

"It's hard to make out," Merle said. "My eyes have seen better days. Here, Hal, what does it say?"

Hal put another pair of reading glasses on top of the ones he was wearing. "It looks like a 'V'. Does it begin with a 'V'?" Addie nodded. "Ver . . . Vera . . . No, it's 'o', Vero, well, we know it's not Vero Beach," and he laughed. "Or is it?"

"It's 'Verona,' " Addie said.

"Isn't that your girlfriend's name?" Hal asked. Merle followed with:

"Isn't it about time you two got married? But that's beside the point. Are you absolutely certain the chest you have is the same one that's in the photo?"

"Only one way to find out," Hal said.

"Which is . . . ," Merle said.

"Open it," Addie said.

"That's not exactly what I had in mind," Hal told Addie.

"Sorry, Hal," Addie said. "Got a bit impulsive there."

"We take the chest to the historical association for verification."

"Is there anybody there who would know?" Addie asked.

"You ought to know," Merle told him. "I believe you speak to her quite frequently."

"Libby," Addie said.

"Precisely," Merle said.

Chapter One Hundred

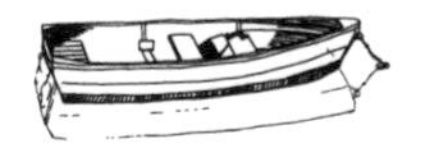

LIBBY BARELY looked up when Addie entered the research library. "Again?" she asked, looking over the top of her glasses.

"Getting to be my regular stomping ground."

"That's *stamping* ground," Libby corrected. Honestly, what was becoming of the language? "Nice story on the missing scalloper, by the way. Terrible tragedy. Lance Willoughby. Don't think I knew him."

"He's not dead yet," Addie said. "Officially, that is."

Libby bristled slightly at Addie's impertinence. "So, is this a social call?"

Addie handed her the photograph of the sea chest. "If you have a magnifying glass, you'll see why I brought this." Libby took a library-issue magnifying glass from her top drawer.

"Is there something in particular I'm supposed to see?"

"Can you see the lettering on the front of the chest?"

"Barely. Spare me the suspense. What is it?"

Addie walked around to stand beside Libby and held the magnifying glass over the lettering. "Look, it says, 'Verona.' This is the ship's chest, Captain Hathaway's chest, the one stolen twenty years ago."

Libby put down the magnifying glass and looked up at Addie. "This isn't a new photo."

"No, Hal took it twenty years ago, when the chest was still on display and before it was stolen."

"We have been busy, haven't we?" Libby took off her glasses and sat back in her chair. "And how may I help you?"

"We were wondering if the historical association might have a record of what's inside the chest."

"A bill of lading, perhaps, or some document relating to the ship's provisions?"

"Yeah, sure."

"Try to say, 'Yes,' Addie, it sounds more professional. I doubt we have anything, but I'll look." She polished her glasses. "Any new riddles to solve?" she asked.

"Just this for now."

She pretended to sigh. "The research librarian is always the last to know. I'm sure I'll read all about it."

"I couldn't do it without you, Libby."

"To that, I'll agree. Which reminds me, I need to get that oral history filed away. Are you going to finish listening to it or not?"

Addie slipped on headphones and advanced the tape to where Cy was talking about the robbery. "I mean they say it was a robbery . . . but whoever took it didn't know what they had." He chuckled. "No sir, couldn't have, but I wouldn't put it past whoever took it that they thought they *did* know what they had. I was pretty sure who took it, too . . . " Now it was getting interesting, Addie thought. " . . . but I was wrong about that, had to be. Now who I *thought* took it was book smart, see, college educated, but that doesn't make him *smart*. I ought to know, I worked with him, well there (pronounced, 'they-yah'), he worked for *me,* for the public works department. Yessuh, book smarts but no *common sense,* know what I mean?

"The reason I thought he took it was because I know what's in it. Used to work for the bank, I did, night janitor. I'd seen that safe in the basement for years, never gave any thought to it; it was stowed off in a corner somewhere. Wouldn't you know one day when I was coming on work they had the safe open, the bank officers of the time. I wasn't much interested, but they called me over. Sure, you hired me, it's your dime, you know? Well now, it was the damndest thing. You know what was in that safe? . . . "

And the tape stopped. Addie whipped off the headphones. He looked at the machine. He looked at the tape. It was at the end! He flipped the tape over and played it, but there was nothing on it. This couldn't be happening. He went up to Libby with the tape and tape player in his hand.

"Something's wrong," he said to her. "There has to be another tape. Something's missing."

"Don't look so sad," Libby said to him. "There are other tapes. Here, let me take a look." He handed it over. Libby inspected the tape and typed something on her computer. "I see," she said.

"What do you see?"

"This tape is incomplete. There are a few like that. Either something went wrong with the recording, or they simply ended the interview there with the expectation of finishing it in the future. That could be it; it just might be incomplete. To whom were you listening?"

"Cy," Addie said.

"I guess that's it, then. He won't be doing any more interviews."

"I guess not."

"Cheer up. By the way, have you checked out the other portrait yet?"

Addie was still thinking about Cy. What was Libby talking about? He looked at her quizzically.

"The painting of Captain Hathaway's wife."

"I'd forgotten about it."

"That might take your mind off this. And here's your photo. We don't have records regarding that particular sea chest. Wasn't it from the bank?"

It sure was. Cy had just confirmed it.

"You might want to check there. Keep in mind, Addie, whatever you're looking for might be somewhere still waiting to be uncovered. Research isn't for the faint of heart."

Chapter One Hundred One

When he got back to the paper, Digit was waiting for him in the newsroom. "Everybody okay?" Addie asked.

"Why wouldn't they be?"

"It's just that you hardly ever come here."

"This couldn't wait. Is there somewhere we can talk?"

Merle and Hal had just left her office and were back in the newsroom. "Merle," Addie said, "do you know Digit Hathaway?"

"Know him, he played football with my son."

"Hello, Mrs. Welfleet," Digit said.

"I think you're old enough to call me Merle," she said. "What brings you in here?"

"Just saying hi to Addie. I've got something to show him."

"Well, show away."

"If it's okay, Mrs. Welfleet —Merle — mind if I spring him for a bit?"

"Paper's out. He can do what he wants."

They left the office by the back door and sat in Digit's truck.

"I meant to bring a photo with me," Addie said. "It pretty much verifies that we've got the missing sea chest."

"Oh, I know we've got the right chest," Digit said. "And we don't need a photo, I've got real proof. That's why I came to see you; I couldn't wait."

"What is it?"

"This," Digit said, and he held up the journal.

"Can I see it?"

"Not here. I'd rather go somewhere private, where we can talk."

Digit drove down the Milestone Road and out behind the airport, taking a long dirt road down to the beach. On the way, Digit told Addie about his discovery.

"It was at the bottom of a box of things that I thought would be useless. I almost took the whole thing to the dump, but, boy, am I glad I didn't. Wait 'til you see it.

"Oh, and I talked to Lance Willoughby." He said it so matter-of-factly that it didn't at first register to Addie. When it did, Addie said:

"He's alive? I mean, you couldn't have."

"I did, although he looks a little different now; he shaved his beard."

Addie still couldn't believe his friend was being so nonchalant. "What happened?" Addie asked. "He didn't drown?"

"No, he didn't drown. I'm not sure how he did it, but he went to a lot of trouble to have Dennison and Caspian think he's dead, which, come to think of it, they probably do. Let's let them think that way for a while — couldn't happen to two more deserving people."

Addie began thinking about the implications of what Digit just told him: there was a story there. Digit interrupted his thoughts.

"Don't go getting carried away. Take a look at this; I think you'll find it a lot more interesting than Lance Willoughby, may he rest in peace." He handed Addie the journal. "I put a bookmark at the pertinent page. Just be careful with it, okay?"

And Addie began to read:

'I had to leave Nantucket. I felt I was going mad, seeing apparitions in the fog. I was fortunate to secure passage not on a packet, but on a fishing boat bound for Gloucester. After three weeks searching the streets of Boston, I found my beloved working at the seaman's sanctuary in the North End. She told me a most fantastical story. After her packet ship had run aground and wrecked, she was in a state of shock. She didn't remember being rescued. Evidently, she wandered away from the Life-Saving station unnoticed, and there began her three months' journey in a state of unknowingness. Were it not for the kindness of the Sisters of Mercy, she couldn't imagine what her fate might have been. The good nuns found her wandering in a near hallucinogenic state, speaking incoherently. They took her in, fed her and sheltered her, but still she could not remember her past. When she became well, but still did not know her name or where she was from, they found her employment as a chambermaid at the seaman's mission, allowing her to continue living with them until she regained her memory.

'It wasn't until the week before I had found her that her memory came back to her, spurred when she thought she heard one of the sailors call out, "Jim, Jim, avast there, Jim." Whether what she heard was true or not, she cannot say, but hearing my name brought her to her senses. She got word to her sister, which evidently arrived after my visit to her, and was about to stay with her, but first she wanted to finish her week at the sanctuary, feeling it was her duty after the sisters had been so kind to her. In her state, she had lost track of time, figuring I wasn't due to arrive back on Nantucket for another month, time enough for her to convalesce at her sister's before getting word to our friends on Nantucket that she was alive and well.

'We have decided to remain in Boston, as she is quite unwill-

ing to make another voyage by boat. I cannot say I blame her, and can only thank God that she is brought back to me.

'And so end my days at sea. After seeing my beloved safely ensconced at her sister's, I traveled on the whaleship Endeavor back to Nantucket. There, I recovered my belongings from the good ship Verona, including the ship's chest, which I entrusted to benefactors at The Pacific National Bank for safe keeping. At some point, I may reclaim these items, but I know they will be secure.

'As I left Nantucket, I watched the inspiring towers of the First and Second Congregational Churches fade from view. Would I ever return to the island again? Perhaps, but not until my darling Rebecca is willing to return with me.'

Chapter One Hundred Two

ADDIE CLOSED the journal, and without looking up said, "Wow." What he thought was, "Libby was right." Revelations come in the strangest places.

"Right?" Digit said. "This is the story, Addie. Forget about Caspian, and Dennison, and Willoughby, they don't matter anymore. It's the history behind the chest that matters, and, besides, we've got it, we've got the chest."

Addie then told Digit about the photo Hal had given him that morning, confirming further they had the right chest. "Even better," Digit said. He looked out at the ocean, proud of his island heritage.

"But I've got some not so great news," Addie continued, and he filled in Digit on Cy's oral history, and how the tape stopped before Cy could tell him what was in the sea chest and who he thought had taken it. "It would tie things up nicely to have that confirmation," Addie said.

"We *know* who stole it," Digit said. "But does that really matter anymore?" He looked at Addie and smiled. "Besides, for all their conniving, what did they gain? '. . . *(F)or there is no folly of the beasts of the earth which is not infinitely outdone by the madness of men.*' "

"Aren't we poetic?"

"It's Melville, nitwit. I thought you were an English major."

"I was."

"Lot of good it did you."

Ignoring Digit's comment, Addie said: "Let's figure this out. We've solved the robbery and we've recovered the stolen chest." He thought for a second. "What do you think happened to the old safe?"

"Willoughby threw it overboard twenty years ago."

"How do you know that?"

"He told me. I was about to leave when he asked me to stay. He told me everything, right down to them originally ditching the safe in my hiding place in the moors. I guess he thought he'd feel better if he unloaded his conscience on me."

"Do you think he does?"

"Doubtful."

"So he was the one who buried it in the cemetery?"

"Yes, he confessed to that, too. And guess which one?"

"The Quaker Burial Ground, just as I told you."

Digit lightly smacked his truck's steering wheel. "Yeah, you were right all along. Maybe I *should* start listening to you," he laughed. "But how did you confirm it?"

"Rebecca. She remembered that Mrs. Worth's friend was a Quaker, and she told Verona who told me. I guess I forgot to mention it to you. I got so sidetracked."

"Yeah, I guess you did."

"What did he say about digging up the chest and finding it gone?"

"He never mentioned it. He only said he had buried it in the Quaker Cemetery."

"But he had to have gone back for it. Why else would he

fake his demise?"

"For a second time, according to that phony lawyer's letter he wrote."

"That's right . . . "

"We didn't talk about that either."

"I wish you would've asked him if he'd tried digging it up, just to know how they buried the dog. Did they put it in anything, or did they just toss it in?"

"You're pretty gruesome, you know that? I suppose I should have told him that we have the chest."

"Oh, well. He can read all about it in next week's newspaper."

"That I *did* tell him."

Addie recalled the last line from Captain Hathaway's journal. "Hey, how about your ancestor's wife's name being Rebecca. You think our Rebecca was named after her?"

Digit pondered the question. "Could be." He paused for a moment. "I'll tell you something strange. Lance told me how he'd remembered where he'd buried the chest, what he'd used for a marker. Said he'd gone there many times over the past ten years, at night mainly, just to look at it." Digit looked over at Addie, as if imploring him to guess.

"And . . . ?" Addie said.

"It was an adjacent gravestone: James and Rebecca Hathaway."

"He had no idea . . . " Addie began.

"That they were related to me. And you know what? I didn't tell him."

Addie became quiet, pensive.

"What's up?" Digit asked him.

"I was just thinking that Captain Hathaway and Rebecca made it back to Nantucket after all."

"Yeah, I guess they did."

And, as he looked out over the gently crashing surf, Digit

let his mind carry him past the waves, and over the ocean, and back to the deck of the whaleship *Verona*, where so many intertwined stories began.

It felt like he'd been sitting on the porch for days. Lance Willoughby looked out at the waters of the upper harbor that sparkled in the spring sunshine. He knew these waters well; too bad he'd soon be leaving them behind.

He was relieved Digit hadn't pressed him on digging up the treasure, on what he'd found: it would have been too embarrassing. It was embarrassing enough that he'd become so absorbed by the whole thing. He wanted to blame Caspian, but couldn't; Caspian didn't control him. No, it was his own fault that he'd allowed himself to believe *he* was in control, as if some kind of right had been bestowed upon him. Control of what?

Good question.

Control of nothing at the moment.

Digit had the chest. He knew that. He knew it by the way Digit *didn't* tell him he had it. Besides, how else would Digit know what was in it?

But who put those bones there? Who replaced the chest with an animal skeleton? He was sure Digit didn't do it, so who did?

That would be one quest he'd leave unexplored. He was finished.

And he laughed, long and hard and loud, at the absurdity of it all.

With the events so fresh in his mind, Addie wanted to get started on the story right away. He suggested, and Digit agreed, that they'd both go back to the paper and powwow with Merle and Hal, just to get some guidance on which angle to take. "I don't think you need to mention Lance," Digit said. "His life's wrecked enough as it is right now." Digit couldn't help but think what a crappy influence Caspian could have had on *his* life had they remained friends.

The two of them practically burst into the newspaper office. "We've got it," Addie said to Merle. "Can we meet with you and Hal in your office?"

"Again? Wasn't once today enough for you?" She looked at Digit, whose smile was almost as wide as his face. "If you don't look like the cat who swallowed the canary," she said. "Well, I guess we'd better meet so I can find out what's got you two so excited."

The reporters and ad salespeople all turned as they walked back to Merle's office. "What could be so important?" one said. "Who knows?" replied another. "Addie always thinks he's on to something big. Somebody ought to remind him he's living on an island."

Merle carefully turned to the bookmarked page in Captain Hathaway's journal and read. When she'd finished, she said: "And you say you have the sea chest?"

"The one and only," Addie said. "I also have my notes about the robbery, and the lengths the perpetrators took to hide it." Digit shot him a look and slowly shook his head. "I mean," Addie continued, "There's so much information, I just need your and Hal's guidance where to begin."

"So you know who did it?" Merle asked. Digit looked up at the ceiling this time, but Addie knew what he was thinking.

"Let's just say Dirk Caspian isn't looking for *Dionis*," Addie said. Digit rolled his eyes.

"And you have a letter addressed to a Mr. Chase, although you say it's really Chief Dennison." Addie nodded.

"Can you prove either of those things?" Hal Humphries

asked, raising an eyebrow. "I mean prove it with further documentation?"

"Well, no, but I guess I could dig a little deeper."

"Give us a minute, will you, Addie?" Merle said. "I'd like to discuss this with Hal."

Addie and Digit went out into the hallway. Merle closed the door. Digit didn't say anything, but Addie knew he wasn't exactly happy. "I didn't mention Willoughby," Addie whispered.

"Just give you another second and you would have," Digit said.

"I swear I wasn't going to. She already knew about Dennison and Caspian. I didn't know anything about Willoughby until you just told me, remember?"

"I suppose," Digit said, and the door to Merle's office opened.

Merle and Hal were both smiling when Addie and Digit stepped in. "We think we've just made your life a lot easier," Merle said to Addie.

"You have the chest, correct?" Hal asked. Addie and Digit both nodded.

"And you have your research into the robbery," Merle noted. Addie nodded again. "Then it's settled," Merle said. "This is a celebration story. After twenty years, the mystery is solved, the stolen sea chest is found in the cellar of a Nantucket house. No need to go into any of the gory details about it's being buried in a cemetery."

"And no need to mention any names of alleged robbers," Hal added. "Any evidence you have is very circumstantial . . . "

"And we don't need any libel suits," Merle said. "No, this is about finding the old sea chest, and how, through diligent research, the origin of why the sea chest was originally discovered in the cellar of the Pacific National Bank can now be told." She looked over at Digit. "You don't mind if we reveal that it's your ancestor's chest, do you?" Digit beamed. "Not at all."

"So, it's settled then. Do you think you can have it written in time for the next edition?" she asked Addie. "Hal and I want time to look it over first, no waiting until deadline, right?"

"Yes, ma'am," Addie said. "One thing, though."

"Yes."

"Should we open it? I've been dying to find out what's inside."

"Absolutely not," Merle said. "Hal, tell them our idea."

"We'll open the chest on Main Street, as originally planned. We'll gather as many people as we can from the first go-round, from the members of the football team to Nantucket's Junior Miss, to whatever bank officers are around. We'll even round up as many kids — kids who are now adults — who took part in the original contest. Part of your story this week will be to announce the big opening."

"And this time," Merle said. "We'll make sure that sea chest is locked up tight, in an undisclosed location. You okay with that, Digit? It is your sea chest now, after all."

"Yes, Mrs. Welfleet. Where should we bring the chest?"

"Bring it here, first, if you don't mind. We want to take pictures.

"And then we'll put it where no one will ever find it, no matter how clever they think they are."

Chapter One Hundred Three

ADDIE STAYED at the newspaper to work on the story. He thought of Ellen. He hadn't spoken with her since she'd left the island. Wait until she hears about this. He picked up his office phone to call her, but stopped: he'd call her after the story came out. He'd go over it with Verona before submitting it to Merle. Verona. His hands touched the keys of his computer, but his mind was on Verona. It was she who'd found the suitcase; Verona who'd helped figure out the very beginning of that riddle. He wondered why . . . . Time to stop wondering, he told himself, and get to work. He began to type:

'A celebrated sea chest that sailed the globe during whaling years, and was stolen twenty years ago on the eve of its contents being revealed to a curious island, at long last has been found . . . . '

While Addie wrote, and before going to Sandy's house to retrieve the chest — as Merle said, his sea chest now — Digit went home to get from his kitchen table something he'd discovered in the same box as the journal. He'd become so excited over the journal's disclosures he'd left behind the smaller, yet equally important, notebook, a ledger of sorts. After he looked through it again, he held the ledger to his lips and laughed. So this is what everyone's been chasing after. And all it took was to open a little book.

"If wishes were horses," Digit thought as he stored the ledger in his sock drawer.

He bounded into Sandy's house, calling out: "Sandy?"

"Sandy's not here, but we are." It was Verona, whose voice came from the living room, the parlor.

Rebecca and Verona were on the couch. In the corner of the room sat the celebrated sea chest, as glorious as an old ottoman. Digit filled them in on what he and Addie had been up to. "I wanted to tell Sandy I was taking this to the newspaper office," he said. "When is she coming back?"

"Soon, I think," Verona said.

"I'll wait, then," Digit said. "Hold on, I've got something to show both of you." He returned with the leather-bound journal and sat between them on the couch. "I thought you might be interested in this. It's Captain Hathaway's diary."

"Let's look at it together," Verona said to Rebecca, to which Rebecca nodded her assent. Digit opened the journal and silently read along with them at first, until Rebecca said: "I think it might be better if you read it aloud to us, Clarence." Digit hadn't heard his given name in a while; his ex-wife Marsha would call him Clarence as a good-natured tease. Coming from Rebecca, he found it heart-warming.

Digit read Captain Hathaway's words about whaling; his observations of the Nantucket zeitgeist of the mid-1800s; his thoughts on being at sea. Before Digit got to the part about the sea chest, Sandy arrived.

"Isn't this a scene?" she said as she entered the living room.

"Almost like the three bears. Am I Goldilocks?"

"Could be," Digit said, standing. "Although I don't think I'd be 'just right.' "

Sandy sidled up to him. "You never know, Digit. You just might be."

"Right. Would you mind if I took the chest? The paper wants to photograph it."

Sandy, Verona and Rebecca looked at him. "What's going on?" they said at once. Digit had been so caught up in the events of the day, he had to think for a second: What *was* going on?

"Addie should be the one to tell you," Digit said.

"No way," said Sandy. "I'm not letting you leave until you tell us, and if you take that chest, I'll call the cops."

"No, you won't," Digit said, sitting back down, realizing they all deserved some explanation. "A lot of it's in that journal." They all looked at him — they weren't going to let him off that easily.

"All right, okay," Digit said. And he told them.

Almost everything. He left out Lance Willoughby.

When he'd finished, he asked Sandy again if he could take the chest to the paper.

"Absolutely," she said. "From what you've told us, that chest rightfully belongs to you anyway. Is it okay with you if they open it on Main Street?"

"I don't think it's mine, any more than you think it's yours," Digit said. "I'm interested to see if anyone still cares."

"Of course they'll care," Sandy said, "especially if Addie gives it a good write-up. This is so exciting." She paused. "So what do you think is in it?"

Digit didn't tell them he knew what was inside. Better for them to find out with everyone else.

Digit carried the chest into the pressroom of *The Looking*

Glass and was about to push through the door into the newsroom when he happened to look through the glass and see Dirk Caspian at the front counter.

Chapter One Hundred Four

DIGIT WALKED quickly back through the pressroom and out the door to his truck. He put the chest beside him on the seat and drove away from the paper, pretty sure that Caspian hadn't seen him — he certainly hadn't seen the chest since Digit hadn't yet pushed open the swinging door. What was Caspian doing at the newspaper? And so what if he had seen the chest? Still, it was best that he hadn't. Digit drove back to Sandy's; there was no rush in getting the chest to the paper, anyway; he liked having it in his possession for a while.

Dirk Caspian asked if he could speak to a reporter. "Addie, there's someone here to see you," the circulation manager said, directing Caspian in the direction of Addie's desk.

Addie didn't look up until Caspian was steps away. He hurriedly covered his notes with his jacket and walked towards Caspian to get away from his computer and the story he was working on. What was this guy doing here? This was all he needed. "How can I help you?" Addie asked when Caspian was still a few feet away.

"Is there somewhere we can sit and talk?" Caspian asked. "At your desk?"

Addie tried to think quickly. "Oh . . . my desk is way too messy; I'd be too embarrassed. Merle, this gentleman is here to see me. Would you mind if we used your office?"

Merle was making notes for the advertising salesperson, hoping the bank would celebrate the sea chest's return with a full-page ad. She looked up, but didn't recognize Caspian. Addie wouldn't ask if it wasn't important. "Be my guest," she said. "You should be feeling right at home in there by now. Third time today."

Addie escorted Caspian to the back of the newspaper office. He needed a notebook, but he wasn't going to go back to his desk to get one. Luckily, he saw one near one of the layout people's desks and he scooped it up. "Hey, Addie," the classified advertising salesperson called as he walked by, "heard you're working on a pretty good story, something about an unsolved . . . "

"Yeah, bad news travels pretty fast around here," Addie interjected.

"Bad news? I thought you'd found . . . "

"Gotta go," Addie said. "Right this way, Mister, Mister . . . "

"Caspian. Dirk Caspian. We've met before, haven't we?"

"I don't think so. Here we are."

Addie took the chair where Hal had sat during their meeting, and motioned for Caspian to take the chair opposite. "So, how can I help you?"

Caspian took a deep breath. "I'm looking for some coverage on a state project I've been working on. Since the initial writeup months ago, your newspaper hasn't written a word, which I find, frankly, unsettling, since my project is of historic significance."

Addie acted coy. "And which project is this?"

"I think you know. But to refresh your memory, I'm hoping

to find the locomotive *Dionis*, of the old Nantucket Railroad."

"Oh, *that* project," Addie said. "I'm sorry, but I wasn't aware there was anything new to report."

Caspian leaned forward, in an effort to be intimidating. To counter his move, Addie leaned forward himself. "You would think a newspaper that fashions itself as the paper of record would take greater interest than it has; there hasn't even been a picture of the excavation site, and nobody's bothered to interview me. To be honest, it didn't matter to me because the *Advocate*, with far greater readership, was being quite informative, but their reporter, unfortunately, has left the island."

"Ellen," Addie said under his breath.

Caspian leaned back. "Yes, Ellen," he said. "I understand you two were something of an item."

What's up with this guy? Addie thought. Just who does he think he is? He kept his composure and stood up. "I'll talk to the editor about your concerns, Mr. Caspian. How can I reach you, if I need to?"

Caspian handed Addie a business card, which listed a Boston telephone number. "That's my office number," Caspian said. "You can leave a message."

Addie had no intention of ever leaving a message. Fortunately, Caspian got the hint when Addie stood; they left Merle's office together. Addie walked in silence, but Caspian had more to say.

"Speaking of Ellen," he said, "did she ever show you a letter addressed to a Conrad Chase?" Addie kept walking. The sooner he got this guy to the door, the better. "I believe she did," Caspian said. "Did it lead you anywhere?"

Addie relaxed. Caspian was fishing. Well, he could fish all he wanted. That's the reason he came to the paper: he was desperate. He was still trying to figure out that riddle. If only he knew what I know, Addie thought. He's lucky we're not going to mention his name in the paper.

When they got to the door, Addie said: "I'll let you know what my editor says," and was just about to turn away when Hal called out: "Addie, do you know when Digit's coming back with that chest? The photographer wants to know."

Caspian took his hand off the door, and turned. His beady eyes were black dots. He seemed to shake when he said to Addie: "You have it."

"I don't know what you're talking about. Now, if you don't mind"

"Oh, I do mind," Caspian said, his voice rising. "I know Digit Hathaway."

"Friend of yours?" Addie asked.

"Yes," Caspian hissed.

"Then I suggest you call him."

Caspian grabbed Addie by both shoulders. "Where is it?" he said. "Where is it?"

Merle walked over, saying in a stern voice: "Addie, what do you need me to do?"

Addie pulled away from Caspian's grasp and said: "Merle, this is Dirk Caspian. I believe he wants to talk to you."

"And I'd be happy to talk to him," Merle said. "Won't you come to my desk, Mr. Caspian?"

But Dirk Caspian didn't hear her. He had bolted.

Chapter One Hundred Five

Digit was sitting in the living room with Sandy, Verona, and Rebecca when his phone rang. " 'Sup," he said to Addie.

"Caspian was here."

"I know. I saw him."

"What?"

"I was coming in the back door of the paper with the sea chest when I saw him at the counter. I bolted."

"So did he."

"What's that? You're not making much sense."

"Let me start over. He came to see me with some phony story about wanting more coverage of his 'big dig.' I've got to be honest, he made me nervous."

"Yes, he has that effect on people."

"Especially when he grabbed me."

"He grabbed you?" Digit was pacing the living room now. "You okay?"

"I'm fine. What he really wanted was to find out if I'd figured out the riddle. That's when I relaxed, when I knew he still had no clue."

"So why did he grab you?"

"Because, not knowing who Caspian was, Hal asked when you were coming back with the chest. That's when he grabbed me. He knows we have it."

"He grabbed you in the newspaper office? Where is he now?"

"I have no idea. He ran out the door when Merle came over to rescue me."

"He's probably on his way to my house. I'll head over there. Thanks, Addie. And don't worry, I'll handle Caspian. It's about time I had a word or two with that guy."

Digit put his phone away. When he looked over at the couch, he saw the concern in their eyes and reported what Addie told him. "Like I told Addie, don't worry. I'll take care of Caspian."

Digit's words were of little comfort to Verona. She didn't want anything to happen to Addie. No matter how much fun he and Digit were having, she couldn't wait for this little adventure to be over. It was beginning to weigh on her mind. Why else would she be seeing things in the fog?

Addie walked over to Merle's desk. "Thanks for helping me out," he said to her.

"Not the first time I've had to rescue a reporter," she said.

"I'm curious, what were you going to say to him?"

"I was going to tell him we had evidence that he stole the safe, and if he didn't want me to call his superiors in Boston, he'd leave this office quietly and not bother anyone here again. Furthermore, if I ever caught him near this newspaper office after today, I'd call the police and have him arrested for trespassing."

"Should I put that in my story, that we believe he was one of the culprits? I'm sorry, alleged culprits?"

"Absolutely not. This is a celebratory story. You stick with the plan."

"Couldn't I mention that Caspian is digging in the exact same spot that is shown on a map created by one of the unknown thieves?"

"Too complicated. Besides, there are no names on that map, no way of tying Caspian to the robbery. The statute of limitations expired years ago anyway. But he doesn't have to know that. Let him think we've got the goods on him."

"He's going to try and get that chest somehow. And he knows Digit has it."

"You may be right. Where is Digit? Tell him to get that chest in here."

Dirk Caspian didn't go to Digit's house; he went instead to Station Brant Point. He didn't bother to acknowledge Boatswain's Mate Murphy and barged into C. C. Dennison's office. "They've got it," Caspian said breathlessly. "They've got the sea chest."

Dennison took too big a swallow of his coffee, burning his throat. "Who's got it?" he wheezed.

"Our old friend Digit Hathaway."

"Who?"

Caspian had forgotten that Dennison wouldn't have known Digit from twenty years ago. And Dennison never told Caspian about his confrontation at the sandbar, which may have revealed that Addie's companion that day was Digit. "Doesn't matter who," Caspian said. "Digit and that stupid reporter have it."

"Addie?"

"That's the one."

Dennison couldn't believe it, but he could believe it. He'd have expected Ellen to uncover the treasure, but didn't think

Addie had it in him. So, it had been a pretty good idea to feed Addie information after all.

"What are you smiling about?" Caspian asked him.

"Oh, nothing. So, what's your plan?"

"Plan?" Caspian hadn't thought about a plan. All he'd wanted to do was get out of the newspaper office — he didn't need a lowbrow editor talking to him. He came to see Dennison because he needed to be somewhere he felt relatively safe; no one on Nantucket was going to bother with the U. S. Coast Guard, even if it did have a simple-minded chief. He just needed to regroup and figure out how to get that chest.

But he shouldn't have rushed over here; now Dennison knew about it. How was he going to cut him out? Maybe if he put Dennison onto that reporter . . . . Dennison interrupted his thoughts.

"Forget it, Dirk, I'm not interested."

"Excuse me?"

"I don't care about that sea chest anymore. In fact, until you showed back up on this island, I had pretty much put it all behind me. But somehow, the memory of twenty years ago poisoned my thinking, got me believing that the sea chest was valuable, worthwhile. Oh, I admit I wanted you out of the picture, badly. I even fed Ellen information to try and get you thrown off the island. And then you come here and start talking and here I go again, listening to you, falling for your charms.

"And I realized how happy, and fulfilled, I'd been since leaving you behind twenty years ago. And I've lately realized how miserable and paranoid I've been since you returned. So have at it, I don't want it. It won't bring you good luck, I'm sure of it now, just misery." Dennison looked Caspian in the eye. "Those last lines of the riddle are what finally did it for me. Did you get that far? Did it mean anything to you? 'What it cost them is their secret?' Well, our secret cost me a bit too much of my life."

Caspian smiled his sardonic grin. “Fine. It’s been a pleasure,” and he held out his hand, but Dennison didn’t take it.

After Caspian left, Dennison felt relief, glad he was out of his life. He had to laugh. For someone who thought he was so smart, Caspian sure wasn’t too observant. If he was, he would have recognized an old safe that now occupied the space behind Dennison’s desk.

Chapter One Hundred Six

DIGIT WAS cleaning out his scallop boat when Caspian pulled into his driveway. Digit heard him close his car door, his feet crunch on the scallop shell drive, but he didn't look up from his work. Caspian stood by the boat, but Digit wouldn't look at him, nor did he speak. Caspian broke the silence:

"Where is it?"

Still Digit didn't speak.

"Where is it?" Caspian asked again.

Digit remained silent. He turned and bent over to untie a line on a dredge, so that his rear end now faced Caspian. Caspian began banging on the side of the boat, saying, "Can you hear me now? Can you hear me now?"

Digit stood up. He had a hammer in his hand. "You put a hole in my boat, I'll put a hole in you."

"Why don't you come down here so we can talk?"

"I can talk fine from right here," Digit said. "What do you want?"

"You know what I want. You've got that sea chest . . . "

"What sea chest would that be?"

Caspian gritted his teeth. "Stop playing games, Digit. I know you have that chest, the guy at the newspaper said so."

"Newspaper? I don't know what you're talking about."

Caspian clenched his fist, stepped closer.

"I meant what I said about hurting my boat," Digit said. "Don't make me prove it."

Caspian smiled, took a different tack. "I know you won't believe this, but I always found it easy to talk to you. I'm not even sure what drove us apart. I often think back to how close we were. Why can't we just talk now? You have something I want. Let's discuss it."

Digit was prepared for this. He knew Caspian would eventually bring up their friendship. All it did was steel Digit's resolve. "I have nothing you want," he said. "I think it's time for you to leave."

"Digit, Digit," Caspian purred, "I've waited too long, and I'm too close now to give up. That chest means nothing to you. You wouldn't even have it now if I hadn't stolen it."

"So you admit it. I should just turn you in."

"I don't think so. They've never suspected me; there's no file on me. If you tell the cops I stole it, I'll just deny it. Even if they believe you, they're not going to waste time, manpower, and money trying to pin this on me. No one cares, Digit."

"Neither do I. Go away." Digit again turned his back on Caspian and went back to work.

"No," Caspian almost yelled. He tried to compose himself. "How much? What's it worth to you?"

"What's it worth to *you?*" Digit asked, without turning.

"So I was right," Caspian said, trying to get the upper hand. "It's money. All along, it's about the money. I should have known. And you acting so moral and high and mighty . . . "

Digit jumped down from his boat and stood toe-to-toe with Caspian. "I'm giving you two seconds to get out of here before I do call the cops." Caspian sneered but remained where he was. "Have it your way, then," Digit said. "I'll wipe the ground with you and then I won't need to call the cops — I'll call an ambulance instead. And if the police do show up? I'll gladly tell them I was protecting my property. Who will they believe then, Dirk? I'll give you a hint: it won't be some coof like you." Digit pushed forward and Caspian fell to the ground. "Now get moving."

Caspian stood up slowly and walked backward to his car. Digit knew he was trying to figure out his next move. When Caspian had his hand on the door handle, Digit said: "I'm going to hide that chest tonight where you'll never find it."

Caspian waited until midnight. He was dressed all in black. He had a strong flashlight with a focused beam. It had been years since he'd been where he was going, but he was certain he knew the way. He drove out of town and out the Polpis Road. He took a right, and headed down a long dirt road. As he turned to climb a hill, he killed his lights. It wouldn't be long now. He could feel his heart in his chest as his car careened along the trail and jostled over bumps, his breathing more rapid with each second.

He knew where to park his car. From there, it was about fifty yards to his destination. The only thing he could hear was his pulse pounding in his ears. Even though he knew there was no one around — no one for miles — he walked with a light tread, as stealthily as he could. He was almost there.

He finally flicked his flashlight on, but held it down, keeping the light close to the ground. Just a few more steps, and, there it was — the secret spot. Ha, ha, he heard in his head, I've got it.

But the chest wasn't there. He moved the branches aside and threw the beam at its base. He must have the wrong bush; he swept the light to the right, then the left, not caring now if the beam carried or not, but there was no other bush like it. He moved the light back to his first choice, pushed back the branches once more, and, on his hands and knees, peered deep into the hole.

Suddenly a light flashed behind him, and a voice asked: "Looking for something?"

He didn't need to turn. It was Digit.

Chapter One Hundred Seven

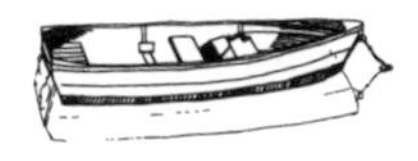

"I'M GOING to guess that you'd thought I'd forgotten that I'd ever shown you this spot in the first place," Digit said calmly. "Now why would you think that, when we must have come here, oh, a dozen times anyway, retrieving our stashes of Ripple wine?" Digit had a state police flashlight that he aimed at Caspian, who looked genuinely stunned. "You said you wanted to talk earlier," Digit continued, "so let's talk." Caspian started to stand but only got to one knee. Every ounce of energy seemed to be sapped from him.

"Yes, let's talk," Digit said. "Let's talk about our friendship. Man, I was totally taken in. And you're good, so good at what you do. I mean, take Cordelia, for example. Oh, I forgot, you *did* take Cordelia. How foolish of me." He shined the strong light into Caspian's eyes, making him wince. "I didn't figure that one out until the end of that summer, the summer you stopped talking to me and started hanging out with your other friends. Isn't it nice you got to hang out with one of them this winter? Too bad the other one died." Caspian said nothing, but Digit could guess what he was thinking. "You've forgotten it's a small island, Dirk;

everyone knows everything about everybody. Now, where was I? Oh, yes, Cordelia. *She* stopped talking to me before *you* stopped talking to me. I have to admit, I was more hurt by you shunning me. Isn't that stupid? Or you might say, 'weak.' I really thought you'd help me to understand, help me get over her, and I couldn't figure out why you wanted nothing to do with me.

"I didn't realize why until after you were arrested. Oh, you needed me then, all right, when I could do something for you, when I could be *useful* to you. And you know, I came so close to telling you forget it, find somebody else to bail you out, but I couldn't. And you know why I couldn't?" He looked hard at Caspian's face, but, as expected, there was no reaction. "Because I've got this stupid idea about friendship, that it's not something you forget about when it's hard to be a friend. And, believe me, you made it awfully hard to be your friend.

"It was shortly after you were booted off the island that I ran into Cordelia again. Isn't that funny? She didn't want to talk to me, but we bumped into each other on Main Street, and I mean, literally. I was turning up Orange Street and had my head down thinking about something, while she had just left the bank and was putting the money in her pocketbook when, wham! What a coincidence, right? Well, she had to talk to me then. And she told me she was sorry that she hadn't written or gotten in touch, but she supposed you had told me everything, since we were such good friends. Did you hear that, Dirk? Even Cordelia thought we were friends, even after you stole her away from me. Yes, she told me that, too — that you two had become an item that winter."

Caspian finally spoke: "And she was good, too."

Without thinking, Digit raised the heavy flashlight and swung — but caught it with his left hand. "You're just not worth it," he said.

Digit then put two fingers into his mouth, and let loose

with a piercing whistle. From the four points of the compass and seemingly out of the bushes came four men brandishing flashlights. They surrounded Caspian.

"Now, these are my friends, too," Digit said. "You don't know them, but they know you. If any of us sees or hears anything about you trying to retaliate against the newspaper, or anyone who works there, well, you really don't want to upset any more islanders, do you?"

The five men then pointed their flashlights back toward Caspian's car. He stood and followed the beam.

As he drove home, Digit felt no satisfaction, only sadness for Caspian. Funny, though, that if Lance hadn't told him where they'd originally hidden the safe, Digit would have forgotten all about that spot. The last time he'd been there, ironically enough, was with Caspian.

Armed with that knowledge, however, Digit knew Caspian wouldn't be able to resist, that he'd take the bait.

Chapter One Hundred Eight

BEFORE HIS midnight rendezvous with Caspian, and after he'd kicked him off his property, Digit called Addie at the newspaper to see if Merle still wanted him to bring the sea chest there. "Slight change of plan," Addie said. "Merle wants to know if you could meet her at her house."

Digit knew why. Merle, an avid birdwatcher, lived out of town, down a dirt road that you'd have to know led to her house; it was so remote that very few people happened upon it by accident.

When Digit arrived, Hal was there with his camera. "Where's Addie?" Digit asked.

"Back at the paper, working on this story," Merle said. "You don't think Caspian will try to bother him, do you?"

"Dirk Caspian's got other things on his mind right now," Digit said.

"Good," Merle said. "Thanks for bringing the chest out here."

"So this is where you're going to hide it?"

"Heavens, no. Too risky, even if I am out in the woods. No,

after he gets his pictures, Hal's going to take it to the last place anybody will look for it."

"And where's that, if you don't mind telling me?"

"Right back where it came from — to the vault of the Pacific National Bank."

That week's edition of *The Looking Glass* featured a banner headline, its first in decades:

> ***A Mystery No More: Whaling Chest Found!***
> ***After 20 years, contents finally to be revealed on Main Street***
>
> 'A sea chest from an 1800s-era whaling ship that had been missing for 20 years, and presumed stolen, has been found. As originally planned two decades ago, the chest will be opened on the steps of The Pacific National Bank next Thursday at noon.
>
> 'After months of investigating the sea chest's mysterious disappearance, the *Looking Glass* uncovered the chest's whereabouts last weekend. The sea chest, which originally sailed aboard the whaleship *Verona* and was the property of ship's captain James Hathaway, was found in the basement of a Nantucket house, hidden amidst a prior owner's effects, with its padlock still intact. The current owner of the house is not a suspect in the chest's disappearance. The prior owner of the house is deceased and also is not suspected of any wrongdoing.
>
> ' "Neither party had any involvement (with the chest's disappearance)," Police Chief Francis Mooney said. He also said the person, or persons, responsible for taking the chest from the old town building will most likely never be apprehended. "It was probably a college prank that got out of

hand," the chief said. "I assume the culprits are long gone because if they were from Nantucket, that kind of thing wouldn't have remained a secret for twenty years; somebody would have talked."

'The chief, who has been on the force for 35 years, and was a sergeant at the time of the robbery, said there have never been any real leads into the identity of the alleged thieves. "We went down every rabbit hole, followed up on every tip. The assumption was that they'd dumped it somewhere, the ocean or even one of the ponds, either because they didn't know what they had, or were afraid of being caught — I suspect they were afraid of being caught. With the recovery of the chest, I consider the case closed."

'Police Chief Mooney will be present at the opening of the chest this Saturday, as will Bertha Stafford, Nantucket's Junior Miss of twenty years ago. Also attending will be Roy Larsen, deputy director of the historical association, past and present officers of The Pacific National Bank, and members of the Nantucket Whalers football team from twenty years ago, who will again hoist the chest onto a ceremonial platform in front of the bank.

'The *Looking Glass* invites all island school children to submit their guesses as to the contents of the chest at special "treasure chest" boxes located at several businesses around the island, including the offices of the *Looking Glass*, the historical association, and The Pacific National Bank. The *Looking Glass* also has the original guesses from twenty years ago. Whoever correctly guesses the contents of the *Verona's* sea chest — past or present — will be awarded with a $100 savings account at The Pacific National Bank. Main Street will be closed to all vehicular traffic Saturday beginning at 9 a.m.

'The chest will be opened after the Town Clock's famed

> Portuguese Bell peals 52 times at noon. The opening duties will be performed by Nantucketers Rebecca Coffin and Clarence Hathaway, the descendants of Captain James Hathaway.'

"I wish I could have put in about the chest being buried at the Quaker cemetery," Addie said to Merle.

"And have every lunatic with a shovel digging up graves all over the island looking for buried treasure? No, thank you. Save it for your memoirs."

"My memoirs?"

"Why certainly. Hal's been working on his for the past thirty years, haven't you, Hal."

"Let's be accurate, Merle," Hal noted. "I've only been working on them for twenty-five. So, Addie, you got your first banner headline. How does it make you feel?"

"That you're only as good as your next story?"

"Give that man a raise, Merle. You've got yourself a reporter."

Addie didn't hear him. He was already working on the next week's follow-up.

Chapter One Hundred Nine

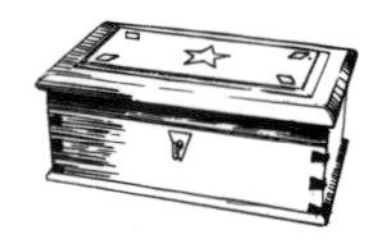

ALTHOUGH A bit windy, April 19 was a beautiful spring day, putting the crowd on Main Street into a festive mood. By eleven o'clock, people jammed the cobblestones in front of the bank, overflowed past the Methodist Church on Centre Street, arced around the other side of the bank past Fair Street, stood four deep on the sidewalks, and flowed down Main Street past the Hub and toward the fountain. Former Nantucket Junior Miss Bertha Stafford stood on the bank steps and from a lightship basket tossed chocolate coins wrapped in gold foil to the children. At 11:30, the chest was carried out the front door of the bank by the former football players — all now twenty years older — and placed on a stand festooned with red, white, and blue bunting. The high school band struck up a rendition of "On, Wisconsin," the Nantucket Whalers football fight song, chosen, apparently, because of its meter.

Addie stood next to Digit, while Verona and Sandy stood behind Rebecca, who had been provided a chair for the occasion. "How many people do you think are here?" Addie asked Digit.

"Beats me. How do you figure out crowd sizes? Looks like a few thousand to me."

"I don't want to overestimate. It'll be safe to say, 'hundreds.' " Addie looked over at the chest, which now seemed a lot smaller than it did in Sandy's living room. "How are you going to open that thing? With a sledgehammer?"

"You won't believe it, but they still had the original key in the bank, complete with ID tag. They never got a chance to use it twenty years ago."

"Think it'll work?"

Digit looked around and whispered in Addie's ear: "It's already unlocked. I figured there might be a problem with it, so I talked it over with the bank president. We got here early this morning to work on it. I used a ton of lubricant, and with a little persuading it clicked. I've got it rigged so it looks locked but it's ready to go."

"Did you look inside?"

"Don't need to."

"You keep saying that. How do you know?"

"I found another diary of Captain Hathaway, a very meticulous guy. He listed everything that was his personal property aboard the *Verona*, probably to prove to the ship's owners that he wasn't taking anything that didn't belong to him. Turns out the contents of this chest didn't."

"Didn't what?"

"Belong to him. It was the property of . . . shhh, I'll tell you later. They're about to start."

A microphone had been placed in front of the bank. By consent, it was agreed that Mr. Larsen of the historical association would make the remarks. After greeting the parties assembled on the steps and acknowledging the crowd, which he estimated to be close to two thousand . . .

Digit turned to Addie, "There's your number."

. . . Larsen began his address. “This is a memorable day for Nantucket,” he said, “a historic day. It is also a day nobody ever thought would happen after the unpleasant events of twenty years ago. Thanks to some good old-fashioned journalism, however,” he nodded to Addie, “we are able to reconvene and celebrate today. It is appropriate that we gather here at the steps of the Pacific National Bank, a bank funded by whaling and named after the vast ocean that Nantucketers explored, mapped, and knew so well that it was commonly referred to as the *Nantucket* ocean. So it is whaling that brings us here today, indeed, that brings us *together* today, to be reminded of our heritage, and to come together as one island. Although we are assembled, ostensibly, to unlock the treasure inside this ancient chest, the real treasure is our regard for our common history, a regard that has not only stirred excitement for this day, but that also has caused us to pause, and ponder that which is important to all of us: our resolve to revere our history and honor those who have walked these same cobblestones before us. That is our real treasure, one that mere riches will never match. We on Nantucket gratefully embrace our past, and learn from it, and respectfully carry these lessons into a bright and compassionate future.”

The crowd burst into applause. Addie took note of the smiles all around him. In this moment, Nantucket truly was one. Larsen continued:

“How fitting that the descendants of the whaling captain who owned this chest are here today to help us unlock the mystery that stoked our curiosity twenty years ago, and proved so beguiling that the chest was spirited away, only to be returned to its rightful place here, on Main Street, an heirloom for us all. Ms. Coffin, Mr. Hathaway, would you please do the honors.”

As practiced, Verona and Sandy stood on either side of Rebecca to steady her as she walked to the chest. Digit handed Rebecca the key. (“Just put it in the lock, don’t turn it,” he quietly reminded her.) With the key in place, Digit pulled on the lock, removed it, and slowly opened the lid.

The crowd buzzed with anticipation; a susurrus of soft whispers carried over the cobblestones. When the lid was fully opened, the crowd surged forward to see.

From his place on the corner of Main and Centre Streets, a spot he had occupied since ten o'clock, Dirk Caspian had a good enough view of the chest to see what was inside when the lid was opened. His palms sweated. He had waited twenty years for this moment, but now he wished the chest would remain closed forever. He dreaded finding out what was inside, fearing that his expectations would be realized, and that the chest contained ivory. "Please, not the *Susan's* Teeth," he said through his own clenched incisors.

On the opposite side of the street, where Orange Street started its incline, a figure wearing a watch cap and hooded sweatshirt lifted binoculars to his eyes as the chest was finally opened. Lance Willoughby had read the *Looking Glass* that week, heartened that Digit remained true to his word and hadn't turned him in. He could begin again, perhaps even reclaim his real name, Nate Powell.

He had planned on being off the island by now, but Digit's telling him that he knew what was inside the chest made him stay. He had to know, after all his plans and machinations, he just had to know.

So, from what he'd gleaned from the paper, someone *had* dug up the chest, probably right after he'd buried it. To think it had been sitting in somebody's cellar all this time. What a joke. What a waste of time.

Still, it had been fun writing that riddle, and watching those other two fall over each other looking for a dead lawyer's office. Good luck, boys, he thought. Can't say it wasn't memorable.

He hoped the document he'd handwritten and slipped into

his truck's glove compartment — a note dated the year before, saying that if anything happened to him while scalloping that his truck and boat should be given to Clarence Hathaway — would be enough to rectify at least some of his deceptions. He liked Digit, had respected his no-nonsense approach to life, and respected him even more now. He wished things could have ended differently — Digit would be a true friend to have — but they hadn't. As soon as he saw what was in the chest, he'd be gone.

C. C. Dennison wasn't on Main Street. With the island's attention focused on the day's happy events, no one was out on the water, and no one was there to notice when he drove a boat through the cut in the east jetty to the backside of Coatue and pushed a certain safe overboard for what he hoped would be the last time.

As he motored back to the dock, he thought he heard a collective gasp emanating from Main Street. He had to get a handle on his overactive imagination, he told himself. Now he was hearing things.

But he wasn't hearing things. When Digit pulled open the lid of the sea chest, the crowd didn't gasp so much as groan. What was inside the old chest surprised everyone — except Digit.

Chapter One Hundred Ten

PEOPLE NEAREST the chest couldn't believe their eyes. "What is it?" Addie heard several people say, almost as one. After a pause of what seemed like minutes, but was in reality mere seconds, Digit leaned in, pulled out a wad of paper, and held it high. "It's money," somebody said, "paper money."

"But it doesn't look like money."

On top of the pile was an envelope, addressed to a Mr. Frederick Parker, Esquire. Digit handed it to Hank Rickenbacker, the president of the bank, who moved to the microphone and read the letter:

'Sir: I beg your indulgence to accept the return of these notes that you so generously provided against the prospects of a successful voyage. I'm most pleased to report the ship Verona was once again blessed with "greasy luck," from which the shipowners should realize a handsome profit. My own profits I wish to exchange for government bonds, since I leave for Boston in a few days' time and will do my banking there. Upon my eventual return from Boston, I will retrieve this chest, but until then entrust it to you for safe keep-

ing. I remain, sincerely and respectfully yours, James Hathaway.'

"What does it mean?" someone in the crowd called out. "Is it money?"

The bank president retrieved one of the notes from the chest and returned to the microphone.

"This is money, in a way, but its years of being legal tender are long gone. This bank, along with most banks in the United States, was authorized to issue its own money, backed by government bonds. When the government consolidated U. S. currency into a central, federal agency in the 1930s, these bank notes were rendered obsolete."

"So it's like Confederate money," someone said.

"Yes, it's worthless, except maybe to collectors. Of course, to the historical association these will be a wonderful addition to their collection. Congratulations."

When Dirk Caspian heard the word 'worthless' his heart skipped and he had to catch himself. He tried getting nearer the chest, but the crowd by now had surged forward, blocking his way and, in fact, pressed him backward. It couldn't be; there had to be something else in the chest, buried underneath. He had to get to the chest. But there was Digit closing the lid, and the football team lifting it up and taking it back inside the bank. Before the high school band could once again play, "On, Wisconsin," Hank, the bank president, said over the microphone: "We've decided that anyone who guessed there was money inside the chest will all be awarded hundred-dollar savings accounts — with real money." The crowd let out a roar of approval and began to disperse.

The chest wasn't yet inside the bank. Caspian, his eyes wild, pushed through people to get to it. The door to the bank was opening, but the chest was still on the outside. As he reached the bank's bottom step, ready to leap, if necessary, a hand was placed atop his shoulder. When he tried to wriggle loose, a voice said,

"Mr. Caspian, if I could have a word . . . . "

He turned to see a man in a suit hold out a badge. "State police. You need to come with me, Mr. Caspian."

Caspian ran up the steps of the bank, opened the door and flew inside, with the plainclothes policeman on his tail. The chest was being taken behind the teller's cages, on its way to the vault. Digit was talking with the bank president; Addie and Verona sat at a table with Mr. Larsen as Addie interviewed him. Everyone looked up when they heard, "Stop!" It was Caspian, reaching for the chest. The policeman pulled out handcuffs and said, "I don't want to have to do this, Mr. Caspian, but I will if you don't desist."

Caspian looked around the room, his eyes darting back and forth like herring rushing upstream. "Digit," he cried, "Digit, tell him it's okay, that you're my friend."

The man showed his badge to Digit. "State Police," he said. "Mr. Caspian needs to come with me."

The look of shock on Digit's face froze Caspian. "You'd better do as he says, Dirk." He turned to the officer, "Can I ask what this is about?"

"I'm afraid not," the man said. "Mr. Caspian, if you'd come with me. Don't make me use these," he said, as he put the handcuffs back on his belt.

Defeated, Caspian was led out of the bank. Digit and Addie looked at each other as if to say, "What was that?"

The plainclothesman escorted Caspian to an SUV parked on the upper Main Street side of the bank. "You can sit in the passenger seat," Caspian was told.

"Mr. Caspian, I have papers here," and he pointed to a briefcase on the back seat, "that find you complicit in defrauding two entities: the Conservation Commission here on Nantucket, and the state historic preservation office, your employer. You not only bribed a state employee to falsify documents naming an obscure wetland on Nantucket a health hazard to the community, you used this false information to procure an emergency certification from the local board." Caspian started to deny the charges, but the policeman put up his hand. "We have depositions and affidavits from all parties involved, Mr. Caspian. These are serious charges, but you do have the right to defend yourself in a court of law. I must advise you, however, that it will come at great cost to you in legal fees alone, and that your chances of acquittal are slim, at best. We have solid evidence against you." The officer let those words sink in, before continuing.

"Due to a backlog of cases, and because of the costs of prosecuting you, the Commonwealth is prepared to offer you an alternative to a court appearance and probable jail time." Caspian looked at the officer. He'd do anything to end this nightmare.

"Mr. Caspian, because of the damage you caused to the wetland, and indirectly to the people of Nantucket, you are to leave the island today, never to return. Also, if you are to reveal, repeat, or divulge any part of this offer, you will be arrested and brought to trial, with no hope of a plea bargain or further considerations. I hope I make myself clear." Caspian could only nod. "Good." The officer reached into the inside pocket of his jacket and handed him a ticket. "The boat leaves at 5:30. Be on it. Goodbye, Mr. Caspian." As Caspian opened the car door, the officer added, "One more thing. You no longer have a position at the historic preservation commission, and don't bother applying for any municipal, state, or government positions."

The plainclothes officer took out his phone and dialed. Their conversation was over. Caspian had to hurry. He only had a little over three hours to pack up his rental in 'Sconset and get off the island.

Chapter One Hundred Eleven

As soon as Caspian left the bank, Addie and Digit burst out laughing. "Did you arrange that?" Addie asked.

"No, but I wish I had. I have to admit when I saw his face . . . "

"You don't have to tell me. The look on your face was priceless. But if you didn't put him up to it, who did?"

"Sandy," said Verona. "With a little help from Ellen."

"Ellen had tried reaching you on your cell, and she didn't want to call the paper, so she called me," Sandy was telling Addie as they all had wine in Sandy's living room. "She said she had some news about Dirk Caspian."

"Which was?" Addie asked.

"That he was about to lose his job." That got everyone's attention. "It seems the chairman of the Nantucket Conservation Commission had friends in a lot higher places than Caspian. That person did some digging of his own and discovered that our friend Caspian had phonied up that order from the state.

Since he hadn't done *too* much damage to the wetland, they were going to make a deal with him: he'd lose his job, but they wouldn't press charges."

"And Caspian didn't know this?" Addie asked.

"This just happened like two days ago. Caspian never told anyone in Boston his Nantucket address, and he'd changed his cell phone, so they called Ellen — who they thought was still working on the island. She thought you'd like to know."

"I've got to call her anyway," Addie said. "Let her know how everything turned out."

"She knows. She has an online subscription to the *Looking Glass*."

"I should have called her sooner."

"She forgives you. She's working on her own story, one welcoming back Chief C. C. Dennison to the Cape."

"When did that happen?"

"He got the news yesterday, right before she called me. There'll be a change of command ceremony at Brant Point next week. Honestly, Addie," she laughed, "you need to stay on top of things better. And, yes, Ellen wants you to call so she can congratulate you."

"But that doesn't explain . . . ," Digit began.

"I know where you're going, Mr. Hathaway," Sandy said, "and no, it doesn't explain. But bear with me for a second." She stopped and smiled at the recollection. "As soon as Ellen and I hung up, I got a call on my landline, from a long-lost friend."

"Chuck Finley," Digit and Addie said in unison, as they both smiled and shook their heads. "The last we heard of him he was . . . "

"In Mexico," Sandy said. "Oaxaca, to be exact, where he's been living the high life for a few years after he hightailed it out of here. He asked me if he thought it was safe for him to return to Nantucket, but before I could answer there was a knock on the door, and there stood Chuck, smiling his Chuck smile. I had no idea he was right outside —calling me on his cell phone, the jerk."

"I *shouldn't* be happy to see him," Addie said, "after what he did to Verona."

"It wasn't so bad, Addie," Verona said. "If you remember, I overreacted."

"And ran away," Addie said.

"But I came back."

"Believe me," Sandy interjected, "I hadn't forgotten how he'd impersonated an FBI agent and convinced the judge that a woman in the courtroom was guilty of identity theft."

"And I thought the judge thought it was me," Verona interjected.

"All because of smiling Chuck," Sandy said. "When he was really trying to convince the judge it was *me*. I was some mad at him that day, which is why, when I saw him, I reminded him he owed me one. That he suddenly appeared right after my conversation with Ellen is the definition of fortuitous, which isn't surprising, considering how Chuck turns up when you least expect him."

"Just like a real cop," Digit said. "But why go after Caspian?"

"Because I don't like him, and I don't trust him. He's so obsessed with that stupid chest. Besides, Chuck is pretty believable. He even had his father's old FBI badge on him."

"But wasn't he pretending to be state police?" asked Addie.

"I don't think Mr. Caspian noticed," Sandy said. "And to see the look on Caspian's face when Chuck approached him . . . "

"You should have seen the look on Addie's and Digit's faces when they saw Chuck," Verona added.

Rebecca, who'd been quietly listening, had a question. "How did Chuck know who Caspian was? They'd never met before."

Sandy answered. "It couldn't have worked out better. When

Verona and I helped you into your seat in front of the bank, I saw Caspian standing in the crowd. I couldn't believe how close he was. I had Chuck waiting on standby over by Fair Street. I don't even think you noticed that I left you with Verona for a little bit, Rebecca, so I could grab Chuck and point out Caspian to him."

"*I* didn't even notice that," Digit said.

"I didn't want you to," Sandy said. "I didn't want anyone wrecking the surprise."

"Well, you sure surprised us," Addie said. "So where's Caspian now?"

"Getting on the 5:30 boat, never to return."

"Not the first time Caspian's heard that," Digit said.

"Which is why I suggested that to Chuck," Sandy said. "I figured it would make it more true to life. Chuck called me right afterwards to tell me he'd bought it."

"Speaking of Chuck," Addie said.

"He's visiting friends, no doubt showing off the brand-new SUV I rented for him, but he'll be back. I told him he could stay with me."

"Let bygones be bygones, eh, Sandy?" Digit noted.

"Forgive and forget, live and let live, take your pick," Sandy said. "Honestly, I missed the crazy bastard."

Chapter One Hundred Twelve

Addie called Ellen the next day. "Great story, Addie," she said. "Nice banner headline. Maybe someday I'll get one."

"You will," Addie said. "I have no doubt. You're not upset I didn't call you before the story ran?"

"Why should you have? That was your story. Besides, you can read my story about C. C. Dennison in tomorrow's *Advocate*. I don't think you'll be seeing him back on Nantucket anytime soon, unless he gets shipwrecked, or something."

"Did he speak to you?"

"Speak to me? He wouldn't shut up, although he didn't have a thing to say when I asked him about that letter from the estate of Nate Powell; said he had more important things to think about and quickly changed the subject. I didn't notice any reporting about the letter in your story, by the way."

"It would have been too confusing. We couldn't mention any names because there was really nothing substantive tying anybody to the robbery. The letter on its own didn't mean anything."

"So they got away with it."

"In a way, but they didn't get the sea chest. Weird."

"What's weird?"

"How people will chase after things that are really only a dream."

"Way too profound for me, Addie. Are you going to write about Caspian getting the axe?"

"Caspian? He's old news. I'm surprised at you, Ellen."

The night before, as Addie and Digit drank wine around Sandy's kitchen table recounting everything leading up to that day, and Sandy and Chuck went in search of a lobster dinner, Verona helped Rebecca to bed.

The events of the day had worn her out, but Rebecca wasn't yet ready for bed. "Would you mind just sitting with me for a while?" she asked Verona, to which Verona smiled. She didn't need to say anything; after all the excitement at the bank, silence was a welcome respite. What a pleasure to be with someone you love and let the simple act of being fill the quiet.

Rebecca retired to her rocking chair. On the windowsill was a small ivory-colored scallop shell that she picked up and held in her fingers. As she gazed into the darkness, she traced the lines of the shell from its rounded, fan-shaped edge towards the narrower hinge. Her father wasn't a scalloper — he was a lighthouse keeper — but he knew how to open scallops and had taught her. She thought now of how the lines on the scallop shell come together at the top, converging in a line that pointed towards her, towards her heart. She looked over at Verona and saw her in silhouette, a real presence now in her life, connected to her and her past, a past that lived on in Verona. She couldn't help but smile. She was tired now, but not weary. "I think I'm ready for bed," she said, and Verona helped her to her feet.

After Rebecca had put on her pajamas, Verona sat beside

her on the bed and combed her snow-white hair. It was a simple act that made her feel closer to Rebecca, as though she'd done it her whole life, although she'd only known Rebecca for several years. "You can stop now, Verona," Rebecca said. "I'd like to lie down."

"May I lie beside you, Mother?" Verona asked.

They both looked at each other wide-eyed. "I'm sorry," Verona said. "I don't know where that came from."

Rebecca's countenance softened into a tender smile. "Don't you, though? You must have been thinking about it."

"No, no," Verona insisted. "It just slipped out. I suppose brushing hair is something a daughter might do for her mother." But Verona wasn't sure if she meant those words or not. True, she did feel close to Rebecca, and as the months went by, the closeness became tangible, as though she could hold it. She certainly felt closer to Rebecca than she might toward an aunt. But that didn't necessarily mean anything. What did mean something was that Verona loved her with a love unlike any she'd ever felt before. It was an unthinking love, a comfortable love, a secure love, a love that was part of her being.

Rebecca took Verona's hands in hers, and gazed lovingly into her eyes. Tears streamed down Verona's cheeks. "You know, don't you?" Rebecca asked softly. Verona nodded and then hugged Rebecca.

"I believe I've always known," Verona whispered. "But it seemed too good to be true." Rebecca reached out to hug Verona, and they both cried tears of happiness.

Two nights later, Verona and Addie huddled in a blanket and watched the sunset. "So she really is your mother?" Verona nodded and kissed him gently. "How come she never told you?"

"She didn't want to hurt me, or take the chance that I might not forgive her for putting me up for adoption. When she first told me she was my aunt, she said she immediately regretted it but felt once the lie was told she couldn't take it back."

"But you've been back together for several years now. It must have been hard for her to keep that secret."

"She said she was just glad to have an opportunity for us to be close." Verona looked out across the water. The sun was making its descent, kissing the blue horizon. She looked into Addie's eyes. "Aunt, mother, what difference does it make when you love someone?"

"You do love her, don't you?"

"With all my heart."

The orange sun flattened as it was swallowed by the sea. Addie could feel Verona's heart beating. With his own heart pounding, he said:

"I love you, Verona, all of you, with every one of my senses. You're my North Star."

She wrapped her arms around him and drew him close. They embraced and kissed and held each other tightly as the last bit of sun disappeared into the ocean.

The afterglow was one to remember.

Chapter One Hundred Thirteen

THANKS TO Libby's intervention, the four of them visited the historical association's storage warehouse: Verona, Addie, Digit and Sandy. After the most recent issue of the *Looking Glass* had been put to bed, Libby called Addie to congratulate him on his write-up, and to remind him of a little unfinished business: namely that he'd never followed up on the painting of Captain Hathaway's wife.

The same worker Addie had met before was waiting for them. "After you left the last time, I was going through our inventory and came across this painting," the warehouse worker said. "What's funny is that I'd never noticed it before, and neither had anyone here. And when I checked the database, it wasn't listed."

"Strange," Addie said.

"Yes. Anyway, we all looked it over and agreed it's probably by the same artist, and if you look on the back," and he took off the protective cloth to show them the back of the painting, "here," and he pointed to the top right corner, "it's penciled in: wife of Capt. Hathaway. So here you go," and he turned the painting to show them.

And Addie nearly fell over.

"Are you all right?" the warehouse worker asked. Addie steadied himself by holding onto the table. He was as unprepared for what he was seeing as anything in his life. It was beyond unbelievable. He looked at the others: Sandy had her hand to her mouth; Digit smiled a half-smile and arched his eyebrows; Verona threw her arms around the three of them and laughed.

"You look like you've seen this painting before," the worker said. "To our knowledge it's never been displayed, nor has it ever been catalogued. It wasn't even near the other one."

Addie could barely whisper. "No, I've never seen it before," he managed to say. "Are you sure it's Captain Hathaway's wife?" he said quietly.

"Pretty sure. I mean, all we've got to go on right now is that inscription on the back, but why wouldn't it be? Unless Captain Hathaway didn't have a wife, and we're pretty sure he did."

"Oh, he did, all right," Digit said.

"So, is this she?" the warehouse worker asked.

Sandy took a step backwards. "It's you, Verona," she said. "The likeness is uncanny."

The warehouse worker glanced at Verona and did a double take. All Addie and Digit could do was slowly nod.

The only calm one was Verona. "Take another look," she said. "It's Rebecca, a younger Rebecca."

And it was.

"Rebecca, you say," the warehouse worker said. "Her name was Rebecca? That's good to know because we've decided to include this painting in the exhibition. According to Libby, she accompanied Captain Hathaway on at least one whaling voyage. It'll be nice to have her name for the catalogue."

"Her name *is* Rebecca," Verona said. "My mother. This is her ancestor, also named Rebecca."

The warehouse worker was flummoxed. "Perhaps I can talk to you all later."

"No need," Addie said. "This painting is Rebecca." He turned to Verona. "She knows."

"Talk to Libby," the warehouse worker said. "I'll go with whatever she says."

He walked the painting back to where it had been sitting when they'd arrived, next to the portrait of Captain Hathaway, which was partially covered by a cloth. Addie hadn't taken particular notice because he'd seen the painting before, but this time it was Verona who did a double take. She lifted the covering. "Who's this a painting of?" she asked the warehouse worker, who looked casually over his shoulder. "That's Captain Hathaway," he said. "Once we confirm the other painting is his wife, they'll be displayed side by side."

Verona stepped closer. She felt as though she'd seen this person before. In the fog.

No, couldn't be. That had been some kind of shadow, a mirage manufactured in the morning mist.

She shook her head as she perambulated back to the group and wrapped her arm around Addie's waist. "You're happy," he said, gazing into her eyes. "Oh, I'm just imagining things again," she said. "My mind can get carried away sometimes."

"Mental meanderings," Addie told her. "Not necessarily a bad thing."

"Will you two quit orbiting," Sandy said, "and come back down to earth."

"Never," they said together.

Digit, meanwhile, lingered by the painting of Rebecca,

baffled by the uncanny resemblance to two people he knew. It just didn't seem real somehow. "Finished?" the warehouse worker asked. Roused from his daydream, Digit nodded. "Oh yeah, sure," he said. "I was just looking."

Putting the cloth back over the painting of Rebecca, and reaching for the frame of the Captain Hathaway portrait, the warehouse worker turned to Digit: "Haven't I seen you somewhere before?"

"Doubtful," Digit said as the warehouse worker re-covered the portrait of Captain Hathaway and carefully set it back in its dolly.

Chapter One Hundred Fourteen

On the last day of spring, near twilight, Addie stood next to Digit on the shores of a secluded beach. The days had lengthened. It was seven-thirty in the evening, but sunset was still more than an hour away. When they heard the first strains of a violin, they turned toward a short boardwalk that led to the beach. Sandy and Rebecca walked towards them, with Sandy supporting Rebecca and leading her to a chair placed close by. Following them was the fiddler, and the most beautiful woman Addie had ever seen.

A crown of flowers adorned Verona's hair, done in a French braid courtesy of her friend Irene. She held a bouquet of purple-flowered lupines as she gracefully walked barefoot onto the beach. Addie's smile was ear-to-ear as Verona took her place beside him. After ensuring Rebecca was settled in, Sandy approached the couple. Having been granted a one-day license to officiate, Sandy performed the simple ceremony. As Verona and Addie kissed, a blue crane swooped in over the water for a graceful landing, and a flock of gulls let loose with their chorus of approval.

The wedding reception was held in Sandy's backyard, with tiki torches lighting the way to the festive tables. Everyone was invited, including Addie's old boss, Ken, and his new boss, Merle. Hal Humphries and Libby were there, as was Irene, who had first befriended Verona when she found her on a Straight Wharf bench, alone and confused, all those years ago. Chuck Finley was there, too, charming as ever, taking on the self-appointed role of Rebecca's date, which he fulfilled with his distinctive brand of duende.

Also there was Ellen, making her first trip back to the island since her elevation to staff writer on the *Advocate.* Addie hadn't forgotten his promise to invite her to the wedding. "C. C. Dennison sends his congratulations," she told him, laughing. "He says if you're ever on the Cape . . . "

"Let me guess," Addie smiled. "Keep going!"

"No, that isn't what he said."

"Maybe not, but it's what he meant."

Digit's toast to the bride and groom was the second time he'd been tasked to give a speech in the last year and a half. Unlike Cy's eulogy, however, of which he was apprehensive, he was thrilled when Addie asked him if he'd be best man.

Digit rose, held his champagne flute aloft, and, when the assembled had quieted down, he began:

"I suppose I serve a dual role here today: first, as Addie's best man, and second, as Verona's newfound relative. Well, cousin, let us both welcome Addie to the family." Tinkling glasses and laughter.

"How often is it that someone walks into your life — through fate, or is it divine intervention — and you know you cannot be complete without that person? How wonderful that these two waltzed into each other's lives. Verona, I never knew what you saw in Addie, but then I realized that you must have told yourself: 'Well, if he's Digit's best friend, there must be *something* about him!' That's it, right? Has to be." More laughter.

"To say Nantucket is integral to your love is an understatement. Your relationship was not only formed on this island, but I'd also guess that it was formed *by* this island, and by the spirits that surround her shores. This much I know: you wouldn't have found each other anywhere else.

"Verona, you were of Nantucket before you ever set foot on the island. You have the soul of an islander, indeed being descended from Nantucketers, the island is in your blood. Little surprise, then, that you were drawn to the island — and we are the luckier for it — but no one more than Addie, the luckiest coof around. Just kidding, Addie, you're no coof. And to those of you who don't know what 'coof' means, as Merle would tell you: 'Look it up!' "

He turned to face the newly-married couple. His eyes glistened over and Digit finished his toast:

"To you both, may you always see the stars in each other's eyes, and may you be each other's compass until all the seas run dry."

They spent the night in an understatedly elegant summer shack on the south shore, far away from town. Addie still had his old convertible, and on the way out to the beach played on the car's indefatigable cassette player what he and Verona now considered their song, Bob Dylan's *New Morning*, which they listened to on their first date. Addie sang along to a particularly relevant verse:

This must be the day that all of my dreams come true

Sitting on the porch sipping champagne, the stars overhead twinkled their approval. The Big Dipper, high in the sky, confidently pointed the way to the Pole Star, the North Star. Cetus had swum southward.

"What is that small cluster of stars near the Milky Way?" Addie asked.

"That's the Dolphin," Verona answered. "Look to the right of that and you'll see the Northern Crown."

"There?" Addie asked.

"I can't see where you're looking," she said. Addie pulled her close and asked, "There?" and began tickling her. She tickled him right back. Love lived within her.

They settled down and sat in silence, the rumbling waves breaking on the shore reassuring in their steadfast reliability. Suddenly, yet calmly, soothingly, came another sound, seeming to emanate from the unseen horizon, a long, low, uninterrupted resonation that slowly rose in pitch and volume as it neared. It was unmistakable to Verona, the siren song of the whale.

And there were two of them.

And they were happy.

Epilogue

November first, the first day of the new scallop season. Digit was on the water early, ready to drop his dredges at the crack of 6:30. It was exhilarating to be back on his boat, the newly-christened *Verona II*. The air smelled sweet as he motored out of the anchorage. It was the start of a new year, with all the expectant promise that association conjured. He would be in early today; he could sense it. In his mind's eye, he could already see the harbor bottom.

Also on the water, another scalloper surveys his new surroundings. He didn't yet have the feel of the area, but knew it wouldn't take him long to adapt: he was a good fisherman and knew his way around a scallop boat. Apart from some variations in customs and traditions, Martha's Vineyard scalloping couldn't be that much different from Nantucket, he thought. At any rate, it would be interesting to find out.

He'd been fortunate to find work on a charter fishing boat out of Edgartown that not only paid him under the table, but provided lodging, of sorts. He had to share a room with two other guys, kids really, no older than he was when he'd first arrived on Nantucket twenty-one years before. The age difference was a blessing: he wasn't at all interested in striking up a friendship with either of them, nor were they interested in him. He was lucky. The arrangement allowed him to save most of his earnings, enough for a down payment on a boat. He wondered if Digit was using *his* boat this season. Probably not. Once you got to know a boat there was little reason to change. He hoped Digit was using his truck, though; it was a lot newer than Digit's old pickup.

Yes, thought Fred Flask — for that was his name now, Lance Willoughby buried along with Nate Powell, both remnants of his past — he was certain Digit was using his truck. He hoped so, anyway. Digit deserved a newer vehicle. It would be one good thing to come out of that whole experience. This time he wouldn't screw it up. Fortunately, in his few months on the Vineyard, he'd never heard anyone even mention Nantucket — the only time the two islands interacted, it seemed, was during the annual high school football game.

The game was on Nantucket this year; he wouldn't be going.

Sea-Fever
By John Masefield

I must go down to the seas again, to the lonely sea and the sky,
And all I ask is a tall ship and a star to steer her by;
And the wheel's kick and the wind's song and the white sail's shaking,
And a grey mist on the sea's face, and a grey dawn breaking.

I must go down to the seas again, for the call of the running tide
Is a wild call and a clear call that may not be denied;
And all I ask is a windy day with the white clouds flying,
And the flung spray and the blown spume, and the sea-gulls crying.

I must go down to the seas again, to the vagrant gypsy life,
To the gull's way and the whale's way where the wind's like
a whetted knife;
And all I ask is a merry yarn from a laughing fellow-rover,
And quiet sleep and a sweet dream when the long trick's over.

"For my mind was made up to sail in no other than a Nantucket craft, because there was a fine, boisterous something about everything connected with that famous old island, which amazingly pleased me."

— Herman Melville, ***Moby-Dick*** Chapter Two

Rounding the Point

VETERAN SCALLOPER and boatman Bruce Cowan was immeasurably helpful and generous with his knowledge about fishing, traditions, and the intricacies and facets of working on the water on Nantucket. He graciously gave of his time and expertise, and never tired of answering countless questions.

Boat captain Andy Castrenze steered me straight on the hows and wherefores of navigating the channel into and out of Nantucket Harbor, and explained the various markers and their meanings. He, too, accepted my follow-up questions with sure hands and a historian's perspective.

Much information was also gleaned from the Nantucket Historical Association's website (nha.org), as well as from the staff of the association's research library, who fielded all my nebulous inquiries with patience and humor.

Thanks, too, to Nantucket's Maria Mitchell Association (mariamitchell.org), for pointing me in the right path around the Pole Star and for clearing up my constellation confusion. Named for the famed Nantucket astronomer who discovered a comet from the roof of the Pacific National Bank in 1847, the Maria Mitchell Association is dedicated to developing "a lifelong passion for science."

H. A. Rey's *The Stars: A New Way to See Them,* was an invaluable resource. Written to be a first guide to the heavens, it is an easily understood trove of information about the constellations, the solar system, and the way stars move throughout the year. It includes star maps, wonderful illustrations, and tips on the best ways to view the constellations all year long. First published in 1952, and continually updated, this educational and highly entertaining book is for curious astronomers of all ages.

About the Author

STEVE SHEPPARD has been a weaver, journalist, magazine editor, freelance writer, musician, and teacher. He lives on Nantucket with his wife, Karin.

About the Recipes

The Baked Scallop recipe is the creation of my mother-in-law, Lia Marks, herself a scalloper.

The Baked Bean recipe is my grandmother's, Anne Isabel Daniels.

The Bacon-wrapped Scallops and Clams Casino recipes are Digit's.

Made in the USA
Middletown, DE
15 October 2021